### Praise for Val McDermid's Kate Brannigan Series

"Kate Brannigan is a sparky, funny and much to be welcomed entrant into the still tiny profession of the female private eye."
—*Times* (UK), on *Dead Beat*

"This is a witty, wickedly good read." —*She*, on *Crack Down*

"Inviting characters, plot, and premise . . . steady building suspense as well. Recommended."
—*Library Journal*, on *Crack Down*

"Kate Brannigan deserves promotion to the top rank, alongside Kinsey Millhone and V.I. Warshawski."
—*Sunday Telegraph* (UK), on *Kick Back*

"Kate's wit has the bite of Fran Leibowitz's."
—*Kirkus Reviews*, on *Kick Back*

"Kate Brannigan is truly welcome. Hot on one-liners, Chinese food, tabloid papers and Thai boxing, she is refreshingly funny."
—*Daily Mail* (UK), on *Kick Back*

"The action, as always, is non-stop, and Kate is a worthy protagonist. Long may she thrive."
—*Books Magazine*, on *Crack Down*

"This Manchester-set series is among the best with a slangy, wise-cracking heroine; good plots and a great cast of characters. A sure winner." —MLB News, on *Clean Break*

# CRACK DOWN

## AND

# CLEAN BREAK

## Also by Val McDermid

# VAL McDERMID

# CRACK DOWN

## AND

# CLEAN BREAK

Grove Press
*New York*

*Crack Down* first published in Great Britain in 1994 by HarperCollins Publishers.
First published in the United States in 1994 by Scribner.

*Clean Break* first published in Great Britain in 1995 by HarperCollins Publishers.
First published in the United States in 1995 by Scribner.

*Printed in the United States of America*
*Simultaneously published in Canada*

First Grove Atlantic edition: July 2018

Text design by Norman E. Tuttle of Alpha Design & Composition.

This book was set in 11.5 pt. Bembo by Alpha Design & Composition
of Pittsfield, NH.

Library of Congress Cataloging-in-Publication data is available for this title.

ISBN 978-0-8021-2830-0
eISBN 978-0-8021-4617-5

Grove Press
an imprint of Grove Atlantic
154 West 14th Street
New York, NY 10011

Distributed by Publishers Group West

groveatlantic.com

18 19 20 21    10 9 8 7 6 5 4 3 2 1

# INTRODUCTION
# TO THE GROVE EDITION

When I started writing crime fiction, I planned to write a trilogy because the book I really wanted to write was the third one, but I couldn't figure out how to get there without writing the first two. And so my first series character, Lindsay Gordon, was born.

I'd always known that I'd move on to something different after those first three books. And what really tempted me was the private eye novel. Sara Paretsky, Sue Grafton, Barbara Wilson and their American feminist sisters had taken that genre by the scruff of the neck and remade it in our image. And I was desperate to see whether I could make that work in the UK, with our different laws and social mores.

Kate Brannigan was the result of that desire. I had three main aims with the Brannigan books. The first—and probably the most important—was that I wanted to stretch myself as a writer. Fledgling writers are often told to write what they know. I took that injunction literally and started my career with a protagonist whose life mirrored my own in many respects. Our personalities were very different, but the superficialities were broadly similar. Ethnicity, gender, occupation, politics.

The question I asked of myself was whether I could create a credible character whose experience of the world was very different from my own. An imaginary best friend rather than an alter ego, I suppose. Because it was important to me that I liked her. If she was going to be a series character, I had to be sure I'd want to come back to her again and again. So I considered my friends. What was it about them I liked and respected? But equally, what was it about them that drove me nuts? Because Brannigan had to be human, not some goody two-shoes who would make me feel perpetually inadequate.

The Kate Brannigan I ended up with grew up in Oxford. Not the dreaming spires of academe—the working class row houses where the workers at the car plant lived. Unlike Lindsay, we know what she looks like—petite, red-headed, a fit kickboxer with an Irish granny. She has a boyfriend, Richard, a rock journalist. Kate knows them both well enough not to live directly with him. They're next-door neighbours whose adjoining houses are linked by a conservatory that runs along the back of both homes.

She's a law school dropout who became an accidental PI. She starts out as the junior partner in Mortensen and Brannigan but eventually becomes her own boss. She has a social conscience but what really drives her is the desire to figure out what is going on. As with most PI novels, we hear the story in the first person. We see things through Kate's eyes and hear her whip-smart wisecracks in real time. Because she always gets to come up with the smart retort that most of us only think of two days later in real life.

There were some tropes of the PI novel I was less comfortable with. For a start, civilians absolutely don't have access to guns in the UK. So I did not have available to me Raymond Chandler's solution to the problem of what to do next: 'Have a man walk through the door with a gun in his hand.' I had to get my kicks in other ways. Literally. With the Thai kickboxing.

More importantly, I felt the new wave feminist crime writers from the US had missed a trick. Most of their protagonists were loners. They maybe let one or two people close but that was the limit. To me, this seemed at odds with my experience of the way women connected. I myself had a nexus of close friends with different backgrounds and skills; we all weighed in and provided help and support both practically and emotionally when needed. This was a pattern I saw all around me. I was determined to reflect that in my work so I gave Kate a network and a significant other. It made the storytelling a damn sight easier too!

The Lindsay Gordon novels had been published originally by a small feminist publishing house, The Women's Press. The advances were small and so were the sales. My second aim was to become a full-time writer of fiction and I knew that to achieve that I had to find a home with a more commercial publisher. So while I didn't tailor my writing to the market place, I knew that the decisions I'd made in giving Kate her personal attributes would mean she'd appeal to a wider audience. I also felt very strongly that I didn't want to live in a ghetto or write in a ghetto. I wanted to embrace the wider world that I inhabited. Kate allowed me to do that, and by giving her a lesbian best friend, I could be inclusive too.

My third goal was political subversion. I've been addicted to crime fiction since childhood. I know how crime lovers read. When we find a new author we like, we search out their backlist and devour that too. What better way to persuade people to read Lindsay Gordon than to give her a seductive sister under the skin? It worked—every time a new Brannigan appeared, there would be a spike in those Lindsay Gordon sales.

The one thing I didn't foresee when I started writing the Brannigan novels was how important their setting would become. The six Brannigan novels are as much a social history of Manchester and the North of England in the 1990s as they are mystery novels. This decade was a fascinating time to live and work there. A former industrial city known in the nineteenth century as Cottonopolis, it had been hollowed out and brought to its knees by the economic policies of Margaret Thatcher's government. But Mancunians don't give up easily. They gritted their teeth and set about reinventing the city throughout the decade. Football, music, financial services and sheer bloody-mindedness produced a reinvigoration and reinvention of the city. Watching that and writing about it was one of the greatest pleasures of writing this series.

I hope reading them gives you as much pleasure.

Val McDermid, 2018

# CRACK DOWN

*For my mother,*
*with love and thanks*

# ACKNOWLEDGEMENTS

I couldn't have written this book without help from several sources. In particular: Diana Cooper, Paula Tyler and Jai Penna all contributed invaluable legal expertise and background information; Lee D'Courcy was generous with specialist knowledge in several key areas; Alison Scott provided me with medical information; Sergeant Cross at the Court Detention Centre kept me on the straight and narrow; Geoff Hardman of Gordon Ford (Horwich) filled in the gaps in my knowledge of the motor trade; and Brigid Baillie provided constructive criticism and encouragement throughout. It would have been a lot less fun without the Wisdom of Julia, the G & R team and the four-legged friends—Dusty, Malone, Molly, Macky, Mutton and Licorice.

Although the book is identifiably set in Manchester and other Northern cities, and many of the locations will be familiar to those who know the patch, all the places and people involved in criminal activities are entirely fictitious. In particular, there is no post office in Brunswick Street, nor any club quite like the Delta. Any resemblance to reality is only in the minds of those with guilty consciences.

# 1

If slugs could smile, they'd have no trouble finding jobs as car salesmen. Darryl Day proved that. Oozing false sincerity as shiny as a slime trail, he'd followed us round the showroom. From the start, he'd made it clear that in his book, Richard was the one who counted. I was just the bimbo wife. Now Darryl sat, separated from the pair of us by a plastic desk, grinning maniacally with that instant, superficial matiness that separates sales people from the human race. He winked at me. "And Mrs Barclay will love that leather upholstery," he said suggestively.

Under normal circumstances, I'd have got a lot of pleasure out of telling him his tatty sexism had just cost him the commission on a twenty grand sale, but these circumstances were so far from normal, I was beginning to feel like Ground Control to Major Tom as far as my brain was concerned. So instead, I smiled, patted Richard's arm and said sweetly, "Nothing's too good for my Dick." Richard twitched. I reckon he knew instinctively that one way or another, he was going to pay for this.

"Now, let me just check that we're both clear what you're buying here. You've seen it in the showroom, we've taken it on the test drive of a lifetime, and you've decided on the Gemini turbo super coupé GLXi in midnight blue, with ABS, alloy wheels . . ." As Darryl ran through the luxury spec I'd instructed

Richard to go for, my partner's eyes glazed over. I almost felt
sorry for him. After all, Richard's car of choice is a clapped-out,
customized hot pink Volkswagen Beetle convertible. He thinks
BHP is that new high-quality tape system. And isn't ABS that
dance band from Wythenshawe . . . ?

Darryl paused expectantly. I kicked Richard's ankle. Only
gently, though. He'd done well so far. He jerked back to reality
and said, "Er, yeah, that sounds perfect. Sorry, I was just a bit
carried away, thinking about what it's going to be like driving
her." Nice one, Richard.

"You're a very lucky man, if I may say so," Darryl smarmed,
eyeing the curve of my calf under the leopard skin leggings that
I'd chosen as appropriate to my exciting new role as Mrs Richard Barclay. He tore his gaze away and shuffled his paperwork.
"Top of the range, that little beauty is. But now, I'm afraid, we
come to the painful bit. You've already told me you don't want
to part-ex, is that right?"

Richard nodded. "'s right. My last motor got nicked, so
I've got the insurance payout to put down as a deposit. Which
leaves me looking for six grand. Should I sort out a bank loan
or what?"

Darryl looked just like the Duke of Edinburgh when he
gets a stag in his sights. He measured Richard up, then flicked
a casual glance over me. "The only problem with that, Richard, is that it's going to take you a few days to get your friendly
bank manager in gear. Whereas, if we can sort it out here and
now, you could be driving that tasty motor tomorrow tea time."
Classic sales ploy; take it off them.

Richard did his personal version of the Fry's Five Boys
gamut, from disappointment to anticipation. "So can we do
that, then, Darryl?" he asked eagerly.

Darryl already had the forms prepared. He slid them across
the desk to show Richard. "As it happens, we have an arrangement with a finance company who offer a very competitive rate
of interest. If you fill in the forms now, we can sort it with a

phone call. Then, tomorrow, if you bring in a banker's draft for the balance, we'll be able to complete the paperwork and the car'll be all yours to drive away."

I looked at the form, not so easy now Darryl had reclaimed it to fill in the remaining blanks. Richmond Credit Finance. Address and phone number in Accrington. It wasn't the first time I'd seen their footprints all over this investigation. I'd meant to check the company out, but I hadn't got round to it yet. I made a mental note to get on to it as soon as I had a spare moment. I tuned back in at the bit where Darryl was asking Richard what he did for a living. This was always the best bit.

"I'm a freelance rock journalist," Richard told him.

"Really?" Darryl asked. Interesting how his face opened up when he experienced a genuine emotion like excitement. "Does that mean you interview all the top names and that? Like Whitney Houston and Beverley Craven?"

Richard nodded glumly. "Sometimes."

"God, what a great job! Hey, who's the most famous person you've ever interviewed? You ever met Madonna?"

Richard squirmed. It's the question he hates most. There aren't that many rock stars he has much respect for, either as people or as musicians, and only a handful of them are names that most members of the public would identify as superstars. "Depends what you mean by famous. Springsteen. Elton John. Clapton. Tina Turner. And yeah, I did meet Madonna once."

"Wow! And is she really, you know, as, like, horny as she comes over?"

Richard forced a smile. "Not in front of the wife, eh?" I was touched. He was really trying to make this work.

Darryl ran a hand through his neat dark hair and winked. In an adult, it would have been lewd. "Gotcha, Richard. Now, your annual income. What would that be?"

I switched off again. Fiction, even the great stuff, is never as interesting when you're hearing it for the nth time. Darryl didn't hang about explaining little details like annual percentage interest rates to Richard, and within ten minutes, he was on to the finance company arranging our car loan. Thanks to the wonders of computer technology, credit companies can check out a punter and give the thumbs up or down almost instantaneously. Whatever Richmond Credit Finance pulled up on their computer, it convinced them that Richard was a sound bet for a loan. Of course, when you're relying on computers, it's important to remember that what you get out of them depends entirely on what someone else has put in.

Twenty minutes later, Richard and I were walking out of the showroom, the proud possessors, on paper at least, of the flashest set of wheels the Leo Motor Company puts on the road. "I do all right, Mrs Barclay?" Richard asked eagerly, as we walked round the corner to where I'd parked the Peugeot 205 Mortensen and Brannigan had been leasing for the six months since my last company car had ended up looking like an installation from the Tate Gallery.

"You wish," I snarled. "Don't push your luck, Barclay. Let me tell you, the longer I spend pretending to be your wife, the more I understand why your first marriage didn't go the distance."

I climbed in the car and started the engine. Richard stood on the pavement, looking hangdog, his tortoiseshell glasses slipping down his nose. Exasperated, I pushed the button that lowered the passenger window. "Oh for God's sake, get in," I said. "You did really well in there. Thank you."

He smiled and jumped in. "You're right, you know."

"I usually am," I said, only half teasing, as I eased the car out into the busy stream of traffic on the Bolton to Blackburn Road. "About what in particular?"

"That being a private eye is ninety-five per cent boredom coupled with five per cent fear. The first time we did that routine, I was really scared. I thought, what if I forget what I'm supposed to say, and they suss that we're setting them up," he said earnestly.

"It wouldn't have been the end of the world," I said absently, keeping an eye on the road signs so I didn't miss the turnoff for Manchester. "We're not dealing with the Mafia here. They wouldn't have dragged you out kicking and screaming and knee-capped you."

"No, but you might have," Richard said. He was serious.

I laughed. "No way. I'd have waited till I got you home."

Richard looked worried for a moment. Then he decided I was joking. "Anyway," he said, "now when we do it, I'm not nervous any more. The only danger is that it's so repetitious I'm afraid I'll blow it out of boredom."

"Well, I'm hoping we won't have to go through it many more times," I said, powering down the ramp on to the dual carriageway. The little Peugeot I chose has a 1.9 litre engine, but since I got the dealership to take the identifying badges off it, it looks as innocuous as a housewife's shopping trolley. I'd be sorry to see the back of it, but once I'd finished this job, I'd be in line for a brand new sporty Leo hatchback. Freemans.

"That's a shame, in some ways. I hate to admit it, Brannigan, but I've quite enjoyed working with you."

Wild horses wouldn't have got me to admit it, but I'd enjoyed it too. In the two years that we'd been lovers, I'd never been reluctant to use Richard as a sounding board for my investigations. He's got one of those off-the-wall minds that sometimes come up with illuminating insights into the white-collar crime that makes up the bulk of the work I do with my business partner Bill Mortensen. But the opportunity to get Richard to take a more active part had never arisen before this job. I'd only gone along with Bill's suggestion to involve him precisely because I felt so certain it was a no-risk job. How could I expose to danger a man who thinks discretion is a fragrance by Calvin Klein?

This job was what we call in the trade a straight up-and-downer. The only strange thing about it was the way we'd got the job in the first place. A two-operative agency in Manchester isn't the obvious choice for an international car giant like the Leo Motor Company when they've got a problem. We'd got lucky because the new head honcho at Accredited Leo Finance was the brother-in-law of a high-class Manchester jeweller. We'd not only installed Clive Abercrombie's security system, but we'd also cracked a major gang of counterfeiters who were giving the executive chronometer brigade serious migraine. As far as Clive was concerned, Mortensen and Brannigan were *the* people to go to when you wanted a slick, discreet job.

Of course, being an arm of a multi-national, ALF couldn't bring themselves to knock on the door and pitch us the straight way. It had all started at a reception hosted by the Manchester Olympic Bid organization. Remember the Olympic Bid? They were trying to screw dosh out of local businesses to support their attempt to kick off the new millennium by holding the Games in the Rainy City. Bill and I are such a small operation, we were a bit bewildered at being invited, but I'm a sucker for free smoked salmon, and besides, I reckoned it would do no harm to flash my smile round a few potentially lucrative new contacts, so I went off to fly the flag for Mortensen and Brannigan.

I was only halfway through my first glass of Australian fizz (as good a reason as any for awarding the Olympics to Sydney) when Clive appeared at my elbow with a strange man and a sickly grin. "Kate," he greeted me. "What a lovely surprise."

I was on my guard straight away. Clive and I have never been buddies, probably because I can't bring myself to be anything more than professionally polite to social climbers. So when the Edmund Hillary of the Cheshire set accosted me so joyously, I knew at once we were in the realms of hidden agendas. I smiled politely, shook his hand, counted my fingers and said, "Nice to see you too, Clive."

"Kate, can I introduce my brother-in-law, Andrew Broderick? Andrew, this is Kate Brannigan, who's a partner in Manchester's best security company. Kate, Andrew's the MD and CEO of ALF." I must have looked blank, for Clive added hurriedly,

"You know, Kate. Accredited Leo Finance. Leo Motor Company's credit arm."

"Thanks, Tonto," I said.

Clive looked baffled, but Andrew Broderick laughed. "If I'm the loan arranger, you must be Tonto. Old joke," he explained. Clive still didn't get it. Broderick and I shook hands and weighed each other up. He wasn't a lot taller than my five feet and three inches, but Andrew Broderick looked like a man who'd learned how to fight his battles in a rugby scrum rather than a boardroom. It was just as well he could afford to have his suits hand-stitched to measure; he'd never have found that chest measurement off the peg. His nose had been broken more than once and his ears were as close to being a pair as Danny DeVito and Arnold Schwarzenegger. But his shrewd grey eyes missed nothing. I felt his ten-second assessment of me had probably covered all the salient points.

We started off innocuously enough, discussing the Games. Then, casually enough, he asked what I drove in the course of business. I found myself telling him all about Bill's new Saab convertible, the workhorse Little Rascal van we use for surveillance, and the nearly fatal accident that had robbed me of the Nova. I was mildly surprised. I don't normally talk to strangers.

"No Leos?" he asked with a quirky smile.

"No Leos," I agreed. "But I'm open to persuasion."

Broderick took my elbow, smiled dismissively at Clive and gently steered me into a quiet corner behind the buffet. "I have a problem," he said. "It needs a specialist, and I'm told that your organization could fit my spec. Interested?"

Call me a slut, but when it comes to business, I'm always open to offers. "I'm interested," I said. "Will it keep, or do you want to thrash it out now?"

It turned out that patience wasn't Andrew Broderick's long suit. Within five minutes, we were in the lounge of the Ramada, with drinks on their way. "How much do you know about car financing?" he asked.

"They always end up costing more than you think," I said ruefully.

"That much, eh?" he said. "OK. Let me explain. My company, ALF, is a wholly owned subsidiary of the Leo Motor Company. Our job is to provide loans for people who want to buy Leo cars and haven't got enough cash. But Leo dealerships aren't obliged to channel all their customers through us, so we have to find ways to make ourselves sexy to the dealerships. One of the ways we do this is to offer them soft loans."

I nodded, with him so far. "And these low-interest loans are for what, exactly?"

"Dealerships have to pay up front when they take delivery of a car from Leo. ALF gives them a soft loan to cover the wholesale cost of the car for ninety days. After that, the interest rate rises weekly. When the car is sold, the soft loan is supposed to be paid off. That's in the contract.

"But if a dealership arranges loans for the Leos it sells via a different finance company, neither ALF nor Leo is aware that the car's been sold. The dealer can smack the money in a high-interest account for the remains of the ninety days and earn himself a tidy sum in interest before the loan has to be paid off." The drinks arrived, as if on cue, giving me a few moments to digest what he'd said.

I tipped the bottle of grapefruit juice into my vodka, and swirled the ice cubes round in the glass to mix the drink. "And you obviously hate this because you're cutting your own margins to supply the low-interest loans, but you're getting no benefit in return."

Broderick nodded, taking a hefty swallow of his spritzer. "Leo aren't crazy about it either because it skews their market share figures, particularly in high turnover months like August," he added.

"So where do I come in?" I asked.

"I've come up with an alternative distribution system," he said simply. Now, all I know about the car business is what I've learned from my dad, an assembly line foreman with Rover in Oxford. But even that little is enough for me to realize that what Andrew Broderick had just said was on a par with the Prime Minister announcing he was going to abolish the Civil Service.

I swallowed hard. "We don't do bodyguard jobs," I said.

He laughed, which was the first time I'd doubted his sanity. "It's so simple," he said. "Instead of having to fill their show-rooms with cars they're then under pressure to sell asap, dealers would carry only one sample of the model. The customer would specify colour, engine size, petrol or diesel, optional extras, etc. The order would then be faxed to one of several regional holding centres where the specific model would be assembled from Leo's stock."

"Don't tell me, let me guess. Leo are fighting it tooth and nail because it involves them in initial expenditure of more than threepence ha'penny," I said resignedly.

"And that's where you come in, Ms Brannigan. I want to prove to Leo that my system would be of ultimate financial benefit to both of us. Now, if I can prove that at least one of our bigger chains of dealerships is committing this particular fraud, then I can maybe start to get it through Leo's corporate skulls that a helluva lot of cash that should be in our business is being siphoned off. And then maybe, just maybe, they'll accept that a revamped distribution service is worth every penny."

Which is how Richard and I came to be playing happy newly-weds round the car showrooms of England. It seemed like a good idea at the time. Three weeks into the job, it still seemed like a good idea. Which only goes to show how wrong even I can be.

# 2

The following afternoon, I was in my office, putting the finishing touches to a routine report on a fraudulent personal accident claim I'd been investigating on behalf of a local insurance company. As I reached the end, I glanced at my watch. Twenty-five to three. Surprise, surprise, Richard was late. I saved the file to disc, then switched off my computer. I took the disc through to the outer office, where Shelley Carmichael was filling in a stationery supplies order form. If good office management got you on to the Honours List, Shelley would be up there with a life peerage. It's a toss-up who I treat with more respect—Shelley or the local pub's Rottweiler.

She glanced up as I came through. "Late again, is he?" she asked. I nodded. "Want me to give him an alarm call?"

"I don't think he's in," I said. "He mumbled something this morning about going to a bistro in Oldham where they do live rockabilly at lunch time. It sounded so improbable it has to be true. Did you check if today's draft has come through?"

Shelley nodded. Silly question, really. "It's at the King Street branch," she said.

"I'll pop out and get it now," I said. "If Boy Wonder shows up, tell him to wait for me. None of that 'I'll just pop out to the Corner House for ten minutes to have a look at their new exhibition' routine."

I gave the lift a miss and ran downstairs. It helps me maintain the illusion of fitness. As I walked briskly up Oxford Street, I felt at peace with the world. It was a bright, sunny day, though the temperature was as low as you'd expect the week before the spring bank holiday. It's a myth about it always raining in Manchester—we only make it up to irritate all those patronizing bastards in the South with their hose-pipe bans. I could hear the comic Thomas the Tank Engine hooting of the trams in the distance. The traffic was less clogged than usual, and some of my fellow pedestrians actually had smiles on their faces. More importantly, the ALF job had gone without a hitch, and with a bit of luck, this would be the last banker's draft I'd have to collect. It had been a pretty straightforward routine, once Bill and I had decided to bring Richard in to increase the credibility of the car buying operation. It must be the first time in his life he's ever been accused of enhancing the credibility of anything. Our major target had been a garage chain with fifteen branches throughout the North. Richard and I had hit eight of them, from Stafford to York, plus four independents that Andrew also suspected of being on the fiddle.

There was nothing complicated about it. Richard and I simply rolled up to the car dealers, pretending to be a married couple, and bought a car on the spot from the range in the showroom. Broderick had called in a few favours with his buddies in the credit rating agencies that lenders used to check on their victims' creditworthiness. So, when the car sales people got the finance companies to check the names and addresses Richard gave them, they discovered he had an excellent credit rating, a sheaf of credit cards and no outstanding debt except his mortgage. The granting of the loan was then a formality. The only hard bit was getting Richard to remember what his hooky names and addresses were.

The next day, we'd go to the bank and pick up the banker's draft that Broderick had arranged for us. Then it was on to the showroom, where Richard signed the rest of the paperwork so we could take the car home. Some time in the following couple of days, a little man from ALF arrived and took it away, presumably to be resold as an ex-demonstration model. Interestingly, Andrew Broderick had been right on the button. Not one of the dealers we'd bought cars from had offered us finance through ALF. The chain had pushed all our purchases through Richmond Credit Finance, while the independents had used a variety of lenders. Now, with a dozen cast-iron cases on the stocks, all Broderick had to do was sit back and wait till the dealers finally got round to admitting they'd flogged some metal. Then it would be gumshields time in the car showrooms.

While I was queueing at the bank, the schizophrenic weather had had a personality change. A wind had sprung up from nowhere, throwing needle-sharp rain into my face as I headed back towards the office. Luckily, I was wearing low-heeled ankle boots with my twill jodhpur-cut leggings, so I could jog back without risking serious injury either to any of my major joints or to my dignity. That was my first mistake of the day. There's nothing Richard likes better than a dishevelled Brannigan. Not because it's a turn-on; no, simply because it lets him indulge in a rare bit of one-upmanship.

When I got back to the office, damp, scarlet-cheeked and out of breath, my auburn hair in rats' tails, Richard was of course sitting comfortably in an armchair, sipping a glass of Shelley's herbal tea, immaculate in the Italian leather jacket I bought him on the last day of our winter break in Florence. His hazel eyes looked at me over the top of his glasses and I could see he was losing his battle not to smile.

"Don't say a word," I warned him. "Not unless you want your first trip in your brand new turbo coupé to end up at the infirmary."

He grinned. "I don't know how you put up with all this naked aggression, Shelley," he said.

"Once you understand it's compensatory behaviour for her low self-esteem, it's easy." Shelley did A Level psychology at evening classes. I'm just grateful she didn't pursue it to degree level.

Ignoring the pair of them, I marched through my office and into the cupboard that doubles as darkroom and ladies' loo. I towelled my hair as dry as I could get it, then applied the exaggerated amounts of mascara, eye shadow, blusher and lipstick that Mrs Barclay required. I stared critically at the stranger in the mirror. I couldn't imagine spending my whole life behind that much camouflage. But then, I've never wanted to be irresistible to car salesmen.

We hit the garage just after four. The gleaming, midnight blue Gemini turbo super coupé was standing in splendid isolation on the concrete apron at the side of the showroom. Darryl was beside himself with joy when he actually touched the bank draft. The motor trade's so far down in the doldrums these days that paying customers are regarded with more affection than the Queen Mum, especially ones who don't spend three days in a war of attrition trying to shave the price by yet another fifty quid. He was so overjoyed, he didn't even bother to lie. "I'm delighted to see you drive off in this beautiful car," he confessed, clutching the bank draft with both hands and staring at it. Then he remembered himself and gave us a greasy smile. "Because, of course, it's our pleasure to give you pleasure."

Richard opened the passenger door for me, and, smarting, I climbed in. "Oh, this is real luxury," I forced out for Darryl's benefit, as I stroked the charcoal grey leather. The last thing I wanted was for him to think I was anything other than brain-dead. Richard settled in next to me, closing the door with a solid clunk. He turned the key in the ignition, and pressed the button that lowered his window. "Thanks, Darryl," he said. "It's been a pleasure doing the business."

"Pleasure's all mine, Mr Barclay," Darryl smarmed, shuffling sideways as Richard let out the clutch and glided slowly forward. "Remember me when Mrs Barclay's ready for a new luxury vehicle?"

In response, Richard put his foot down. In ten seconds, Darryl Day was just a bad memory. "Wow," he exclaimed as he moved up and down through the gears in the busy Bolton traffic. "This is some motor! Electric wing mirrors, electric sun roof, electric seat adjustment . . ."

"Shame about the clockwork driver," I said.

By the time we got home, Richard was in love. Although the Gemini coupé was the twelfth Leo car we'd "bought," this was the first example of the newly launched sporty superstar. We'd had to confine ourselves to what was actually available on the premises, and we'd tended to go for the executive saloons that had made Leo one of the major suppliers of fleet cars in the UK. As we arrived outside the pair of bungalows where we live, Richard was still raving about the Gemini.

"It's like driving a dream," he enthused, pressing the remote control that locked the car and set the alarm.

"You said that already," I muttered as I walked up the path to my house. "Twice."

"No, but really, Kate, it's like nothing I've ever driven before," Richard said, walking backwards up the path.

"That's hardly surprising," I said. "Considering you've never driven anything designed after Porsche came up with the Beetle in 1936. Automotive technology has moved along a bit since then."

He followed me into the house. "Brannigan, until I drove that, I'd never wanted to."

"Do I gather you want me to talk to Andrew Broderick about doing you a deal to buy the Gemini?" I asked, opening the fridge. I handed Richard a cold Jupiler and took out a bottle of freshly squeezed pink grapefruit juice.

He opened the drawer for the bottle opener and popped the cap off his beer, looking disconsolate. "Thanks, but no thanks. Can't afford it, Brannigan."

I didn't even think about trying to change the mind of a man with an ex-wife and a son to support. I never poke my nose into his finances, and the last thing that would ever make the short journey across his mind is curiosity about my bank balance. We never have to argue about money because of the way we organize our lives. We own adjacent houses, linked by a conservatory built across the back of both of them. That way, we have all the advantages of living together and almost none of the disadvantages.

I opened the freezer and took out a bottle of Polish vodka. It was so cold, the sobs of spirit on the inside of the bottle were sluggish as syrup. I poured an inch into the bottom of a highball glass and topped it up with juice. It tasted like nectar. I put down my glass and gave Richard a hug. He rubbed his chin affectionately on the top of my head and gently massaged my neck.

"Mmm," I murmured. "Any plans for tonight?"

"'Fraid so. There's a benefit in town for the girlfriend of that guy who got blown away last month in Moss Side. You remember? The innocent bystander who got caught up in the drugs shoot-out outside the café? Well, she's four months pregnant, so the local bands have got together to put on a bit of a performance. Can't not show, sorry."

"But you don't have to go for a while, do you?" I asked, running my fingers over his shoulder blades in a pattern that experience has demonstrated usually distracts him from minor things like work.

"Not for ages," he responded, nuzzling my neck as planned. Nothing like exploiting a man's weaknesses, I thought.

I wasn't the only one into the exploitation game, though. As I grabbed my drink and we did a sideways shuffle towards the bedroom, Richard murmured, "Any chance of me taking the Gemini with me tonight?"

I jerked awake with the staring-eyed shock that comes when you've not been asleep for long. The light was still on, and my arm hurt as I peeled it off the glossy computer gaming magazine I'd fallen asleep over. I reached for the trilling telephone and barked, "Brannigan," into it, simultaneously checking the time on the alarm clock. 00:43.

"Did I wake you?" Richard asked.

"What do you think?"

"Sorry. That kind of answers the question," he said cryptically.

My brain wasn't up to it. "What question, Richard?" I demanded. "What question's so urgent it can't wait till morning?"

"I just wondered if you were at the wind-up, that's all. But you're obviously not, so I'd better come home and call the cops."

I was no further forward. I massaged my forehead with my spare hand, but before I could get any more sense out of him, the pips sounded and the line went dead. I contemplated going back to sleep, but I knew that was just the fantasy of a deranged mind. You don't become a private eye because you lack curiosity about the doings of your fellow man. Especially when they're as unpredictable as the man next door. Whatever Richard was up to, I was involved now too. Heaving a sigh, I got out of bed and struggled into my dressing gown. I went through to my living room, unlocked the patio doors and walked through the conservatory to Richard's house.

As usual, his living room looked like a teenager's idea of paradise. A Nintendo console lay on top of a pile of old newspapers by the sofa. Stacks of CDs teetered on every available surface that wasn't occupied by empty beer bottles and used coffee mugs. Rock videos were piled by the TV set. A couple of rock bands' promotional T-shirts and sweat shirts were thrown over an armchair, and a lump of draw sat neatly on a pack of Silk Cut, next to a packet of Rizlas on the coffee table. If vandals ransacked the place, Richard probably wouldn't notice for a fortnight. When we first got together, I used to tidy up. Now, I've trained myself not to notice.

Two steps down the hall, I knew what to expect in the kitchen. Every few weeks, Richard decides his kitchen is a health hazard, and he does his version of spring cleaning. This involves putting crockery, cutlery and chopsticks in the dishwasher. Everything else on the worktops goes into a black plastic bin liner. He buys a bottle of bleach, a pair of rubber gloves and a pack of scouring pads and scrubs down every surface, including the inside of the microwave. For two days, the place is spotless and smells like a public swimming pool. Then he comes home stoned with a Chinese takeaway and everything goes back to normal.

I opened the dishwasher and took out the jug from the coffee maker. I got the coffee from the fridge. Richard's fridge contains only four main food groups: his international beer collection, chocolate bars for the dope-induced raging munchies, ground coffee and a half-gallon container of milk. While I was waiting for the coffee to brew, I tried not to think about the logical reason why Richard was coming home to call the police.

I realized the nightmare was true when I heard the familiar clatter of a black hack's diesel engine in the close outside. I peeped through the blind. Sure enough, there was Richard paying off the cabbie. I had a horrible feeling that the reason he was in a cab rather than the Gemini had nothing to do with the amount of alcohol he had consumed. "Oh shit," I muttered as I took a second mug from the dishwasher and filled it with strong Java. I walked down the hall and proffered the coffee as Richard walked through the front door.

"You're not going to believe this," he started, taking the mug from me. He gulped a huge mouthful. Luckily, he has an asbestos throat. "Cheers."

"Don't tell me, let me guess," I said, following him through to the living room, where he grabbed the phone. "You came out of the club, the car was gone."

He shook his head in admiration. "Ever thought of becoming a detective, Brannigan? You don't ring 999 for a car theft, do you?"

"Not unless they also ran you over."

"When I realized the car was on the missing list, I wished they had," he said. "I thought, if Brannigan doesn't kill me, the money men will. Got a number for the Dibble?"

I recited the familiar number of Greater Manchester Police's main switchboard. Contrary to popular mythology about private eyes, Bill and I do have a good working relationship with the law. Well, most of the time. Let's face it, they're so overworked these days that they're pathetically grateful to be handed a stack of evidence establishing a case that'll let them give some miserable criminal a good nicking.

Richard got through almost immediately. While he gave the brief details over the phone, I wondered whether I should call Andrew Broderick and give him the bad news. I decided against it. It's bad enough to lose twenty grand's worth of merchandise without having a night's sleep wrecked as well. I must point that out to Richard some time.

# 3

Two nights later, it happened again. I was about to deal Kevin Costner a fatal blow in a game of Battle Chess when an electronic chirruping disturbed our joust. Costner dissolved in a blue haze as I struggled up from the dream, groping wildly for the phone. My arm felt as heavy as if I really was wearing the weighty medieval armour of a knight in a tournament. That'll teach me to play computer games at bedtime. "Brannigan," I grunted into the phone.

"Kate? Sorry to wake you." The voice was familiar, but out of context it took me a few seconds to recognize it. The voice and I came up with the answer simultaneously. "Ruth Hunter here."

I propped myself up on one elbow and switched on the bedside lamp. "Ruth. Give me a second, will you?" I dropped the phone and scrabbled for my bag. I pulled out a pad and pencil, and scribbled down the time on the clock. 02:13. For a criminal solicitor to wake me at this time of night it had to be serious. Whichever one of Mortensen and Brannigan's clients had decided my beauty sleep was less important than their needs was going to pay dear for the privilege. They weren't going to get so much as ten free seconds. I picked up the phone and said, "OK. You have my undivided attention. What is it that won't keep?"

"Kate, there is no way of making this pleasant. I'm sorry. I've just had Longsight police station's custody sergeant on to me. They've arrested Richard." Ruth's voice was apologetic, but she was right. There was no way of making that news pleasant.

"What's he done? Had a few too many and got caught up in somebody else's war?" I asked, knowing even as I did that I was being wildly optimistic. If that was all it was, Richard would have been more interested in getting his head down for a kip in the cells than in getting the cops to call Ruth out.

"I'm afraid not, Kate. It's drugs."

"Is that all?" I almost burst out laughing. "This is the 1990s, Ruth. How much can they give him for a lump of draw? He never carries more on him than the makings for a couple of joints."

"Kate, it's not cannabis." Ruth had that tone of voice that the actors on hospital dramas use when they're about to tell someone their nearest and dearest probably isn't going to make it. "If it was cannabis, believe me, I wouldn't have bothered calling you."

I heard the words, but I couldn't make sense of them. The only drug Richard ever uses is draw. In the two years we've been together, I've never known him to drop so much as half a tab of E, in spite of the number of raves and gigs he routinely attends. "It's got to be a plant, then," I said confidently. "Someone's had it in for him and they've slipped something into his pocket."

"I don't think so, Kate. We're talking about two kilos of crack."

Crack. Fiercely addictive, potentially lethal, crack cocaine is the drug everybody in narcotics prevention has the heebie-jeebies about. For a moment, I couldn't take it in. I know two kilos of crack isn't exactly bulky, but you'd have to notice you had it about your person. "He was walking around with two *kilos* of crack on him? That can't be right, Ruth," I managed.

"Not walking around. Driving. I don't have any details yet, but he was brought in by a couple of lads from traffic. I'm afraid it gets worse, Kate. Apparently the car he was in was stolen."

I was out of bed, pulling knickers and tights out of the top drawer. "Well, who was he with, then? He can't have known he was in a hot motor!"

My stomach knotted as Ruth replied, "He was on his own. No passengers."

"This is like a bad dream," I said. "You know what he's like. Can you see Richard as a major-league car thief and drug dealer? Where are you now, Ruth?" I asked.

"I'm on my way out the door. The sooner I get in to see him, the sooner we can get this business straightened out. You're right. Richard's no villain," she said reassuringly.

"Too true. Look, Ruth, thanks for letting me know. I appreciate it." I fastened my bra and moved over to the wardrobe door.

"I'll keep you posted," she said. "Speak to you soon."

Sooner than you think, I told myself as I shrugged into a cream polo-neck knitted cotton top. I grabbed my favourite knock-'em-dead suit, a lightweight wool number in a grey and moss green weave. Of course, dressing on the run, my legs tangled in the trousers as I made for the hall and I ended up sprawled on the floor, face smacked up against the skirting board, forced to recognize that it was too long since I'd cleaned the house. Cursing in a fluent monotone, I made it as far as the porch and pulled a pair of flat loafers out of the shoe cupboard. On my way out of the door, I remembered the route I was planning to go down, and hurried back into the living room, where I picked up the slim black leather briefcase I use to impress prospective clients with my businesslike qualities.

As I started the car, I noticed Richard's Beetle wasn't in its usual parking space. What in God's name was going on? If he'd gone out in his own car, what was he doing driving round in the middle of the night in a stolen car with a parcel of heavy drugs? More to the point, did the owners of the drugs know who'd driven off with their merchandise? Because if they did, I didn't give much for Richard's chances of seeing his next birthday.

I pulled up in the visitors' car park at Longsight nick a couple of minutes later. There wasn't much competition for parking places that time of night. I knew I'd have at least fifteen minutes to kill, since Ruth had to drive all the way over from her house in Hale. Usually, I don't have much trouble keeping my mind occupied on stakeouts. Maybe that's because I don't have to do it too often, given the line of work Mortensen and Brannigan specialize in. A lot of private eyes have to make the bulk of their income doing mind-and-bum-numbing bread-and-butter surveillance work, but because we work mainly with computer crime and white-collar fraud, we spend a lot more of our backside-breaking hours in other people's offices than we do outside their houses. But tonight, the seventeen minutes I spent staring at the dirty red brick and tall blank windows of the rambling, mock-Gothic police station felt like hours. I suppose I was worried. I must be getting soft in my old age.

I spotted Ruth's car as soon as she turned into the car park. Her husband's in the rag trade, and he drives a white Bentley Mulsanne Turbo. When she gets dragged out of bed in the middle of the night, Ruth likes to drive the Bentley. It doesn't half get up the noses of the cops. Her regular clients love it to bits. As the dazzling headlights in my rear-view mirror dimmed to black, I was out of my car and waving to Ruth.

The driver's window slid down with an almost imperceptible hum. She didn't stick her head out; she waited for me to draw level. I grinned. Ruth didn't. "You'll have a long wait, Kate," she said, a warning in her voice.

I ignored the warning. "Ruth, you and I both know you're the best criminal lawyer in the city. But we also both know that being an officer of the court means there is a whole raft of things you can't even think about doing. The kind of shit Richard seems to have got himself in, he needs someone out there ducking and diving, doing whatever it takes to dig up the information that'll get him off the hook with the cops and with the dealers. I'm the one who's going to have to do that, and the most efficient way for that process to get started is for me to sit in on your briefing."

Give her her due, Ruth heard me out. She even paused for the count of five to create the impression she was giving some thought to my suggestion. Then she slowly shook her head. "No way, Kate. I suspect you know the provisions of PACE as well as I do."

I smiled ruefully. The Police and Criminal Evidence Act hadn't exactly been my bedtime reading when it became law, but I was reasonably familiar with its provisions. I knew perfectly well that the only person a suspect was entitled to have sitting in on their interview with the police was his or her solicitor. "There is one way round it," I said.

There's something about the mind of a criminal solicitor. They can't resist discovering any new wrinkle in the law. Dangle that as a carrot and they'll bite your arm off faster than a starving donkey. "Go on," Ruth said cautiously. I swear her eyes sparkled.

"Trainee solicitors who are just starting criminal work usually learn the ropes by bird-dogging a senior brief like yourself," I said. "And that includes sitting in on interviews in police stations."

Ruth smiled sweetly. "Not in the middle of the night. And you're not a trainee solicitor, Kate."

"True, Ruth, but I did do two years of a law degree. And as you yourself pointed out not five minutes since, I do know my way around PACE. I'm not going to blow it out of ignorance of the procedures." I couldn't remember the last time I'd had to be this persuasive. Before I knew where I was, I'd be down on my knees begging. This was going to be the most expensive night out Richard Barclay had ever had.

Ruth shook her head decisively. "Kate, if we're going to quote each other, let me remind you of your opening speech.

As an officer of the court, there are a whole lot of things I can't even think about doing. I'm afraid this is one of them." As she spoke, the window rose again.

I stepped back to allow Ruth to open the door and get out of her living room on wheels. She let the door close with a soft, expensive click. She took a deep breath, considering. While I waited for her to say something, I couldn't help admiring her style. Ruth looked nothing like a woman whose sleep had been wrecked by the call that had dragged her out of bed. There was nothing slapdash about her understated make-up and her long blonde hair was pulled back in a neat scalp plait, the distinguished silver streaks at the temples glinting in the streetlights. She was in her middle thirties, but the only giveaway was a faint cluster of laughter lines at the corners of her eyes. She wore a black frock coat over a cream silk shirt with a rolled neck, black leggings and black ankle boots with a high heel. The extra height disguised the fact that she had to be at least a size eighteen. We'd been friends ever since she'd been the guest speaker at my university Women in Law group, and I'd never seen her look anything other than immaculate. If I didn't like her so much, I'd hate her.

Now, she put a surprisingly slim hand on my arm. "Kate, you know I sympathize. If that was Peter in there, I'd be moving heaven and earth to get him out. I have no doubt whatsoever that Richard's first demand will be that I get you on the case. And I'll back that one hundred per cent. But give me space to do what I'm best at. As soon as I'm through here, I'll come straight round and brief you, I promise."

I shook my head. "I hear what you're saying, but that's not enough, I'm sorry. If I'm going to do what *I'm* best at, there are questions I need to ask that won't necessarily have anything to do with what you need to know. Ruth, it's in your client's best interests."

Ruth put an arm round my shoulder and hugged me. "Nice try, Kate. You really should have stuck to the law, you know.

You'd have made a great advocate. But the answer's still no. I'll see you later."

She let me go and walked across the police car park towards the entrance, the heels of her boots clicking on the tarmac. "You'd better believe it," I said softly.

Time to exploit the irregular verb theory of life. In this case, the appropriate one seemed to be: I am creative, you exaggerate, he/she is a pathological liar. I gave Ruth ten minutes to get through the formalities. Then I walked across to the door and pressed the intercom buzzer. "Hello?" the intercom crackled.

Giving my best impression of a panic-stricken, very junior gopher, I said, "I'm with Hunter Butterworth. I was supposed to meet Ms Hunter here; I'm her trainee, you see, only, my car wouldn't start, and I got here late, and I saw her car outside already. Can you let me through? Only, I'm supposed to be learning how to conduct interviews by observing her, and when she rang me she said Mr Barclay's case sounded like one I could learn a lot from," I gabbled without pause.

"Miss Hunter never said anything about expecting a trainee," the distorted voice said.

"She's probably given up on me. I was supposed to meet her twenty minutes ago. Please, can you let me through? I'll be in enough trouble just for being so late. If she thinks I haven't showed up at all, my life won't be worth living. I've already had the 'clients rely on us for their liberty, Ms Robinson' lecture once this week!"

I'd struck the right chord. The door buzzed and I pushed it open. I stepped inside and pushed open the barred gate. The custody sergeant grinned at me from behind his desk. "I'm glad I'm not in your shoes," he said. "She can be a real tartar, your boss. I had a teacher like her once. Miss Gibson. Mind you, she got me through O Level French, which was no mean feat."

He asked my name, and I claimed to be Kate Robinson. He made a note on the custody record, then led me down a well-lit corridor. I took care not to trip over the cracked vinyl floor tiles whose edges were starting to curl. It was hard to tell what colour they'd started out; I couldn't believe someone had actually *chosen* battleship grey mottled with khaki and bile green. Halfway along the corridor, he paused outside a door marked "Interview 2" and knocked, opening the door before he got a reply. "Your trainee's here, Miss Hunter," he announced, stepping back to usher me in.

Like a true professional, Ruth didn't bat an eyelid. "Thank you," she said grimly. Typically, it was Richard who nearly gave the show away. His whole face lit up in that familiar smile that still sends my hormones into chaos.

He got as far as, "What are you—" before Ruth interrupted.

"I hope you don't mind, Mr Barclay, but my colleague is a trainee who is supposed to be learning the tricks of the trade," she said loudly. "I'd like her to sit in on our consultation, unless you have any objections?"

"N-no," Richard stammered, looking bewildered.

I stepped into the room and the sergeant closed the door firmly behind me.

Simultaneously, Richard said, "I don't understand," and Ruth growled softly, "I should walk out of here right now and leave you to it."

"I know. I'm sorry. I couldn't not. It's too important. But look on the bright side: if I can blag my way into the secure interview room of a police station, aren't you glad you've got me on the team?" I added an apologetic smile.

Before Ruth could find an answer for that particular bit of cheek, Richard said plaintively, "But I don't understand what you're doing here, Brannigan."

"I'm here because you need help, Richard. I know you spend most of your time on another planet, but here on earth, it's considered to be a pretty serious offence to drive around in a stolen car with enough crack to get half Manchester out of their heads," I told him.

"Look, I know it sounds like I'm in deep shit. But it's not like that." He ran a hand through his hair and frowned. "I keep trying to tell everybody. It wasn't a stolen car. It was *our* car. The one we bought in Bolton on Tuesday."

# 4

Before I could pick the bones out of that, Ruth interrupted. "Let's just hold everything right there. Kate, you are here on sufferance. I, on the other hand, am here because Richard asked me to be. I've got a job to do and I intend to do it, in spite of your interference. So let me ask my questions, and then if there's anything we haven't covered, you can have your turn."

It wasn't a suggestion, it was an instruction. I knew what I'd done was bang out of order. I'd taken a big risk on the strength of my friendship with Ruth, and I didn't want to risk damaging those bonds any further. Besides, I like watching people who are really good at what they do. "That's absolutely fine with me," I said.

"You mean she really isn't meant to be here?" Richard asked, his grin irrepressible even in the face of Ruth's frown.

"If you weren't facing such serious charges, I'd have bounced her out of the door. It didn't seem like a good time to generate even more suspicion on the part of the police. Now, Richard, let's get to it. I don't have all night." Ruth picked up her pencil and started to write. "Let's start at the beginning. What happened tonight?"

Richard looked uncertain. "Well, the beginning isn't tonight. I mean, depending on what you mean, the beginning's either Tuesday night or three weeks ago."

It was my turn to grin. I didn't envy Ruth her task. I love him dearly, but the only time Richard can tell a story in a straight line from beginning to end is when he's sat in front of a word processor with the prospect of a nice little earner at the end of the day.

Ruth squeezed the bridge of her nose. "Maybe you could give me the short version, and I'll stop you when I don't understand something."

"It's this job Kate's got on. I've been helping her out with it. We have to buy these cars, you see, and then we give them back to the car company." Richard paused hopefully.

Ruth's grey eyes swivelled round and fixed on me. "Perhaps you'd like to elaborate . . . ?"

I nodded. "My clients are the finance arm of the Leo Motor Company. They suspect some dealerships of committing fraud. It's our job to provide them with evidence, so Richard and I have been posing as a married couple, buying cars with money supplied by Leo, who then take the cars back from us," I said.

"Thanks. So, you've been buying these cars. What happened on Tuesday night?" she asked.

"We'd picked up this really ace motor, the Gemini turbo super coupé," Richard said enthusiastically. "Anyway, I had to go into town, and I decided to treat myself and drive the coupé, since we'd only got it for a day or two. Then when I came out of the club, the car was gone. So I came home and reported it stolen to the police."

Ruth looked up from her pad. "Did they send anyone round?"

"Yeah, a copper came round about an hour later and I gave him all the details," Richard said.

"And I informed my client first thing on Wednesday morning, if that's any help," I added.

This time Ruth didn't scowl at me. She just made another note and said, "So what happened next?"

Richard took off his glasses and stared up at the ceiling.
A line appeared between his brows as he focused his memory.
"I went into town about nine tonight. I had to meet a couple
of women in the Paradise Factory. They're the singers in a jazz
fusion band, and they've just signed their first record deal. I'm
doing a piece on them for one of the glossies. It was too noisy
in the Factory to hear ourselves talk, so we left and went round
to Manto's." Trust Richard to spend his evening in the trendiest
café bar in the North West. Looking at his outfit, I was surprised
the style police had let him in. "We stayed till closing time," he
went on. "The girls were going on to the Hacienda, but I didn't
fancy it, so I went off to get my car. I'd parked it off Portland
Street, and I was walking past the gardens on Sackville Street
when I saw the car." He put his glasses back on and looked
expectantly at Ruth.

"Which car, Richard?" Ruth asked patiently.

"The coupé," he said, in the injured tones of someone who
thinks they've already made themselves abundantly clear. Poor
misguided soul.

"You saw the car that you had reported stolen in the early
hours of Wednesday morning?"

"That's right," he said. "Only, I wasn't sure right away if it
was the same one. It was the right model and the right colour,
but I couldn't see if it was the right registration number. It had
trade plates on, you see."

"Trade plates," Ruth repeated as she scribbled. I was
intrigued. Any self-respecting car thief would have smacked
fake plates on a stolen car right away. I couldn't for the life of
me see why they'd use the red and white plates garages use to
shift untaxed cars from one place to another. It was just asking
to be noticed.

"Yeah, trade plates," Richard said impatiently. "Anyway,
I went over to this car, and I lifted up the trade plate on the
front, and it was the same reg as the one that got nicked on

Tuesday night," Richard said triumphantly. He put his glasses on and grinned nervously at both of us. "It's going to be OK, isn't it?" he added.

Ruth nodded. "We'll get it sorted out, Richard. Now, are you absolutely certain that this was the same car?"

"I still had the keys on my key-ring," he said. "It had one of those little cardboard tags on it with the number of the car, so I wasn't just relying on my memory. It was the identical number. Besides, the key I had opened the car, and there was still one of my tapes in the cassette. Isn't that proof enough?"

"Somehow, I don't think the point at issue is going to be the car," I muttered quietly. Ruth gave me a look that would have curdled a piña colada.

"Did you call the police and tell them you'd found the car?" Ruth asked.

"Well, I figured that if I wandered off to look for a phone, the guy that had nicked it could easily have had it away again while I was busy talking to the Dibble. So I thought I'd just repo it myself and call the cops when I got home," Richard explained. It wasn't so unreasonable. Even I had to concede that.

"What did you do next?" Ruth said.

"Well, I did what any reasonable person would have done," Richard said. My heart sank. "I took the trade plates off and cobbed them in the gutter."

"You cobbed them in the gutter?" Ruth and I chorused, neck and neck in the incredulity stakes.

"Of course I did. They didn't belong to me. I'm not a thief," Richard said with a mixture of self-righteousness and naïvety that made my fingers itch with the desire to get round his throat.

"It didn't occur to you that they might be helpful evidence for the police in catching the car thieves?" Ruth said, all silky savagery.

"No, it didn't, I'm sorry. I'm not like you two. I don't have a criminal sort of mind."

Ruth looked like she wanted to join me in the lynch mob. "Go on," she said, her voice icy. "What did you do after you disposed of your corroboration?"

"I got in the car and set off. I was nearly home when I saw the flashing blue lights in my rear-view mirror. I didn't even pull over at first, because I wasn't speeding or anything. Anyway, they cut me up at the lights on Upper Brook Street, and I realized it was me they were after. So I stopped. I opened the window a couple of inches, but before I could say anything, one of the bizzies opened the door and dragged me out of the motor. Next thing I know, I'm spread-eagled over the bonnet with a pair of handcuffs on and his oppo's got the boot open.

"They kept on at me about the car being stolen, and I kept telling them, yeah, I knew that, 'cos I was the person it had been stolen off, but they just wouldn't listen. Then the guy looking in the boot came round with this Sainsbury's plastic bag, and he's waving it in my face saying, 'And I suppose the villains that nicked your car decided to leave you a little something for your trouble?' Well, I had no idea what was in the boot, did I? So I told them that, and they just laughed, and bundled me into their car and brought me here. Next thing I know is they're on at me about a parcel of crack. And that's when I thought, uh-oh, I need a brief."

Richard sat back and looked at the two of us. "It's an unexpected bonus, getting Brannigan as well," he added. "How soon can you get me out of this dump, Ruth?" he asked, gesturing round the shabby interview room.

"That depends on several things. Being absolutely honest, Richard, I'm not optimistic that I can avoid them charging you, which means you won't be going anywhere until I can get you in front of a magistrate and apply for bail, which we can probably manage tomorrow morning. I still have some questions, though. Have you at any time opened the boot of the coupé?"

Richard frowned. "I don't think so," he said hesitantly. "No, I'm pretty sure I haven't. I mean, why would I?"

"You didn't check it out when you bought it? Look to see if there was a spare wheel and a jack?" Ruth asked.

"The salesman showed us when we took it for a test drive," I interjected. "I certainly don't remember Richard ever going near it."

He managed a grin. "We didn't have it long enough for Brannigan to take it shopping, so we didn't need the boot."

"Good," Ruth said. "This carrier bag that they produced from the boot. Had you ever seen it before?"

Richard shrugged. "Well, I don't know. It was just an ordinary Sainsbury's carrier bag. Brannigan's got a drawer full of them. There was nothing about it to make it any different from any other one. But it wasn't in the boot when that rattlesnake showed us the car on Monday. And I didn't put it there. So I guess it's fair to say I'd never seen it before."

"Did you touch it at all?"

"How could I? I said, I'd never seen it before," Richard said plaintively.

"The officer didn't throw it to you, or hand it to you?" Ruth persisted.

"He couldn't, could he? His oppo had me cuffed already," Richard replied.

"Yes, I'm a little surprised at that. Had you put up a struggle? Or had you perhaps been a little over-energetic in the verbal department?" Ruth asked carefully.

"Well, I wasn't exactly thrilled at being bodily dragged out of what was, technically, my own motor when I hadn't even been speeding and I'd been on the Diet Coke all night. So I suppose I was a bit gobby," Richard admitted. If my heart could have sunk any further, it would have done. Add resisting arrest to the list, I thought gloomily.

Ruth was clearly as cheered as I was by this news. "But you didn't actually offer any physical violence?" she asked, the hope in her voice as obvious as a City supporter in a United bus.

"No," Richard said indignantly. "What do you take me for?"

Diplomatically, neither of us answered. "The keys for this coupé—did you have both sets?"

Richard shook his head. "No, Brannigan had the others."

"Have you still got them?" she asked me.

I nodded. "They're in the kitchen drawer. No one but the two of us has had access to them."

"Good," Ruth said. "These two women you were with—can you give me their names and addresses? I'll need statements from them to show you were talking about their record contract, rather than sitting in some dark corner negotiating a drug deal."

"You're not going to like this," Richard predicted. Correctly, as it turned out. "I only know their stage names. Lilith Annsdaughter and Eve Uhuru. I don't have any addresses for them, just a phone number. It's in my notebook, but the boys in blue have taken that off me. Sorry." He tried a smile, but the magic didn't work on either of us.

Ruth showed her first real sign of tiredness. Her eyes closed momentarily and her shoulders dropped. "Leave that with me," she said, her voice little stronger than a sigh. Then she took a deep breath, straightened her shoulders and pulled a packet of extra-long menthol cigarettes out of her briefcase. She offered them round, but got no takers. "Do you suppose this counts as Thursday's eleventh or Friday's first?" she asked. "Either way, it's against the rules." She lit the cigarette, surprisingly, with a match torn from a restaurant matchbook. I'd have had Ruth marked down as a Dunhill lighter.

"One more thing," Ruth said. "You've got a son, haven't you, Richard?"

Richard frowned, puzzled. "Yeah. Davy. Why?"

"What does he look like?"

"Why do you want to know that?" Richard asked. I was glad he had; it saved me the bother.

"According to the custody sergeant, when the officers searched the car more thoroughly, they found a Polaroid photograph that had slid down the side of the rear seat. It shows a young boy." Ruth took a deep breath. "In a rather unpleasant pose. I think they're going to want to ask some questions about that too."

"How do you mean, a rather unpleasant pose?" I demanded.

"He's stripped down to his underpants and handcuffed to a bed," Ruth said.

Richard looked thunderstruck. I knew just how he felt. "And you think that's got something to do with *me*?" he gasped, outraged.

"The police might," Ruth said.

"It couldn't be anything to do with us," I butted in. "Neither of us has been in the back seat since we got the car. The only person who'd been in the back seat that I know of is the salesman, on the test drive."

"OK, OK," Ruth said. "Calm down. All I was thinking is that the photograph might possibly have an innocent explanation, and that it might have been your son."

"So what does this kid look like?" Richard said belligerently.

"I'd say about ten, dark wavy hair, skinny."

Richard let out a sigh. "Well, you can count Davy out. He's only eight, average size for his age, and his hair's straight like mine, and the same colour. Light brown." The colour of butterscotch, to be precise.

"Fine. I'm glad we've cleared that up," Ruth said. "Any questions, Kate?"

I nodded. Not that I had any hopes of a useful answer. "Richard, when you were in Manto's, did you see anyone you recognized from the club the other night? Anyone a bit flash, a bit hooky, the type that just might have nicked the motor?"

Richard screwed up his eyes in concentration. Then he shook his head. "You know me, Brannigan. I don't go places to look at the punters," he said apologetically.

"Did you do a number on anybody about the car?"

"I didn't mention it to a soul. I'd just have looked a dick-head next week, back with my usual wheels," he said, with rare insight.

"I don't suppose you know who's doing the heavy-duty stuff round town these days?"

Richard leaned forward and stared into my eyes. I could feel his fear. "I've got no interest," he said, his face tense. "I bend over backwards to avoid taking any interest. Look, you know how much time I spend in the Moss and Cheetham Hill with new bands. Everybody knows I'm a journo. If I showed the slightest interest in the gangs and the drugs, I'd be a dead man, blown away on the steps of some newspaper office as a warning to other hacks not to get any daft ideas in their heads about running a campaign to clean up Manchester. You ask Alexis. She's supposed to be the crime correspondent. You ask her the last time there was a heavy incident in Moss Side or Cheetham Hill where she did anything more than toddle along to the police press conference! Believe me, if I thought for one minute that the gang that owns these drugs knows it was me that drove off with them, I'd be begging for protective custody a long, long way from Manchester. No, Brannigan, I do not know who's doing the heavy stuff, and for the sake of both our healths, I suggest that you remain in the same blissful state."

I shrugged. "You want to walk away from this? The only way you're going to do that is if we give them a body to trade," I turned to Ruth. "Am I right?"

"Regardless of that, you're probably going to have to spend another few days in police custody," Ruth warned him.

Richard's face fell. "Is there no way you can get me out sooner? I've got to get out of here, double urgent," he said.

"Richard, in my opinion, the police will charge you with possession of a Class A drug with intent to supply, which is not a charge on which magistrates are inclined to allow bail. I'll do my best, but the chances are heavily stacked against us. Sorry about that, but there we go." Ruth paused to savour a last mouthful of smoke before regretfully stubbing out her cigarette.

"Oh, shit," Richard said. He took off his glasses and carefully polished them on his paisley silk shirt. He sighed. "I suppose I'll have to go for it. But there's one slight problem I haven't mentioned that Brannigan seems to have forgotten about," he said sheepishly, looking short-sightedly in my direction.

My turn to sigh. "Give," I said.

"Davy's due on the seven o'clock shuttle tonight. Remember? Half-term?"

As his words sank in, I got to my feet, shaking my head. "Oh no, no way. Not me."

"Please," Richard said. "You know how much it means to me."

"There isn't that much dosh in the world," I said, panicking.

"Please, Kate. That bitch is just looking for an excuse to shut me out," he pleaded.

"That's no way to talk about the woman you married, the mother of your child, the former joy of your existence and fire of your loins," I said, slipping defensively into our routine banter. It was no use. I knew as I looked down at the poor sod that I'd already given in. A dozen years of efficient contraception, and what does it get you? Someone else's kid, that's what.

# 5

I had to sit through the whole tale a second time for the CID's preliminary taped interview with Richard. Ruth had instructed him to co-operate fully, in the hope that it might predispose them towards letting his bail application go through. Looking at their faces as they listened to Richard's admittedly unlikely story, I didn't rate his chances of seeing daylight for a while.

After the interview, Ruth and I went into a brief huddle. "Look, Kate, realistically, he's not going to get bail tomorrow. The best chance we have of getting him out is if you can come up with evidence that supports his story and points to the real criminals." I held my tongue; Ruth is one of the few people I allow to tell me how to suck eggs.

"The crucial thing, given the amount of drugs involved, is that we keep him out of the mainstream prison system so he's not in contact with criminals who have connections into the drug scene. What I'm going to suggest to the CID is that they use the excuse of the 'stolen' car and the possibly pornographic photograph to exploit paragraph five of the Bail Act," she went on.

I must have looked as blank as I felt, for she deigned to explain. "If the suspect's been arrested for one offence and the police have evidence of his implication in another, they can ask for what we call a lie-down. In other words, he remains in police custody for up to three days for the other matters to be investigated. That'll give us a bit of leeway, since the meter doesn't start running till the day after the initial hearing. That gives us Saturday, Sunday, Monday and Tuesday. He'll appear in court again on Wednesday, by which time you might have made enough headway for me to be able to argue that he should be let out."

"Oh whoopee," I said. "A schedule so tight I'll be singing soprano and an eight-year-old too. Go for it, Ruth."

I left Ruth to her wheeling and dealing with the CID just after half past four and drove into the city centre. Chinatown was still lively, the late-night trade losing their shirts in the casinos and drunkenly scoffing Chinese meals after the clubs had closed. Less than a mile away, in the gay village round Chorlton Street bus station, the only sign of life was a few rent boys and hookers, hanging around the early-morning street corners in a triumph of hope over experience. I cruised slowly along Canal Street, the blank windows of Manto's reflecting nothing but my Peugeot. I didn't even spot anyone sleeping rough till I turned down Minshull Street towards UMIST.

The street was still. I pulled up in an empty parking meter bay. There were only three other cars in the street, one of them Richard's Beetle. I'd have to come back in the morning and collect it before some officious traffic warden had it ticketed and clamped. At least its presence supported Richard's story, if the police were inclined to check it out. I took my pocket Nikon out of my glove box, checked the date stamp was switched on and took a couple of shots of the Beetle as insurance.

Slowly, I walked round to Sackville Street, checking doorways and litter bins for the trade plates. I didn't hold out much hope. They were too good a prize for any passing criminal, never mind the guys who had stuck them on the coupé in the first place. As I'd expected, the streets were clear. On the off chance, I walked round into the little square of garden in Sackville Street and searched along the wall and in the bushes, being careful to avoid touching the unpleasant crop of used condoms. No joy.

Stumbling with exhaustion, I walked back to my car and drove home. The prospect of having to take care of Davy weighed heavily on me, and I desperately wanted to crack on and make some progress towards clearing Richard. But the sensible part of me knew there was nothing I could do in the middle of the night. And if I didn't get some sleep soon, I wouldn't be fit to do what had to be done come daylight.

I set my alarm for half past eight, switched off the phones and turned down the volume on the answering machine. Unfortunately, I couldn't do the same thing with my brain. I tossed and turned, my head full of worries that wouldn't lie down and leave me in peace. I prayed Ruth's stratagem would work. While he was still in police custody, Richard was fairly safe. But as soon as he was charged and remanded to prison, the odds would turn against him. No matter how much the police tried to keep the lid on this business, it wouldn't take long in the leaky sieve of prison before the wrong people learned what he was in for. And if the drugs belonged to one of the Manchester gangs, some warlord somewhere would decide that Richard needed to be punished in ways the law has long since ceased to contemplate.

We'd both gone into this relationship with damage from past encounters. From the start, we'd been honest about our pain and our fears. As a result, we'd always kept it light, by tacit agreement. Somewhere round about dawn, I acknowledged that I couldn't live with myself if I let anything happen to him. It's a real bastard, love.

I was only dozing when the alarm went off. The first thing I did was check the answering machine. Its friendly red light was flashing, so I hit the "replay" button. "Hello, Kate, it's Ruth." Her voice was friendlier than I deserved. "It's just before six, and I thought you'd be pleased to hear that I've manged to persuade the divisional superintendent that he has most chance of obtaining convictions from this situation if he keeps Richard's arrest

under wraps. So he's agreed, very reluctantly, not to hold a press
conference announcing a major drugs haul. He's not keen, but
there we go. Was I put on earth to keep policemen happy? He's
also receptive to the idea of a lie-down, but he wants to hang
on till later in the day before he makes a final decision. Anyway,
I hope you're managing some sleep, since working yourself to
the point of exhaustion will not serve the interests of my client.
Why don't you give me a call towards the end of the afternoon,
by which time we both might have some information? Speak to
you soon, darling. It'll be all right." I wished I could share her
breezy confidence.

As the coffee brewed, I called my local friendly mechanic
and asked him to collect Richard's Beetle, promising to leave
a set of keys under the kitchen window box. I also phoned in
to the office and told Shelley what had happened. Of course, it
was Richard who got the sympathy. Never mind that I'd been
deprived of my sleep and landed with a task that might have
caused even Clint Eastwood a few nervous moments. Oh no,
that was my job, Shelley reminded me. "You do what you've got
to do to get that poor boy out of jail," she said sternly. "It makes
me feel ill, just thinking of Richard locked up in a stinking cell
with the dregs of humanity."

"Yes, boss," I muttered rebelliously. Shelley always makes
me feel like a bloody-minded teenager when she goes into
Mother Hen mode. God knows what effect it has on her own
two adolescents. "Just tell Bill what I'm doing. I'll be on my
mobile if you need me urgently," I added.

I washed two thick slices of toast down with a couple of
mugs of scalding coffee. The toast because I needed carbohy-
drate, the coffee because it was a more attractive option than
surgery to get my eyes open. I pulled on jogging pants and
a sweat shirt without showering and drove over to the Thai
boxing gym in South Manchester where I punish my body on
as regular a basis as my career in crime prevention allows. It
might not be the Hilton, but it meets my needs. It's clean, it's

cheap, the equipment is well maintained and it's mercifully free of muscle-bound macho men who think they've got the body and charm of Sylvester Stallone when in reality they don't even have the punch-drunk brains of Rocky.

I wasn't the only person working out on the weights that morning. The air was already heavy with the smell of sweat as half a dozen men and a couple of women struggled to keep time's winged chariot in the service bay. As I'd hoped, my old buddy Dennis O'Brien, burglar of this parish, was welded to the pec deck, moving more metal than the average Nissan Micra contains. He was barely breaking sweat. The bench next to him was free, so I picked up a set of dumbbells and lay back to do some tricep curls. "Hiya, kid," Dennis said on his next outgoing breath. "What's the world been doing to you?"

"Don't ask. How about you?"

He grinned like a Disney wolf. "Still doing the police's job for them," he said. "Got a real result last night."

"Glad somebody did," I said, enjoying the sensation of my flabby muscles tightening as I raised and lowered the weights.

"Fourteen grand I took off him," Dennis told me. "Now that's what I call a proper victim."

He was clearly desperate to tell the tale, so I gave him the tiny spur of encouragement that was all he needed. "Sounds like a good 'un. How d'you manage that?"

"I hear this firm from out of town are looking for a parcel of trainers. So I arrange to meet them, and I tell them I can lay my hands on an entire wagonload of Reeboks, don't I? A couple of nights later, we meet again and I show him a sample pair from this truck I'm supposed to have nicked, right? Only, I haven't nicked them, have I? I've just gone down the wholesaler's and bought them." As he got into his story, Dennis paused in his work-out. He's physically incapable of telling a tale without his hands.

"So of course, they fall for it. Anyway, we arrange the meet for last night, out on the motorway services at Sandbach. My mate Andy and me, we get there a couple of hours before the meet and suss the place out. When these two bozos arrive, Andy's stood hiding behind a truck right the far side of the lorry park, and when the bozos park up beside my car, I make sure they see me giving him the signal, and he comes over to us, making out like he's just come out of the wagon, keys in his hand, the full monty." Dennis was giggling between his sentences like a little lad outlining some playground scam.

I sat up and said, "So what happens next?"

"I say to these two dummies, 'Let's see the money, then. You hand over the money, and my mate'll hand over the keys to the wagon.' And they do no more than hand over their fourteen grand like lambs. I'm counting the money, and when I've done, I give Andy the nod and he tosses them the keys. We jump into the motor and shoot straight off. I tell you, the last thing I see is the pair of them schmucks jumping up and down beside that wagon, their mouths opening and shutting like a pair of goldfish." By the end of his tale, Dennis was doubled over with laughter. "You should've seen them, Kate," he wheezed. "The Dennis O'Brien crime prevention programme scores another major success."

The first time he said that to me, I'd been a bit baffled. I didn't see how ripping someone off to the tune of several grand could prevent crime. So Dennis had explained. The people he was cheating had a large sum of money that they were prepared to spend on stolen goods. So some thief would have to steal something for them to buy. But if Dennis relieved them of their wad, they wouldn't have any money to spend on stolen goods, therefore the robbery that would have had to take place was no longer necessary. Crime prevention, QED.

I moved over to a piece of equipment designed to build my quads and adjusted the weights. "A lot of dosh, fourteen grand," I said. "Aren't you worried they're going to come after you?"

"Nah," he said scornfully, returning to his exercise. "They're from out of town. They don't know where I hang out, and nobody in Manchester would be daft enough to tell them where to find me. Besides, I was down Collar Di Salvo's car lot first thing this morning, trading the BMW in. They'll be looking for a guy in a red BM, not a silver Merc. Take a tip, Kate—don't buy a red BMW off Collar for the next few days. I don't want to see you in a case of mistaken identity!"

We both pumped iron in silence for a while. I moved around the machines, making sure I paid proper attention to the different muscle groups. By ten, I was sweating, Dennis was skipping and there were only the two of us left. I collapsed on to the mat, and enjoyed the complaints of my stomach muscles as I did some slow, warm-down exercises. "I've got a problem," I said in between Dennis's bounces.

Just saying that brought all the fear and misery right back. I stared hard at the off-white walls, trying to make a pattern out of the grimy handprints, black rubber skidmarks and chips from weights swung too enthusiastically. Dennis slowed to a halt and walked across to the shelves of thin towels that the management think are all we deserve. Like I said, it's cheap. I suppose it was their version of crime prevention; nobody in their right mind would steal those towels. Dennis picked up a couple, draped them over his big shoulders and sat down on the bench facing me. "D'you want to talk about it?"

I sighed. "To be honest, I'm not sure I can." It wasn't that I didn't trust Dennis. Quite the opposite. I trusted his affection for me almost too much to tell him what had happened to Richard. There was no knowing what limits Dennis would go to in the attempt to take care of anyone threatening my happiness and wellbeing. Considering the different perspective we have on the law of the land, we find ourselves side by side facing in the same direction more often than not. For some reason that neither of us quite understands, we know we can rely on each other. And just as important, we like each other too.

Dennis patted my left ankle, the only part of me he could comfortably reach. "You decide you want an ear, you let your Uncle Dennis know. What d'you need right now?"

"I'm not sure about that either." I wiped the back of my hand over my mouth and upper lip and tasted the sharp salty sweat. "Dennis. Why would you put trade plates on a stolen motor rather than false plates?"

"What kind of stolen motor? Joyrider material, stolen to order, or just somebody stuck for a ride home?"

"A brand new Leo Gemini turbo super coupé. Less than a ton on the clock."

He pondered for a moment. "Temporary measure? To keep the bizzies off my back till I got it delivered where it was supposed to be going?"

"In this instance, we're talking a couple of days after the car was lifted. Plenty of time to have dropped it off with whoever, I'd have thought," I said, shaking my head.

"In that case, you're probably talking right proper villainy," he replied, rubbing the back of his neck with one of the towels.

"Run it past me," I said.

Dennis pulled a packet of Bensons and a throw-away lighter out of the pocket of his sweat pants and lit up. "They never have any bloody ashtrays in here," he complained, looking round. The paradox clearly escaped him. "Anyway, your professional car thief goes out on the job knowing exactly what motor he's going for. He doesn't do things on spec. He'd have a set of plates on him that he'd already matched up with another car of the same make and model, so that if some smart-arsed traffic cop put him through the computer he'd come up clean. So he wouldn't need trade plates. Your serious amateurs, they might use trade plates just to get it across town to their dealer. But they're not that easy to come by. OK so far?"

I got off the floor and squatted on a low bench. "Clear as that Edinburgh crystal you offered me last month," I said.

"Your loss, Kate," he said. "Now, on the other hand, if I wanted a fast car for a one-off job, I'd do exactly what the guy you're interested in has done. I'd nick a serious set of wheels, smack some trade plates on it from my local friendly hooky garage when I was actually using it, then dump it as soon as I'd finished the job."

"When you say proper villainy, what exactly did you have in mind?" I asked.

"The kind of stuff I don't do. Major armed robbery, mainly. A hit, maybe."

I began to wish I had the sense not to ask questions I wasn't going to like the answers to. "What about drugs?"

He shrugged. "Not the first thing that would spring to mind. But then, I don't hang out with scum like that, do I? At a guess, it'd only be worth doing if you were shifting a parcel of drugs a reasonable distance between two major players. Say, from London to Manchester. Otherwise there'd be so many cars running around with trade plates that even the coppers would notice. Also, trade plates are ten a penny on the motorway. Whereas brand new motors with or without trade plates stick out like a sore thumb on the council estates where most of the drugs get shifted. You want to get a pull these days, you just have to park up in Moss Side in anything that isn't an old banger," he added bitterly.

"What would you say if I told you there were a couple of kilos of crack in the boot of this car?"

Dennis got to his feet. "Nice chatting to you, Kate. Be seeing you. That's what I'd say."

I pulled a face and stood up too. "Thanks, Dennis."

Dennis put a warm hand on my wrist and gripped it tightly enough for me not to think about pulling away. "I've never been more serious, Kate. Steer clear of them toerags. They'd eat *me* for breakfast. They wouldn't even notice you as they swallowed. Give this one the Spanish Archer."

"The Spanish Archer?" This was a new one on me.

"El Bow."

I smiled. "I'll be careful. I promise." I thought I'd grown out of promising what I can't deliver. Obviously I was wrong.

# 6

I walked into the office to find my partner Bill looming over Shelley like a scene from *The Jungle Book*. Bill is big, blond and shaggy, the antithesis of Shelley, petite, black and immaculately groomed right down to the tips of her perfectly plaited hair. He looked up and stopped speaking in midsentence, finger pointing at something on Shelley's screen.

"Kate, Kate, Kate," he boomed, moving across the room to envelop me in the kind of hug that makes me feel like a little girl. Usually I fight my way out, but this morning it was good to feel safe for a moment, even if it was only an illusion. With one hand, Bill patted my back, with the other he rumpled my hair. Eventually, he released me. "Shelley filled me in. I was just going to phone you," he said, walking over to the coffee machine and busying himself making me a cappuccino. "This business with Richard. What do you want me to do?"

On paper, Bill might be the senior partner of Mortensen and Brannigan. In practice, when either of us is involved in a major case and needs help from the other, there's never any question of the gopher role going to me just because I'm the junior. Whoever started the ball rolling stays the boss. And in this instance, since it was my lover who was in the shit, it was my case.

I took the frothy coffee he handed me and slumped into one of the clients' chairs. "I don't know what you can do," I said. "We've got to find out who stole the car, who the drugs belong to and to make out a strong enough case against them for the police to realize they've made a cockup. Otherwise Richard stays in the nick and we sit back and wait for the slaughter of the innocents."

Bill sat down opposite me. "Shelley," he said over his shoulder, "stick the answering machine on, grab yourself an espresso and come and give us the benefit of your thoughts. We need every brain we've got working on this one."

Shelley didn't need telling twice. She sat down, the inevitable notepad on her knee. Bill leaned back and linked his hands behind his head. "Right," he said. "First question. Accident or intent?"

"Accident," I said instantly.

"Why are you so sure?" Bill asked.

I took a sip of coffee while I worked out the reasons I'd been so certain. "OK," I said. "First, there are too many imponderables for it to be intentional. If someone was deliberately trying to set up Richard, or me, they wouldn't have bothered with the trade plates. They'd just have left it sitting there with its own plates, so obvious that he couldn't have missed it. Why bother with all of that when they could have planted the drugs in either of our cars at any time?"

Shelley nodded and said, "The thing that strikes me is that it's an awful lot of drugs to plant. Surely they could have achieved the same result with a lot less crack than two kilos. I don't know much about big-time drug dealers, but I can't believe they'd waste drugs they could make money out of just to set somebody up."

"Besides," I added, "why in God's name would anyone want to frame Richard? I know *I* sometimes feel like murdering him, but I'm a special case. Not even his ex-wife would want him to spend the next twenty years inside, never mind be willing to splash out—what, two hundred grand?"

Bill nodded. "Near enough," he said.

"Well, even she wouldn't spend that kind of dosh just to get her own back on him, always supposing he paid her enough maintenance for her to afford it. It's not as if he's an investigative journalist. The only people who take offence at what he writes are record company executives, and if any of them got their hands on two kilos of crack it would be up their noses, not in the boot of Richard's car." My voice wobbled and I ran out of steam suddenly. I kept coming up against the horrible realization that this wasn't just another case. My life was going to be irrevocably affected by whatever I did over the next few days.

Thankfully, Bill didn't notice. I don't think I could have handled any more sympathy right then. "OK. Accident. Synchronicity. What are the leads?"

"Why does somebody always have to ask the one question you don't have the answer to?" I said shakily.

"Has his solicitor got anything from the police yet?" Bill asked. "Who's looking after him, by the way?"

"He's got Ruth. If the cops have got anything themselves yet, they've not passed it on. But she asked me to call her this afternoon." I stirred the froth into the remains of my coffee and watched it change colour.

"So what have we got to go at?"

"Not a lot," I admitted. "Frankly, Bill, there aren't enough leads on this to keep one person busy, never mind the two of us."

"What were you planning on doing?" he asked.

"I don't know anybody on the Drugs Squad well enough to pick their brains. So that leaves Della."

Bill nodded. "She'll be as keen to help as me and Shelley."

"She should be," I agreed. Not only did Detective Chief Inspector Della Prentice owe me a substantial professional favour in return for criminals translated into prisoners. Over the past few months, she'd also moved into that small group of women I count as friends. If I couldn't rely on her support, I'd better send my judgement back to the manufacturer for a major service.

"The only other thing I can think of is cruising the city centre tonight looking for another serious motor with trade plates on it."

"The logic presumably being that if they've lost the car they were counting on, they'll need another one?" Bill asked. "Even though the drugs have gone?"

"It's all I've got. I'm hoping that our man will be out and about, trying to find out who's got a parcel of crack they shouldn't have. But that's a one-person job, Bill. Look, leave me numbers where I can reach you, day or night. I promise, if I get anywhere and I need an extra pair of hands, I'll call you right away."

"That's truly the only lead you've got? You're not holding out on me?" he asked suspiciously.

"Believe me, Bill, if I thought there was anything for you to do, I'd be on my hands and knees begging," I said, only half joking.

"Well, let's see what Della has to say. Right, team, let's get some work done!" He strolled back over to Shelley's desk. "This bit here, Shelley. Can we shift it further up the report, so all the frightening stuff hits them right at the beginning?"

Shelley rolled her eyes upwards and got to her feet, squeezing my arm supportively as she passed me on the way to her desk. "Let me have a look, Bill," she said, settling into her chair.

As I headed for my own office, Bill looked up and smiled. I think it was meant to reassure me. It didn't. I closed my door and dropped into my chair like a stone. I put a hand out to switch on my computer, but there didn't seem a lot of point. I swivelled round and looked out of the window at the city skyline. The lemon geranium on the sill was drooping. Knowing my track record with plants, my best friend Alexis had given me the geranium, confidently predicting it was indestructible. I tried not to see its impending death as an omen and turned away. Time was slipping past, and I didn't seem to be able to take any decisive action to relieve the sense of frustration that was burning inside me like indigestion.

"Come *on*, Brannigan," I urged myself, picking up the phone. At least I could get the worst job over with. When the phone was answered, I said, "Andrew Broderick, please."

Moments later, a familiar voice said, "Broderick."

"Andrew, it's Kate Brannigan. I have good news and bad news," I said. "The good news is that we've found the car, undamaged."

"That's tremendous," he said, his astonishment obvious. "How did you manage that?"

"Pure chance, unfortunately," I said. "The bad news, however, is that the police have impounded it."

"The police? But why?"

I sighed. "It's a bit complicated, Andrew," I said. Brannigan's entry for the understatement of the year contest. When I'd finished explaining, I had an extremely unhappy client.

"This is simply not on," he growled. "What right have they got to hang on to a car that belongs to my company?"

"It's evidence in a major drugs case."

"Jesus Christ," he exploded. "If I don't get that car back, this operation is going to cost me about as much as the scam. How the hell am I going to lose that in the books?"

I didn't have the answer. I made some placatory noises, and got off the line as fast as I could. Staring at the wall, I remembered a loose end that was hanging around from Broderick's job, so I rang my local friendly finance broker.

Josh Gilbert and I have an arrangement: he runs credit checks on dodgy punters for me and I buy him dinner a lot. Anything else he can help us with we pay through the nose for.

It turned out that Josh was out of town, but his assistant Julia was around. I explained what I wanted from her and she said, "No problem. I can't promise I'll get to it today, but I'll definitely fax it to you by Tuesday lunch time. Is that OK?"

It would have to be. The one free favour Josh had ever done me was introducing me to Detective Chief Inspector Della

Prentice. My next call was to her direct line. She answered on the second ring. "DCI Prentice," she said crisply.

"Della, it's Kate," I said. Even to me, my voice sounded weary.

"Kate! Thanks for getting back to me," she said.

"Sorry? I didn't know you'd been trying to get hold of me," I replied, shuffling the papers on my desk in case I'd missed a message.

"I spoke to your machine an hour or so ago. When I heard what had happened to Richard," Della said. "I just wanted you to know that I don't believe a word of it."

I felt a lump in my throat, so I swallowed hard and concentrated very hard on the jar of pencils by my phone. "Me neither," I said. "Del, I know it's not your manor, but I need all the help I can get on this one."

"Goes without saying, Kate. Look, it's not going to be easy for me to get access to the case information or any forensic evidence, but I'll do what I can," she promised.

"I appreciate that. But don't put your own head in the noose in the process," I added. No matter how much they spend on advertising to tell us different, anyone who has any contact with real live police officers know that The Job is still a white, patriarchal, rigidly hierarchical organization. That makes life especially hard for women who refuse to be shunted into the ghetto of community liaison and get stuck in at the sharp end of crime fighting.

"Don't worry about me. I'll find out who's on the team and see who I know. Meanwhile, is there anything specific I can help you with?"

"I need a general backgrounder on crack. How much there is of it around, where it's turning up, who they think is pushing the stuff, how it's being distributed. Anything there is, including gossip. Off the record, of course. Any chance?" I asked.

"Give me a few hours. Can you meet me around seven?"

I pulled a face. "Only if you can get to the airport," I said. "I have a plane to meet."

"No problem."

"Oh yes it is. Richard's son's going to be on it. And the one thing he mustn't find out is that his dad's in the nick on drugs charges."

"Ah," Della said. It was a short, clipped exclamation.

"I take it that response means you don't want to share the child-minding?"

"Correct. Count me out. Look, I'll dig up all I can and meet you at Domestic Arrivals in Terminal I, at the coffee counter, just as you come in. Around quarter to seven, OK?"

I didn't want to wait that long, but Della wasn't the sort to hang around either. If quarter to seven was when she wanted to meet, then quarter to seven was the soonest she could see me with the information I needed. "I'll see you then. Oh, one other thing. I don't think it's got anything to do with the drugs, but there was a Polaroid picture of a young kid in handcuffs—you know, bondage-style—in the car. Probably just dropped by one of the villains. But maybe you could ask around and see if there's anybody that Vice have in the frame for paedophilia who's also got form for drugs."

"Can do."

"And Della?"

"Mmm?"

"Thanks."

"You know what they say. A friend in need . . ."

"Is a pain in the ass," I finished. "See you." I put the phone down. At last I felt things were starting to move.

The conversation with Della had reminded me of the part of the problem I'd deliberately been ignoring. Davy. Not that he was in himself a problem. It's just that I wasn't very good at keeping eight-year-old boys happy when I was eight myself, and I haven't improved with age. According to Richard, Davy was the only good thing to come out of his three-year marriage, and his ex-wife Angie seemed more determined with each passing year to reduce his contact with the only child he was likely to have if he stayed with me. So it was imperative that Davy didn't go back from his half-term holiday with lurid tales of Daddy in the nick.

Which sounded simple if you said it very fast. Unless we could spring Richard in the next day or two, however, it was going to be extremely complicated. Richard and I had agreed an initial lie, which should hold the fort for a day or two. After that, it was going to get complicated. While Davy might just believe his dad had had to dash abroad on an urgent, chance-in-a-lifetime job, it wasn't going to be easy to explain why Richard couldn't get home again. There may be parts of the world where the transport isn't too reliable on account of wars and famine, but unfortunately most of them don't run to major rock venues. Either way, whether it took hours or days, I was going to need some assistant minders, if only to baby-sit while I rambled the city centre streets looking for fast cars with trade plates. And there aren't very many people I'd trust to do that.

I picked up the phone again and tapped in Alexis Lee's office number. *"Chronicle* crime desk," a young man's voice informed me.

"Alexis, please."

"Sh'not'ere," came the snippy reply.

"I need to speak to her in a hurry. You wouldn't happen to know where I can get hold of her?" I asked, clinging to my manners by my fingernails. My Granny Brannigan always said politeness cost nothing. But then, she never had to face the humiliation of dealing with lads who still think a yuppie is something to aspire to.

"'Zit'bout'story?" he demanded. "You c'n tell me if it is."

"Not as such," I said through clenched teeth. I could hear my Oxford accent becoming more Gown than Town by the second. "Not yet, anyway. Look, I know you're a very busy person, and I don't want to waste any of your precious time, but it's awfully important that I speak to Alexis. Do you know where she is?"

There's a whole generation of young lads who are either so badly educated or so thick skinned they don't even notice when they're being patronized. The guy on the phone could have featured in a sociology lecture as an exemplar of the type. "Sh's a' lunch," he gabbled.

"And do we know where?"

"Gone f'r a curry."

That was all I needed to know. There might be three dozen curry restaurants strung out along the mile-long stretch of Wilmslow Road in Rusholme, but everybody has their favourite. Alexis's current choice was only too familiar. "Thanks, sonny," I said. "I'll remember you in my letter to Santa."

I was out of my seat before I'd put the phone back. I crossed my office in five strides and walked into the main office. "Shelley, I'm off to the Golden Ganges. And before you ask how I can eat at a time like this, don't. Just don't."

# 7

If the gods had struck me blind the moment I entered the Golden Ganges, I'd still have had no problem finding Alexis. That unmistakable Liverpudlian voice, a monument to Scotch and nicotine, almost drowned out the twanging sitar that was feebly trickling out of the restaurant's speakers, even though she was seated a long way from the door. The volume told me she wasn't working, just routinely showing off to her companion. When she's doing the business with one of her contacts, the sound level drops so low that even MI5 would have a job picking it up. I walked towards the table.

Alexis spotted me two steps into the room, though there was no pause in the flow of her narrative to indicate it. As I approached, she held up one finger to stop me in my tracks a few feet away, interrupting her story to say, "Just a sec, Kate, crucial point in the anecdote." She turned back to her companion and said, "Thomas Wynn Ellis, a good Welsh name, you'd think you'd cracked it, yeah? I mean, she's not *crazy* about the Welsh, but at least you've got a fair chance that he's going to speak English, yeah? So she fills in all the forms to be taken on as a patient, then makes an appointment to see him about her back problem. She walks into the surgery, and what does she find? Straight from Karachi, Dr Thomas Wynn Ellis, product of the Christian orphanage, colour of a bottle of HP sauce! She was sick as a parrot!"

Alexis's companion giggled. I couldn't find a laugh, not just because I'd heard her ridicule the casual racism of her colleagues before. I sat down at the table. Luckily they'd progressed to the coffee. I don't think I could have sat at the same table as a curry, never mind eaten one. I didn't recognize the young woman sharing the table, but Alexis didn't leave me in the dark too long. "Kate, this is Polly Patrick, she's about to take up a post at the university, doing research into psychological profiling of serial offenders. Polly, this is my best mate, Kate Brannigan, PI."

Polly looked interested. I winced. I knew what was coming. "You're a private investigator?" Polly asked.

"No," Alexis butted in, unable to resist her joke of the month. "She's Politically Incorrect!" She hooted in mirth. In anyone else, it would wind me up to some tune, but Alexis's humour is so innocently juvenile she somehow manages to be endearing, not infuriating.

This time, I managed to dredge up a smile. "Actually, I am a private investigator. And I'd be fascinated to have a chat with you some time about what you do."

"Ditto," said Polly. Unusually for a psychologist, she had some people skills, for she took the barely indicated hint. "But it'll have to be another time. I've got to dash. Perhaps the three of us could do lunch some time soon?"

We all made the appropriate farewell and let's-get-together-soon noises, and a few minutes later, Polly was just a memory. Alexis had ordered more coffee somewhere during the good-byes, and I sat staring at the froth on mine as she lit a cigarette and settled into her seat. "So, Sherlock," she said. "What's the problem?"

I reckoned I was about to ask her something that would test our friendship to the limits. But then, the last time she'd asked me a major favour, it had nearly got me killed, so I figured I didn't need to beat myself up about it too much. I took a deep breath and said, "I need to talk to you about something important. It's personal, it's big and it's got to be off the record. Can you live with that?"

"We're friends, aren't we?"

"Yeah, and one good turn deserves the lion's share of the duvet."

"Go on, girl, spill it," Alexis said. She opened a shoulder bag only marginally smaller than mine and ostentatiously pressed the button that switched off her microcassette recorder. "Your secret is safe with me."

"Why d'you suppose that line terrifies me?" I said, in a weak attempt at our usual friendly banter.

Alexis ran a hand through her wild black hair. Coupled with her pale skin and the dark smudges under her eyes, I sometimes think she looks worryingly like one of Dracula's victims in the Francis Ford Coppola version. Luckily, her linguistic vigour usually dispels such ethereal notions pretty damn quick. "Shit, KB, if that's the best you can do, there's clearly something serious going down here," she said. "C'mon, girl, spit it out."

"Richard's been arrested," I said. "He was technically driving a stolen car that not-so-technically had two kilos of crack in the boot."

Alexis just stared at me. She even ignored her burning cigarette. The woman who had heard it all could be shaken after all. "You're at the wind-up," she finally said.

I shook my head. "I wish I was." I gave her the full story. It didn't take long. Throughout, she kept shaking her head in disbelief, smoking so intensely it seemed to be all that was keeping her in one piece. When I'd brought her up to speed, she carried on smoking, head weaving like a Wimbledon spectator.

"It could only happen to Richard," she finally said in tones of wonder. "How does he do it? The poor sod!" Alexis and Richard play this game of cordially disliking each other. I'm not supposed to know it's a game; things must be bad if Alexis was letting me see she actually cared about the guy. "I take it you want me to dig around, see what the goss is out on the streets?"

"I don't want you to take any chances," I said, meaning it. "You know as well as I do that most of the drug warlords in this city would blow you away at the slightest provocation. Don't tread on anybody's toes, please. I don't want you on my conscience as well as Richard. What I'm after is more practical." I broke the news about Davy's imminent arrival.

"Sure, we'll help out. I like Davy. He's good fun. Besides, it gives me and Chris a great excuse to bunk off a weekend's labouring and have a giggle instead." Alexis and her architect girlfriend Chris are members of a self-build scheme, which means they spend most of their spare daylight hours pushing wheelbarrows full of cement along precarious wooden planks. A dozen of them bought a piece of land, and Chris designed the houses in exchange for other people's skills in exotic areas like plumbing, wiring, bricklaying and roofing. It's my idea of hell, but they love it, though not so much that they're not glad of an excuse to give it the body swerve from time to time. I knew taking care of Davy fitted the bill perfectly; it had a high enough Goody Two Shoes element to assuage any guilt at skiving off the building site.

Hearing Alexis confirm my hopes almost brought a genuine smile to my lips. "So can you be at the house tonight about eight?"

Alexis frowned. "Not tonight I can't. I'm having dinner with a contact."

"No chance you can rearrange it?"

"Sorry. The guy's only in town for a few days." She stubbed out her cigarette and washed the taste away with a swig of coffee. She must have felt the need to justify herself, for when I didn't respond, she carried on, "I was at college with him, and we stayed in touch. He's one of your high-flyers, a whiz-kid with the Customs and Excise, if that's not a contradiction in terms. Anyway, he's in Manchester for a briefing session with the Vice Squad. Apparently, there's been a new range of kiddie porn mags and vids hitting the market, real hard-core stuff, and they think the source is somewhere in the North West. Can you believe it, girl? We're actually exporting this shit to Amsterdam and Denmark, that's how heavy it is. So my mate Barney's up here to tell the blue boys what they should be looking for, and I've pitched him into letting me buy him dinner. Sorry, Kate, but I've already promised the editor a splash and a feature launching a campaign for Monday's paper."

I shrugged. "Don't worry about it. I'll get someone else lined up for tonight, and you can weigh in when you're clear."

"Don't do that. Chris'll see you right tonight, I'm sure she will. All she's got planned is a night in front of the soaps and a bottle of Muscadet in the bath. You got the talking brick with you?" Alexis held out her hand, and I passed her my mobile phone. I couldn't help thinking I'd be less than thrilled if Richard had offered me up for a night's baby-sitting when I'd got my heart set on a night in with *Coronation Street* and a Body Shop selection box.

"All right, darling?" Alexis began the conversation. "Listen, Kate needs your body tonight . . . Girl, you should be so lucky. No, it's a bit of a crisis, you know? I'll fill you in later. She needs somebody she can trust to mind Davy round at Richard's . . . Eight, she said, is that OK? . . . Darlin', you'll get your reward in heaven. See you at home about six. Love you too." Alexis pressed the "end" button with a flourish. "Sorted. I'll give her my keys for your house so she can let herself in." She folded the phone closed and handed it back to me.

"I appreciate it," I said. I meant it too. I hoped I wasn't going to run out of favours and friends before I managed to get Richard out of jail. "One more thing—when you're chatting up your porn expert, can you ask him if there's any suggestion of a tie-in with drugs?"

"Why do you ask?" Alexis demanded, her brown eyes suddenly alert.

I groaned. "It's not a story, trust me. It's just that there's an outside chance one of the people involved in this business of Richard's might be into paedophilia."

"What makes you think that?" she asked, suspicious that she might be missing out on something that would plaster her by-line across the front pages of the *Chronicle*.

"It'd be cruel to tell you," I said. "You'd only be upset because you couldn't use it."

Alexis shook her head, a rueful smile twitching the corners of her mouth. "You know me too well, girl."

I stood on the pavement outside the Golden Ganges, watching Alexis's car pull away from the kerb into a death-defying U-turn. The air was heavy with the fumes of traffic and curry spices, the sky bleak and overcast, the distant sounds of police and ambulance sirens mingling with the wail of a nearby car alarm. I turned the corner of the side-street where I'd left my car, and the ululations of the alarm increased dramatically. It took me a moment or two to realize that it was my car that was the focus of attention for the two black lads with the cordless hand-drill.

"Hey, shitheads," I yelled in protest, breaking into a run without even thinking about it.

They looked up, uncertainty written all over their faces. It only took them seconds to weigh up the situation and decide to leg it. If it had been after dark, they probably would have brazened it out and tried to give me a good kicking for daring to challenge their right to my stereo. Shame, really. I had so much pent-up frustration in me that I'd have relished the chance to show them my Thai boxing skills weren't just for keeping fit.

By the time I reached the car, they were round the next corner. The mashed metal of the lock wasn't ever going to make sweet music with a key again. I pushed the control button that stopped the alarm shrieking. Sighing, I pulled the door open and climbed in. At least having the lock replaced would kill one of the hours I couldn't find a way to fill usefully. Before I started the engine, I called Handbrake the mechanic, checked he'd collected the Beetle without a hitch and told him I needed a new driver's door lock. That way, I wouldn't have to hang around answering his phone while he nipped out to collect the part.

I turned left on to Oxford Road and headed away from the city centre. I was clear of the curry zone in a few minutes, and straight into the heart of university residences and student bedsits. I pushed the "eject" button on the stereo. Goodbye Julia Fordham. Plangent and poignant was just what I didn't need right now. I raked through my cassettes and smacked the Pet Shop Boys' *Discography* into the slot. Perfect. A thrusting beat to drive me onwards and upwards, an emotional content somewhere below zero. At the Wilbraham Road lights, I cut across to Kingsway and over to Heaton Mersey where Handbrake operates out of a pair of lock-ups behind a down-at-heel block of flats. Handbrake is a mate of Dennis's who's been team mechanic to Mortensen and Brannigan for a few years now. And, for his sins, he also gets to play with Richard's Beetle. He's called Handbrake because he used to be a getaway driver for armed robbers, and he specialized in 180-degree handbrake turns when the pursuit got a bit too close for comfort. He did a six-stretch back in the early eighties, and he's gone straight ever since. Well, only a bit wobbly. Only now and again.

There was a Volkswagen Golf in one of Handbrake's two garages. As I pulled up, Handbrake emerged from under the bonnet. Anyone less likely to adopt the anonymous role of a getaway driver it would be hard to imagine. He's got flaming red curls as tight as a pensioner's perm and a face like a sad clown. He'd have no chance in an identity parade unless the cops brought in a busload of Ronald McDonalds. Handbrake wiped his hands on his overalls and gave me a smile that made him look like he was about to burst into tears.

"Gobshites get you?" he greeted me.

"Caught them in time to save the stereo," I told him, leaving the door open behind me.

"That's saved you a few bob, then. The lad'll be back with the locks any minute," Handbrake said, giving the door the judicious once-over. "Nice clean job, really."

"No problem with the Beetle?"

He shook his head. "Nah. Piece of piss. I left it outside your house, stuck the keys back through the letter box. Mr Music out of town, is he?" I was saved from lying by the arrival of a young black kid on a mountain bike. "All right, Dobbo?" Handbrake called out.

The lad hauled back on his handlebars to pull up in mid-wheelie. "My man," he affirmed. He shrugged out of a smart leather backpack and took a new set of locks for my Peugeot out of it. He handed it to Handbrake, quoted what seemed to be an interestingly low price and added on a tenner for delivery. Handbrake pulled a wad out of his back pocket and counted out the cash. The lad zipped it into his leather bum bag and cycled off. At the corner, he stopped and took out what looked like a mobile phone. He hadn't looked a day over fourteen.

"Don't take offence, Handbrake, but these parts aren't a little bit moody, are they?" I hate having to be such a prissy little madam, but I can't afford to be caught out with a car built from stolen spares.

Handbrake shook his head. "Nah. Him and his mates have got a deal going with half the scrap yards in Manchester. Product of the recession. Not so much drugs around, not so much dosh to be made ferrying them round the town, so Dobbo and a couple of his mates spent some of their ill-gotten gains on a computer. One of them checks with the scrap yards every morning to see what new stock they've got in. Then when punters like me want a part, we ring in and the dispatcher works out where they can get it from and sends one of the bike boys off for it. Good game, huh?"

"You're not kidding." I watched Handbrake pop the remains of the lock out of my car door. "Handbrake? You know anybody on the drugs scene that moves their merchandise in stolen motors?"

Handbrake snorted. "Ask me another. I try not to know anything about drugs in this town. Like the man said, a little learning is a dangerous thing." Handbrake did A Level English while he was inside. Who says prison doesn't change a man?

"OK. How would someone get hold of a set of trade plates?"

"You mean if you're not a legitimate person?"

"Why would I be asking you about legitimate people?"

He snorted again. "Well, you can't just cobble them together in a backstreet workshop. It's only the Department of Transport that makes them, and the numbers are die-stamped into the metal, not like your regular licence plates. You'd have to beg, borrow or steal. There's enough of them around. You could nick them off a garage or a motor in transit, though that way they'd be reported stolen and you wouldn't get a lot of mileage out of them. Beg or buy a loan of a set off a delivery driver. Best way is to borrow them off a slightly dodgy garage. Why, you need some?"

Handbrake likes to wind me up by pretending he's the innocent abroad and I'm the villain. But I wasn't in the mood for it right then. "No," I snarled. "But I think I might be about to deprive someone of some."

"Better be careful where you use them, then."

"Why?"

"'Cos you'll get a tug is why. The traffic cops always pull you if you're using trade plates. Not so much on the motorway, but defo if you're cruising round. If they so much as think you're using them for anything except demos, tuition or delivery, you've had it. So you better have a good cover story."

I was glad of the tip. I didn't think this was the right weekend for a roadside chat with the traffic division.

# 8

I kicked my heels for the best part of an hour in Ruth's waiting room while she was dealing with a client. I'd have been better employed catching up on my sleep. After I'd stood on for a major bollocking for my outrageous behaviour at Longsight nick, we sat glumly staring at each other across her cluttered desk, depressed by the lack of information we had to trade. "I suspect the officers actually working the case don't believe a word Richard's saying," Ruth said. "All I get is the condescending wink when I suggest that if they really want to make a major drugs bust they should be on the phone to every villain who's ever grassed in his life. Anything to get a lead on the car thieves. But of course, they don't really believe in the car thieves," she added cynically. "The one lucky break we have so far is that none of the police officers we've dealt with has made the connection between Richard and you. At least the superintendent is prepared to go along with the idea of a lie-down, even though he stressed that it was for his team's benefit and not mine."

I got to my feet. "I suppose it's a step in the right direction. I'll let you know as soon as I get anything," I said grimly.

Out in the street, the city carried on as usual. I cut across Deansgate and through the Victorian glass-domed elegance of

the Barton Arcade into the knots of serious shoppers bustling
around the designer clothes shops of St Ann's Square. Nobody
had told the buskers outside the Royal Exchange that this was not
a day for celebration and their cheery country rock mocked me
all the way across the square and into Cross Street. I'd abandoned
the car on a single yellow line round the back of the NatWest
bank, and to my astonishment, I didn't have a ticket. It was the
first time all day that I'd got the benefit of an even break. I had
to take it as an omen.

Back home, I checked Richard's answering machine and
saved the handful of messages. I returned a couple of the more
urgent calls, explaining he'd had to go out of town at a moment's
notice and I wasn't sure when he'd be back. I also checked his
diary, and cancelled a couple of interviews he'd arranged for the
early part of the coming week. Luckily, he didn't have much
planned, thanks to Davy's visit. God only knew how he was
going to write this week's magazine column. Frankly, it was
the least of my worries.

Manchester's rush hour seems to have developed middle-aged
spread. When I first moved to the city, it lasted a clearly defin-
able ninety minutes, morning and evening. Now, in the evening it seems to start at four and continue till half past seven.
And on Fridays, it's especially grim. Even on the wide dual
carriageway of Princess Parkway, it was a major challenge to
get into third. It felt like a relief to be in the airport. That's
how bad it was.

I was ten minutes early for our meeting, but Della was
already sitting in the domestic terminal with a coffee. When
the automatic doors hissed open to let me in, she glanced up
from her *Evening Chronicle*. Even from that distance I could see
the anxiety in her deep-set green eyes. She jumped to her feet
and pulled me into a hug as soon as I got close enough. "Poor
you," she said with feeling, steering me gently into a seat. The

sympathy was too much. Seeing the tears in my eyes, Della patted me awkwardly on the shoulder and said, "Give me a sec, I'll get you a coffee."

By the time she returned, I was as hard-boiled as Philip Marlowe again. "Like the hair," I remarked. Her shining chestnut hair, normally controlled to within an inch of its life in a thick plait, was loose around her shoulders, held back from her face with a wide, sueded silk headband.

"Thanks." She pulled a face. "Think it'll impress a forty-year-old merchant banker?"

"Business or pleasure?"

"He thinks pleasure, I suspect business." Detective Chief Inspector Della Prentice is the operational head of the Regional Crime Squad's fraud task force. She's a Cambridge graduate, with all the social graces that implies, which means that when she's got some bent businessman in her sights he's more likely to think this charming woman who's so fascinated by his work is a corporate headhunter rather than a copper. The problem is, as Della once explained with a sigh, the best con men are often the most charming.

"We never sleep, eh?" I teased.

"Not with people we suspect might have their hands in a rather interesting can of worms," Della said. "Even if he is buying me dinner at the Thirty-Nine Steps." I felt a momentary pang of jealousy. Since Richard only ever wants to eat Chinese food, I don't often get the chance to eat at the best fish restaurant in Manchester. As if reading my thoughts, Della said, "But enough of my problems. Any news on Richard?"

"Not a sausage. I feel so frustrated. I just haven't got any handles to get a hold of. I don't suppose you've got anything for me?" I asked morosely.

"We . . . ell, yes, and no," Della said cautiously, lighting a cigarette with her battered old Zippo.

The ticket-free windscreen *had* been an omen. "Yeah?" I demanded.

"The fingerprint SOCO who went over Richard's car did some work for me a while back when I was looking into forged insurance policies, and we got quite pally. So I bought her a butty at lunch time."

"What did she find?" I asked.

"It's what she didn't find that's significant. She was being a bit cautious. Understandably, because she's not had time yet to analyse all the prints thoroughly. But it looks like Richard's fingerprints were on all the surfaces you'd expect—door handle, gear stick, steering wheel, the cassette in the stereo. But there were none of his prints on the boot, or the carrier bag or the plastic bags that the rocks were in. In fact, there were no prints at all on any of those. Just the kind of smudges you get from latex gloves. And Richard had no gloves on his person, nor were there any in the car." Della gave a tentative smile, and I found myself reflecting it.

"D'you know, that's the first good news I've heard all day?"

Della looked apologetic. "I know it's not much, but it's a start. If I hear any more on the grapevine, I'll let you know. Now, as to the other thing. You owe me, Kate—I thought when I left the West Yorkshire fraud squad that I'd never have to drink with another patronizing, sexist Yorkshireman. Today I discovered they actually get worse when they're in exile on the wrong side of the Pennines. According to DCI Geoff Turnbull of the Drugs Squad, it's understandable that a nice woman like me should be interested in drugs. After all, even if I didn't manage to fulfil my womanly role by reproducing myself before my divorce, I must have contemporaries whose kids are in their late teens and therefore at that dangerous age," Della growled through clenched teeth.

"Oh dear," I sympathized. "And when exactly are they letting him out of intensive care? I know a choir that's short on sopranos."

Della managed a twisted smile. "Once he'd finished condescending, he did actually come up with some interesting information. Apparently, when crack first started to appear in this country, it was in relatively small amounts and in quite specific areas. The obvious inference was that there were only a handful of people involved in the importing and distribution of it, and while its presence was worrying, its level of penetration wasn't seriously disturbing. However, during the last few months, small quantities of crack have been turning up all over the country along with some unusual designer drugs. The really worrying thing is that these finds have been coming out of routine operations." Della paused expectantly.

I didn't know what she was expecting. I said, "Why is that so worrying?"

"It's turned up where they didn't expect to find it. The operations have been targeted at something else, say Ecstasy or heroin, and they've ended up producing a small but significant amount of crack as well. And it's not localized. It's dotted all over the shop." Della looked serious. I could see why. If small finds were appearing unexpectedly, the chances were that they were only the tip of a very large iceberg.

"Any particular geographical distribution?" I asked.

"Virtually all over the country. But it's mostly confined to bandit country."

"Meaning?" I asked.

"The sort of areas that are semi-no-go. Inner city decayed housing, satellite council estates both in the cities and in bigger towns. The kind of traditional working-class areas where people used to leave school and go into the local industry, only there's no industry any more so they graduate straight to the dole queue, the drink and drugs habits and the petty crime that goes with them." Della stubbed her cigarette out angrily.

"I bet your Yorkshire DCI didn't put it quite like that."

"How did you guess?" Della said cynically. "Anyway, the bottom line is that it looks like we've got a crack epidemic on our hands. And they suspect that whoever is dealing this crack has a very efficient distribution network."

That ruled out the post office. "And they think Richard is part of that?"

"I didn't ask. But they clearly think he's important enough to be worth sweating." Della sighed. "It doesn't look good, Kate, I'm bound to say."

I nodded. She didn't have to tell me. "Any suggestions as to where I might start looking?"

Della looked at me. Her green eyes were serious. "You're not going to thank me for this, but I don't think you should be looking at all. These are very dangerous people. They will kill you if they think you're any kind of threat."

"You think I don't know that? What option have I got, Della? If I can't get the real villains behind bars, they'll kill Richard. As soon as they find out just who drove off with their parcel of crack. You know they will. They can't afford not to, or every two-bit dealer in town'll think they can give them the run-around." I swallowed the last of my coffee. I should have gone for camomile tea. The last thing I needed was to get even more hyped up.

"Did you get the chance to ask about the Polaroid?" Anything to avoid another unnerving gypsy warning.

"I spoke to a woman DS in Vice. She said she couldn't think of anyone off the top of her head, but she'd ask around. But the DCI running Richard's case doesn't seem particularly interested in it, probably because in itself it isn't technically obscene." Della lit another cigarette, but before she could say more, bodies started flowing through the doors leading from Domestic Arrivals. Judging by the high proportion of men in suits clutching briefcases that seemed as heavy as anchors after a hard day's meetings, the London shuttle was down. I stood up. "I think this is Davy's flight," I said.

Della was at my side in a flash. She gave me a quick hug, threw a glance over her shoulder to make sure she wasn't about to be accosted by a small boy, and said, "Stay in touch. I'll bell you if I hear anything." And she was gone.

The first rush had subsided, leaving the stragglers who had had to wait for luggage from the hold. After what felt like a very long time, the double doors swung open on a woman in British Airways uniform, carrying a small holdall. By her side, Davy trotted, looking like he was auditioning for the moppet role in the next Spielberg film, hair flopping over his forehead in a slightly tousled fringe, big brown eyes eager. He was proudly wearing an outfit he'd chosen with his dad on his last visit, topped by the New York Mets jacket Richard had sent him from a recent trip to the States, still too baggy for his solid little frame. Then he saw me. All in a moment, he seemed puzzled, then disappointed. He looked around again, then realizing Richard really wasn't there, he waved uncertainly at me and half smiled. My heart sank. As far as Davy was concerned, I was clearly a poor substitute. As if I needed the confirmation.

It turned out a lot better than I expected. On the way to the car park, I told Davy the lie Richard and I had prearranged. Dad was in Bosnia; he'd had to fly off suddenly because he'd had an exclusive tip that Bob Geldof was out there organizing some sort of Bosnia Aid concert. I almost believed it myself by the time I'd finished the explanation. Davy took it very calmly. I suppose after eight years, he's grown accustomed to a dad who doesn't behave quite like other kids' fathers. At least he's not shy; that's one thing that being around Richard and his crazy buddies in rock and journalism has cured him of. "You remember Chris and Alexis?" I asked him as we drove out of the airport towards the M56.

He nodded. "Alexis is funny. And Chris is good at drawing and painting and building things with Lego. I like them."

"Well, they're going to help me look after you, because I've got some work to do over the weekend."

"Can't I come with you to work, Kate?" he wheedled. "I want to be a private detective like you. I saw this film and it was in black and white and it had an American detective in it, Mum said he was called Humpty something, and he had a gun. Have you got a gun, Kate?"

I shook my head. Depressingly, he looked disappointed. "I don't need one, Davy."

"What about if you were fighting a bad man, and he had a gun? You'd need one then," he said triumphantly.

"If I was fighting someone who had a gun, and he knew I had a gun, he'd have to shoot me to win the fight. But if he knows I haven't got a gun, he only has to hit me. That way I stay alive. And, on balance, I think I prefer being alive."

Chris was waiting when we got home. I'd rung ahead to give her ten minutes' warning, so she was just assembling home-made cheeseburgers as we walked in. I could have kissed her. The three of us sat round the breakfast bar scoffing and telling the sort of jokes that eight-year-olds like. You know: why do bees hum? Because they've forgotten the words.

After we'd pigged out, I showed Davy the latest Commander Keen game I'd got for us both. I extracted a promise from him that he'd go to bed in half an hour when Chris told him to, and left him bouncing on his pixel pogo stick through Slug Village. Ten minutes split between the bathroom and the bedroom was enough to knock me into shape for the night. My lightweight walking boots; my ripped denim decorating jeans over multi-coloured leggings; a Bob Marley T-shirt I won at a rock charity dinner; and a baggy flannel shirt that belonged to my granddad that I keep for sentimental reasons. I tucked my auburn hair into a Day-Glo green baseball cap, and slapped on some make-up that made me look like an anaemic refugee from Transylvania. Grunge meets acid house. I found Chris in front of the television, watching the news. Bless her, she didn't turn a hair at the apparition. "I really appreciate this. And believe me, Richard will need a bank loan to express his appreciation when all this is over. I take it Alexis filled you in?" I said quietly, perching on the arm of the sofa.

"She did, and it's horrifying. What's happening? Any progress?" That's probably the shortest contribution to any conversation I've ever heard Chris make.

"Not really. That's why I'm going out now. I've got one or two leads to follow up. Are you OK to hang on here?"

Chris patted my knee. "We're staying till this is all sorted out. I brought a bag with me, and I've moved us into Richard's room, I hope that's all right, but it seemed the most sensible thing, because then Davy can sleep in his usual bed in Richard's house so you can come and go as and when you please without worrying about waking any of us, and then we're on hand to take over the child minding as and when you need us." I swear she's the only person I know who can talk and breathe at the same time.

I gave Chris a swift hug and stood up. "Thanks. I'll see you in the morning then." I walked out of the house, feeling a sense of purpose for the first time since I'd had Ruth's phone call.

# 9

I started off at the Delta, known to Richard and his cronies, for obvious reasons, as the "Lousy Hand." That's where he'd been the night the car was stolen. The Lousy Hand occupies a handful of railway arches in a narrow cul-de-sac between the GMEX exhibition centre and the Hacienda Club. Since it was only half past nine, there was no queue, so I sailed straight in.

The décor in the Lousy Hand has been scientifically designed to make you think you've dropped a tab of acid even when you're straight. God knows what it does to the kids who are really out of their heads. Everywhere I looked there were psychedelic fractals mingling at random with *trompe-l'œil* Bridget Riley-style monochrome pop art extravaganzas. There were only a few dozen punters in that early, but most of them were already on the dance floor, mindlessly happy as only those high on Ecstasy can be. The dancing was something else, too. Scarcely co-ordinated, the dancers looked like a motley assortment of marionettes jerked around by a five-year-old puppet master with all the elegance and skill of Skippy the bush kangaroo. The music had the irritating insistence of a bluebottle at a window, the heavy bass beat so loud it seemed to thump inside my chest. I'd have sold my soul to be back home with a nice restful video like *Terminator 2*.

Feeling about a hundred and five, I crossed to the bar. As well as the usual designer beers, the optics of spirits and the Tracy-and-Sharon specials like Malibu and Byzance, the Lousy Hand boasted possibly the best range of soft drinks outside Harrods Food Hall. From carrot juice to an obscure Peruvian mineral water, they had it all, and most of it was carbonated. No, officer, of course we don't have a drug problem here. None of our clients would dream of abusing illegal substances. And I am Marie of Roumania.

The bar staff looked like leftovers from the club's previous existence as a bog-standard eighties yuppie nightclub. The women and the men were dressed identically in open-necked, wing-collar white dress shirts and tight-fitting black dress trousers. The principal differences were that the men probably had marginally more gel, wax and mousse on their hair, and their earrings were more stylish. I leaned my elbows on the bar and waited. There weren't enough customers to occupy all the staff, but I still had to hang on for the obligatory thirty seconds. God forbid I should think they had nothing better to do than serve me.

The beautiful youth who halted opposite me raised his eyebrows. "Just a Diet Coke, please," I said. He looked disappointed to be asked for something so conventional. He swivelled on one toe, opened the door of a chill cabinet and lifted a can off the shelf, all in one graceful movement. I don't know why he bothered. I couldn't have looked less like a talent scout from MTV.

"Wanna glass?" he asked, dumping the can in front of me. I shook my head and paid him.

When he came back with my change, I said, "You know the street outside? Is it safe to park there? Only, I'm parked right up near the dead end and there's no streetlights, and I wondered if a lot of cars get nicked from out there?"

He shrugged. "Cars get nicked. Outside here's no worse than anywhere else in town. A thousand cars a week get stolen in Manchester, did you know that?" I shook my head. "And two thirds of them are never recovered. Bet you didn't know that." Never mind the Mr Cool image, this guy had the soul of a train spotter in an anorak.

Ignoring him, I went on, "Only, it's not really my car, it's my boyfriend's and he'd kill me if anything happened to it."

"What kind is it?" he asked.

"Peugeot 205. Nothing fancy, just the standard one."

"You're probably all right, then." He leaned his elbows on the bar and elegantly crossed his legs. I prepared myself for a lecture. "Six months ago, you couldn't park a hot hatch anywhere between Stockport and Bury and expect to find it there when you went back to it. But with these new insurance weightings, the bottom's dropped out of the second-hand market for boy-racer cars. So the professionals gave up on the sports jobs and started nicking boring old family cars instead. Less risk as well. I mean, if you was the Old Bill, would you think the Nissan Sunny cruising past you was being driven by any self-respecting car thief?"

I giggled. Not because he was funny, but because he clearly expected it. "Only," I persisted, "my boyfriend's mate had his car nicked from outside here the other night, and he was really pissed off because he'd only bought it that day. And it was a beauty. A brand new Leo Gemini turbo super coupé."

"I heard about that," he said, pushing himself upright again. "That was the night they had the benefit, wasn't it?"

"I dunno."

"Yeah, that's right. The gig was finished, because we'd shut up the bar and the lights were up. The guy came storming back in, ranting about his precious motor and demanding a phone." So much for not mentioning the car to a soul. "Mate of yours then, was he?" the barman asked.

I nodded. "Mate of my boyfriend's. He reckoned somebody saw him parking it up and coming in here. He said he thought they must have been coming to the club too, or else why would they be down the cul-de-sac?"

The barman grinned, unself-conscious for the first time. "Well, he'd have plenty thieves to choose from that night. Half Moss Side was in here. Drug barons, car ringers, the lot. You name it, we had them."

With a flick of his ponytail, he was gone to batter someone else's brain with his statistics. I swigged the Coke and looked around me. While I'd been standing at the bar, there had been a steady stream of punters arriving behind me. Already, the place looked a lot fuller than it had when I entered. If I was going to have a word with the bouncers before they had more important things to think about, I'd better make a move.

There were two of them in the foyer, flanking the narrow doorway that had been cut in the huge wooden door that filled the end of one of the arches occupied by the club. They both wore the bouncer's uniform: ill-fitting tux; ready-made velvet bow tie that had seen better days. As I approached, the older and bulkier one slipped through the door and into the street. Intrigued, I got my hand stamped with a pass-out and followed him. He walked about fifty yards up towards the dead end. I slipped into the shadows beyond the club and watched him. He looked around, then simply turned and walked back, carrying on past the club for another fifty yards or so before strolling back inside.

I stuck my head round the door and said, "Where's the best place to park around here? Only, I don't want to get the car nicked. It's my boyfriend's."

The smaller bouncer flashed a "Right one we've got here" look at his oppo. "Darling, you don't look like the kind of girl who'd have a boyfriend with a car worth nicking," he said, smoothing back his hair with a smirk.

"Mind you don't wear out the rug," I snarled back, pointing to his head. Although he was only in his early twenties, his dark hair was already thinning so it was a fair bet that would be a tender spot.

Right on the button. He scowled. "Piss off," he quipped wittily.

"Does the management know you're this helpful to customers who only want to avoid giving the club a worse name than it's already got?" I asked sweetly.

"Don't push it," the bouncer with the wanderlust said coldly, glowering down at me. Now I could see him in the light, he seemed familiar, but I couldn't place him, which surprised me. I don't often forget guys that menacing. He was a couple of inches over six feet, thick dark hair cut in an almost military short back and sides. He wasn't bad-looking if you ignored the thread-thin white scar that ran from the end of his left eyebrow to just underneath his ear lobe. But his eyes wrecked any illusion of attractiveness. They were cold and blank. They showed as much connection to the rest of humanity as a pair of camera lenses.

"Look, I just don't want to get my car nicked, OK?" I gabbled. "It seems to happen a lot around here, that's all."

The big bouncer nodded, satisfied I'd backed down. "You want to be safe, leave it on one of the main drags where there's decent street-lighting."

"You want to be really safe, don't bring the car into town. In fact, why don't you do us all a favour and leave yourself at home as well?" the balding Mr Charm sneered.

I winked and cocked one finger at him like a pistol. "I might just take your advice." I let the door bang shut behind me and walked back to my car. Even if anyone at the Lousy Hand knew anything about the coupé's disappearance, I couldn't see a way of getting them to talk to me. It had been a long shot anyway. Sighing, I climbed into the car and started cruising the city centre streets. There were plenty of clubs for the dedicated seeker of pleasure to choose from, and even more restaurants catering to the late-night trade, which gave me plenty of kerbs to crawl. I prayed the Vice Squad weren't doing one of their occasional random trawls of the red-light zones. The last thing I needed was to have to explain to a copper why I was doing an impersonation of a dirty old man.

I drove systematically down the streets and back alleys for a good couple of hours without spotting a single red and white trade plate. If I'd been working for a client, I'd have given up right then. But this was different. This was personal, and the man lying in a cell worrying about the charges he was facing was the man I'd chosen to share my life with. I might not be getting anywhere out on the streets, but I could no more jack it in and go home to bed than I could set Richard free with one mighty bound.

Just before midnight, I realized I was ravenous. I'd been so hyped up on adrenaline all evening that I was suddenly right on the edge of a low blood sugar collapse. I phoned an order through, then drove back through Chinatown, double parked outside the Yang Sing and picked up some salt and pepper ribs, paper wrapped prawns and pork dumplings. I couldn't help a pang of guilt, thinking about prison food and Richard's conviction that if it didn't come out of China or Burger King it can't be edible.

I drove back to the Lousy Hand. If the car thief plied a regular patch, I might just catch him at it. It was as good a place to eat my takeaway as any. I drove slowly up the cul-de-sac, looking for a space. Nothing. I turned round in the dead end and drove back down. I got lucky. Someone was pulling out just as I passed. I tucked the car in against the kerb and opened the sun roof so the smell of the Chinese wouldn't linger in the car for the next six months. I started on the prawns, wanting to polish them off before they became soggy.

I looked around as I ate. Nothing much was moving. There was a short queue outside the Lousy Hand, but it seemed to be static. The only car I could see worth stealing was a new Ford Escort Cosworth, but its ridiculous spoiler, like the tail of a blue whale, was so obvious that I couldn't imagine many thieves having the bottle to go for it. Besides, it was bright red and you know what they say about red cars and male sexual problems . . .

In my wing mirror, I noticed the man mountain bouncer emerging from the Lousy Hand again. Clearly time for another walkabout. As he reconnoitred the street, I thought he still looked nigglingly familiar, but I couldn't think where from, unless we'd had a brief encounter one night when I'd been on the town with Richard. After all, bouncers shift around the clubs about as fast as cocktail waitresses, and I wasn't always one hundred per cent *compos mentis* when we crawled out of clubs in the small hours.

He headed in my direction. Instinctively, I slid down in my seat till I was below window level. I heard his footsteps on the pavement, then, when he was level with me, he stopped. I held my breath. I don't know what I expected, but it wasn't the familiar bleating of a mobile phone being dialled. I inched carefully up till I could just see him. He had his back to me and a slimline phone to his ear.

"Hiya," he said, his voice low. "Ford Escort Cosworth. Foxtrot alarm system. Been in about ten minutes . . . No problem." The phone beeped once as he ended the call. I slid back down below eye level as he turned back towards the club. Valet parking I'd heard of. But valet stealing?

I watched in the wing mirror till he was safely back indoors, then I pulled off the Day-Glo cap and got out of the Peugeot, still clutching my Chinese. I melted into the shadows of one of the railway arches which had a deep door recess. I could hardly believe it wasn't already occupied by one of the city's cardboard-box kids. I didn't have long to wait. I still had half my spare ribs left when a black hack coughed up the cul-de-sac. It stopped outside the Lousy Hand, and a man got out. In the lights of the club entrance, I got a quick look. Thirtyish, medium height, slim build. He walked into the club, fast, like a man with a purpose other than a dance, a drink and a legover.

He was out again in seconds, carrying a small holdall. He walked briskly towards the Cosworth. As he came closer, I clocked a heavy thatch of dark hair, high cheekbones, hollow cheeks, surprisingly full lips, a double-breasted suit that hung like it was made to measure. He stopped a few feet away from the Cosworth, flashed a quick, penetrating glance around him then crouched down. Through the gap between cars, I could just see him take something out of the holdall. It looked a bit like an old-fashioned TV remote, bulky, with buttons. I couldn't see any details, but he seemed to be hitting buttons and moving a slider switch on the side. This routine lasted the best part of a minute. Then, three sharp electronic exclamations came from the Cosworth, the hazard lights flashed twice and I heard the door locks shift to "open." He dropped the black box back into the holdall and took out a pair of trade plates.

The man stood up and gave that quick, frowning glance round again. Still clear, he thought. One plate went on the back of the car, hiding the existing number. He fastened the other over the front plate, then almost ran to the driver's door. He was in the car in seconds. It took less than a minute for the engine to roar into life. The car shot out of the parking space. Rather than drive to the end of the cul-de-sac and do a time-wasting three-point turn, as I'd expected, he simply shot back down the street in reverse.

Caught flat-footed, I leapt for the Peugeot. By the time he'd reversed on to the main drag and headed off towards Oxford Road, I was behind him, just far enough for him not to get twitchy. Interestingly, he didn't drive the Cosworth like a boy racer. If anything, he drove like my father, a man who has never had an accident in twenty-three years of driving. Mind you, he's seen dozens in his rear-view mirror . . . The speedo didn't rise above twenty-eight, he stopped on amber and he didn't even attempt any traffic-light grand prix stuff. We crossed Oxford Road and carried on sedately down Whitworth Street, into Aytoun Street and past Piccadilly Station. Then it was time for a quick whizz through the back doubles before he pulled up outside Sacha's nightclub and blasted the horn. Luckily I was far enough behind him to stay tucked away on the corner. I cut my lights and waited.

Not for long. If the speed of her response was anything to go by, patience wasn't her boyfriend's strong suit. Depressingly, she looked like she'd walked straight off the bottle-blonde production line. Expensive bimbo, but bimbo nevertheless. Bimbos are the last women in the world wearing crippling high heels and make-up that could camouflage a Chieftain tank. This one must have had enough hair spray on her carefully tumbled locks to lacquer a Chinese cabinet, since it didn't even move in the chill wind that had sprung up in the last hour.

She jumped into the waiting Cosworth and we were off again. He was still driving like a pursuer's dream. I dumped the Pet Shop Boys and let Annie Lennox entertain me instead. Round Piccadilly, down Portland Street, down to Deansgate, out along Regent Road. I had to hang well back now, because there wasn't a lot of traffic around, and the thief was driving so law-abidingly that any reasonable driver would have overtaken him long ago. At the end of the dual carriageway, instead of heading straight on down the motorway, he hung a left, heading towards Salford Quays. I can't say I was totally surprised. He looked the sort.

The Quays used to be, unromantically, Salford Docks. Then the eighties happened, and waterfronts suddenly became trendy. London, Liverpool, Glasgow, Newcastle, Manchester. They all discovered how easy it was to part fools and their money when you threw in a view of a bit of polluted waterway. Salford Quays was Manchester's version of greed chic. It's got it all: the multi-screen cinema, the identikit international hotel for jet-set business people, more saunas per head of population than Scandinavia, its very own scaled-down World Trade Center for scaled-down yuppie losers and more *Penthouses* than penthouses. The only thing it lacks is any kind of human ambience.

I noticed that the Cosworth was slowing. I pulled into the parking bay of a small block of flats and killed my lights just as he drew up. He'd stopped outside a long block of narrow three-storey town houses with integral garages on the ground floor.

He got out of the Cosworth, but I could see a whisper of exhaust in the cold night air that told me the engine was still running. He waved a hand in the direction of the garage door and it rose slowly to reveal a two-year-old black Toyota Supra. He swapped the cars over, leaving the Supra on the hard standing and the Cosworth tucked safely away inside the garage.

I watched for another twenty minutes or so as lights went on and off in various rooms. When the house went dark, I decided that if Richard's car thief was entitled to sleep, so was I.

I got home just after two. The house was silent, the bed chilly. If I didn't get him out of jail soon, I was going to have to buy a hot-water bottle.

# 10

I dreamed I was walking down a corridor filled with breakfast cereal, going snap, crackle and pop with every step. Cautiously, I opened one eye. It was only half a dream. Davy was sitting on the edge of the bed, tucking into a bowl of one of Richard's noisier cereals, a tumbler of orange juice on the bedside table next to him. He was watching me, and as he registered the rising eyelid, he smiled uncertainly.

"Did I wake you?" he asked. "I didn't want to miss you."

I propped myself up on one elbow and shook my head. "Not really," I lied. Things were bad enough without me giving Davy a bad time. I glanced at the clock. Five past seven. I couldn't even summon up the energy to groan.

"Have you got to work today?" he asked.

"I'm afraid so," I said.

He looked crestfallen. "Can't I come with you?" he asked wistfully. "I could help."

"Sorry, hon, not today. But I don't have to go out for a couple of hours yet, so we could play some computer games first, if you want?"

He didn't have to be asked twice. When Chris and Alexis stumbled through the conservatory just after half past eight looking like Beauty and the Beast, Davy and I were absorbed in a game of Lemmings. Alexis threatened to pull the plug out of the socket unless we reverted to normal English usage. Guess which one is the Beast?

I got up and said I had to go. Before Davy's disappointment could turn into a sulk, Alexis asked if he'd brought his trunks and if he fancied spending the afternoon at a fun pool. Nobody invited me, which is probably just as well, since the temptation of playing on the slides and surfing in the wave pool might just have proved too much.

Before the grown-ups could go into a huddle about how we were going to amuse him till lunch time, Davy solved the problem. "Kate, is it all right if I go out and play this morning?" he asked.

"Who with?" I asked, trying to act like a responsible co-parent. Judging by the look on Davy's face, he was afraid I was turning into the wicked stepmother.

"Daniel and Wayne, from the estate. I *always* play with them when I come and see my dad."

I didn't see a problem, and as soon as the deal was struck, Davy was gone. "I've got to run too," I said, heading for the shower.

"What's happening with Richard?" Alexis demanded, following me down the hall as Chris disappeared into the kitchen and started brewing some more coffee.

"They've charged him with possession with intent to supply," I shouted over the sound of the spray and the pump from my new power shower.

"Oh shit," Alexis said.

"I'm hopeful we can keep the lid on it," I said. "Will there be any reporters in the magistrates' court this morning?"

"Well, if I don't go down, there won't be anyone from the *Chron*," Alexis said. "And with it being a bank holiday weekend, the court agency probably won't bother with cover either. You might just get away with it. If you do drop unlucky, there are two courts sitting. If there is a reporter kicking around, ask your solicitor to get the case called in one court while the reporter's in the other one. Shouldn't be a problem. I take it that Plan A is for you to find the evidence that will clear Richard before his next court appearance?"

"Got it in one," I said. "And unless you've got any bright ideas about how I'm going to do that, sod off and let me have my shower in peace."

Alexis chuckled. "OK. I'm going in to the office in a bit to write up my copy from dinner last night. That'll be my alibi for ignoring the mags. If anybody asks me, I'll say I checked it out with the clerk and there was nothing of any interest coming up. I'll be at my desk till lunch time if you need me for anything."

"Thanks. I might just take you up on that. How did your evening go, by the way?"

Alexis pulled a face. "That depends on whether you're asking the cold-hearted bastard journalist or the human being. As a journo, it was a major coup. There is definitely a big-time child porn ring operating somewhere in Greater Manchester, and I'm the only journo that knows about it. We're talking million-pound industry here. But Barney showed me some of their stock in trade. And as a human being, I have to say it was one of the nastiest experiences of my life. It made me fucking glad I don't have kids of my own to worry about."

"I don't need child porn to make me feel like that," I said gloomily. "Temporary custody of Davy's quite enough. Did you ask him about any tie-ins with drugs?"

"I did, and if there are any, he doesn't know about them. Most likely, one of your drug dealers is a pervert. Which doesn't really help, does it?"

I love to start the day with the good news.

Saturday morning, Manchester Magistrates' Court. The one day of the week the marble corridors of the court don't resemble the supermarket chill cabinet—there's hardly a headless chicken in sight. The only cases dealt with at the Saturday court are the overnighters—breaches of the peace, drunk and disorderly, soliciting, the occasional assault. And Richard. Because his was such a major charge and he was arrested after midnight, the police hadn't been inclined to process the paperwork fast enough for him to appear at Friday's court, so he'd spilled over into Saturday. Although it probably didn't feel like it to Richard, that had its advantages. As Alexis had confirmed, the chances were good that it would escape press attention, so the people whose drugs Richard had driven off with wouldn't be picking up their *Evening Chronicle* and finding "Rock journalist charged with massive drug haul" splashed all over the front page.

According to Ruth, Richard had been moved the night before from the nick at Longsight into the custom-built secure detention cells inside the magistrates' court building. As we'd arranged, I made my way to the duty solicitor's interview room on the fifth floor. Normally at quarter to ten on a court morning, the place is heaving with defendants, their families, their kids and their harassed lawyers. The air's usually thick with cigarette smoke and recriminations. Today, while it wasn't as silent as the executive floor lobby of a multi-national, it was a lot quieter than weekdays.

I pushed open the glass door of the small office and sat on the far side of the round table, commanding a view of the entire length of the foyer outside the courtrooms. It was nearly ten when Ruth swept into sight, a nervous-looking man almost trotting to keep up with her. Ruth shoved the door open and subsided into the chair opposite me with a huge sigh. "God, that holding area depresses the knickers off me," she complained, lighting a cigarette. "Kate," she added through a mouthful of smoke, "this is Norman Undercroft, the duty solicitor. Norman, this is Kate Brannigan, my client's partner."

Norman ducked his head politely, looking up at me from under mousey brows. Close to, he looked a lot older than my first impression. His papery skin was covered in a network of fine lines, placing him in his late forties. He opened his mouth to speak, but Ruth beat him to it. "Right, Kate. Listen very carefully, I only have time to run this past you once. This morning, Richard will be represented by Norman here. Norman will get up on his hind legs and tell the court that this is a complicated matter about which his client has not yet had the opportunity to consult his own solicitor fully. Therefore, Norman will be asking the court to remand Richard in custody for the weekend. The prosecution will leap to their feet indignantly and respond that Richard is a menace to society, and furthermore, the police are investigating other serious charges in relation to him. They'll ask for a lie-down so that these matters can be resolved. And the mags will smile sweetly and agree. Any questions?"

"When can I see him?" I asked.

"Between seven and nine in the evening. Any visit is at the discretion of the duty inspector, so don't be stroppy. You go round to the back entrance in Gartside Street opposite the car park. That it? Sorry to be so abrupt, but I've got twenty for lunch and Peter has not got the knack of getting the caterers to do any work." She got to her feet. "Have you made any progress, by the way?"

"It's early days yet, but I think I might just be getting somewhere."

"OK. Look, I've arranged to see Richard tomorrow morning. Why don't we meet afterwards? Say eleven, in the Ramada. You can buy me brunch."

"Make it Salford Quays," I called after her. "I might need to be down there."

"The Quays it is," she tossed over her shoulder as she disappeared round the corner. The room seemed to double in size now only Norman and I were left. I gave him a friendly smile.

"Overwhelming," I said.

"Mmm," said Norman. "Good, though. I'd choose her if I was ever charged with anything, especially if I'd done it."

I hoped everyone else wouldn't assume Richard was guilty just because he'd hired the best criminal lawyer in town. Wearily, I followed Norman round to Court 9. There didn't seem to be a journalist in the court, unless the court reporting agency had taken to hiring elderly women who look one step away from bag ladies and have such excellent powers of recall that they don't need a notebook.

I sat on one of the flip-down seats at the back of the court-room. There were two magistrates on the bench, a man and a woman, both middle-aged, both decidedly middle class. After two breaches of the peace and a soliciting, I decided she was a teacher and he owned his own small business. She had that unmistakable air of wanting to tell them all to behave, and he had the blunt style of the self-made man who has no conception of why everybody can't be like him.

Richard was the last case of the morning. Watching him walk into the dock, I realized just how hard it is for people to get justice. After thirty-six hours in custody wearing the same clothes, not having shaved or showered, he looked like a bad lad even to me, and I was on his side. The very structure of the court itself made the accused appear to be some sort of desperado. Richard stood in the reinforced dock, behind a barrier of heavy Perspex slats, the door into the court locked to avoid any pos-sibility of him escaping. Behind him stood an alert prison officer. The system made it clear who was the sinner here.

Although he was familiar enough with court procedures from his days as a local paper journalist, Richard looked around the court with all the bewilderment of an animal that went to sleep in the jungle and woke up in the zoo. His hair seemed to have gone lank and dead overnight, and he pushed it back from his forehead in a gesture I'd noticed hundreds of times when he was working. When he saw me, one corner of his mouth twitched in a half-smile. That was a half more than I could manage.

There was no chance for Richard even to protest his innocence. He was treated like a parcel that has to be processed.
As Ruth had predicted, the magistrates made little difficulty
about remanding Richard in custody. The prosecuting solicitor obligingly explained that not only were the police pursuing further inquiries but they were also keen that Richard be
kept away from other prisoners to avoid any collusion with his
alleged co-conspirators. They all looked as if the very idea of
a bail application on a charge like this was the best joke they'd
heard since Margaret Thatcher announced the National Health
Service was safe in her hands. The whole thing took nine and a
half minutes. As Richard's prison officer escort led him out of
the dock, he turned his back to the bench, wiggled his fingers
at me and blew a kiss. I could have wept.

Instead, I thanked Norman Undercroft politely for his
efforts and walked briskly out into the fresh air. Since I was
only round the corner from Alexis's office, I cut through Crown
Square and entered the building via the underground car park.
I had wheeled the door combination out of Alexis ages ago;
you never know when you're going to need a bacon sandwich
at four in the morning, and the motto of the canteen staff of
the Manchester *Morning Sentinel* and *Evening Chronicle* is "We
never run out."

I took the lift up to the editorial floor. Things were fairly
peaceful. Most of the sports staff hadn't come in yet, and Satur-
days are such quiet news days that there's only ever a skeleton
team in the newsroom. Alexis sat hunched over her keyboard
in a quiet corner cut off from the rest of the room by a dense
thicket of various interesting green things. I recognized the
devil's ivy and the sweetheart plant. I've killed cuttings from
both of them. I edged round the plants. Alexis flapped a hand
at me, indicating I should sit down and shut up. I did.

With a flurry of fingers over the keyboard, Alexis reached
the end of her train of thought, leaned back, narrowed her eyes
and re-read her last paragraph, absently reaching out for the

cigarette in her ashtray. It had already burned down to the tip, and she looked at it in astonishment. Only then did I merit any attention. "All right?" she asked.

"As predicted. Remanded till Wednesday to allow for further police inquiries relating to other serious crimes. And unless the court agency has taken to hiring the Invisible Man for Saturday shifts, we're clear there too."

"It's only a matter of time before somebody gets a whisper," Alexis warned. "It's too good a story for the Old Bill to sit on. It's not every day they capture a parcel that size."

"So let's get a move on," I said.

"What's with the 'us'? Isn't unpaid child-minding enough?"

"That's only the start. I need to look at your copy of the electoral roll."

Alexis nodded and tipped back dangerously in her chair till she could reach the filing cabinet behind her. She pulled out the bottom drawer. "Help yourself," she said. I don't know exactly where she gets it from, but Alexis always has an up-to-date copy of the city voters' list. She keeps it next to another interesting document which fell off the back of a British Telecom lorry, a list of Greater Manchester names and addresses sorted by phone number. In other words, if you've got the number, you can look up the address and name of the subscriber. Very handy, especially when you're dealing with the kind of dodgy customer Alexis and I are always running up against.

I looked up the relevant street in the electoral roll and discovered the occupant was listed as Terence Fitzgerald. The phone book revealed no listing for Terence Fitzgerald, but I checked Directory Enquiries on my mobile phone and discovered there was a mobile listed for him.

"Find what you wanted?" Alexis asked.

"Maybe," I said. I had a way to go before I could be sure that the car thief and Terence Fitzgerald were one and the same. Thanks to the poll tax fiasco, the electoral roll has ceased to be an accurate guide to who actually lives at any particular address.

"Time for a coffee?" Alexis asked.

I shook my head. "Places to go, people to see. Thanks all the same."

For the briefest possible time, she looked concerned. "Take care of yourself, KB."

"I'll be fine," I lied. I waved goodbye and headed for the lifts. As I drove out of the car park, I stared up at the grim concrete façade of the court building and tried not to think about Richard sitting in a windowless cell, nothing to do but stare at the walls and sweat with fear. I'd once been behind the heavy iron bars of the CDC, while I'd still thought that being a lawyer was a fit and proper job for a grown-up. A criminal solicitor friend had let me shadow him for a day's duty. I'd woken up sweating for weeks afterwards.

Luckily, fighting with the city traffic didn't give me much opportunity to brood. It was just after eleven when I tucked myself into the little parking bay that gave me a perfect view of Terence Fitzgerald's town house. The black Supra was still sitting on the drive, and the bedroom curtains were still shut.

I took my Nikon out of the glove box and fitted a stubby telephoto lens to it. Then I settled back to wait and watch. God knows, it was a thin enough lead. But it was all I had. I'd give it today and see what turned up. If nothing did, it looked like a bit of breaking and entering might be on the agenda.

# 11

I have friends who believe we can transmit psychic energy that reaches out and touches other people, impelling them to follow certain courses of action. They'd reckon their theory gained credibility when Terence Fitzgerald's bedroom curtains opened five minutes after I took up station outside his house. Me, I think it probably had more to do with Terence's alarm clock than the waves of anxiety and urgency I was generating.

Twenty minutes later, Terence emerged, hair still damp from the shower. He wore a chocolate leather blouson over baggy brown trousers, cream shirt and splashy tie. I banged off a couple of shots as he got into the car, then I started my engine. He passed me without a second glance, and I tucked into the traffic a couple of cars behind him as we hit the main road. He headed towards town, turning off at the big new Harry Ramsden's fish and chip shop at Castlefield, an area on the edge of the city centre which the powers that be are desperately trying to transform from post-industrial desert into tourist attraction. So far they've got the chippie, a couple of museums and Granadaland, Manchester's dusty answer to Disneyland and Universal Studios. And, of course, the expensive hotels that British tourists can't actually afford.

I pulled into the garage just beyond Harry Ramsden's and pretended to check my tyre pressures while I kept watch. He came out of the takeaway section a few minutes later with an open package which he carefully laid on the passenger seat as he got back into the car. Just the thought of the fish and chips had me salivating.

He shot back into the traffic again, and we were soon belting down the Hyde Road. No granddad driving today. The only time my speedo dropped below forty-five was at the traffic lights. I nearly lost him when he went through an amber as it turned to red but I put my foot down and caught him at the next set of lights, just before the motorway. It looked like we were heading over the Woodhead Pass to Sheffield. There was no chance to take in the magnificent scenery today. I was too busy concentrating on keeping the car on the road as I powered round the bends and up the long moorland inclines in the wake of the Supra. We hit the outskirts of Sheffield around one, and Terence slowed down, clearly less familiar with the Steel City than he was with Manchester.

We skirted Hillsborough, driving more carefully now since the police were already out in force for a Sheffield Wednesday home game. I can't understand how anybody can bear to go there to watch football these days. I know *I'll* never forget those newspaper photographs of dying Liverpool fans, nearly a hundred of them, crushed to death on a sunny spring afternoon just like this one. I tried to clear the morbid memories by focusing on the Supra's rear end, twitching now-you-see-it-now-you-don't round the next corner like a rabbit's tail.

We cut through backstreets lined with blank, silent buildings, monuments to an industry that once employed a city and made Sheffield steel world-famous. The captains of industry tell us that Sheffield produces more steel than ever before, and with a quarter of the old workforce. It just doesn't feel like it, driving through what appears to be an industrial graveyard.

Beyond the mills, we climbed steeply. Like Rome, Sheffield's a city built on seven hills. Difference is, you get better pizzas in Sheffield. Soon, we were engulfed by a sprawling council estate, sixties terraces and low-rise maisonette blocks as far as the eye could see. Terence seemed to know where he was now, for he speeded up again, scattering mongrels as he went. It was becoming more difficult to maintain an unobtrusive tail, since virtually every car in sight looked like it had at least one wheel in the grave.

The Supra signalled a right turn as it approached a large asphalted area beside a low, square building. I carried straight on, turning into the first side-street. I gave it a few minutes, then I headed back the way I'd come. A couple of hundred yards from the building, I parked the car, made sure the alarm was on, and walked the rest of the way on foot. As I got closer, I could see a battered sign which told me that Suzane was a slag, that Wayne shags great and that Fairwood Community Centre had been opened in 1969. All the casual visitor needed to know, really.

There was a blackboard outside the centre, surrounded by a knot of teenagers who looked like Sheffield's entry for the Wasted Youth of the Year contest. I'd have felt threatened if I didn't know I could kick the feet out from under any of them. As it was, I was wary, avoiding eye contact as I glanced at the blackboard. On it was written in sprawling capitals, "Q Here 4 Sale. 3pm and 6pm. Bargins Galore." Stapled to the corner was a bundle of flyers. I detached one as I walked on by and stuffed it into my pocket.

I rounded the corner of the community centre to the sound of a wolf whistle and a couple of suggestions as to what the youth of Sheffield would like to do to me. In the car park, as well as the Supra, there was a Cavalier and a three-ton truck. The truck was reversed hard up against the hall, its doors opened back parallel with the wall. I crouched down to tie my shoelace and sneaked a look under the van. Beyond it, the double doors of what was obviously the hall's fire exit were open. Short of crawling under the truck and into the hall, there was no way I could see what was in either of them.

I was about to walk back to the car when my phone chirruped. I felt incredibly exposed, answering a mobile phone right there, so I hurried round to the far side of the truck. At least I was out of sight from the road now. Irritated with myself for not having the sense to remember to leave the phone in the car, I barked, "Brannigan," into the phone.

"Kate? Where are you? Are you near home?" It was Alexis, but Alexis as I'd never heard her before. Even in those few words, I could hear panic. And panic meant only one thing.

"Davy?" I said, my fear rising instantly to equal hers.

"Kate, can you get home? Now?"

"What's happened?" I was already skirting round the back of the community centre, crossing a scrubby playing field and heading back to the car. "He's not . . . gone missing?" My immediate terror was that, somehow, someone had discovered who had driven off with the drugs and that Davy was either a hostage or the potential victim of a vicious reprisal.

"No, nothing like that. It's just . . ."

I could hear Chris's voice saying in the background, "For God's sake, Alex, give me the phone, you're only winding her up." Then Chris's voice replaced Alexis's. "Don't panic," she said. "Davy's come back to the house and he's in a bit of a state, like he's high on something. I think he might have been given drugs or something, and I think we ought to take him to hospital. How long will it take you to get home?"

I was at the car, switching the alarm off, shoving the key in the ignition, all on automatic pilot while I digested what Chris was saying. I felt as if I'd been punched in the stomach. Taking Davy to hospital was the nightmare scenario. There was no way we could do it without everything coming on top. Angie would discover that not only was her ex-husband in jail but her son had been put at risk by said ex-husband's fancy woman and her lesbian friends. The chances of Richard ever seeing his son again without a social worker shrank to the size of a terrorist's conscience.

Chris cut into my racing thoughts. "Hello? Kate? Are you still there?"

"Yeah, I'm here," I said, powering down the street and heading back towards the Manchester Road. "Look, you can't take him to hospital. Oh shit, this is the worst possible thing . . . Give me a minute." I thought furiously. On the other hand, if he was really ill, we couldn't *not* take him to hospital. The one thing Richard would never forgive was if I let anything happen to Davy. Come to that, I'd have a hard job forgiving myself. "How bad is he?" I asked.

"One minute he's shivering, the next he's sweating. He keeps going off into crazy giggling fits and he keeps pointing at nothing really and giggling and then cuddling up to us," Chris said. There was a note of desperation in her carefully controlled voice.

My brain had finally accessed the relevant information. "Give me five minutes, Chris," I said.

"I don't know," she said. "He's not at all well, Kate."

"Please. Five minutes, max." I cut off the connection before Chris could argue any more. I pulled up with a screech of rubber and the blast of a horn from the car behind. I nipped open my Filofax and found the number I was looking for. I punched the number into the phone and moved back into the traffic. Sinful, I know, but getting to Davy was a greater imperative than the interests of other road users.

If anyone could help me, it was Dr Beth Taylor. Beth divides her time between an inner city group practice and a part-time lectureship at the university in medical ethics. A few years ago, she had a fling with Bill which lasted about three months, which is probably a record for my business partner. Now, she's Mortensen and Brannigan's first port of call whenever we're investigating medical insurance claims. She also repairs broken bits of Brannigan from time to time.

The phone answered on the second ring. "This is Beth," the distant voice said. "I'm not here right now, but if you want me to call you back you can leave a message after the tone. If

it's urgent, you can try me on my mobile, which is . . ." I keyed
the number into the phone as she recited it, then ended the call
and dialled her mobile, praying to God she not only had it with
her but was also in a decent reception area.

The phone rang once, twice, three times. "Hello, Beth
Taylor." I'd never heard a more welcome sound.

"Beth? It's Kate Brannigan."

"Hi, Kate! Long time no see. Which I suppose is a good
thing, in your case. Is this a professional call? Only, I'm on my
way to play hockey."

I bit back the frustrated sigh. "It's an emergency, Beth."

"What have you done this time?" Underneath the warm
humour in her voice, there was no mistaking the concern.

"It's not me. It's my partner's son. The friends who are
looking after him think he might have been given drugs."

"Then it's not me you want, Kate, it's the casualty department at MRI. You should know that."

"Beth, I can't. Look, I can't explain now, not because I'm
not prepared to, but because there isn't time. Please, Beth, I *need*
this favour. I'm on my way back to my house now, and as soon
as I get there, I'll tell you why I can't take him to hospital unless
it's a matter of life and death," I pleaded.

"If it's drugs, it could well be that," Beth warned.

"I know, I know. But please, you're the only doctor I know
well enough to trust with this."

There was a moment's silence. "I shouldn't do this," she
said with a sigh. "It's against all my better judgement."

"You'll go?"

"I'll go. Where is he?"

"He's at my house. You remember it?"

"I remember," Beth said. "I'll be there in about ten minutes. Oh, and Kate?"

"Yeah?"

"You owe Crumpsall Ladies Hockey Club a round of
drinks for every five minutes I'm late for the game." The

phone went dead before I could tell Beth it would be worth
every penny.

I rang Chris straight back and told her Beth was on her
way. The relief in her voice told me exactly how much fear she'd
been hiding when she'd spoken to me before. "Thank God!"
she exclaimed. "He's just been sick. We're really scared, Kate."

"It's not your fault, Chris. This would have happened
whether Richard had been there or not, believe me. Look,
phone me if there's any change, OK? I'll be back as soon as
I can."

I might have broken all records driving to Sheffield. But I
shattered them driving back.

I barrelled through my front door like the Incredible Hulk on
speed. There wasn't a sound from anywhere, and it took me
less than ten seconds to discover they weren't in the house. I
ran through the conservatory and yanked open the patio doors
leading to Richard's living room. Still no one. By now, I was
convinced they'd had to rush him to hospital. All the way home,
I'd been plagued by a vision of Davy lying in the subdued lighting of intensive care, more tubes than Central London coursing
in and out of his little body.

I crossed the room in half a dozen strides and hauled the
door open, cannoning into Chris, who stepped backwards into
Beth, who continued the domino effect with Alexis. "Ssh," Beth
said before I could say a word. I backed into the living room
and the other three trooped behind me. Alexis shut the door.

"How is he? What's happening?" I demanded.

"Calm down," Beth instructed. "Three deep breaths." I
did what she told me. I even sat down. "Davy's going to be
fine. I've just given him a mild sedative and tranquillizer which
have calmed him down and sent him to sleep. He'll probably be
more or less zonked out till morning. He might feel a bit groggy
tomorrow, but basically he'll be OK."

"What was the matter? What happened?" I asked.

"He presented like someone who has absorbed a significant amount of an hallucinogenic drug," Beth said. "Nothing life-threatening, thank God."

"But how? Where did he get it from? He only went out to play with a couple of other kids from the estate! Who'd feed drugs like that to kids?"

"I said 'absorbed' advisedly," Beth said. She ran a hand through her spiky blonde hair and frowned. "You know those temporary tattoos that kids use? They wet the transfers and the pictures slide off on to their skin?"

I nodded impatiently. "Yeah, yeah, Davy loves them. Some nights he gets in the bath looking like the Illustrated Man."

"Did he have any transfers on his body this morning when he went out?"

"Not that I noticed," I said. "Did either of you notice last night?"

Chris and Alexis both shook their heads.

"He must have thirty or forty on his arms or chest now," Beth said. "And that's the source of the problem, I reckon. I've heard of a couple of cases like this, though I've not actually seen one before."

"But I don't understand. It can't be something in the trans-fers, surely. He often has them covering the whole of his arms and his chest. He's crazy about them, like I said. He'll put on as many as Richard will buy for him."

Beth sighed. "You're right, it's not the transfers as such. It's what's been done to them. They've been doctored. They've been impregnated with a drug not unlike acid or Ecstasy, probably one that's been designed to provide a feeling of mild euphoria, general friendliness and energy. But taken in the dose Davy seems to have absorbed, it also produces hallucinations. We dumped him in the bath and washed them all off so he won't absorb any more, and luckily he seems to have had a pleasant trip rather than a terrifying one."

Beth's words seemed to reverberate long after she'd finished speaking. None of us seemed able to come up with an adequate response. Finally, it was Alexis's journalistic instincts that hit the ground running ahead of my private investigator's. "What do they look like, these transfers?" she asked.

"Some are geometric. Blue and gold stars, about the size of a 10p. Red and pink triangles, too. Others have pictures of clowns, cars, Batman and Superman logos and dinosaurs. The only difference between them and the straight ones is the packaging, so I've been told. Apparently the dodgy ones come in little foil packets, like those individual biscuits you get on aeroplanes. Sorry, I don't know any more than that."

"I can't believe I've not heard about this on the grapevine," Alexis said, outraged.

"She's a journo," I explained to Beth.

"Why haven't there been any warnings about this?" Alexis continued. "It's scandalous."

"Presumably, the powers that be didn't want to start a panic," Beth said. "I can understand why, since it seems to be such a rarity."

"Never mind the story, Alexis. What about Davy? Will he definitely be OK?" Chris demanded.

"He'll be absolutely fine, I promise you. In future, make sure he finds another bunch of friends to play with. Look, I've got to run. My hockey match starts in ten minutes. I'll swing by tomorrow morning, just to be on the safe side, but the best thing you can do is let him sleep it off in peace."

Beth's departure left us in an awkward silence. Alexis broke it. "It's nobody's fault," she said. "We're all going to beat ourselves up, we'll all be fighting each other to take the blame, but it's nobody's fault."

"I know," I said. I got to my feet. "I just want to take a look at him." I walked down the hall to the spare room and pushed the door open. Davy was lying on his back, arms above his head, legs in a tangle of kicked-off duvet. There was a smile on his sleeping face. I leaned over and pulled the cover up over him. He stirred slightly, grunting. I didn't know what else to do so, feeling awkward, I backed out of the room and closed the door behind me.

I went back through to the kitchen. Alexis was sitting on her own, rolling a modest joint from Richard's stash. "Don't you think there's been enough drug-taking for one day around here?" I asked. I was teasing, but only just.

Alexis shrugged. "The doctor says too much stress is bad for me. Chris is making a pot of coffee. You got time for a cup before you go back to wherever you were before you were so rudely interrupted?"

I raised my eyebrows. "I wasn't planning on going back."

"Why? Had you finished what you were doing?"

"Well, no," I admitted.

"So get back on the road. There's nothing you can do here. Davy's zonko. Beth said he'd sleep till morning. Anybody can baby-sit a sleeping kid. But you're the only one that can get Dick out of jail."

"Don't call him Dick," I said automatically. "You know how it depresses me." I looked at my watch and sighed. I had plenty of time to drive back to Sheffield and still be in time for the six o'clock sale. With luck, it would be over early enough for me to get back to Manchester in time to visit Richard. I got to my feet just as Chris came in with a tray of coffee.

"Aren't you stopping for a brew?" she asked.

I put on my FBI face. "You expect me to drink coffee at a time like this?" I asked sternly. "People, a girl's got to do what a girl's got to do."

Chris giggled. Alexis guffawed. I don't know why it is that people just don't take me seriously.

# 12

Literary critics punt the theory that private eyes are society's outsiders. That might have been true in 1940s Los Angeles, but it's a joke in 1990s Britain. These days, if you want to last more than five minutes as a private investigator, you've got to have the instincts of a chameleon. Gumshoes that stand out in a crowd are as much use to the client as a chocolate chip pan. I've had to pass as everything from lawyer to temp, including high-class hooker and journalist, sometimes both on the same day. At least tonight I'd already cased the venue, which gave me a pretty substantial clue as to dress code.

I pulled the crumpled flyer out of my pocket and gave it the once-over. Whoever had put it together wasn't going to win any awards for grammar or graphic design. The one-day sale promised bargains of a lifetime—video recorders for £69.99, camcorders for £99.99, microwaves for £49.99, plus hundreds of other exclusive, unique, etc. Already, and for free, we'd been presented with more exclamation marks than any reasonable person could use in a decade. With all this in mind, I dressed for the occasion. Tight faded Levis, a black Tina Turner *Simply the Best* sweat shirt (because black always makes me look like I have a major vitamin deficiency), and Richard's three-sizes-too-big Washington Redskins jacket. I finished the ensemble with a pair of white stilettos with a two-inch heel, bought, I hasten to add, solely for professional purposes. I gathered my auburn hair into a top knot and held it in place with a gold Lurex elasticated band. Never mind a million dollars, I looked about threepence halfpenny. I'd fit in like a flea in a cattery.

I was back in Sheffield at half past five. I dumped the car in a city centre car park and found a cab to take me out to the council estate. I tipped the cabbie a fiver, which persuaded him to come back for me later. At quarter to six, I joined the queue snaking along the pavement outside the community centre. There were getting on for a hundred punters, and none of them looked like they'd be allowed to carry a donor card, never mind a gold card. I reckoned the youngest were under two, slumped slack-mouthed and sleeping in their pushchairs. The oldest were never going to see seventy again. The rest included harassed-looking women, middle-aged at twenty-five, to lads who looked fifteen till you clocked the eyes. I'd calculated well. Nobody gave me a second glance.

At ten to six, the doors opened and we streamed in. The hall was brightly lit, empty except for a raised dais in front of the "Fire Exit" sign. On the dais was a high counter, piled higher still with cardboard boxes claiming to be filled with microwaves, camcorders, videos and TVs. Other boxes had garish pictures of pan sets, dinner services, game consoles, canteens of cutlery, radio alarms, toasters, battery chargers and socket sets. It looked like a cut-price Aladdin's cave. Behind the stack of boxes I could see a burly man with a perm like a 1970s footballer. If his suit had been any sharper he'd have been arrested for possession of an offensive weapon. He fiddled with a mike, clipping it on to a tie so loud I expected a shriek of feedback. "Ladies and gentlemen," he cajoled, "don't hang back. Come right down to the front where I can see you, and I mean that especially for you lovely ladies. I want to feast my eyes on your charms, because I have to tell you that even though I'm supposed to stand up here being scrupulously fair with you ladies and gentlemen, I'm only human. And I'd have to be more than human to resist some of the lovely ladies I can see in here tonight." Unbelievable. Even more unbelievable, they obeyed. Like lemmings.

Sticking with the flow of the crowd, I moved forward, edging out towards the side of the hall. I looked around, searching for Terence. I spotted him after a few moments, one of several men flanking the dais. Their ages varied from late teens to early forties. I wouldn't have trusted one of them to hold the dog while I went for a pee. I reached the far wall and stopped about ten feet away from the platform. I took a good look round. The punters were eager, many of them patting the pockets that held their money, reassuring themselves it was still there. It wouldn't be for much longer, I suspected, and not because of pickpockets, either.

Now, most of the men by the platform, including Terence, were fanning out among the crowd, keeping one eye on the auctioneer as he "entertained" the audience with a steady stream of patter consisting of *risqué* remarks, old jokes and jocular encouragement to the crowd to move forward and prepare to enjoy themselves. I tuned back in. "I want you to promise me one thing tonight, ladies and gentlemen. I want you to promise me that you'll be good to yourselves. You're going to be offered the bargains of a lifetime here tonight, and I don't want to see you holding back because you don't think you deserve them. I am here tonight to treat you, and I want you to promise me you won't be afraid to treat yourselves. Is that a promise? Will you do that for me?"

"Yeah," they roared back. I couldn't believe it. The guy looked like they'd minted the word "spiv" just for him, yet the punters lapped it up like free beer.

"Now, who wants to start the ball rolling with me tonight? Who needs a cigarette lighter?" A few hands shot in the air. "Who could use a pack of five blank cassettes?" A forest of hands joined them. "And is there anyone out there who would like a pack of three brand new video tapes?" I was probably the only person in the room not waving wildly. I buried my pride and stuck my hand up. The salesman grinned. "Now if it was up to me, I'd be giving these items away, but unfortunately, the law of the land forbids me from exercising my natural generosity. So, you need to give me a token payment for these little tasters of what's to come."

He paused for dramatic effect. The crowd hung on his words, rapt as a nineteenth-century congregation in thrall to some lunatic visionary minister. "I'm going to be as fair as I can be. My team of lads are keeping a careful eye on you all, to see who qualifies. Now, I've got twenty of these disposable lighters here, and the first twenty to stick their hands in the air . . ." He paused again, and half a hundred arms flew wildly into the air. "The first twenty to stick their hands in the air *after* I give the word, those lucky people can purchase a lighter for only one penny. Now, I can't say fairer than that, can I?"

The crowd obviously thought not. The salesman waved a ridiculous gavel in the air. "Now, I'm going to bang me little hammer three times, and when I hit the counter the third time, that's the signal. Then the lucky twenty will be privileged to be allowed to buy a cigarette lighter for only one penny." There was a pregnant pause. The hammer descended once, then twice. Half the hands in the room flailed in the air at the moment the hammer should have fallen the third time. Embarrassed, they dropped their hands again. "Don't be greedy now," the salesman admonished. "I promise you, everybody who wants a bargain here tonight will get one." As he ended his sentence, the hammer banged for the third time, and a thicket of hands straggled into the air. The salesman made a pretence of looking around to see who was first, nodding histrionically as he caught the eye of his henchmen scattered round the room. Twenty punters with waving hands were selected for the cigarette-lighter bargain. It looked to me as if they'd been chosen at random. As we progressed through the cassette tapes (fifty pence), the videos (one pound) and non-stick frying pans developed as a by-product of the American space programme (two pounds), the same arbitrary selections were made. The salesman's assistants only seemed interested in checking out the contents of people's wallets.

The salesman had them in the palm of his hand now. The initial loss leaders had convinced them that tonight they really were going to get bargains. The salesman tossed back his curls and fastened the top button of his jacket, as if to signal it was time to get down to serious business. "Ladies and gentlemen, I'm not going to insult your intelligence here tonight. I bet you all watch *That's Life*. You know that there are unscrupulous people out there who want to part you and your money. Now, I'm not like that. So here's what I'll do. If you put your trust in me now, I will see to it that your trust does not go unrewarded. Ladies, this is something that will change your lives. Gentlemen, this is something that will change your luck. Every now and again, in the perfume laboratories of Paris, men in white coats come up with something that transforms the woman who wears it from the everyday to the absolutely sensational. With the right perfume, any housewife can make the man in her life feel like she's Liz Taylor, Joan Collins and Michelle Pfeiffer rolled into one. It's a scientific fact. They did it with Chanel No. 5. They did it with Giorgio. Now, they've done it with this!"

He brandished a box in the air. Candyfloss pink and silver stripes. It looked unlike anything I'd ever seen before. "Here it is, ladies and gentlemen. My brother is in the import/export business, and he has secured a case of this unique Parisian perfume for my customers before it goes on general sale. This exclusive perfume, Eau d'Ego, will be the subject of a major advertising campaign right through the summer, ladies and gentlemen. It's going to be the hottest seller this Christmas, I promise you that. And tonight, you can be the very first people in Britain to own a bottle of Eau d'Ego."

I struggled to keep a straight face. My French might not be up to much, but when Richard and I had spent a romantic weekend in Paris, we'd done a tour of the city sewers. I don't think you'd find many chic Parisians wearing a perfume whose name sounds suspiciously like *eau d'égout*—sewage.

The salesman was still in full flow, however. "Now, we have a massive selection of bargains here tonight. But inevitably, we don't have enough of our most popular items to go around. My boss puts limits on me. I mean, how many of you would like to buy a camcorder for under a hundred pounds?"

Nearly half the punters waved frantically at him. He gave a satisfied smirk. "Exactly. Now, my boss would sack me if I was to sell more than three of our bargain camcorders in one evening. So I have to ration you. Now, I have fifty bottles of Eau d'Ego here on this platform tonight. If you trust me enough to buy a bottle of this exclusive Parisian fragrance, I will give you first refusal on the lots I'm selling here tonight. I'm not saying you *can't* buy a camcorder if you don't buy the perfume, because that would be illegal, ladies and gentlemen. What I am saying is that the people who trust me enough to become my customers now will be given priority when it comes to buying the lots where we have restricted numbers. Now, I think you'll agree, I can't say fairer than that." His tone left no space for argument. It wasn't a particularly clever pitch, and he wasn't the world's greatest spieler, but they loved it.

"I warn you, ladies, if you get a taste for Eau d'Ego, you are never going to be called a cheap date again. When this marvellous perfume goes on sale in the shops, it will have a recommended retail price of forty-nine pounds ninety-five. Now, I'm not expecting you to pay forty-nine pounds ninety-five tonight. After all, you've not seen the advertising campaign, you've not read all the magazines raving about it, you've not seen the effect it has on me. All you've got is my word. And if I tell you that the wife helped herself to a bottle and I've gone home every night since, that should tell you something!" He winked. I winced.

"I'm not even asking you to pay half-price for the privilege of wearing this fragrance. Ten pounds, that's all. For only a tenner, you can be among the first women to wear a perfume that's destined to be the scent of the stars. Now, when my hammer falls for the third time, my assistants will have their eagle eyes peeled and the first fifty hands in the air will be given this exclusive opportunity." This time, there was no pause. The hammer banged once, twice, three times. The audience proved Pavlov's theory of stimulus-response, the hands high above their heads as soon as the hammer hit.

All the assistants ran around distributing perfume and grabbing tenners. Terence seemed to be doing exactly the same as everyone else. At least, I couldn't see any difference. I began to wonder if I was wasting my time.

The salesman had moved on from the perfume. Now, he was putting together bundles of items. I reckoned I could buy their equivalent down any high street in the land for less than they were asking. But common sense had died somewhere in the salesman's pitch, and he had stomped the corpse into the dust with his patter. They were *fighting* to be allowed to pay over the odds for crap that would explode, disintegrate, tarnish, break or all of the above within weeks.

The hysteria rose as he went through the charade of selling serious bargain lots to five hand-picked mug punters. I had to admire his style as he relieved them of between a hundred and fifty and three hundred pounds for bundles of goods they thought they'd bought at a huge discount. I wouldn't mind betting that at the end of the sale, they'd find that they hadn't been granted the special lots at all. All they'd get would be goods worth rather less than they'd paid, and a wide-eyed assurance that the parcel they'd "bought" had been sold to that (non-existent) man standing right behind them . . . I was watching carefully, and *I'd* lost track of what was going on. The mug punters had no chance.

But the most extraordinary was yet to come. "Have I been good to you tonight, or have I been good to you tonight?" the salesman demanded. He was greeted with a reasonably warm murmur. "Do you think I'm someone you can trust? You, madam—would you trust me?" He went through half a dozen members of the audience, pinning them with his stare, demanding their loyalty. Every last one of them bleated a "yeah" like so many sheep.

He smiled, revealing what he'd been doing with some of the profits. "I told you about my brother earlier, didn't I? The one in import and export? Well, he knows how I love to treat you people, so he's always on the look-out for bargains that I can pass on to my customers. Now, a lot of these things come from outside the EEC, and according to EEC regulations, we can't display them in the same way. So what we do is we make them up into parcels. Even I don't know what's in these parcels, because we make them up at random. But I can guarantee that each of these parcels contains goods to a value well in excess of what I'm asking for them. All I ask of you is that you take the goods home with you before you unwrap them. Not because we want you to buy a pig in a poke but because the contents vary so much. If the person standing next to you sees you've got a state-of-the-art food processor for a tenner and he's only got a toasted-sandwich maker, a set of heated rollers and a clock radio, it can often cause jealousy, and the last thing we want is fights breaking out because some of our bargains are such outrageously good value for money. Now, I'm going to start with ten-pound parcels. Who's spent money with me here tonight and would like to take advantage of my insane generosity?"

I couldn't help myself. My mouth fell open. A couple of dozen people were waving their bottles of perfume in the air. Most of them looked like Giro Day was the biggest financial event in their lives. Yet they were shelling out hard-hoarded cash on a black bin liner that could have contained a bag of sugar and a half-brick. I wouldn't have believed it if someone had told me about it. Then, as the salesman moved on to fifty-pound lucky bags, I noticed a change in the pattern. It was hardly noticeable, but it was enough. For the first time that evening, I began to believe I was in the right place at the right time.

# 13

I drove back to Manchester, replaying what I'd just seen, wondering what it meant. If I hadn't been totally focused, I could so easily have missed the tiny alteration to the pattern. It had happened just after the fifty-pound lots had started. Terence had emerged from behind the platform with a black bin liner, just like all the others. Then he'd snaked through the crowd to a short guy in his early twenties with a red baseball cap and a black leather jacket. Even though the guy didn't have his hand stuck in the air, Terence had passed over the bag in exchange for a fat brown envelope. It looked to me like it contained a lot more than fifty pounds, unless the guy in the red hat was paying in roubles.

They said nothing to each other, and the whole exchange took the same few seconds every other transaction had taken. Terence was back serving punters within the minute. But unlike the other mugs, the guy in the red hat wasn't sticking around. As soon as he'd collected his bag of goodies, he was off, shouldering his way through the crowd towards the door, pulling off the red hat and stuffing it inside his jacket. I contemplated following him, but I had no wheels, and besides, I wanted to carry on watching Terence to see what else he'd get up to.

The answer was, nothing. For the short time that remained, he did exactly the same as the other floor men, dishing out black bin liners in exchange for crumpled notes, fending off punters who thought they'd not had the treat they'd been promised at the start of the evening.

Then, with bewildering suddenness, it was over. While the salesman was still speaking, most of his assistants switched their attention from the audience to the platform. With astonishing speed, the boxes that remained on the dais disappeared into the back of the van. By the time his closing speech was over, the platform was bare as my fridge the day before I hit the supermarket.

I worked my way back to the door, joining the punters who were slowly coming back down to planet earth to the depressing realization that they'd been comprehensively ripped off in a completely legal way with no comeback. By the time I made it outside the hall, the satisfied murmurs had turned into discontented mutterings, growing in volume as people began to examine the contents of their blind buying spree. My taxi was waiting, and I didn't hang around to watch them turn into a lynch mob. Neither did the sales crew. As my taxi pulled away from the kerb, I saw the van and the two cars move across the car park. By the time the crowd got angry enough to do anything about it, the lads'd be halfway back across the Pennines.

I pondered all the way to Manchester. It was still almost too slender even to be called circumstantial, but all my instincts told me I was following the right track. I was pretty sure I'd just witnessed the handover of a parcel of illegal substances. I just hoped that it wasn't wishful thinking that was shunting my instincts down the trail of Terence Fitzgerald.

❧❀❧

It was nearly twenty to nine when I abandoned the Peugeot on a double yellow line a couple of streets away from the sprawling court complex round Crown Square. I was cutting it fine, since visiting ended at nine. I'd covered my back by phoning ahead *en route* from Sheffield, telling the duty inspector I'd been delayed by a puncture but that I would definitely be there within visiting hours. Looking on the bright side, I'd only have been allowed fifteen minutes anyway. I kicked off the tart's shoes and pulled on the pair of Reeboks I always keep in the car, yanked off the hair band and shook my wavy auburn hair free. I grabbed the plastic bag I'd packed in Richard's bungalow, then I jogged round to the back of the Magistrates' Court building.

I slowed down as I entered the covered walkway that cuts into the ground floor of the building and into the range of the video cameras. I didn't want to look like I was storming the building. I pressed the door intercom buzzer. "Can I help you?" asked a voice with more static than a taxi radio.

"I'm here to visit a prisoner. Richard Barclay. I'm his girl-friend," I said.

"Go through the double doors to the lift and press the but-ton for the seventh floor," the voice told me as the door buzzed and the lock was released.

The lift door opened on a different world from the spiffy smartness of the courts. No wood panelling or cool marble floors here. The paintwork was chipped and dirty, the floors pocked with cigarette burns, the walls adorned only with anti-crime posters to intimidate the visitors. I was signed in by a cheerful police officer who ushered me into a tiny cubicle, with two low stools bolted to the floor. The cubicle was divided in half by a metal-topped counter beneath a thick Perspex screen. On each side of the counter, there was a telephone handset. I stared through the screen. The other side was identical, except that there was no handle on the inside of the door. I could get up and go any time I wanted, but the prisoner didn't even have that amount of control. I glanced at my watch. It was just after quarter to.

The door opened and Richard walked in, giving a depress-ing little wave. He sat down, and I found myself noticing all the things I had come to take for granted. The smooth fluidity of his movements. The way his smile starts on the left side of his mouth before becoming symmetrically cute. I blinked hard and nailed a smile on. His mouth moved, but I couldn't hear a thing. I picked up the phone, waving at him to do the same thing. "I was beginning to think you weren't coming," I heard through the earpiece. It wasn't an accusation. His voice sounded strange, disembodied but immediate, not like a normal phone conversation.

"Sorry, but it was your fault I'm so late. I was out there on the mean streets working for you," I said with a ghost of our usual sparring.

"How's Davy?" he asked.

I swallowed. "He's fine," I lied, hoping it didn't show. "He's in bed asleep." That bit was true at least.

His eyebrows rose in perfect arcs, just like Paul McCartney's. "Before nine o'clock? On a Saturday night?"

"Alexis runs a tight ship," I said confidently. "She's having so much fun child-minding that she's worn him out. Movies, computer games, swimming, enough thick shakes to eliminate the EC milk mountain. Or should that be lake?"

"Depends if it's gone sour yet," he said. "Is he missing me?"

"When he has the time to notice you're not there," I said drily. "I'm the one that's missing you."

This time, the smile only made it halfway. "I feel like Tom Jones in 'The Green, Green Grass of Home,'" he said. He rubbed a hand over his face. He looked exhausted.

"You don't look like him, thank God," I told him. "They treating you OK?"

He shrugged. "I guess. I've got a cell to myself, which is an improvement on last night. And the food's just about edible. It's the boredom. It's doing my head in. I'd kill for a decent book and a clean shirt."

I waved the plastic bag. "Clean shirt, boxers, socks and a couple of books. Alexis chose them." He looked bemused. I wasn't surprised. "She says it doesn't mean anything's changed between you," I added.

He relaxed. "Thank God for that. I can stand most things, but I don't know if I could bear to go through the rest of my life being grateful to Alexis. Thanks, Brannigan. I appreciate it."

"You better had," I growled. "I don't do this for my clients, you know. You're going to be working flat out till Christmas as it is just to pay me." I brought him up to speed, stressing how tentative it all was. That didn't stop him looking like a kid who was expecting Santa to turn up with a ten-speed mountain bike *and* a Sega Mega Drive.

"OK, I hear you. Gimme the bottom line. Are you going to get me out of here in time to spend some time with Davy?" he asked. The trust I could read in his eyes pushed my stress levels into the stratosphere.

"I sincerely hope so." I had a horrible feeling that if I didn't, my failure would mean more than one disappointed kid.

Leaving Richard wasn't something I'd relished. But the fresh air outside the court building was. I breathed deep, staring up at the sky, not caring that there was a blur of light rain in the air. I can't remember the last time I felt so low. I checked in with the baby-sitters and Chris told me Davy was still spark out. I drove round by Terence Fitzgerald's house, but the place was in darkness and there was no car outside. I contemplated a bit of burglary, but I knew it was madness. The second rule of successful burglary is: Always make sure you know enough about their lives to know when they're likely to come back. I didn't know nearly enough about Terence's nasty habits. And I didn't relish the thought of being trapped on the top floor with no visible means of escape.

I didn't feel like going home yet. I gunned the car engine into life and cruised back into town. Almost without thinking, I headed for Strangeways. In the long shadow of the Victorian prison commerce thrives. The narrow streets are packed with wholesalers' warehouses, lock-ups and shop fronts, selling casual clothes, electrical goods, jewellery, beauty supplies and furniture. They're mostly family businesses, and the ages of the businesses are like the strata in a geological map. The Jews were here first, then the Cypriots, then the Asians, then a handful of boat people. We're expecting the Bosnians any day now.

A lot of the business that goes on in Strangeways is entirely legitimate. And then, a lot of it isn't. A diligent Trading Standards Officer spending a Sunday poking around the market could find enough infringements to keep a court busy for a week. They regularly do. Only nobody ever answers the summonses.

On a Saturday night, Strangeways looks as empty, dark and moody as a Hollywood film set. Except for the Jewish café, that is. Formally the Warehouse Diner, it's an unpretentious dive frequented by the traders, petty criminals and occasional visitors like me. It's the only decent eating place outside Chinatown that stays open till four in the morning, which makes it handy for all sorts of reasons. Besides, they do the best salt beef sandwiches in town, and the best fry-ups. Some dickhead nominated it for one of those "cheap and cheerful" good food guides, which means that every now and again a bunch of tourists arrives to gawp at the regulars. I've always enjoyed the atmosphere, though if you want certain items, you have to pick your time carefully. The rabbi's a regular visitor, and the mornings he's due there's no bacon butties and only beef sausages.

I'd hit a lull; the early trade had eaten and gone and the nighthawks weren't in yet. As I'd expected, there were a few familiar faces in the diner. The one I was most pleased to see was Dennis. He waved to me to join him and his two buddies, but what I wanted to talk about wasn't for public consumption. I shook my head and sat at a table on my own. As my tea and sandwich arrived, so did Dennis. "What do you know, Kate?" he greeted me, pulling out the chair opposite me.

"Not a lot. Life's a bitch and then you die," I said wearily.

"Nah," he said. "Life's a bitch and then you marry one."

"That's no way to talk about the love of your life."

He grinned. "Me and the wife, we're modern. Into all the latest fashions. That's what keeps a marriage alive. These days we have an S&M relationship."

I knew I was walking into it, but I walked anyway. "S&M?"

"Sex and meals." Dennis roared with laughter. It wasn't that funny, but it was great camouflage. Now everyone would think I was just another victim of Dennis's funny stories.

"Nice one. You know a bloke called Terence Fitzgerald? Lives on the Quays. Drives a black Toyota."

"Terry Fitz? We were in Durham together." He didn't mean on holiday. Durham jail is one of the meanest, bleakest places a man can do time. They don't send you there for non-payment of fines.

"What was he in for?"

"A blag with a shooter. He was the wheels man. Like Handbrake, only nasty. They never got him for it but he run over an old dear when they was having it away on their toes after a job in Skelmersdale, and he never stopped. Slag," Dennis added contemptuously.

"He been out long?"

Dennis shrugged. "A year or so. I don't know what he's doing these days."

"I do," I said. "He's working as a floor man for an outfit doing hall sales." I handed Dennis the crumpled flyer. "This outfit."

Dennis nodded sagely. "This is his brother-in-law's team. Tank Molloy. He married Fitz's sister Leanne. Good operation he's got there. Makes a lot of money. And he does it all dead legal. He shafts them, but he shafts them within the letter of the law. The BBC had a team following him round for weeks, trying to turn him over, but they couldn't get nothing on him except for being immoral so they had to back off. Burly bloke, hair like a poodle, terrible taste in ties, that's Tank. He's usually the top man."

I raised one eyebrow. "The top man?"

"The one that does the patter."

I nodded. "Sounds like him. Any drug connection?"

Dennis looked shocked. "What? Tank Molloy? No way. He's an old-fashioned villain, Tank. He's like me. Wouldn't touch drugs with a bargepole. I mean, where's the challenge in that?"

"What about Terry Fitz?"

Dennis took his time lighting a cigarette. "Fitz has got no scruples. And he don't give a shit who he works with. If he's got in with the drug boys, you don't want to tangle. He's sharp, Fitz. The only thing he's stupid about is shooters. He thinks they're a tool of the trade. He wouldn't think twice about blowing you away if there was just you standing between him and a good living."

# 14

It's a piece of cake, being a lawyer or a doctor or a computer systems analyst or an accountant. Libraries are full of books telling you how to do it. The only textbooks for private eyes are on the fiction shelves, and I don't remember ever reading one that told me how to interrogate an eight-year-old without feeling like I was auditioning for the Gestapo. It didn't help that Alexis was standing in the doorway like a Scouse Boadicea, arms folded, a frown on her face, ready to step in as soon as I stepped out of line.

Davy sat in bed, looking a bit pale, but otherwise normal. I figured if he was well enough to wolf scrambled eggs and cheese kabanos, he was well enough to answer a few simple questions. Somehow, it didn't work out that straightforwardly. I sat on the bed and eventually we established that he was feeling OK, that I wasn't going to tell his mum and we'd negotiate about his dad at a later stage. Already, I felt exhausted.

"Where did you get the transfers from?"

"A boy," he said.

"Did you know the boy?" I asked.

Davy shook his head. He risked a quick glance at me from under his fringe. I could see he was going to grow up with the same lethal cuteness as his father. However, since I've yet to discover any maternal instincts and I'm not into little boys till they're old enough to have their own credit card, the charm didn't work on me. I stayed firm and relentless. "You don't usually take presents from strangers, do you, Davy?"

Again, the shake of the head. This time, he mumbled, "He wasn't a proper stranger."

"How do you mean?" I pounced.

"Daniel and Wayne knew him," he said defiantly. "I wasn't going to, but they said it was all right."

"Were you playing with Daniel and Wayne?"

This time he nodded. His head came up and he looked me in the eye. He was on surer ground now. Daniel and Wayne were two of the kids from the council estate. He knew I knew who he was talking about. I stood up. "OK. In future, don't take things from people unless *you* know them. Is that a deal?"

Looking stubborn rather than chastened, he nodded. "OK," he dragged out.

"I'm really not cut out for this game," I muttered to Alexis as I left.

"It shows," she growled. Walking down the hall, I heard her say, "You going to lie in your pit all day, soft lad? Only there's a pair of skates at Ice World with your name on, and if you're not ready in half an hour I'm going to have to go on my own."

"Can't we go later, Alexis?" I heard Davy plead.

"You're not going to lie there half the day, are you?"

"No. But I want to go and watch my dad's team playing football this morning. We always go and watch them when I'm here."

Silence. I bet standing on a freezing touchline watching the local pub team kick a ball badly round a muddy pitch was as much Alexis's idea of hell as it was mine. I smiled as I headed through the conservatory and back into my own territory. It was nice to know that even Alexis got stiffed now and again. I pulled on last night's jeans. I opened the wardrobe and realized I wasn't going to be able to take a rain check on my date with the iron for much longer. I'd hire someone to do it, but on past experience it only causes me more grief because they never, but never, get the creases in the right places.

Irritated, I grabbed a Black Watch tartan shirt, a leftover from my brief excursion into grunge fashion, hastily abandoned when Della told me I looked like a refugee from an Irish folk group. At least it gave me an excuse to wear the battered old cowboy boots that are more comfortable than every pair of trainers I possess. I put a white T-shirt on under the tartan and headed out the door in search of Daniel and Wayne's mum.

I crossed the common to the rows of four-storey council flats where Cherie Roberts lived. After all this time, I'm still capable of being surprised by the contrast with the neat little enclave where I live. At the risk of sounding like Methuselah at twenty-eight, I can remember council estates where the Rottweilers didn't go around in pairs for security. Oxford isn't famous for its pleasant public housing, but I had school friends who lived out on Blackbird Leys when it was the biggest council housing estate in Western Europe, and it was OK. I don't remember obscene graffiti everywhere, lifts awash with piss and shit, and enough rubbish blowing in the wind between the canyons of flats to mistake the place for the municipal dump. Thank you, Mrs Thatcher.

I walked on to the corner and looked down the narrow cul-de-sac, trying to remember which block Cherie's flat was in. I knew it was on the top floor and on the left-hand side. I'd know it when I saw it, but if I could avoid climbing six sets of stairs, I'd be happier. There was nobody around to ask either. Half past nine on a Sunday morning isn't a busy time on the streets where I live. I set off, chewing over what I knew of Daniel and Wayne's mum.

Cherie was a pale thirty-year-old who looked forty except when she smiled and her bright blue eyes sparked. She didn't smile that often. She was a single parent. She hadn't ever been anything else in practice, even though she'd been married to

Eddy Roberts for eight years. Eddy was a Para who'd fallen in love with violence long before Cherie ever got a look-in. They'd married in a moment of madness when he was waiting to be shipped to the Falklands to help win Mrs Thatcher's second term. He'd come back with his head full of Goose Green and gone just crazy enough for them to invalid him out. He stuck around for the few days it took to impregnate Cherie, but before Daniel was much more than a tadpole, her soldier of fortune was off fighting somebody else's war in Southern Africa. He dropped in a year later for long enough to give her a couple of black eyes and another baby before he vanished into Central America.

Davy is the reason I know all this. He'd been coming up to visit regularly for a few months when Cherie turned up on my doorstep one night. Davy had obviously been boasting about my brilliance as a private eye, for Cherie had a task for me. She explained, right up front, that she couldn't afford to pay me in money but she was offering a skill swap. Her cleaning and ironing for my detecting. I was tempted, till she told me about the job. She wanted me to find Eddy. Not because she wanted him back, but because she wanted a divorce.

I'd explained gently that Mortensen and Brannigan don't handle missing persons, which happens to be no less than the truth. I could tell she didn't believe me, even though I spent an hour outlining a few suggestions on how and where she might track down her errant husband. Relations between us weren't helped when the agency was all over the papers a couple of months later because of a very high-profile missing person case that I'd cracked . . . Since then, whenever we'd met in the post office or in the dentist's waiting room she'd been frigidly polite, and I guess I'd stood on my dignity. Not the most promising history for a successful interview.

I struck lucky on the third attempt. I recognized Cherie's door as soon as I hit the landing. Daniel's Ninja Turtle stickers were unmistakable, and obviously difficult to remove. Nothing so embarrassing to a kid as the evidence of last year's cult. Taking a deep breath, I knocked. No reply. I banged the letter box, and was rewarded with a scurrying behind the door. The handle turned and the door swung open a couple of inches on a chain and the sound of the TV blasted me, but I couldn't see anybody. Then a small voice said, "Hiya," and I adjusted my eye level.

"Hiya, Daniel," I said to the pyjama-clad figure. I had a fifty per cent chance of being right.

"I'm Wayne," he said. I hoped that wasn't a sign from the gods.

"Sorry. Hiya, Wayne. Is your mum in?"

He shrugged. "She's in bed."

Before he could say more, I saw a pale blue shape in the background and heard Cherie's voice say sharply, "Wayne. Come away from there. Who is it?"

I cocked my head round the crack in the door and said, "Hi, Cherie. It's me, Kate Brannigan. Sorry to wake you, but I wondered if I could have a word."

Cherie appeared at the door in a faded towelling dressing gown and shoved Wayne out of the way. "I wasn't asleep."

I was glad about that. She'd have had to be seriously hearing impaired to have slept through the volume her kids seemed to need from the TV. "Yeah, right," I said diplomatically.

"What is it?" she asked.

"I just wanted a word. Em . . . Can I come in?"

Cherie looked defensive. "If you want," she said, grudging every word.

"I don't want the whole neighbourhood to hear me," I said, trying desperately not to sound like I was about to give her a bad time.

"I've nothing to be ashamed of," she said defensively. She let the chain off and opened the door wide enough to let me in. After I'd entered, she stuck her head out and gave the landing the quick one-two to check who had spotted me.

I pressed against the wall to let her pass and lead me into the living room. "Out," she said curtly. Daniel reluctantly uncurled himself from the sofa and walked out of the room. Cherie switched off the TV and stared aggressively at me. "D'you want a brew, then?" It was a challenge.

I accepted. While she was in the kitchen, I looked around. The room was scrupulously clean and as tidy as my place on a good day. Given she had two kids, it was impressive. It was a shame she didn't have enough cash to upgrade from shabby. The leatherette upholstery of the sofa was mended with parcel tape in places, and in others it had completely worn away. The walls were covered in blown vinyl in a selection of patterns, clearly a job lot of odd rolls. But the paint was still white, if not quite brilliant, and she'd pitched some video shop manager into letting her have some film posters to brighten the place up.

"Seen enough?" Cherie demanded, returning from the kitchen on bare and silent feet. There was nothing I could say about her home that wouldn't sound patronizing, so I said nothing, meekly accepting the mug of tea she held out to me. "There's no sugar," she said. "I don't keep it in."

"That's OK, I don't use it."

The door opened a couple of inches and Daniel's head and one shoulder appeared. "We're going round to Jason's to watch a video," he said.

"OK. Behave yourselves, you hear me?"

Daniel grinned. "You wish, Mum," he giggled. "See ya."

Cherie turned her attention back to me. She'd found a moment to drag a brush through her shoulder-length mouse-coloured hair, but it hadn't improved the image a whole lot. She still looked more like a woman at the end of her day rather than the beginning. "So what's this word you wanted to have with me?"

I swallowed a mouthful of strong tea and dived in at the deep end. "I'm really worried about something that happened yesterday, and I think you probably will be too. Davy's up for the week. He was out playing yesterday morning for a couple of hours, and when he came in, he was in a hell of a state. He was really hyper, he was sick, and his temperature was all over the place. I got a friend of mine who's a doctor to come around and have a look at him. The bottom line is, he was out of his head on drugs."

The words were barely out of my mouth before Cherie jumped in. "And it has to be something to do with my kids, doesn't it? It couldn't be any of those nice middle-class kids from your street, could it? How do you think kids around here get the money for drugs?"

That wasn't one I was prepared to answer. Reminding her of the muggings, burglaries and dole frauds that are the everyday currency of life at the bottom of the heap wasn't going to earn me the answers I was looking for. "I'm not blaming your lads, Cherie. From what I can gather, they're as likely to be victims as Davy was."

That wasn't the right response either. "Don't you accuse my lads of taking drugs," she said dangerously, her eyes glinting like black ice. "We might not have much compared to you, but I take care of my kids. You've no shame, have you?"

That was when I lost it. "Will you for Christ's sake listen to me, Cherie?" I snarled. "I've not come here to have a go at you or your kids. Something scary, something dangerous, happened to Davy and I don't want it happening to any other kids. Not yours, not anybody's. You and me smacking each other over the heads with our prejudices isn't going to sort things out."

In the silence that followed, Cherie gave me the hard stare. Gradually, the sullen look left her face. But the suspicion was still there in her eyes. "OK. You got somebody else's kicking. I had them bastards from the Social round the other day, doing a number about how Eddy's not paying any maintenance and I must know where he is."

I pulled a face. "Pick a war, any war."

"That's more or less what I told them. So, what's all this business with Davy got to do with me?" The adrenaline rush had subsided and her eyes had dulled again, emphasizing the dark blue shadows beneath them. She sat on the arm of the sofa, keeping her eyes firmly fixed on mine.

"These drugs were absorbed through the skin. From those tattoo transfers that the kids stick all over themselves. According to my doctor friend, the tattoos are impregnated with drugs. I don't know why. Maybe it's to give kids the taste for it. You know, a few freebies to get them into the habit, then it's sorry, you've got to cough up some readies."

Cherie pulled a pack of cheap cigarettes out of her dressing-gown pocket and lit up. "I've seen my two with a few transfers," she admitted. "I know they must have got them from one of the other kids because I don't buy them the stickers, and they've had them some times when they've not had spends. But I've never seen them out of their heads, or anything like it. Mind you, the way they wind each other up, you probably couldn't tell," she added, in a grim joke.

I mirrored her thin smile. "The problem seems to have arisen because Davy OD'd on the transfers. He loves them, you see. Given half a chance and a year's pocket money, he'd cover himself from head to foot with them. Especially if they were *Thunderbirds* ones. Now, Davy says he was playing with Wayne and Daniel yesterday. A boy he didn't know gave him the transfers, and he seems to have handed over as many as Davy wanted. He says he thought it was OK to take the transfers from the boy because Wayne and Daniel knew him," I said.

"I suppose you want to ask my pair who this lad was," Cherie said with the resignation of a woman who's accustomed to having her autonomy well and truly usurped by the middle-class bastards. Once upon a time I'd have been insulted to be taken for one of them, but even I can't kid myself that I'm still a working-class hero.

I shook my head. "If you don't mind, I'd rather you asked them. I think you're more likely to get the truth out of them than me. They'd only think I was going to bollock them."

Cherie snorted. "They'll *know* I'm going to bollock them. OK, I'll ask them when I see them. It'll be a few hours, mind you. Once they get stuck into a pile of videos, they lose all track of time."

"Great. If you get anywhere, can you let me know? I'm going to be in and out a lot, but there'll probably be somebody in next door in Richard's. Or else stick a note through the door. I'd really appreciate it." I got to my feet.

"You going to hand the slags over to the cops?" Cherie asked. Behind her bravado, I could sense apprehension.

"I don't think people that hand out drugs to kids should be out on the street, do you?"

Cherie shook her head, a despairing look on her face. "Put them away, another one jumps in to take their place."

"So we just let them carry on?"

"No way. I just thought you'd know the kind of people that'd put them off drug dealing for life. And put off anybody else that was thinking it would be a good career move."

People get strange ideas in their heads about the kind of person a private eye hangs out with. The worrying thing for me was that Cherie was absolutely right. I knew just the person to call.

# 15

Ruth hadn't hung around waiting for me in reception. I spotted her behind the *Independent on Sunday* from the other side of the coffee lounge. There was already a basket of croissants and a selection of cold meats and cheeses on the table. Whipped cream in Alpine peaks was gently subsiding into her hot chocolate, and somehow she'd managed to get a whole jug of freshly squeezed orange juice all to herself. Luckily, she'd chosen a window table which commanded a view of the Quays. On the way to meet her, I'd swung round by Terry Fitz's flat and been relieved to see the Supra sitting on the drive and the curtains still firmly closed. From the hotel, I'd be able to see if he left home.

I sat down and said, "If I rush off suddenly, it's not because of something you've said."

She lowered the paper and groaned. "Oh God, not melodrama over Sunday brunch? Frankly, I can see why you copped out of the law. Not nearly exciting enough to keep you going."

"I'm not grandstanding," I bristled. "I'm trying to get Richard out of jail."

"You and me both," Ruth said calmly, dumping her paper, reaching for a croissant and dunking it into her chocolate. I felt faintly sick. "Any progress?" she asked.

I brought her up to speed. It didn't even fill the gap between me ordering coffee and wholemeal toast and them arriving. Ruth listened attentively in between mouthfuls of soggy croissant. "How fascinating. It's a novel way of distributing drugs. This sounds very promising for Richard," she said as I ground to a halt. "But you're going to need a lot more than that before we can persuade the Drugs Squad that Richard was merely an innocent abroad."

"What are the next moves, from your point of view?" I asked.

"That depends to some extent on you. If you can come up with enough by Tuesday morning for the Drugs Squad to get going, then I've got a slight chance of getting bail on Wednesday."

"How slight?" I asked.

Ruth studied the cold meat and speared a slice of smoked ham. "I'd be lying if I said it looked good. Failing that, what I can go for is a short remand, say an overnight or a couple of days, arguing that investigations are in progress which may produce a significantly different picture within twenty-four hours. If the Drugs Squad then mount a successful operation based on information received from you, the chances are we can then get Richard out on bail. It'll take a little longer to get the charges dropped, but at least he won't be languishing in the CDC while I'm working on it." She split a croissant and loaded it with ham, followed by a slice of cheese. I envied her appetite. I stared morosely at the toast and poured myself a coffee.

I didn't even have time to add milk. A flash of light as the sun hit the windscreen of Terry Fitz's car alerted me. He was turning out of his drive. I hit the ground running. "Sorry!" I called back to Ruth. "Send me the bill."

"Don't worry about it," she shouted. "I'll charge it to the client."

And I thought I padded my bills. One thing about hanging out with lawyers: they don't half make you feel virtuous.

This time, we headed up the M6. I had no trouble with the tail at first, since half of the North West of England had decided the only place to be on the sunny Sunday of a bank holiday weekend was in a traffic jam on the motorway. Things improved after Blackpool, but there were still a lot of families having the traditional bank holiday argument all the way to the Lakes. The Supra was an impatient outside-lane hogger and flasher of lights, but he had few chances to hammer it till the traffic thinned out after the Windermere turn-off. Then he was off. I prayed he was keeping a look-out for traffic cops up ahead as I watched the speedo creep up past a ton. The last thing I needed was a driving ban.

He slowed as we approached the Carlisle turning, and I hung back till the last minute before I shot off in his wake. His destination was only five minutes off the motorway, a sprawling concrete pillbox of a pub sandwiched between a post-war council estate of two-up two-down flats built to look like semis, and a seventies estate of little "executive" boxes occupied by sales reps, factory foremen and retail managers struggling with their mortgages. I drifted past the Harvester Moon Inn, watching as he parked the Supra by the truck I recognized from the previous day. I slowed to a halt, twisted my rear-view mirror round and watched Terry Fitz climb out of his car, pick up a black bin liner from the rear seat well and head into the pub.

I parked round the corner from the pub and walked back. The blackboard stood outside the main entrance, announcing today's sales at two p.m. and five p.m. in the pub's upstairs function room. Depressed at the very thought of it, I dragged myself into the pub. It was a huge barn of a place, arbitrarily divided into bar and lounge by a wooden partition at head height. Well, head height for someone with a bit more than my five feet and three inches. The whole place was in dire need of a face-lift, but judging by the desperate tone of the notices on the walls, it wasn't making enough to persuade the brewery to spend the necessary cash. Monday night was "the best trivia night in town," Tuesday was "Darts Open Night, cash prizes," Wednesday was "Ladies Night! With Special House Cocktails," Thursday offered "Laser Karaoke, genuine opportunities for Talent!" while Friday was "Disco Dancing! Do the Lambada with Lenny. The Harvester's very own king of the turntables." And people say Manchester's provincial.

The clientele was marginally up-market of the down-at-heel decor. There were, naturally, more men than women, since somebody has to baste the chicken. I felt out of place, not because of my gender, but because I was the only person who wasn't part of the locals' tribal rituals. The customers sat or stood in tight groups, taking part in what was clearly a regular Sunday lunch-time session with unvarying companions. I carried on walking past the bar, gathering a few inquisitive stares on the way, and through a door at the rear marked "Harvest Home Lounge." It led to a small foyer, with stairs climbing upwards, and a set of double doors leading out into the car park. With half an hour to go before the sale, I'd clearly beaten the Carlisle crowds to the draw.

I walked back to the car and headed into the town centre till I found a Chinese chippy next to a corner shop. I drove back crunching worryingly cubic sweet-and-sour chicken, with a bag of apples for afters to make me feel virtuous. I joined the queue for the sale with only a few minutes to go. This time, I hung back as we filed in so I could have a good view of the rest of the punters. The sale followed the same pattern as the previous evening's. The only change was that Molloy, the top man, only offered forty bottles of perfume. I put that down to the slightly smaller crowd that they had drawn. When we got down to the pig-in-a-poke lots, I kept my eyes fixed on Terry Fitz.

The night before hadn't been a fluke. Soon as Molloy announced the fifty-pound lots, Terry appeared with a black bin liner that looked identical to the others. But he took it straight over to a punter I'd already singled out as the man most likely to. Just like the previous night's mark, he was wearing a black leather jacket and a red baseball cap. It was a different guy, there was no question about it. But the clothes were identical.

As soon as I saw the handover, I eased myself away from the audience and ran downstairs. I slipped inside the door leading to the pub and held it open a crack. As I'd expected, Red Cap was only moments behind me. He didn't even pause to look around him, just headed straight out into the car park. I was behind him before he'd gone a hundred yards.

He wasn't hard to tail. He bounced on his expensive hi-tops with a swagger, his red cap jauntily bobbing from side to side. Across the car park, over the road and into the council estate. We walked for half a mile or so through the estate until we came to three blocks of low-rise flats arranged in an H-shape. Red Cap went for the middle block, disappearing into a stairwell. Cautiously, I followed, keeping a clear flight below him as he climbed. I caught a glimpse of his jacket as he turned out of the stairs on the third floor, and I ran the last flight. I cleared the stairs and hit the gallery in time to see a door close behind him. Trying to look as if I belonged, I strolled along the gallery. His was the third door. The glass had been painted over and heavy curtains obscured the windows. I turned and walked back, my eyes flicking from side to side, desperately seeking a vantage point.

One of the legs of the H looked as if it was in the process of being refurbished or demolished. The windows were mostly boarded up and there was no sign of life. I hurried back down the stairs and across to the deserted block. Sure enough, the stairwell was boarded up. It had been padlocked, but the housing had been crowbarred off, some time ago, by the looks of it. I pulled the door open far enough to squeeze round it and cautiously made my way up the gloomy stairs. From what little I could see, it looked like HIV alley, condoms slithering and syringes crunching underfoot. Once I passed the first floor it

became lighter and cleaner. I went all the way up to the fourth
floor and emerged on the gallery at an oblique angle to Red
Cap's front door. Then I settled down to wait.

Half an hour later, there had been four visits to the flat:
two separate youths, one couple in their teens and a pair of lads
with a girl in tow. Red Cap had opened the door to all of them,
and they'd slipped inside, only to emerge less than five minutes
later looking a lot happier. I've seen chemists' shops with fewer
customers. After the fourth visit, I thought it was time to risk
collecting some firm evidence, so I left my sentry post and
jogged back to the car. I drove into the private housing estate
and headed in the general direction of the flats. I didn't want
to leave the car in an exposed place like a pub car park once I'd
revealed that it held more than yesterday's newspapers. I parked
in a quiet side-street and opened my photographic bag. I put on
the khaki gilet Richard brought me back from a business trip to
LA. It's got more pockets than a snooker club. I put the Nikon
body with the motor drive in one, and slipped my telephoto
lens and doubler into inside pockets.

Within ten minutes, I was back on the fourth floor, the
long lens resting on the edge of the balcony, focused on Red
Cap's front door, motor drive switched on. I didn't have long
to wait. In less than an hour, I had six separate groups on film.
If I didn't win the Drugs Squad's Woman of the Year award, it
wouldn't be for want of trying.

# 16

I called it a day on the surveillance at half past four and walked back to the car. I swapped cameras, choosing a miniature Japanese one that slots into a pocket in the gilet. The pocket has a hole in it that corresponds to the lens of the camera. I loaded the camera with superfast film so it would capture an image without the need for flash, plugged in the remote shutter release cable and threaded it through the lining so the button sat snugly in the pocket I'd have my hand stuffed into. Before I set off for the five o'clock sale, I called home. There was no reply, either at my house or Richard's, so I assumed everybody was having a good time.

The five o'clock sale ran to the same formula. If I had to do this many more times, I'd be able to take over the top man's job. This time, I'd got near the front of the queue and waited till the red cap and the black leather jacket appeared. This time, it wasn't a man. Nice to see that equal opps is finally making its way into criminal circles. She was about my age, taller, bottle blonde and pale as Normandy butter. I manoeuvred my way through the crowd till I was standing at an angle to her, perfectly positioned for my camera to do the business. The handover came right on cue, the bulky envelope exchanged for a black bin liner. This time, Terry Fitz winked. I'm not sure if it was because she was a woman, or because he knew her, but it was the first time I'd seen him display any kind of recognition towards the happy recipients of his little parcels.

I thought about following the woman, but decided I'd rather stay with Terry Fitz. I knew where the drugs were going now; what I didn't know was where they were coming from. With his record, I couldn't see Terry Fitz standing on for having them stashed in his house. I waited till the woman in the red baseball cap was well clear, then I nipped out ahead of the masses and got my car in position between the pub and the motorway.

Just before eight, Terry Fitz shot past me at a disgraceful speed. On the way back, the bank holiday traffic trapped us again, but in spite of that we were still in Salford by half past nine. As we turned into the Quays, I hung back. I was a good half-mile away when he pulled up on the street outside his house. He jumped out of the car, trotted up the path and opened the garage, re-emerging seconds later behind the wheel of the Escort Cosworth, still with its trade plates.

I waited till it zoomed past me sounding like Concorde with a frog in its throat before I spun the Peugeot round and sped off in its wake. Back down the motorway, on to the M63, this time heading south towards Stockport. As we drove over Barton Bridge, the elevated section above the Manchester Shit Canal (so called because of the sewage works that huddle along its banks), I stayed right over in the fast lane. I came rather too close to checking out whether or not there's an afterlife one night on Barton Bridge, and it left me more than a little wary of trusting in the crash barriers.

As we descended the long curve of the bridge, I let my breath out again. I stayed with his tail-lights past Trafford Park and Sale, but I nearly missed him as he cut across three lanes of traffic to shoot off on the slip road for the M56 and the air-port. We didn't stay on the motorway for long. He came off at the junction for the sprawling council estate of Wythenshawe, bypassed the shopping centre and made for the far side of the

airport, over towards the cargo holding areas. The job suddenly
got awkward.

The Cosworth turned right down a narrow lane that
wound alongside the perimeter fence of the airport. Following it down there was a risky venture. Sighing, I doused my
lights and turned right. My car was black, which meant I had
less chance of being spotted. The downside was that anything
coming in the opposite direction wouldn't see me either. The
things we do for love.

The lane was fairly straight, so I managed easily to keep the
lights of the Cosworth in sight for a mile or so, then, abruptly,
they disappeared sharply on the right. Time for a gamble. Since
that was the airport side of the road, I didn't think Terry Fitz had
turned off on to another minor road. I decided he'd arrived at a
rendezvous. I spotted a field gateway a couple of hundred yards
ahead on the left, and pulled into it, killing the engine fast. I
got out of the car and pushed the door gently to. The click of
the lock made me jump, but I told myself it wouldn't carry far,
not so close to the airport.

I took a good look round before I crossed the road and
moved cautiously towards the spot where the Cosworth had
vanished. There was a narrow gap in the hedgerow, and I edged
my head round. A rutted, stony track led a few yards off the
road, angling round sharply to the double doors of a wooden
building. Small barn, large garage, take your pick. The Cosworth was outside, parked next to a Mercedes 300SL with the
personalized plate TON 1K. I could see a thin line of yellow
light along the top of the door, but nothing more. The side of
the lock-up was only feet away from the airport fence.

I felt seriously exposed where I was, so I slipped across the
track and inched up to the corner, checking the hedge as I went.
Just on the corner, there was a bit of give and I wriggled into
the bushes, trying not to think of all the nocturnal creatures
that lurk in the English countryside. If you ask me, extinct is
quite the best state for mice and rats and most other small furry

animals with sharp teeth. Not to mention all the creepy insects that would take one look at my hair and decide it was a better habitat than the filthy maze of the hedgerow.

I gave an involuntary shudder that rippled through the hedge with a noise like *Wuthering Heights* meets *The Wind in the Willows*. "Get a grip, Brannigan," I muttered under my breath. I took a deep breath and my nose filled with dust. Predictably, just like the worst kind of wimpy heroine, I felt a sneeze welling up inside. I pinched the bridge of my nose so tight my eyes watered, but not so much that I missed the garage door opening. Terry Fitz appeared in the doorway, called back, "No problem, speak to you in the week," and walked briskly to the Cosworth.

He was carrying three Sainsbury's carrier bags, but I didn't think he'd come all the way out to the airport to pick up some groceries. He opened the boot, and in the glow of the courtesy light, I saw him lift the carpet and stow the carrier bags underneath. From the look of it, they were packed into the well where the spare wheel should be. Fitzgerald slammed the boot shut, then got into the Cosworth. He bounced the car round in a tight three-point turn, then he was off, leaving a cloud of dust hanging in the moonlight. I didn't even think about trying to follow him.

Instead, I waited to see who else was lurking inside the garage. I didn't think that anyone who owned a motor like that was likely to be spending the night there. Besides, with Richard behind bars, I had nothing better to do with my Sunday evening.

It was a long half-hour before there was any sign of life. With no warning, the door swung open. Before I had the chance to see who emerged, the inside light snapped off. A tall, burly man in an overcoat came out and turned his back to me as he fastened a couple of big padlocks that closed the heavy steel bars protecting the doors. Then, still with his back to me, he headed towards the Mercedes. I backed out of the hedge, coming out on the track out of his sight, and raced back towards the road as his engine started. I reckoned I had a couple of minutes while he turned the big car around. With a bit of luck, he'd be heading the way my car was facing and I might be able to pick him up. If I lost him, at least I had the car registration number to go at.

I dived behind the wheel of the Peugeot just as his headlights swept the hedge opposite the gap. The gods were smiling. He drove away from me, so I started the engine, left the lights off and followed. I was beginning to feel like I'd got the sucker role in a very bad road movie.

We were only a mile from the main road. I let him glide off before I switched my lights on and rejoined the respectable. I hoped this wasn't going to be a long chase, because my fuel gauge told me I'd soon be running on fumes. At least Mercedes Man didn't drive like a speed freak. I suppose when you're driving round in that much money you don't need to prove anything to anybody.

We cruised through Wilmslow, the town where car dealers aren't allowed to sell anything that costs less than five figures. They're all here—Rolls-Royce, Porsche, BMW, Mercedes, Jaguar, even Ferrari. Just before the town centre, the Merc turned right and, a couple of hundred yards down the road, he pulled on to the forecourt of a small car pitch. EMJ Car Sales. Even the second-hand motors were all less than three years old.

The driver got out of the car and let himself into the car showroom. A light came on inside. Now at least I knew where Terry Fitz had come by his trade plates. And why he seemed to go for seriously expensive motors. Five minutes later, the interior light snapped off and the driver got back into his Merc. I still hadn't had a good enough look at him to attempt identification. We drove back into the town centre. It was quiet; not even the designer clothes shops had attracted late-night browsers. We passed the station and headed out of town. By now, I had a shrewd suspicion where we might be headed.

Prestbury has more millionaires per head of population than any other village in England, according to the media-hype types. The only way you'd guess from hanging round in the main street is from the motors parked outside the deli and the *chocolatier*. They don't have sweetie shops run by Asians in places like Prestbury. They don't have anything that isn't one hundred per cent backed up by centuries of English Conservative tradition. But then, in Prestbury, you don't get the kind of *nouveau* millionaire celebs that give the paparazzi palpitations. We're talking captains of industry, backroom boys and girls, the high rollers whose names mean nothing to anyone outside a very select circle. You can tell it's posh, though. They haven't got pavements or streetlights. After all, who needs them when you go everywhere by car or horse?

About a mile from the centre of the village, the Merc signalled a left turn. I signalled right, then killed my lights and pulled on to the verge. Someone was going to have a major tantrum when they saw my tyre marks in the morning. I jumped out of the car and sprinted towards the gateway he'd entered. I crouched behind the gatepost. The deeply incised letters told me I was outside Hickory Dell, the land that taste forgot. The house was built on the side of a slope, a split-level monstrosity that could have housed half Manchester's homeless and still have had room for a wedding reception. A four-car garage bigger than any house on my estate stood off to one side. One garage door was open, the drive outside it spotlit with high-wattage security lights. I heard the soft slam of a car door, then the heavy-set man emerged. As he swung round to check the door was closing behind him, I got a good look at his face.

I'd seen him before, no question about it. The problem was, I didn't have a clue where or when.

# 17

I stopped running and took a couple of seconds to work out exactly where I was. I could feel the prickle of sweat under my helmet as I swivelled my head from side to side. I turned sharp right and started running again. As I rounded the next corner, my heart sank. I'd hesitated too long. The tank was heading straight for me, blocking the entire width of the street. Desperately, I turned back, in time to see the helicopter closing off my retreat by dropping a block of what looked remarkably like granite into the street.

Resigned to defeat, I pulled off my helmet and glove. In the next playing area, Davy was still inside his helmet, one hand on the joystick that controlled the tank, the other punching the air triumphantly. I hate kids. They're *always* better at the computer games where hand-eye co ordination is vital.

I tapped the top of his helmet and undid the straps. Reluctantly, he let go the joystick and climbed out of the seat. "Time up, cybernaut," I said. I glanced at my watch. "They'll be closing soon." The brand new VIRUS Centre (Virtual Reality UniverSe, I kid you not) had proved to be the best possible way of amusing Davy without doing my head in. It had only opened a month before, and secretly I'd been dying to try out the twenty game scenarios promised in their lavish brochure.

I'd been wary about coming on a bank holiday Monday, but it had been surprisingly quiet. I blame the parents. Not that I'm complaining—their absence gave me and Davy a lot more scope for enjoying ourselves.

I suppose I should have felt guilty, indulging myself with swords and sorcery while Richard was still languishing, but he seemed to think that his son's enjoyment was just as important as my attempts to get him released. Besides, Alexis had had to go into the office anyway to do some last-minute work on the child porn exposé that would launch the *Chronicle*'s latest campaign. At least I'd pitched her into trying to find out who lived at Hickory Dell.

We headed back to the car via the souvenir shop. "Enjoy yourself?" I asked. Pretty redundant question, really.

"It was boss. Top wicked." I took that to mean approval. "It was a lot better than Ice World," he said judiciously. "Skating gets boring after a while. Your ankles get sore. And the other stuff was pretty boring. You know, all that discovering the South Pole stuff. The models are really naff, and they don't *do* anything. "'S not surprising there was hardly anybody there," he added, dismissing Alexis's attempts to entertain him.

"Wasn't there?" I asked, more for something to say than out of interest.

"There was *no* queues," he said indignantly. "Anything worth doing always has queues." He looked around the souvenir shop, where we were the only customers. "Except this place," he qualified.

How bizarre to be part of a generation where queues are a sign of approval. Me, I'd pay money to avoid standing in line. I'm the driver everyone hates, the one who jumps the queue of standing traffic on the motorway and sneaks in just as the three lanes narrow to two. I nearly said something, but Davy was already delving through a box of transfers.

I left him to his browsing and ambled over to the ego board by the door. It displayed five-inch by three-inch colour photographs of the creators and senior staff of the VIRUS Centre, captioned with their names and executive titles. They all looked interchangeable with the mugshots on the board down the local supermarket. I turned back to check on Davy, and suddenly my subconscious swung into action. No queues at Ice World, coupled with the ego board, had finally woken my memory. The answer had been there all the time, only I'd been too dozy to spot it.

When we got back, Alexis was sitting in my conservatory, trying to look like she was engrossed in the evening paper. I knew she was only pretending; Chris gave the game away. "You were right," she said to Alexis in a surprised voice. "It *was* Kate's car. Hello, you two. Have a good day?"

That was all the encouragement Davy needed. He launched into a blow-by-blow account of the VIRUS Centre. Like an angel, Chris steered him off towards the kitchen, seducing him with promises of fish fingers and baked beans. I collapsed on the sofa and groaned. "Thank God for contraception," I muttered.

"I don't know what you're going on about," Alexis said. "He's good as gold. You want to spend a day looking after my nephew. He's hyperactive and his mother's the kind of divvy who fills him up with E numbers. Any more complaints from you and I won't tell you what I've found out today."

I closed my eyes and leaned back. "The occupant of Hickory Dell is Eliot James," I intoned. "Boss man at Tonik Leisure Services. Owners of, among other things, Ice World. Which, if what Davy says is right, must be struggling. If you're half-empty on a cold bank holiday Sunday morning, you're not going to weather the recession indefinitely." I sneaked an eyelid half-open. Alexis's expression moved from fury to disappointment to amusement. Luckily for me, it stopped there.

"Nobody loves a smartass," she growled. "OK, clever clogs. So what else have you dug up about Jammy James while you've supposedly been off entertaining me laddo? I mean, I don't know why I bother putting myself out when you just bugger off and do it yourself anyway!"

I sat up and tried to look apologetic. "I haven't been doing any digging, I promise you. Like I said this morning, I knew I'd seen him before, I just couldn't get a handle on it. Then Davy told me Ice World was as lively as Antarctica on a Saturday night, which set me wondering how these theme parks cover their overheads when the punters haven't got enough money to take the family out on a bank holiday. We were in the souvenir shop, and they've got one of those boards with the flattering photos of the top brass that are meant to make you think this is a really user-friendly operation. I was staring at that, and then I remembered that I'd seen the guy I trailed on one of those ego boards. Add that to the personalized number plate on the car . . ."

"What personalized plate?" Alexis protested. "You never said anything to me about a personalized plate!"

I gave a guilty smile. "I . . . ah . . . I forgot to mention that. TON 1K. Sorry. I've got a lot on my mind."

Alexis shook her head. "I don't know. It's worse working for you than for my brain-dead newsdesk. So what else have you remembered?"

"That's it," I promised. "Have you got anything?"

Alexis pulled a face. "Bits and pieces. Nothing really. But I've arranged to meet one of my contacts in half an hour, and he's promised me the full SP on Jammy. Oh, and by the way—Ruth's coming round at nine o'clock for a powwow. And so's Della."

"What?" I howled.

Alexis shrugged. "Della rang up after Ruth had arranged to come round. I thought they might as well come together to save us having to go over everything twice."

"Oh God," I groaned. "I don't suppose it occurred to you that I might not want them to know the same things?"

Alexis looked amused. "Which one were you planning on lying to—the lawyer or the copper?"

I left Davy to Alexis and Chris, and headed for the office to develop the films I'd shot in Carlisle. In the cool silence of the darkroom, I concentrated on the job in hand, forcing myself to switch off from the ins and outs of the case. That way, I hoped, my subconscious would get on with processing the information in peace, and come up with some useful inspirations.

I shoved the finished prints into a folder, and headed downstairs to the Mexican restaurant to fortify myself for another soul-destroying visit to the cells. The place was empty, except for one guy sitting alone at a table towards the rear of the restaurant. He gave me a brief glance as I entered, then returned to the magazine he had propped up beside his bowl of chilli. With a jolt of surprise, I recognized the menacing bouncer from the Lousy Hand. If he was a regular here—and I couldn't see any other reason for frequenting the place on a bank holiday Monday, since the food isn't that great—it explained why he'd seemed familiar at the club. Relieved to have cleared that one up, I settled into a window table with my back to his cold eyes and ordered some guacamole and a plate of frijoles. As I ate, I thought about the evening ahead.

Now I'd calmed down, I was pleased Alexis had fixed up the brainstorming session, because I suspected that the dynamic between the four of us might just spark off some fresh ideas. I was desperate for any insight that might take us a step nearer getting Richard out of jail. The hardest thing about being grown-up is realizing there are no magic formulas to release the ones we love from pain. Maybe that's why I enjoy computer games so much: you get to be God.

The girls were ready and waiting when I got back from the nick. Alexis had taken charge in my absence. I found it hard to recognize my living room. A flip chart on an easel had materialized from somewhere, and she'd arranged the chairs so we could all see it. She'd also found my cache of Australian Chardonnay and distributed glasses to the other two. I mumbled that I'd stick with the vodka and disappeared into the kitchen to fix myself a lemon Absolut with freshly squeezed pink grapefruit juice. By the time I got back, Alexis was copying some complicated tree structure from her notebook on to the flip chart. Ruth and Della looked as bemused as I felt.

"Alexis, I don't want to be difficult, but . . ."

"Chris is putting Davy to bed, so you don't have to worry about him butting in, if that's what's bugging you," she said, not even pausing.

"It wasn't, actually. I just wondered what you were doing."

"I need the diagram to explain about Jammy's empire," Alexis said in the condescending tones I use to small children and she uses to news editors.

"Maybe Kate could bring us up to date," Ruth said. "Then perhaps we'd all have a clue what you're up to, Alexis." Ever the diplomat.

It took a disturbingly short time to fill everyone in on my weekend activities. "I waited till James went into the house, then I came home," I finished up. "Oh, and I've developed and printed up the films I shot in Carlisle."

There was a slight pause. I could see Alexis gathering herself together to leap into the breach when Ruth said, "I'm impressed, Kate. When you told me how little we had to go on, I thought we had as much chance of establishing the identity of the real criminals as I have of becoming Lord Chief Justice."

"You're right, Kate's done an impressive job, but the Drugs Squad are going to have mixed feelings about it," Della said ruefully. "They've been chasing this crack epidemic for some time now, and while there are senior officers who are going to be bloody glad to get a solid handle on it, a lot of people are going to be very pissed off at being shown up by a private eye. And a woman private eye at that."

"Tell me about it," I sighed.

"And then there's the question of the accused," Della went on. "I've only been in Manchester a matter of months, but that's long enough to know that Eliot James is a name that means money, power and influence."

Alexis finally managed to get a word in. She jumped to her feet. "And that's where I come in," she announced. "I've been doing some digging into Mr Eliot James." She picked up her marker pen and attacked the flip chart. For a full fifteen minutes she blinded us with science, taking us on a whirlwind tour of Jammy James's leisure and property empire, his constant efforts to muscle in on the Olympic bid consortium, the parlous state of his marriage and the debts, loans and mortgages that, added together, put him in what building societies euphemistically call a negative equity situation.

"It's like Maxwell," she concluded with a flourish. "On the surface, it looks like everything's hunky-dory. But underneath, there's this huge iceberg of debt ready to smash into Jammy's hull and turn Tonik into the *Titanic*."

"She's got a way with words, that girl," I said. "Ever thought of becoming a writer, Alexis?"

Della was shaking her head in amazement. "I think I'll just go and shoot myself now," she said. "This has been a bad evening for the police. First, Kate does the Drugs Squad's job. And now you do my job. From what you've said, it looks very like our Mr James is trading while insolvent, so we're looking at one criminal offence at least. I think when the boys from the DS have finished with him, I'll be wanting a word."

Ruth, who had been unusually quiet, said, "It certainly explains why he needs the kind of cash injection that the drugs trade can bring. It does, however, give me a slight problem."

"You're not his brief, are you?" I asked, the cold hand of panic squeezing my chest.

"Thankfully, no," Ruth said. "But he does play golf with Peter. My husband," she added for Della's benefit. Peter hadn't been at Mortensen and Branningan's Christmas party, where the two women had first met. "And he's supposed to be coming to dinner on Saturday."

"Who with?" Alexis demanded cheekily. "The wife or the mistress? Both, incidentally, called Sue. I suppose that way he doesn't run the risk of using the wrong name in bed."

"Ignore her; it's gone to her head, getting something right for once," I said.

"Yo, wait till I break this little gem in tomorrow's paper!" Alexis exclaimed.

"No way!" Ruth shouted.

"Don't you *dare!*" Della thundered in unison. "We want Jammy James nailed down watertight, not leaping up and down about trial by media."

"Never mind that," I butted in. "Personally, I don't give a toss about nailing Jammy James. This is about getting Richard out of jail. And you printing daft stories in the *Chronicle* is not the way to do that, so forget it, Alexis, OK? What comes next, Ruth?"

Ruth spoke slowly, measuring what she said as she spoke. "Kate's right, Alexis. I know this must be burning a hole in your notebook, but I think it would be disastrous for Richard if you wrote a story about this."

Alexis pulled a face. "All right," she sighed. "But when I *can* write about it, I want all of you to talk to me on the record."

We all nodded wearily. "Ruth?" I asked.

"Kate, you're going to have to talk to the police. You're also going to have to persuade them to move quickly; the sooner the better from Richard's point of view."

Della interrupted. "On that point, they'll already be anxious about how current your information is. These days, most drug dealers alter their distribution patterns every few weeks. Eliot James's team might not be doing that, but as far as the Drugs Squad is concerned, stress that this is up-to-the-minute info and the situation could change any day. There is one significant gap in your evidence, however, which might make them cautious."

"What's that? Something I've got time to fix?" I asked anxiously. I'd been right to decide I needed other people's eyes on this case.

Della pulled a face. "It's not exactly a matter of time. It's a matter of legality. We don't know what's inside this shed out at the airport. If it's just an empty shell, it's not going to be easy to establish a direct connection between James and Fitzgerald. A good brief would argue that James had gone there for reasons entirely unconnected with the drug trade; he could even postulate a hypothetical third party that they were both there to meet."

I nodded, grateful for the advice. "Supposing I had that information, how quickly is quickly, in Drugs Squad terms?"

Della shrugged. "I don't know this lot well, but given your info they should be able to plug straight into the surveillance. If this team is as busy as your material suggests, they could have the bare bones of their evidence within twenty-four to forty-eight hours."

"Which means what, in terms of Richard's imprisonment?" I asked Ruth.

She bought time by lighting a cigarette. "Best case, you talk to the Drugs Squad first thing and they stand up in court and support my bail application. Chances of that: almost nil. Worse case, they use your information, make a bundle of arrests and refuse to accept Richard was an innocent bystander. Chances of that: probably low. Most likely scenario, if you get to the Drugs Squad tomorrow, when I argue for bail on Wednesday, it will be refused but the magistrates will agree to a short remand, say till Thursday or Friday, to give the police the chance to evaluate the fresh evidence."

My disappointment must have been obvious, for Alexis hugged me and Ruth shrugged apologetically. "Well, we'd better get you fixed up with an appointment to see the Drugs Squad, hadn't we?" Della said briskly. "Where's the phone?"

I pointed it out, and she wandered into the conservatory to make her call. I watched her through the patio doors. Her face was animated, her free hand expressive. Whatever she was saying, she wasn't pleading. As she ended the call, I remembered something else I wanted to talk to the Drugs Squad about. I turned to Alexis. "Do you know if Cherie Roberts has been around today? Or if she's left me a note?"

Alexis shook her head. "Not that I know of. Chris didn't say anything."

Typical, I thought. Just as well I wasn't relying on Cherie to help get Richard out of jail.

# 18

It was midnight before I got the house to myself. Much as I enjoy their company, I couldn't wait for the three of them to go home. Ironically, they probably thought they were doing me a favour, keeping me from brooding over Richard's absence. And of course, I couldn't explain why I wanted rid of them, not with two of them being officers of the court. My impatience wasn't helped by the fact that I'd stopped drinking after my first vodka; if discovering what the shed contained was the key to releasing Richard, then I was going to have to get inside there. Preferably before my nine o'clock appointment with DCI Geoff Turnbull of the Drugs Squad.

I went through to my bedroom and changed into the black leggings and black sweat shirt I save for the sort of occasion when nobody I want to impress is likely to see me; illicit night forays, decorating, that sort of thing. I didn't have any black trainers, but I did have a pair of black canvas hockey boots which I'd bought in a moment of madness years before when they'd briefly looked set to be the next essential fashion item. I'd been a first-year student at the time, which is as good an excuse as any. I stuffed my hair inside a black ski cap, and I was all set. I know the Famous Five burned corks and rubbed their faces with the ash, but I couldn't bring myself to do anything that ridiculous.

Besides, I had to drive right across town to get to the airport, and I didn't rate my chances of convincing any passing traffic cop that I was on my way to a Hallowe'en party.

On my way out the door, I stopped in my study and picked up one of those compartmentalized mini-aprons that tradesmen stuff with obscure tools. Mine contains a set of lock picks, a glass cutter, a kid's arrow with a sucker on the end, a couple of pairs of latex gloves, a Swiss Army knife, a small camera with a spare film, pliers, a high-powered pencil torch, a set of jeweller's screwdrivers, a couple of ordinary screwdrivers, a cold chisel, secateurs and a toffee hammer. Don't ask. Before I set off, I filled up a mini jug kettle that runs off the car cigarette lighter. Like I said, don't ask.

Less than half an hour later, I was cruising down the country lane I'd been in the night before. I pulled up in the same gateway and plugged in the kettle. As the water boiled, I lifted the lid and let the car fill up with steam. I got out and looked at the windows, satisfied. Anyone passing would be more likely to be jealous than suspicious.

I set off, hugging the infested hedgerows, just in case. I eased round the corner of the track, and saw with relief that there were no cars parked outside the shed. I crept slowly round the edge of the clearing till I was parallel to the big front doors. A quick look around, then I slipped across into the shadow of the shed. I took out my torch and shone it on the lower of the two padlocks. My heart sank. Some locks you can pick after ten minutes' training. Some locks give experts migraine. This wasn't one of the easy ones. I wished I'd brought Dennis with me. I gave it twenty minutes, by which time my hands were sweating so much inside the latex gloves that I couldn't manipulate the picks properly. In frustration, I kicked the door. It didn't swing open. I just got a very sore foot.

I shone the torch on the other padlock, but it was another of the same. The steel bars didn't look too promising either. Muttering the kind of words my mother warned me against, I

skirted the corner of the shed and worked my way down the far
side. Although it didn't look much, it was actually a deceptively
solid building. I'd have expected to find the odd loose board,
perhaps even a broken window. But this shed looked like it
had been given a good going over by the local crime prevention officer. There was one window on the airport side, but it
was barred, and behind it was opaque, wire-reinforced glass. I
reached the far corner, but I couldn't get down the back of the
shed at all because of the insidious creeping of the undergrowth.
Frankly, I doubt if Mickey Mouse could have squeezed through
that lot. With a sigh, I turned back. No chance. That was when
the spotlight pinned me to the wall.

At least, that's what I thought at first. I froze like a dancer
in a strobe, not even daring to blink. Then, as the light swept
over me and my brain clocked on, I realized it was only the
cyclops headlight of a tow truck from the cargo area. I threw
myself to the ground and wriggled back to the front of the shed.
Not a moment too soon. As I reached the doors, a battery of
floodlights snapped on, bathing an area fifty yards away with
harsh bleaching light. A truck was towing a train of boxes from
one cargo holding area to another. This wasn't the time or place
for burglary, I decided.

I inched backwards on my stomach towards the short drive
leading to the road. And that's when I spotted the skylight.
Gleaming in the blackness of the roof, it reflected the lights
like a mirror. Even though it was a good twelve feet above the
ground, the really exciting thing about it was the two-inch gap
at the bottom. I gauged the distances involved, and saw there
was a way inside the shed.

Getting out again was going to be the problem, I realized as I
hung from the edge of the skylight, torch between my teeth. I
tried to direct the beam downwards, to see what I was going to
land on when I let go. I saw what looked like a chemistry lab

constructed by a bag lady. If I dropped from here, I was going to end up either impaled on a Bunsen burner or shredded by the shards of a thousand test tubes. That probably explained why the skylight on the blind side of the roof was open. Even with fume hoods, cooking up designer drugs is a disgustingly smelly occupation. The chemists doubtless decided the need for fresh air was greater than the security benefit of being hermetically sealed. At least having a factory out in the middle of nowhere meant there weren't any neighbours to complain about the pong.

With a groan, I flexed my complaining shoulder muscles and hauled myself back up and out again. I sat on the edge of the skylight and stared into the night. I'd only let myself over the edge in the first place because my torch hadn't been powerful enough to reveal the contents of the shed. And if the torch wasn't, the flash probably wouldn't be either. I had to come up with another idea, and quickly. I'd already had to wait an hour for the cargo area to go dark again, and I didn't know how long it would be before they took it into their heads to shuffle the packing crates again.

I could come up with only one possibility. Sighing, I eased myself off the skylight until my feet were in the guttering. Spread-eagled against the roof, I edged along until I came to the end of the roof. Slowly, cautiously, I slid down the corrugated asbestos until I was crouching, most of my weight on the guttering. I gripped the edge and half rolled off the roof, stretching my legs downwards as far as they would go. Then, thanking God for all the Thai boxing training I'd done, I gradually let myself down. I couldn't feel the roof of the Peugeot under my toes. I'd just have to pray I was in the right place. I released my handholds.

The drop was only a few inches, but it seemed to last minutes. Gasping for the breath I'd been holding, I slithered down the hatch back on to blessedly solid ground and opened the boot. I lifted the carpet, and there, tucked into the spare wheel, was the answer to my prayers. I grabbed the tow rope,

coiled it round me like a mountaineer, gently closed the hatch
and clambered back up the car and on to the roof.

I fixed the rope to a downpipe that was conveniently near
the skylight and dropped it through the hole. I bit on the torch
again and slowly started the precarious descent. Needless to say,
the tow rope wasn't long enough to take me all the way to the
floor, but it left an easy drop of a couple of feet, and I'd be able
to reach it again if I moved a lab stool under it.

Getting in was the hard part. Doing the business with the
camera was easy. I just started by the doors and worked my way
through the shed, photographing the battered equipment, the
jars of chemicals, the lists of instructions taped to the walls above
the benches, and the plastic bags of white crystalline powder that
made my gums numb. I don't know a lot about the drug world,
but it looked to me as if there was much, much more than a bit
of crack coming out of Jammy James's kitchen.

What there wasn't was paperwork. No filing cabinets, no
safe, nothing. Wherever Jammy James kept his records, it wasn't
here. I decided I paid enough in taxes. I'd done most of the
work; it was time the Drugs Squad did their bit.

Wearily, I shifted a lab stool under the rope and climbed
on top of it. My shoulder muscles were threatening to phone
the cruelty man as I dragged myself up the rope and over the
sill. I carefully lowered the skylight, restoring it to its previous
position, give or take a millimetre or two. Then I untied the
rope, did my crab imitation along the roof again. This time, the
transfer of weight from feet to arms didn't go quite so smoothly;
my shoulders were too tired for a gradual lowering, and my arms
jerked uncomfortably in their sockets, making me let go sooner
than I should have. I wondered how I was going to explain the
depression in the roof to the car-leasing company.

My body wanted to get into bed as soon as possible, but my
head was singing a different song. I had two films from the shed
that needed developing. It would help my case if I could show
the prints to Turnbull. The devil on my shoulder told me to go

home and crash out for a few hours, then go into the office early to develop my films. But I knew myself well enough to know what my reaction would be when the alarm shattered my sleep at seven. And it wouldn't be to leap out of bed bright-eyed and bushy-tailed, ready to rush to the office and fill my lungs with the noxious fumes of photographic chemicals. With a groan, I shoved *The Best of Blondie* into the cassette player and opened the window all the way. If cold air and Debbie Harry's frantic vocals couldn't keep me awake, nothing would.

I managed nearly four hours' sleep. Never mind what Richard owed me in fees; he owed me more sleep than I'd ever catch up on. For once, it wasn't Davy who woke me. It was Chris. She stuck her head round the bedroom door, followed by a hand waving a mug of coffee like a white flag. "Come in," I grumbled. "Time is it?" I would have rolled over to look at the clock, but I couldn't find the energy.

"It's quarter past eight," she said apologetically, sliding round the door and holding out the mug at arm's length. Alexis had obviously warned her I'm not at my sparkling best first thing.

"Shit!" I growled, as I leaped upright. Or rather, tried to. As soon as I moved, my shoulders went into spasm, and I let out a muffled screech of pain. I managed to shuffle up the bed enough to drink without a straw and seized the mug gratefully. "Sorry I yelled. I'm in pain, and I've got to be at Bootle Street nick first thing with my brain firing on all four cylinders. So far, it's not looking good."

Chris tried a smile that turned into a *Spitting Image* grimace. "I just thought I'd better tell you that I'm off to work now," she said. Belatedly, I noticed she was suited up, her hair dried and sprayed into the kind of neatly sculpted shape that Frank Lloyd Wright would have turned into an art gallery. "Davy's had a shower and breakfast, and he's dressed and sitting in front of breakfast telly, which should keep him quiet for approximately twelve minutes, which is when the next news bulletin is due."

"Has Alexis left?" Pointless question. Alexis is invariably at work by seven.

"'Fraid so," Chris apologized. "She said she expected to be finished by three, and that you should ring her at the office if you wanted her to pick up Davy later. I'm really sorry we can't help out today."

"Don't be," I said. The power of speech seemed to have returned with the second mouthful of coffee. "You two have done more than enough. Richard owes you."

Chris smiled, a genuine one this time. "I know you'll find it hard to believe, but we've enjoyed ourselves. I live with Alexis, don't forget, so I'm used to dealing with the demands of small children, and she loves having someone to play with."

"You're not getting broody, are you?" I asked suspiciously. It's bad enough that all my straight friends seem to be hellbent on repopulating the world without the lesbians joining in.

"Building a house is more than enough to be going on with," Chris replied as she headed out the door. In the hall she turned back and gave me a mischievous smile. "Ask me again in a couple of years."

If my neck hadn't seized up, I'd have turned my face to the wall. As it was, I gulped the rest of the brew and slowly, excruciatingly, dragged my body out of bed and into an upright position. I walked to the bathroom stiff as a guardsman. Unfortunately, I'd slept too late to have a bath so had to settle for a shower. I tried to relax as the hot water did the business, but I'd only been under for a couple of minutes when I heard Davy's voice outside the door.

"Kate?" he shouted. "Can I play with your computer?"

"Not here, Davy. I've got to go to work in a minute, so I thought maybe you'd like to play on my machine in the office," I spluttered.

Silence. That was more unnerving than anything he could have said. I switched off the shower, wrapped myself in a bath sheet and opened the door. He leaned against the wall, looking dejected. My breath stuck in my chest. The line of his body, the angle of his head, the slight frown was so like his father it hurt. He looked up through his long lashes at the sound of the door opening. "When's my dad coming home?" he asked plaintively.

I managed to get my lungs working again. "Not for a couple of days, I don't think. I spoke to him on the phone last night, after you'd gone to sleep. He said he misses you too and he'll get back as soon as he can get a plane. I'm sorry, I know I'm not a lot of fun." I hugged him. Surprisingly, he didn't pull a face and draw away. He hugged back.

"It's not that," he said. "I'm having great fun. I just wish he was here too."

You and me both, pal, I thought but didn't say.

I broke my personal land speed record getting out the door that morning. Dressed in under five minutes, second cup of coffee down the neck in less than a minute, breakfast one of the Pop-Tarts I'd bought for Davy. It tasted like sugar-coated polystyrene, but at least it raised the blood sugar level. By the time I parked on the single yellow line round the corner from the office, I was almost functioning.

I hustled Davy up the stairs and into my office, checking the clock as I walked through the door. Seventeen minutes till deadline. Shelley was already at her desk, earphones in, fingers flying over the keyboard. I strode past her with a little wave, shooing Davy into my office. I switched on my PC, showed him the games directory and made him promise not to interfere with any of the other files on the machine. He dumped his backpack by the desk and was absorbed in Lemmings 2 before I'd had time to walk back out. I closed my office door behind me and perched on Shelley's desk, nailing what I hoped was a pathetic and appealing smile on my face.

"No, Kate." She hadn't even looked up from her screen. "I am *not* a child-minder and this is an office, not a crèche."

"I know it's not a crèche. A crèche is what happens when two BMWs collide in Sloane Street."

"Not funny," she retorted, not pausing long enough to let her sense of humour kick in.

"Please, Shelley. He'll be no trouble. Just for this morning. Just till I can get back from court. I promise I'll sort something else out for tomorrow."

"There's no such thing as an eight-year-old boy who's no trouble. I'm a mother, don't forget. I've told the same lies you're telling now."

"Shelley, please? I have a meeting with the Drugs Squad in ten minutes. Richard's freedom depends on it. I don't think they're going to be mega-impressed if I turn up with Davy in tow." I was practically begging. I'd done so much of it lately it was beginning to become second nature. Another bad habit to lay at Richard's door. What's worse is that it doesn't work.

I got up from the desk and went into Bill's office, where I helped myself to his portable TV, a gift from a grateful client who had Mortensen and Brannigan to thank for the ending of his little software piracy problem. I marched through the outer office, wrestled with the door handle and staggered into my office, where I put it down on one of my cupboards. "There's the TV, in case you get fed up with the computer," I said to Davy. I can't swear to it, but I don't think he even looked up.

I stalked back into the office and gestured over my shoulder with my thumb. "Look at that. You're telling me that's more than you can cope with? God, Shelley, am I disappointed in you."

When all else fails, go for the ego. The only trouble is, sometimes the ego bites back. Shelley smiled like Jaws and said sweetly, "Just this once, Kate. And by the way, Andrew Broderick's been on again. He says if he doesn't get his car back soon he's going to have to come to some arrangement about reducing our fee."

There's nothing like keeping the customer satisfied. I checked the fax machine on the way out, but nothing had arrived from Julia. I hoped that didn't mean it was going to be one of those days. Not when the next item on the agenda was a close encounter with the Drugs Squad.

# 19

Q: What's the difference between a schneid watch and a police-man? A: Schneid watches keep good time. By the time DCI Geoff Turnbull deigned to fit me into his busy schedule, I'd worn a furrow in the floor tiles of the front office. I was getting more wound up than an eight-day clock.

When he finally appeared, it took all my self-control not to bite his head off. Instead, I smiled sweetly and meekly fol-lowed him through the pass door into the real world of the city centre nick. We stopped outside a door that said "Drugs Squad—Private." I thought at first that was a joke, till I saw Turnbull pull out a key to unlock the door. He noticed me noticing and said, "You can't be too careful, the stuff we have in here. These days, we've got more civilian support staff than we have coppers, and some of them have got more loyalty to their bank balances than they have to The Job."

How to win friends and influence people, I thought as I smiled what I hoped would pass for agreement and approval. I followed him into an overcrowded office, crammed with desks, VDUs, bulging files, and not an officer in sight. The walls were lavishly adorned with colour photographs of vil-lains. By the look of the pics, most of them were snatched, like mine. If anything, mine were sharper. Maybe Turnbull would be so impressed with my work that he'd offer me a job as a police photographer.

Turnbull's personal office was partitioned off in one corner. He'd managed to bag the only window, not much of a deal since it looked out on a brick wall all of five feet away. He squeezed his rugby player's frame behind the loaded desk and gave me the hard stare with small sharp blue eyes. He couldn't have looked less like my idea of a Drugs Squad officer. I'd expected an emaciated hippy lookalike with a distressed leather jacket and a pair of jeans. Either that or a flash bastard dripping with personal jewellery who could pass for a major dealer. But Turnbull looked like the only drug you'd suspect him of using was anabolic steroids. He lived up to his name: short curly hair with a forelock like a Charolais, the no-neck and shoulders to match, with the gut of a man whose stomach muscles have given up the unequal struggle with Boddingtons Bitter. I put him in his late thirties, well along the road to the coronary unit.

He rubbed a beefy hand over his jaw, massaging plump flesh. "So, you're Miss Kate Brannigan," he said consideringly. He managed to make the "Miss" sound like an obscenity. "Not much of you, is there?"

I shrugged. "Enough to do the job. I don't get many complaints."

He leered automatically. "I bet you don't."

I raised my eyebrows and gave him the bored look. "DCI Prentice told me you were the person to talk to. I've got some information for you on one of your cases. Richard Barclay?"

"Oh aye," he said, his Yorkshire accent deliberately exaggerated. "The boyfriend." He picked up his phone and dialled an internal number. "Tommo? Any time you like." He replaced the receiver and shook his head. "I suppose you expect me to believe your fella's been fitted up? Well, you're in for a disappointment. It wasn't Drugs Squad officers that picked him up, it was Traffic, and even if they wanted to plant drugs on him, they wouldn't have access to anything like those amounts. So you're barking up the wrong tree there."

"I don't think he's been fitted up," I said patiently. "But the drugs in the car were nothing to do with Richard, and the sooner you realize that, the lower the compo's going to be for the wrongful arrest."

Turnbull guffawed. "Was that a threat creeping out of the woodwork? By heck, Miss Brannigan, you like living dangerously."

Before I could reply, a doorbell sounded. Turnbull leaned back and pressed a button on the wall behind him. I heard the door of the main room open behind me. I resisted the temptation to turn around and see who owned the heavy feet crossing the floor towards me.

Somehow, I wasn't too surprised when the custody sergeant from Longsight walked into Turnbull's office. "That her?" Turnbull asked.

The sergeant nodded. "No question about it, sir. That's the woman who purported to be Miss Hunter's assistant the other night. She claimed her name was Kate Robinson."

"Thank you, Sergeant. I'll talk to you later."

"Sir," the sergeant said.

We both held our peace as the feet retreated back across the Drugs Squad office. Turnbull stared at me, a triumphant little smile on his cupid's-bow lips. I kept my eyes on his, determined not to show any weakness. As the door closed behind the custody sergeant, Turnbull said scathingly, "It's not just you amateurs that can make deductions. I've been wanting to talk to you, Miss Brannigan. DCI Prentice's phone call just made it a bit easier for me to get you in here without a brief hanging on our every word. Especially since your brief's left herself wide open to charges of unprofessional conduct. I'm sure the Law Society would be fascinated to hear about her interpretation of professional ethics. And now we both know there's at least one offence I can hang on to you for, mebbe we can cut the crap and get down to the business."

I said nothing. When his bluster ran out, he was going to have to charge me or let me go. Either way he was going to have to listen to what I had to tell him. And I felt sure that his threats against Ruth were emptier than a dosser's bottle. The last thing coppers like him want to do is to antagonize the tightly knit club of criminal solicitors. Turnbull carried on staring at me and started drumming his fingers on the desk. Then he opened his desk drawer and took out a packet of cigars. When I rule the world, the European Court of Human Rights is going to outlaw the obtaining of confessions under cigar- and pipe-smoke torture.

He lit his panatela, the only slim thing about him, and said, "Soon as I heard the story behind this car, soon as I heard that technically it was your responsibility, I wanted to talk to you. I mean, what better cover for a drug dealer's wheels than supposedly investigating some daft car-finance scam? Count yourself lucky you didn't spend the weekend in the CDC like your boyfriend."

I shook my head. Clearly, I wasn't going to get anywhere being sweetness and light. Time for No More Ms Nice Guy. "I don't believe I'm hearing this," I snarled. "I come along here with enough information to close down a major drug ring and hand you a bloody great score sheet of arrests, and you treat me like *I'm* the criminal? Jesus, it's no wonder you lot are always whingeing you don't get support from the public. If you threaten to arrest everybody that tries to give you a tip-off, it's a bloody miracle anybody tells you what day it is."

He leaned forward and sneered. I bet he wouldn't have if he could have seen how badly his teeth needed a scale and polish. I was surprised his breath didn't strip them down to the bare enamel on a daily basis. "You were supposed to be the bloody lawyer the other night. I shouldn't have to tell you that it's an offence to withhold information about a criminal offence. So cough, Miss Brannigan, or I'll have you banged up so fast your head'll spin."

I stood up and leaned on Turnbull's desk. I was getting good and tired of being jerked around by the legal system.

"Listen, Turnbull," I said coldly. "You threaten me once more and I walk out that door and you don't get another word out of me till you've formally arrested me, cautioned me and allowed me to talk to my solicitor. I might not be a qualified lawyer, but I'd be willing to bet I'd score more points than you on a PACE quiz. Now, are we going to talk like grown-ups, or are we going to carry on playing silly boys' games?"

"Let's be clear about one thing," he said, still not willing to let the macho bravado slip. "I'm not doing any deals with you. None of this 'I show you mine and you let my boyfriend go' routine. As far as I'm concerned, Mr Richard Barclay's in this up to his fancy tortoiseshell specs."

I raised my eyes to the ceiling and sighed. "I just love a man with an open mind. Mr Turnbull, by the time you've heard me out, you'll be dying to release Richard, because if you don't, you're going to look like dickhead of the year after the papers have finished with you. And that's *not* a threat, it's my considered opinion."

"Sit down," he growled. "Let's hear what you've got to say."

Ignoring his order, I leaned against the wall. I took my miniature tape recorder out of my bag and pressed the "record" button. "Since you don't seem inclined to tape our little chat, I'll do it for you," I said. "It'll save me having to come back later and make a statement. I know all your instincts tell you not to believe a word that anybody in custody says, but in this instance, you really should have listened. That's all I did. The only clue in Richard's story, as far as I could see, was the business with the trade plates. So I did what any good copper should do: I followed my instincts." Turnbull looked like he wanted to throttle me, but the part of him that had taken him to the rank of DCI was obviously dying to know what I'd dug up, and right now his curiosity was stronger than his belligerence.

I took him through it from start to finish, omitting only the details of how I came by the photographs of the inside of Jammy James's kitchen. "Careless of them, leaving the door unlocked, but then, you just can't get the help these days," I finished up, taking the pics out of my bag and spreading them in a fan across Turnbull's desk.

He poked at the pics with the end of a Biro, as if they'd soil his fingers. Then he shook his head. "You expect me to believe this taradiddle?" he asked scornfully. "Eliot James? As in, Eliot James who plays golf with the Chief Constable? Eliot James who runs charity schemes for underprivileged kids at his leisure centres? *That* Eliot James?"

"The same," I said. "Having friends in high places doesn't stop you being a crook. Look at the Guinness trails. And if doing charity work was a guarantee of staying out of jail, the Krays would still be running London. Look, James is hanging on to his business empire by his fingernails. Check it out. Go down Ice World, The Dinosaur Adventure, Laser Land, or any of his leisure complexes. They're all empty. His cash flow doesn't. The only reason DCI Prentice isn't running a full-scale fraud inquiry into the sleazeball is that she thinks the drugs angle deserves the first bite of the cherry. But if you're not interested, I know she'll be after James like a greyhound out of a trap."

Turnbull leaned back in his chair. The legs sounded like an avant-garde string quartet. "It's funny, isn't it, how you've managed to find all this out so easily when we've been trying to get something on this mob for ages?" he speculated. "If I was a suspicious man, I might think it was because you and your boyfriend were in it up to your eyeballs, and you decided to shop the rest of the team to try and get him off the hook. You wouldn't be the first private dick caught out by the recession who decided to turn their limited knowledge of crime on its head."

The only thing that stopped me being arrested for assaulting a police officer was the realization that I'd be as much use to Richard as a chocolate fireguard if I ended up behind bars too. So I smiled sweetly at the insult. "If I was going to turn to crime, Mr Turnbull, I wouldn't have to leave the house. Computer crime. That's where the real, no-risk money is these days. And I've forgotten more about computers than you'll ever know. Look, I'm not asking you for a major favour. I haven't once said, 'I'll tell you what I know in return for you letting Richard walk away from all of this.' I'm handing you all this on a plate, and all I'm asking is that you don't oppose Ruth Hunter's request for a short remand so you can start to test the value of what I've given you."

"And that's all, is it?" he asked, utter disbelief riddling his voice like a virus in a computer.

"Pretty much, yeah. You see, Mr Turnbull, in spite of your performance this morning, I happen to think you're an honest copper. I don't think you want innocent men put away just to make your clean-up rate look better. And I know the strength of what I've given you. I think after forty-eight hours you'll have the same gut feeling I've got about Richard's innocence, and I don't think you'll be opposing bail then. But I'm not asking for any promises."

"Just as bloody well," he grumbled, "for you'd not be getting any." He stared down at the photographs on his desk, slowly sifting through them, assessing what he was seeing with the eyes of an expert. Turnbull eventually looked up. "So, what has Ruth Hunter told you to ask for?"

"I want you to call the Crown Prosecution solicitor and ask that they don't oppose Ruth's request for a short remand."

"That it?"

"That's it. Now, are you going to give me something back, or am I going to develop profound amnesia about the events of the last three days?"

He grinned. "You know, for a girl, you're not short on bottle. OK, I'll do it. I can't say fairer than that, now can I?"

"That's fine," I said. "You won't mind if I hang on while you make the call?"

This time he laughed delightedly, his hand making a half-hearted gesture that, if I'd been a bloke, would have turned into a clout on the back that would have brought my breakfast back. "You're not a Yorkshire lass by any chance, are you? No? Pity."

I waited while he did as I'd demanded. He was no more charming to the Crown Prosecution Service's solicitor than he'd been to me, but he seemed to achieve the right result. On my way out of the door, I said, "By the way—Mr Broderick wants to know when you're going to release his very expensive motor from your compound."

Turnbull snorted. I almost expected him to paw the ground. "He's been on to you as well, has he? You tell your Mr Broderick that he can have his poncey set of wheels back when I'm good and satisfied that it's going to yield up no more clues to me. And that could be after your boyfriend's trial. Now, bugger off and let me get on. Oh, and leave me that tape, will you? Like you said, it'll save me having to keep you here all day making a statement."

I handed the tape over with a grim little smile. "One other thing," I said. "Nothing to do with Richard. You know those transfers that kids use—temporary tattoos, that sort of thing?"

Turnbull nodded. "I've got a seven-year-old that gets in the bath looking like a merchant seaman. What about them?"

"Ever heard of them being impregnated with drugs and used to get kids high?"

Turnbull pulled a face. "I've heard rumours, but I've never actually come across a case. It's one of them urban legends, isn't it? It always happens to a friend of a friend's cousin's dog. Crap, as far as I'm concerned. If I was wanting to get kids stoned, I'd just stick something in sweets or fizzy drinks. Helluva lot easier. Why d'you ask?"

"Like you said, urban legend. A friend of a friend's cousin's dog asked a doctor I know about it. She said the same as you." I got to my feet. "Sorry to have troubled you. Thanks. For phoning." And I was gone, quitting while I was still ahead. Let's face it. Telling Geoff Turnbull about Davy's brush with the hallucinogens wasn't the way to get his daddy out of jail.

# 20

I walked back through the office door on the stroke of twelve. The door to my office was closed. I raised my eyebrows in a question at Shelley. She pursed her lips and said, "I had to shut the door in case any clients walked in."

Curious, I opened my door a couple of feet and stuck my head round. I saw instantly what she meant. Davy was still intent on the computer, but now Bill was sitting next to him, clutching his own joystick. Neither of them looked up at the sound of the door. I cleared my throat. Bill glanced up. As soon as he realized it wasn't Shelley with some troublesome business query, I could see his attention leave the game and focus sharply on me. He got up, saying, "I've got to go and talk to Kate, Davy. Thanks for the game."

Davy didn't even look up as he said, "But Bill, you've got one more life!"

"Well, since you've still got four, I guess I'll have to concede. You win," Bill said, pretending to be petulant about it.

In the glow of the screen, Davy grinned, his body shifting strangely in the chair as he controlled whatever it was that was currently conquering the universe. Bill steered me out of the room and through into his office. "He's a nice kid," Bill said. "No bother." I was beginning to wonder if there was something wrong with me. Was I the only person on the planet who liked to live in a child-free zone?

Bill sat down and stretched his long legs in front of him. "So, how did it go?"

I filled him in on the weekend's events. Maybe I should just ring Richard Branson and ask him to release it on CD. It would save me a lot of time. Then I ran through my interview with Geoff Turnbull.

"You think he really will keep an open mind about Richard?" Bill asked.

"I doubt it. I think the only chance he's got is for Turnbull to make a lot of arrests. When he realizes none of them even know Richard's name, he's going to have to unclamp his jaws from off Barclay's leg."

"But he did go along with the short remand request?"

"Sure, but that's no skin off his nose, is it?" My early jubilation at getting Turnbull to look properly at my evidence had evaporated. I wondered fleetingly how the families of the Guildford Four and the Birmingham Six had put up with this dislocating ordeal for the years it had taken them to have their loved ones released. I took a deep breath. "And now," I said, "I want to ask you a favour."

"Ask away," he said. "Hacking? Bugging? Your wish is my command."

"None of the above. It's just that I've had enough aggro for one day. Will you phone Andrew Broderick and tell him what Turnbull said about the car? It's hard enough keeping my head together without having to deal with someone else's disappointments."

Bill jumped up and engulfed me in a bear hug, his thick blond beard tickling my ear. "Poor old Katy," he said softly. "It's not always easy, being as tough as old boots, is it?"

I let myself be held, wallowing in the illusion of security. There's something very solid about Bill. I felt like I was being given a tranquillity transfusion. After a few minutes, I drew back, standing on tiptoe to kiss his beard. "Thanks," I said. "Now, I'm going to take Davy for a swim and a pizza, and then the pair of us are going to get a pile of videos and completely indulge ourselves."

"You deserve it," Bill said. "You've done a helluva job, considering you started with virtually nothing to go at. Richard's a lucky guy."

"What do you mean, lucky? When he sees our bill, he'll be wishing he was back inside," I said. "See you in the morning, Bill. Unless you want to come round and play computer games with Davy tonight?"

"I'll pass," he said. "I've got some rather different games in mind for tonight. Abstinence makes the heart grow fonder, you know." Somehow, I found it hard to believe the heart was the organ in question. I wondered who the lucky woman was this week. One day, he's going to meet one with fancier footwork than him, and that'll be a battle worth seeing. Till then, he's working his way through the intelligent female population of the north of England. He once told me he's never been to bed with a woman yet who didn't teach him something. I don't *think* he was talking about sex.

There were only a couple of dozen people in the fun pool at Gorton, so Davy and I made the most of the slides and the waves, treating the place as our personal pleasure dome. Although my shoulders screamed in complaint at first, the water therapy seemed to help. Afterwards, both ravenous, we scoffed huge pizzas and enough salad to keep Watership Down's bunnies going for a week. Then we hit the video shop and chose more movies than we'd have time to watch. I didn't care. Part of me felt a holiday sense of release. I'd done everything I could to get Richard freed. Now all I could do was wait, and I owed it to Davy to do that as cheerfully as possible.

As we drove across Upper Brook Street and into Brunswick Street, the traffic slowed to a crawl. I couldn't see what the problem was, only that there was no traffic heading past us in the opposite direction. Eventually, craning my neck, I could see that the road ahead was cordoned off, and that traffic was being diverted down Kincardine Road by a uniformed policeman. Curious, I swung the car out of the queue, and indicated to the policeman that I wanted to turn right, heading back home. He gave me the nod, and I pulled round the corner and parked. I couldn't help myself. There's no way I could ignore something looking that interesting on my own doorstep. At the very least, it looked like someone had raided the local post office. I sometimes wonder whether I chose the career or it chose me. I turned to Davy and said, "Wait here a minute. I just want to see what's going on." He flicked a glance heavenwards, sighed and pulled a comic out of his backpack.

I got out of the car and locked it up, then cut through the council estate so that I'd emerge at the mouth of a narrow alley off Brunswick Street, but further down than the road block. I was almost opposite the pelican crossing, and I could see that there was a second road block a little further down in the other direction. On the pedestrianized little shopping precinct on the other side of the street, two police cars and an ambulance were standing, doors open, just outside the post office. Around them milled a bewildered-looking knot of people, police officers trying to keep them away from the person the ambulance crew were crouched over. The wailing cries of a child rose and fell like a siren. While I watched, another pair of police cars arrived.

One of the ambulance crew stood up and shook his head while his colleague continued to crouch on the ground. There was a commotion at the heart of the crowd, then a stretcher was loaded into the ambulance. The spectators parted, and the ambulance reversed on to the road and sped off. The crowd stayed back long enough for me to see a policewoman ushering two young boys into the back of a police car, which shot off in the wake of the ambulance, blue light flashing. It was hard to

be certain from that distance, but they looked disturbingly like
Wayne and Daniel.

By this time, I was a question mark on legs. I'd also spotted
a familiar mane of black hair bobbing around on the fringes of
the crowd, tapping people on the shoulders and thrusting a tape
recorder in their faces. I checked that none of the cops were looking my way, then I nonchalantly nipped out of the alley, crossed
the street and headed for Alexis. If anyone had tried to stop me,
I'd have insisted I was on my way to a dental appointment in the
precinct. If the police were suspicious enough to check it out,
Howard's receptionist knew me well enough to back me up.

As I drifted closer, I could see the police officers were working their way through the crowd, taking names and addresses
rather than attempting statements. I could hear odd snatches of
shocked conversation: "all over in seconds . . ."; ". . . balaclava
over his head . . ."; "thought it was a car backfiring . . ."; "police
should *do* something about them druggies . . ." Alexis was over
on the far side, tape recorder shoved under the nose of a uniformed inspector. I took my notebook and tape recorder out of
my handbag and rushed round the fringe of the crowd to Alexis's
side. I arrived in time to hear him say in harassed tones, "Look,
I can't tell you any more now, you'll have to wait till we have
a clearer idea ourselves." Then, seeing me and falling for my
instant disguise, he added, "And I haven't got time to go through
it all again. Get the details from her," he said, gesturing towards
Alexis with his thumb. She turned and clocked me. Her face,
already paler than usual, seemed to go even whiter.

"For Chrissake, what are you doing here?" she hissed.

"I could say the same to you. What's happened? Somebody
taken a pot at the post office? And where's the rest of the pack?"

"Still on their way, if they even know about it. I just happened to be driving back to your house when it all came on
top. Kate, you've got to get out of here! Now! Move it!" Alexis
started hustling me away, back towards the side-street where
I'd left my car.

"Why?" I protested. "What's it got to do with me?"

"Where's Davy?" she demanded, still shooing me away from the crowd and back across the street.

"He's in the car." We'd reached the opening of the alley and I stepped in, then stopped in my tracks. I wasn't going another pace further until she enlightened me. "What is going on, Alexis? What happened back there?"

She ran a hand through her unruly hair and pulled a crushed packet of cigarettes out of her bag. She lit up and took a deep drag before she spoke. "I'm sorry, but there is not a gentle way of saying this. Cherie Roberts just got killed," she said.

I felt like I'd been punched in the chest. The air emptied out of me like a burst balloon. "A robbery? She got in the way?" I asked.

My face must have betrayed my hope that this had been no more than a horrific accident, a tragic and malignant twist of fate, for Alexis turned her face away and shook her head, smoke streaming down her nostrils in twin plumes. "No. It was a hit."

I squeezed the bridge of my nose between my fingers. I didn't want to believe what Alexis was saying. "That can't be right," I said half-heartedly. "For fuck's sake, she was no big deal. She was just another single mum, trying to get through the days and keep her kids out of trouble."

"I've covered too many stories like this over the last couple of years in the Moss and Cheetham Hill," Alexis said bleakly, referring to the violent drug wars that have practically doubled Manchester's homicide figures. "According to the eyewitnesses, Cherie was coming out of the post office after cashing her child benefit. There was a car parked on the other side of the road. When she came out, the car revved up, shot across the road, mounted the pavement and drove towards her. When they were a few feet away from her, she got blasted from the rear window with both barrels of the shotgun. It was, variously, a metallic blue Sierra, a silver Toyota, a grey Cavalier, and nobody's admitting to getting the registration number."

I closed my eyes and leaned against the wall. I could feel the brick rough against my fingertips. "Dear God," I breathed. I'd asked her to find out who had given her kids drug-laced transfers. And two days later, Cherie Roberts was on her way to the mortuary, stamped with the familiar hallmarks of a drug-related murder. Suddenly, my eyes snapped open. "Davy!" I gasped. I turned on my heel and ran down the alley, panic pumping the blood till my ears pounded with the drum of my heartbeat.

I rounded the corner, imagination painting scenes of bloodshed and violence that even Sam Peckinpah would draw the line at, making all sorts of ridiculous bargains with a god I don't believe in. I skidded to a halt by the car, feeling deeply foolish as Davy waved at me and mouthed, "Hi," through the glass. Alexis rushed up behind me, slightly breathless. "We need to talk," she said. "What did you ask Cherie on Sunday?"

"The wrong question, obviously," I said bitterly. "I asked her to ask the kids who they got the transfers from. That's all. She must have taken it further than that. Shit, Alexis, I need a drink. Are you finished here, or do you need to talk to some more people?"

"I'm too late for the final edition anyway. I've got the eyewitness stuff for tomorrow's paper. It'll be a while now before the police issue a full statement. Let's go back to your place, eh?" She squeezed my arm sympathetically. "It's not your fault, KB. It wasn't you that pulled the trigger."

So why did I feel so guilty?

It took less than a minute to drive round to my house. I parked in the bay outside Richard's house and walked towards mine. Davy hung behind, bouncing up and down at the end of the path, waiting for Alexis to get out of the car so he could show her the videos we'd chosen. You can't see my porch from the parking bays. There's a six-foot, gold and green conifer in the way. I'd never thought much about it before. But that afternoon, I was more glad than I can say that the tree was there.

I passed the tree and glanced towards my house. What I saw made me stumble and nearly fall. I regained my balance and took a couple of steps closer to make sure my eyes weren't playing tricks on me. Then I felt sick. The white uPVC of the lower half of the door was pocked with hundreds of little black puncture holes. The glass in the upper half was crazed and starred, no match for the close-range blast it had sustained. Whoever had terminated Cherie Roberts had left me their calling card.

# 21

I wheeled round as fast as I could and nailed a smile on my face as I headed back towards Alexis and Davy, in a huddle looking at videos. "We might as well go in through Richard's," I said, trying to sound breezy. "I've got some paperwork to do later, and that way you won't have to worry about disturbing me."

It didn't entirely work. Alexis looked up sharply at the cracked note in my voice. "All right," she said casually. "His video's just as good as yours, and we're nearer the ice-cream there."

I steered them up the path, carefully using my body to shield Davy from the sight of my front door. I needn't have bothered; he was so engrossed in his chatter with Alexis that he didn't even glance in that direction. She did, though, and I could see from the momentary tightening of her lips that she'd spotted the damage. I unlocked the door and Davy ran into the house ahead of us. "What the hell's going on, KB?" Alexis demanded.

"Your guess is as good as mine," I hissed. "You think this happens all the time?"

Alexis put her arm round my shoulders and squeezed. "OK, sorry. But we need to get him out of here," Alexis murmured. "It's not safe."

"You think I don't know that? What can we do? Where can we take him?" I asked.

"I'll pitch him into coming to the pictures, then I'll take him back to our house. Fill him up with burgers and popcorn and let him crash out with us while you get this sorted out," she said softly.

"Gee thanks," I said, my frustration bubbling up to the surface. "And how exactly do you suggest I go about that?"

"Calm down, girl," Alexis protested. "I was talking about getting the door fixed, not solving the mysteries of the universe."

I sighed. "Sorry. I'm kind of edgy, you know?"

Alexis put the other arm round my shoulders and gave me a quick hug. "I'll go and get Davy before he gets stuck into one of those videos." She headed down the hall. I leaned against the wall and took some deep breaths, doing the mental relaxation exercises my Thai boxing coach taught me. I heard her say, "Hey, soft lad, you can't watch a film without popcorn. Tell you what, why don't we go to the proper pictures? Then we can go to the McDonald's drive-in near my house and take the burgers back and watch your videos there."

"What are we going to go and see?" Davy demanded.

"Hang on a minute," Alexis said. She emerged from the living room and said, "Did I see the local freesheet scrunched up in the porch? They've got the multi-screen listings in, haven't they?"

"I think so," I said, exhaling the last of the twenty breaths.

Alexis moved past me and picked up the crumpled newspaper that had been stuffed gratuitously through Richard's letter box some time over the weekend. "You know, I really object to trees being cut down so that rubbish can be dumped in my porch without my permission or invitation," I grumbled.

"I hate freesheets too," Alexis said, flicking through the pages. "Because they get distributed to so many homes, advertising managers just lie about how many people read the bloody things, so local businesses spend their limited budgets advertising in wastepaper rather than taking an ad in the *Chronicle*. So the number of pages we print decreases, so we don't hire as many journalists. And the freesheets don't take up the slack on account of they're crap editorially," she added for good measure.

"Not that you're biased or anything," I muttered. "Found the listing yet?" As I spoke, a rumpled sheet of blue writing paper slid out from between the newspaper's pages and fluttered to the floor.

"Mmm," Alexis said, frowning in concentration as she moved back down the hall.

Absently, I bent down and picked up the paper. It was a sheet from a writing pad, folded in half. On the outside, in unfamiliar writing, I read: "Kate Brannigan." Before I opened it, I knew what it was. I closed my eyes until the wave of nausea passed, then, slowly, apprehensively I unfolded it.

The hand was uncertain but perfectly legible. "Kate—I came round Monday afternoon but there was nobody in. I asked the boys where they got the transfers from, and they told me who's handing them out. I spoke to the lad and found out where he's getting them from, and there's more to it than the drugs. You're right, it shouldn't be going on, and I'm going round tonight to tell him so. If you want to come with me, come to my flat about seven o'clock. Yours sincerely, Cherie."

I slid down the wall till I was crouching in a tight bundle. I'd let Cherie down. I'd been so busy running around being a hero for Richard that I hadn't made the time to check back with her. And now she was dead, all because I hadn't managed to prevent her from sticking her head into a hornet's nest.

I'd probably have stayed like that forever if I hadn't heard wagons roll from the living room. Davy was shrieking with delight over some movie or other, Alexis's rumble of enthusiasm a lower counterpoint. "Come on then, I'll race you to the car," I heard her say. I forced myself into an upright position and I'd managed to find something approximating a smile by the time Davy was close enough to notice.

"See you later, super troopers," I said as they passed at a run.

"We'll be at our house," Alexis said. "Phone Chris and tell her, would you? Only, don't tell her why, she'll only get fear of loss. I'll tell her when she gets home."

I watched them drive off in the car. I don't think I've ever been so sorry to see Alexis leave. I pulled myself together with the assistance of a strong vodka and grapefruit juice and cut through the conservatory to my house. I didn't think I was up to approaching from the front. What amazed me was that the place wasn't crawling with police. But then, my bungalow's on the end of the row. No one overlooks the front of it, and even though it's got a postcode that whacks my insurance up into the stratosphere, it's still the kind of area where people assume a loud bang is a backfire from one of the MOT failures that sit on bricks all over the council estate, and not the shoot-out at the O.K. Corral.

From the inside, the front door looked just about as lethal. Time to call in a favour. I rang the office, and told Shelley I was on my way in. "Oh, and Shelley? I'd like to make a contribution to your household budget."

"You what?"

"I need a new front door. Pronto monto. I mean tonight. Can you get Ted to see to it?" Ted Barlow is the man Shelley strenuously insists she's not actually, technically, living with. They fell in love when he turned up in our office looking forlorn, with the bank about to foreclose on his conservatory business. While I was busy sorting out the mess, the pair of them gazed into each other's eyes and whispered sweet nothings. Now Shelley's got a conservatory that takes up a good half of her back garden, and Ted tends to answer her phone first thing in the morning.

"What's happened? Have you had a burglary?"

"I wish," I said with feeling. "Unfortunately, it's a little bit more personal than that. I'll tell you all about it when I come in."

"What about a key? Shall I get him to come by the office and pick one up?"

I pictured the door. "I think a key's a bit academic," I said. "If I can get the key in, I'll leave the outside door unlocked, OK? So if it's still locked, he'll know just to kick it in." I couldn't believe the words that were coming out of my mouth. I was instructing someone to kick my door in? Sooner or later, somebody was going to pay for all this. For scaring me, for killing Cherie, for giving drugs to little kids.

I felt safer in the office. Illogical, I know, but fear and logic are hardly ever on speaking terms, never mind pals. I perched on the edge of the leather sofa in Bill's office and told him all about the latest crisis. "I'm sorry to lay it all on you," I apologized, "but I need to talk it through."

His blue eyes smiled. "We're partners, aren't we? In my book, that makes this as much my business as yours."

"I know, but, I feel like it's always me that's in the shit up to the neck. I seem to be accident-prone these days. I remember when this agency never did anything more dramatic than prowling through somebody else's database. Now I seem to spend half my life in a state of panic."

Bill chewed his beard and shrugged. "So walk away from it." He saw my look of instant outrage and grinned. "You see?" he teased. "You like answers too much, Kate. But this time, I think we really should walk away from it. This is one for the cops."

I shook my head vehemently, my nervous fingers plaiting the streamers from the waste basket of his shredder. "No can do, Bill. Sorry."

Bill prowled the room like a huge blond bear who's forgotten where he left the honey jar. "It's too much of a risk," he insisted. "These people are serious, Kate. They've given you a warning. If they think you're ignoring that, then they won't hesitate to give you the same treatment they dished out to that poor woman. And frankly, I haven't got the time to find another partner right now."

"I *can't* go to the police, Bill. I'm not just being bloody-minded!"

"It wouldn't be the first time," he said, a wry smile counteracting the bitter edge to his voice.

I stood up, his restlessness infecting me. I walked across to his desk and perched on the edge of it and explained. "Bill, the Drugs Squad are supposedly checking out the info I handed over to them, and if it stands up, Richard will be released on bail on Thursday morning. If I go to the bizzies now and say, 'Excuse me, some drug dealer's hit man's just taken a shotgun to my front door, but it's got absolutely nothing to do with the fact that you've got my partner locked up on drugs charges,' they're going to fall about. There's no way they're not going to connect it to what's happened to Richard, and that'll be the end of any chance he's got of being turned loose."

Bill stopped pacing and threw himself down on the sofa. He breathed out deeply through his nose. "Kate, I don't want you to take this the wrong way, but hadn't you considered the possibility that it just might be connected to Richard's case rather than Cherie's death?"

"It's hard for me to get my head round the idea that there were two lunatics with shotguns wandering round Ardwick at the same time. The only credible explanation is that when Cherie fronted up whoever is pushing these drugs to kids, she mentioned my name. She might even have used me as an insurance policy. You know—'if anything happens to me, Kate Brannigan knows where to come looking.' If that's what happened, then hiring some psycho with a sawn-off to kill Cherie gets even more cost-effective. It not only gets rid of someone who knows more than the dealer wants her to, it also serves as a warning to me to keep my nose out and to stay away from the cops investigating the shooting. And it lets everybody else who's involved with the racket know just what's coming to them if they step out of line. A real bargain, when you think about it," I added angrily.

Bill said, "But I don't necessarily think that there *were* two psychos driving round Ardwick with a shooter. Manchester isn't LA. Having a gun in your glove box or under your car seat so the girls all know you're a big man and the yobs all know to give you a wide berth is a different kettle of fish from being a hired gun. It could be that while there was only one gunman, there were two paymasters. That would explain why Cherie was killed and you were only warned."

Suddenly, I saw the flaw in Bill's theory. "It was *my* front door," I said.

"Yes?" Bill said.

"Not Richard's. It was *my* front door. Don't you see?" I was excited now, banging the desk with my fist. "If they'd wanted to warn me off the case, they'd have blasted Richard's front door. *He's* the one that's vulnerable, *he's* the one that's banged up with a load of villains, *he's* the one with the eight-year-old pressure point. Besides, the only people who know there's any connection between me and Richard are the Drugs Squad."

Bill slumped in his office chair and chewed a pencil. "And we trust the Drugs Squad not to have a leak? We think they don't have any bent officers who might just be in Eliot James's golf club?"

I sighed. "I don't exactly *trust* Geoff Turnbull. Not even on Della's say-so. But he's an ambitious man, and self-interest's one of the most powerful engines there is. I bet the thought of nailing a smooth operator like Eliot James is a bigger aphrodisiac than oysters to a man like Turnbull. And he'll want all the credit for himself; I doubt very much if he's told a living soul he got his information from a private eye."

"I can't argue with that," Bill said, resignation all over his face. "So, what now?"

I told him. And since his only alternative was to betray me by going behind my back to the police, Bill reluctantly agreed to help where he could.

The main problem for me now was that I'd argued myself out of any chance of feeling secure. At least if I'd believed the shooting had anything to do with Jammy James and his merry men, I'd have known that the Drugs Squad were about to rob the gunman of any future playdays from that direction. Now, I had to live with the uncomfortable fact that some complete stranger out there wanted me to give up an inquiry so badly that they'd blown a hole in my front door. If I was going to stop them doing the same thing to me, I'd better find out who they were. And fast.

# 22

The rush-hour traffic had already started to build by the time I left the office. I sat smouldering in the jam at the top of Plymouth Grove, listening to GMR cheerily telling me where the traffic black spots were. I could have crossed town faster on foot than I was managing by car. I watched the seconds tick past on my watch, muttering darkly about what the transport policy would be when I ruled the world. It was twenty to five by the time I'd inched up Stockport Road and turned off into the car park behind the Longsight District Centre. I parked illegally as near as I could get to the Social Services office. I wanted to make sure I didn't miss my target.

Like the rest of the city's social workers, the family placement officer theoretically knocks off work at half past four. But like most of her colleagues, Frankie Summerbee knows that the only way to come close to dealing with her workload is to stay at the office long after the town hall bureaucrats have gone home. So, like most of her colleagues, Frankie's chronically over-tired, over-stressed and prone to making decisions that don't always look too wonderful in the cool light of day under cross-examination. That's what I was relying on this afternoon.

I've known Frankie almost as long as I've known Richard. Before he moved in next door to me, he lived in

Chorlton-cum-Hardy, that Manchester suburb whose trendiness quotient rises and falls in tandem with the Green Party's electoral share. He lived in the downstairs flat of an Edwardian terraced cottage. Frankie had the flat upstairs. Luckily for her, that included the attic. I don't know if that had always been her bedroom, but after Richard moved in downstairs I suspect that sleeping at least two floors away from his stereo became an imperative.

Of course, as a trained social worker, she couldn't avoid helping him out: cooking the odd meal, picking up his washing from the launderette, grabbing a stack of pizzas every now and again as she whizzed past the chill cabinet in the supermarket on her weekly shop. I don't expect she got any thanks, but he did take her out to dinner a few times, and so she became another victim of the Cute Smile.

The bonking bit didn't last too long. I suspect they both realized after the first time that it was a big mistake, but they're both much too kind to have hurt the other's feelings by saying so. Luckily, Frankie also has the good social worker's ruthless streak, otherwise they'd probably both still be hanging on till the last minute every Saturday night because nice people come second. Under normal circumstances, I was glad she'd forced a return to uncomplicated friendship so he was unencumbered when he met me. After the events of the past few days, I wasn't so sure.

I could have short-circuited the waiting period by picking up my mobile phone and dialling Frankie's direct line, but I was glad of a breathing space to try to organize my thoughts into something approaching order. I didn't get one.

I'd been sitting there less than ten minutes when Frankie's spiky black hair appeared like a fright wig on top of a stack of files. The files teetered forward above a pair of black leggings and emerald green suede hi-tops. I jumped out of the car and rushed forward to help her. "Hi, Frankie," I said, putting my arms out to steady the files as I stopped her in her tracks.

The hair tilted sideways and two interested brown eyes peered round the stack of files. Her granny glasses were slowly sliding down her nose, but not so far that she didn't recognize me. "Hi, Brannigan," she said. She didn't sound surprised, but then she's been a social worker for the best part of ten years. Nothing surprises Frankie any more.

"Let me help," I said.

"The car's over there," she said, sounding slightly baffled as I grabbed the top half of her pile. "The red Astra."

I carried the files over to the car and we did small talk while she fiddled with her keys and unlocked the hatchback. It wasn't easy, avoiding the subject of Richard's incarceration, but I managed it by dragging Davy's visit into the conversation two sentences in. We loaded the boot, and Frankie slammed it shut, then leaned against it, catching me eye to eye. Not many people manage that, but Frankie and I are so alike physically that if I ever get signed up to star in a movie with nude scenes I could get her to be my body double. "This is not serendipity, is it?"

I shook my head sheepishly. "Sorry."

She sighed. "You should know better."

"It's not business, Frankie," I said in mitigation. "It's personal, and it's not for me."

She raised her eyebrows and looked sceptical. I can't say I blamed her. "I'm in a hurry," she said. "I've got a meeting this evening. I was on my way to grab a quick curry since I skipped lunch. If you think there's any point in telling me what you're after, follow me to the Tandoori Kitchen. You're buying. Deal?"

"Deal," I said. I've always liked the Tandoori Kitchen. The food's consistently good, but the best thing of all is the chocolate-flavoured lollipops they give you when they bring you the bill. I wasn't particularly hungry, but I ordered some onion bhajis and pakora to keep me occupied while Frankie worked her way through the biggest mushroom biryani I've ever seen.

"So what's this favour you're after, Brannigan?"

"Who said anything about a favour?" I said innocently.

"A person doesn't need to have A Level Deduction to know you're after something more than a share in my poppadums when you turn up on the office doorstep. What are you after?" Frankie persisted.

So much for gently working round to it. I plunged in. "You took a couple of kids into care this afternoon. Daniel and Wayne Roberts. Their mum was shot in Brunswick Street?"

Frankie nodded cautiously. "Mmm?"

"I knew Cherie quite well, because Davy always plays with Daniel and Wayne when he's staying with Richard. Also, I helped her out when she was trying to get a divorce from Eddy, her ex." I paused, but Frankie didn't lift her eyes from her curry.

Nothing for it but to soldier on. "I was driving home with Davy this afternoon just after Cherie had been shot. The place was jumping with police and ambulance crews, and we saw the boys being taken away in a police car. Then when we got home, all the neighbours were talking about Cherie being shot. The bottom line is that Davy's in a hell of a state. He's terrified because Cherie's been shot, but he's even more frightened because Daniel and Wayne have been carted off in a police car."

"Not particularly surprising," Frankie said sympathetically. "Poor Davy. So what do you want me to do?"

"I just wondered if there was any chance you could fix up for me to take Davy to see Daniel and Wayne this evening. I know it's bending the rules and all that, but I don't see how I'm going to get him to sleep otherwise. He's climbing the walls. He thinks Daniel and Wayne have gone to prison, you see." I sighed and shrugged. "I've tried to explain, but he won't believe me."

"I wonder why not," Frankie said drily. She gave me a shrewd look. "Are you sure you're asking for Davy and not for yourself?"

"Give me a break, Frankie," I complained. "You know I don't do murders. Strictly white collar, that's Mortensen and Brannigan."

She snorted, not a wise move when you're dealing with curry spices. After she'd finished spluttering and sneezing, she said, "And Patrick Swayze's strictly ballroom. OK. I believe you. God knows why. But if I find out you've been lying to me, Brannigan, I'll be really disappointed in you."

Just as well I'm not a Catholic or I'd never get out of bed in the morning with the weight of guilt on my shoulders. I smiled meekly and said, "You won't regret this, Frankie."

"Where is Davy now?" she asked. "Is he with Richard?"

"My friend Alexis is looking after him. She was going to take him to the pictures to see if she could take his mind off what's happened." I glanced at my watch. "They should be back within the next half-hour or so."

Frankie ran a hand through her spiky hair. "I hope for your sake I don't live to regret this, Brannigan. I'll tell you what would make me feel happier, though."

"What's that?" I asked, willing to go along with anything half-reasonable so long as I still had the chance to hit the boys with a few questions.

"I'd be a lot happier if Richard brought Davy along rather than you. Then I could be sure there wasn't a hidden agenda." Frankie said calmly.

I hoped the dismay I felt didn't reach the surface. I pulled a face and said, "You and me both. But the boy wonder is out of town tonight. He's gone to Birmingham to see some international superstar I've never heard of at the NEC. He went off this afternoon early. He doesn't even know about Cherie."

Frankie sighed. "I'll just have to live with it, then. OK. We've placed Wayne and Daniel with emergency foster parents in Levenshulme. Normally, it would take a few days to organize a visit while we checked out the credentials of the person claiming to be friends or family, but in this case, I don't see why we shouldn't speed the wheels of bureaucracy since I know both you and Davy. Besides, it might just help the boys to settle, feel less abandoned. After we've eaten, I'll find a phone box and call the foster parents, see what time will fit in with their arrangements."

I put my mobile phone on the table. "Have this one on me," I said, nudging it towards her.

Frankie shook her head, smiling wryly. "Since I've known you, I've come to realize what the essential quality of a private investigator is," she said, reaching across and picking up the phone.

"What's that?"

"You simply don't recognize the point where the rest of the world backs off," she said. "Now, how do I work this thing?"

It was just after seven when Davy and I pulled up outside a trim between-the-wars semi off Slade Lane. The street was quiet, one of the few in the area that motorists driven demented by traffic don't think is a short cut to anywhere. I'd had a difficult half-hour with Davy, explaining what had happened to Cherie and the boys. I thought I should keep it low-key so I wouldn't frighten him, but I'd forgotten how small boys like things to be gory. He hadn't seen it happen right in front of his eyes, so it was no more real, no more frightening than a cartoon or a video. I was glad Frankie had gone off to her meeting; anything less like a terrified nervous wreck than Davy it would be hard to imagine.

You couldn't say the same for Daniel and Wayne. They sat huddled together on a settee in the front room. The television was on and their eyes were pointing at it, but they weren't watching. They didn't look up when the foster mother showed Davy and me into the room, but when she spoke, they both turned their heads towards us, a look of bafflement on their faces. They had the bewildered, desperate air we've all grown used to seeing in endlessly recurring TV film of refugees from disaster areas.

"Hi, lads," I said. "Davy and I were wondering if you fancied going to the ice-cream parlour."

Wayne got to his feet and, after a moment, Daniel joined him. I felt like a monster, dragging these two shattered kids out of the nearest thing they were going to have to a home, just to satisfy my curiosity. Then I looked at Davy and remembered my front door. That reminded me there was a lot more at stake than my nosiness. "Or we could go somewhere else, if you'd rather," I said.

"It's good there," Davy said anxiously, disturbed by his friends' silence.

"I want to go home," Wayne said. "That's where I want to go."

The foster mother, a bulky, comfortable-looking woman in her late thirties, stepped past me and gave Wayne a hug. "You've got to stay with us for a while, Wayne," she said in a soothing voice. "I know it's not the same as home, but tomorrow we'll go back to your house and get your clothes and the rest of your stuff and you can be at home here, OK?"

"We'll go to the ice-cream place, then," he said grudgingly to me. Wayne shrugged off the woman's arm and pushed past her into the hall, where he stood expectantly by the door. Daniel followed him, and, after a quick glance at me for permission, so did Davy.

"I'll have them back in an hour," I promised.

"Don't worry about it," she said. "Quite honestly, love, the more worn out they are tonight the better."

For the first twenty minutes, I said nothing about Cherie or the shooting. We pumped money into the Wurlitzer, we argued the relative merits of everything on the menu. Then I sat back and watched while the boys wolfed huge ice-cream sundaes, gradually returning to something approaching normal behaviour, even if it was tinged with a kind of hysteria. I even joined in some of their fun, dredging my memory for old and sick jokes. When I reached the point where the only one I could remember was the one about the Rottweiler and the social worker, I reckoned it was time to change tack.

"Davy got a lot of new transfers yesterday, didn't you?" I said brightly.

"Where did you go?" Daniel asked.

"VIRUS," said Davy and proceeded to enthuse about the virtual reality centre.

"Maybe we could all go together the next time Davy's up," I suggested. "Show them your tattoos, Davy."

He took off his New York blouson to reveal tattoos that spread up from his wrists and finally disappeared into the sleeves of his T-shirt. Wayne and Daniel studied the intergalactic warriors and dinosaurs, desperately trying not to look impressed.

"Huh," Wayne finally said. "I've had ones just as good as that."

"Where from?" Davy challenged.

"From Woody on the estate. You know, him that gave you a load last week."

There is a god. "I don't think I know Woody," I said. "Where does he live?"

"Up the top. Near the Apollo. Where the chip van parks," Daniel said positively.

"Wasn't your mum going to go and see him last night?" I asked, feeling like I was walking on eggshells. It was the first time Cherie had been mentioned, and I didn't know how they would react.

Wayne stared into his sundae dish, scraping his spoon round the sides. But Daniel didn't seem bothered. "Nah," he said scornfully. "It wasn't Woody she went to see. She'd already seen Woody and gave him a right gobful about giving things to us. And Woody said he was just doing what he was told to do, and she said he was a waste of space and who told him, and he said, the guy in the house on the corner. And that's where she went."

"What guy is that, do you know?"

Daniel shook his head. "Don't know his name. We don't go there."

"What house is it?"

"You know I said where Woody lives? Well, if you was standing at the chip van and you looked across the street that way," he said, gesturing with his right arm, "it's the house on the corner. That's where my mum went last night," he added.

I was impressed. "Were you with your mum when she saw Woody?" I asked. Daniel's information seemed almost too good to be true.

"'Course *we* weren't," Wayne said contemptuously. "She didn't even know we were out. We followed her. We always follow her. She says we're the men of the house and she needs us to take care of her, so we follow her, but she don't know. We watch and listen so we'll know if anyone did bad things to her and we could get them back later. She never saw us," he added proudly.

"I wish I was that good at following people," I said. "It would come in really handy in my job. You'll have to give me lessons one of these days. Where did you learn your tricks? From the TV?"

Wayne shook his head, swinging it elaborately from side to side. "Our dad showed us. He trained us to be silent and deadly, just like the Paras."

I felt a chill in my heart. According to Cherie, Crazy Eddy hadn't been near the kids in years. "When was this?" I asked casually.

"For ages. He just turns up at the common where we go with our bikes and takes us up Levenshulme and trains us. But he made us promise we wouldn't tell anybody because he didn't want Mum to know. But now Mum's not here, it doesn't matter about telling, does it?" Wayne's face crumpled and he rubbed his eyes savagely with his fists.

"No, it doesn't matter. Your dad must be really proud of you. When did you see him last?"

"We saw him yesterday," Daniel said. "But he's been around for ages. He came back at Easter."

# 23

I knew that if I betrayed my surprise I wouldn't get another word out of Daniel or Wayne. Somehow, I had to keep superficially calm at the news that Crazy Eddy was back in town. I breathed softly and thought about something restful: a room freshly painted barley white, actually. "I thought your dad worked away," I said.

Daniel stuck his chest out like a sergeant major. "He does. He's a warrior, my dad. He teaches whole armies how to fight like him. But when they've learned how to do it, he comes home and sees us."

"Does he come home often?" I asked.

"Once or twice a year," Wayne muttered. "The first time was just after I was five. We were playing in the playground at school at break time and this soldier came up to us, and he crouched down beside us and said, 'You know who I am, don't you?' And we did, because Mum had his picture on her dressing table." At the mention of the photograph, something clicked inside my head. Wayne looked up and met my eyes. "Do you think we can go and live with him now? Be soldiers with him?"

"You'll have to ask your foster mother about that," I said, distracted by the piece of the jigsaw that had just fallen into place. "Where does your dad stay when he's here?" I tried to sound casual.

"In the Moss. With a man that used to be one of his squaddies," Daniel said. "He's never taken us there. He's too busy training us."

"Of course he is. It's a tough job, being a good soldier." Out of the corner of my eye, I could see Davy getting restive. I pretended to be stern. "And you soldiers are letting the side down now." All three looked puzzled. "Do you know what's wrong with this picture?" I asked, gesturing at the table. They all held their breath and shook their heads. "Empty plates!" I mock-roared. "Time for seconds! Who wants more?"

I didn't have to ask twice. After the waiter had brought the second round of ice-creams, I said, "So what training were you doing with your dad yesterday?"

"Tracking and observation," Daniel reported. "We met Dad round the common, and then we went and hid across the main road, on the waste ground. We had binoculars, and we watched the outside of the flats and we waited for Mum to come out, then we trailed her and spied on her talking to Woody. Dad said she should keep her nose out of other people's business when we told him she was on about the transfers."

"Did he know about the transfers, then?" I asked through a mouthful of chocolate hazelnut. I'd succumbed the second time around.

"'Course he does," Wayne said, scornful again. "He told us to get the transfers off Woody and get the other kids to use them. He said they'd all want them and that way they'd do what we told them to. But we don't use the ones we take off Woody. Dad said that would be a sign of weakness, so we don't."

Eddy wasn't wrong about the transfers being a sign of weakness. I couldn't help wondering just how much he knew about what was going on in the house on the corner. It was time I paid it a visit. But first, I had to keep my side of the bargain I'd made with myself. I'd had my needs met; now,

Daniel and Wayne were entitled to the same thing. I dug my hand in my pocket and dumped a handful of change on the table. "Who wants to play?" I demanded, gesturing with one thumb towards the array of video-game machines at the far end of the ice-cream parlour.

I kept half an eye on them as I struggled with the significance of what Wayne had told me without realizing. Now I knew why the big bouncer at the Lousy Hand seemed so familiar. It wasn't because he was a regular in the Mexican restaurant downstairs from the office.

I'd once seen that photograph that Cherie kept in her bedroom. She'd shown me it when she'd asked me to hunt her husband down. He'd been in uniform, the maroon beret of the Paras cocked jauntily on his head. He'd been nearly ten years younger too. But that scar clinched it. The man who was fingering cars for Terry Fitz was none other than Crazy Eddy Roberts. At the very least, it was a strange coincidence.

It takes more than bereavement to divert small boys from arcade games. By the time they'd fought in the streets, driven several grand prix, played a round or two of golf and done enough terminating to get us jobs with Rentokil, the effects of the afternoon's trauma had receded noticeably. When we all piled back into my car, the haunted look had left their eyes. I didn't doubt that it was only a temporary respite, but even that was enough to ease my guilt at having taken advantage.

I dropped them off, promising that we'd keep in touch, then I drove Davy back to Alexis's. Of course, he was fired with curiosity as to why they'd moved back to their house and why he was staying with them there instead of with me in Coverley Close. Luckily, he was tired enough to be fobbed off with the excuse that Alexis and Chris needed to be at home now they were back at work because all their clothes and stuff were there. Alexis greeted him like a long-lost friend and hustled him off to the spare room, where she'd moved the video and the portable TV from their bedroom. I made the coffee while she made sure he was sufficiently engrossed in *The Karate Kid* for the dozenth time.

"You all right, girl?" Alexis asked when she returned. "You look about as lively as a slug in a salt cellar."

"Gee thanks. Remind me to call you next time my self-confidence creeps above the parapet. I'm just tired, that's all. I've not had a decent night's kip since last Wednesday."

"Why don't you crash out here now? You can have the sofa bed in the study."

"Thanks, but no thanks. I've got to go and sit outside a house in the dark."

"Hey, the sofa bed's not that bad," Alexis protested, joking. "I've slept there myself."

"Sorry to hear that, Alexis," I said, pretending deep concern. "I hadn't realized your relationship was in such a bad way."

"Hey, carry on getting it that wrong and you could get a job on the *Chronicle*'s diary column."

"Tut-tut," I scolded. "And you the one that's always telling me how unfairly you journos are maligned for your inaccuracies. Anyway, enough of this gay repartee. I've got work to do, and you've got a child to mind. I'll call you later." I headed for the door. "And Alexis? I know you probably think I'm over-reacting, but don't open the door to anyone unless you know them." I was through the door before she could argue.

I got in the car, revved up noisily, and drove round the corner. I gave it a couple of minutes, then turned back on to Alexis's street, stopping as soon as I had a clear view of the path leading to the house. I picked up my mobile and dialled a familiar number. It rang out, then I heard, "Hello?"

"Dennis? It's Kate. Are you busy tonight?"

"I don't have to be," he said, his voice too crackly for me to hear whether he sounded pissed off or not.

"I need a major favour."

"No problem. Whereabout?"

I gave him brief directions and settled back to wait. OK, so I was being paranoid. But like they say, that doesn't mean they're not out to get you. There was no way I was leaving this street until I was sure that Davy, not to mention Alexis and Chris, had someone to watch over them. And there was no minder I'd trust more than Dennis. He had an added advantage. Years of earning his living as a burglar had developed in him an astonishing ability to stay awake and alert long after the rest of us are crashed out snoring with our heads on the steering wheel. If he was sitting outside the house in his car, I'd feel a lot less worried about the possibility of Jammy James wanting to use me or Davy as a lever against Richard. Not that I believed for one minute that the demolition of my front door was a message from James. I just thought it was better to be safe than sorry. Or something.

While I was waiting, I wondered how Richard was coping. I felt bad about missing the evening's visit, but I figured he could live without seeing me for a day. Whereas, if I didn't do all I could to finger the people who were responsible for the holes in my door, he might have to get used to the idea of not seeing me again. Ever. It wasn't a comforting thought.

The house on the corner of Oliver Tambo Close wasn't the ideal place for a stakeout. The chip van's presence meant a constant flow of people up and down the street, as well as the gang of local yobs who hung round the van every evening just for the hell of it. Add to that the general miasma of poverty and seediness up this end of the estate, and I knew without pausing to think that the Peugeot would stick out like a sore thumb as soon as that evening's rock audience from the Apollo had gone home. I swung round by the office lock-up and helped myself to the Little Rascal van we've adapted for surveillance work.

I stopped behind the chip van, bought fish, chips and cholesterol and ostentatiously drove the Little Rascal back round the corner on to the street running at right angles to Oliver Tambo

Close. From the tinted rear windows of the van, I had a perfect view of the house, front door and all. I pulled down one of the padded jump seats and opened my fragrant parcel. I felt like I'd done nothing but eat all day, yet as soon as I smelled the fish and chips, I was ravenous. I sometimes think we're imprinted with that particular aroma while we're still in the womb.

While I tucked in, I checked out the house. I'd once been inside one of the other houses on the estate demanding action against the toerag who'd been anti-social enough to smash my car window and walk off with my radio cassette. Sparky, who runs the car crime round here, wasn't too pleased about a bit of private enterprise on his patch, especially from someone who was too stupid to work out which cars belonged to locals and which were fair game. Incidentally, he's not called Sparky because he's bright; it's because he uses a spark plug whirling on the end of a piece of string to shatter car windows. Anyway, I thought it was fair to assume this house would have the same layout as Sparky's. It looked the same from the outside, and Manchester City Council's Housing Department has never been renowned for its imagination.

The door would open into a narrow hall, the kitchen off to the right and the living room to the left. Behind the kitchen was the staircase, a storage cupboard underneath. I'd gone upstairs to use the bathroom and noted two other doors, presumably leading to bedrooms. That checked out with what I could see of the house on the corner. My job wasn't made any easier by the vandals who had busted the streetlamp in front of it. I could see heavy curtains were drawn at every window, even the kitchen. That was unusual in itself. If you've *got* curtains for all your windows in Oliver Tambo Close, the Social Security snoopers come round and ask where you're getting your extra income from.

I could see a crack of light from a couple of the windows, but apart from that there was no sign of life until nearly half past ten. The front door opened a couple of feet and spilled a long tongue of pale light on to the path. At first, there was no one to be seen in the doorway, then, sudden as sprites in an arcade game, two kids barrelled down the hall and out on to the path. They were both boys, both good-looking in the way that most lads have grown out of by adolescence. Unfortunately for the teenage girls. I'd have put them around nine or ten, but I'm not the best judge of children's ages. One had dark curls, the other had mousey brown hair cut in one of those trendy styles, all straight lines and heavy fringes that remind me of BBC TV versions of Dickens.

The two boys seemed in boisterous, cheerful moods, pushing each other, staggering about, giggling and generally horsing around. They stopped on the corner and pulled chocolate bars out of the pockets of their jeans. They stood there for a few minutes, munching chocolate, then they ran off down the street towards the blocks of flats where Cherie Roberts had tried to bring her kids up as straight as she knew how. A slow anger had started to burn inside me when those kids appeared on the path, all alone at a time of night that's a long way from safe in this part of town. Apart from anything else, it's an area that's always full of strangers in the evening, since the city's major rock venue is just round the corner. If a child was lifted from these streets, the police would have more strange cars to check out than if they clocked every motor that cruises the red-light zone.

I bit down on my anger and carried on watching. About twenty minutes later, the door opened again, more widely this time, and a young man appeared. He couldn't have been more than five-six, slim build, blond, late twenties, cheekbones like chapel hat pegs. He had his jacket collar turned up and sleeves rolled up. Clearly no one had told him *Miami Vice* is yesterday's news. He walked with a swagger to a Toyota MR2 parked at the kerb. I toyed with the idea of following him, but rejected it. I didn't know that he was anything to do with the drugs being foisted on kids, and besides, chasing a sports car in a delivery van is about as much fun as that nightmare where you're sitting an exam and you don't understand any of the questions, and then you realize you're stark naked as well.

So I stayed put. The MR2 revved enough to attract the envy of the chip-van gang, then shot off, leaving a couple of hundred miles' worth of rubber on the road. Ten minutes later, the door opened again. This time, the hall light snapped off. Two men emerged. In the dimness, it was hard to see much, except that they both looked paunchy and middle-aged. They walked towards my van, near enough for me to see that they both wore Sellafield suits—those expensive Italian jobs that virtually glow in the dark. Surprisingly, they got into an elderly Ford Sierra that looked perfectly in keeping with the locale, and drove off.

I carried on with my vigil. There were no lights on that I could see, but I figured there might still be someone in the bathroom, or the bedroom at the rear of the house. The chip van packed up at midnight, and the gang wandered off to annoy someone else. By half past midnight, it had started to drizzle and the street was as quiet as it was ever going to get. There was still no sign of life at the house. I unlocked the strongbox in the floor of the van, and helped myself to some of the essential tools of the trade. Then I pulled on a pair of latex surgical gloves.

I got out of the van and walked towards the narrow alley that runs up the back of Oliver Tambo Close so the bin men have more scope to strew the neighbourhood with the contents of burst black rubbish sacks. As nonchalantly as possible, I made sure I wasn't being watched before I nipped smartly down the alley. The house on the corner had a solid fence about seven feet high, with a heavy gate about halfway along. Luckily, one of the neighbours was trusting. A couple of doors down was a dustbin. I retrieved the bin and climbed on top of it.

The rear of the house was in darkness, so I scrambled over the fence and dropped into a tangle of Russian vine. Come the holocaust, that's all there will be left. Cockroaches and Russian vine. I freed myself and stood on the edge of a patchy lawn staring up at the house. There was a burglar alarm bell box on the gable end of the house, but I suspected it was a dummy. Most of them round here are. Even if it was for real, I wasn't too worried. It would take five minutes before anyone called the cops, and by the time they got here, I'd be home, tucked up in bed.

The back door had two locks, a Yale and a mortise. The patio doors looked more promising. You can often remove a patio door from its runners in a matter of minutes. All it takes is a crowbar in the right place. Only problem was, I was fresh out of crowbars. With a sigh, I started in with the lock picks. The mortise took me nearly twenty minutes, but at least the rain meant nobody with any sense was out walking curious dogs with highly developed senses of smell and powerful vocal cords. When the lock clicked back, I stretched my arms and flexed my tired fingers. The Yale was a piece of cake, even though I couldn't slide it open with an old credit card and had to use a pick. Cautiously, I turned the handle and inched the door open.

Silence. Blackness. I slipped into the carpeted hall and left the door on the latch. Slowly, painstakingly, I inched forward down the hall, my right hand brushing the wall to warn me when I reached the living-room doorway. As my eyes grew accustomed to the dark, I made out a patch of lesser blackness on the left. The stairs. As I drew level, I paused and held my breath. I couldn't hear a thing. Feeling slightly more relaxed, I carried on.

The living-room door was open. I moved through the doorway tentatively, scared of tripping over furniture, and closed the door softly behind me. I switched on the big rubber torch I'd taken from the van's glove box and slowly played it over the room.

It was like two separate rooms glued together in the middle. In the far end of the room, the walls were painted cream. There was a cream leather armchair, a pair of school desks with child-sized chairs, and a pair of bunk beds complete with satin sheets. Where there should have been a light fitting hanging from the ceiling there was a microphone. At the midpoint of the room,

a camcorder was fixed on a tripod, flanked by a couple of photographer's floodlights.

The other half of the room, where I was standing, was like
the distribution area of a video production company. There was
one of those big video-copying machines that do a dozen copies
at a time, a desk set up for home video editing, boxes of Jiffy
bags and shelf upon shelf of videos, one title to a shelf. Titles
like, *Detention!, Bedtime Stories* and *You Show Me Yours* . . . There
were also sealed packets of photographs. Now I began to understand why kids were being handed free drugs that would smash
their inhibitions to smithereens and make them see the funny
side of being exploited to hell. I could only come up with one
explanation of what was going on here, and the very thought of
it was so sickening that part of me didn't want to hang around
checking the evidence. The only thing that forced me to do it
was the thought of some smartass from the Vice Squad doing
the "so if you didn't look at these videos, how do you know
they weren't Bugs Bunny cartoons?" routine on me.

I picked a title at random and slotted it into the player on
the editing desk. I turned on the TV monitor. While I waited
for the credits to come up, I slit open a packet of photographs.
Twelve colour five-by-sevens slid out into my hand. I nearly lost
my fish and chips. I recognized the blond man who'd left earlier
in the Toyota, but the children in the shots were, thank God,
strangers. I'd have been fairly revolted to see adults in some of
those poses, but with children, my reaction went beyond disgust.
At once, I understood those parents who take the law into their
own hands when the drunk drivers who killed their kids walk
free from court.

If the photographs were bad, the video was indescribably
worse, all the more so because of the relentlessly suburban locations where these appalling acts were taking place. I could barely
take five minutes of it. My instincts were to empty a can of petrol
on the carpet and raze the place to the ground. Then common
sense prevailed and reminded me it would be infinitely preferable

if those bastards ended up behind bars rather than me. I switched off the video and ejected the tape. I picked up the photographs and stuffed them inside my jacket. I grabbed another couple of videos off the shelf. The night relief at Longsight police station were in for an interesting shift.

I stood up. I heard a sickening crunch. My eyes filled with red, shot through with yellow meteors. A starburst of pain spread from the back of my head. And everything went black.

# 24

Mosquito. Unmistakable. High-pitched whine circling my head, in one ear and then in the other. Bluebottle. Low, stuttering buzz mixing in with the mozzie. You wouldn't think two little insects could make enough noise to give you a splitting headache, I thought vaguely as I surfaced.

Then the pain hit. You know when you catch your finger in a door? Imagine doing that to your head, and you'll start to get the picture. The sharp edge of the agony snapped my brain back into gear. In the tiny gaps between waves of pain and nausea, I started to remember where I'd been and what I was doing when something seriously brutal put my memory on pause.

As that memory returned, so my senses started to catch up. I still couldn't force my eyes open, but my hearing had recovered from its dislocation. I wasn't hearing a mozzie and a bluebottle. I was hearing a voice. The words drifted in and out, like listening to a pirate radio station on the edge of its transmission area. "I don't fucking *know* how she got in," I heard. "I was fucking sleeping, wasn't I? Look, it's your job to sort out problems . . ." The voice tailed off. The silence was blissful.

Moments later, the voice started yapping again. This time, I registered that it was a man. "I don't give a shit what you're doing. Look, you're paid to do this sort of thing. I'm just paid

to copy videos and *be* here, not whack people over the head
with tripods. You'd better get your arse over here now and deal
with this cow." Silence again. Then the voice, higher pitched,
angry. "You've already been paid once to warn her off, and it
didn't work, did it? So you'd better come round here and finish
the job or else I'll have to ring Colin and tell him you're not
prepared to turn out, and he won't be pleased about that, not
being disturbed this time of night."

It finally dawned on me that this was me he was talking
about. If I'd had the energy to be afraid, I'd have been gibber-
ing. As it was, the immediate prospect of being executed helped
focus my mind even more. My eyes still refused to open, but I
became aware of a shooting pain in my shoulders and managed
to work out my position. I was suspended by my wrists, which
were manacled by something warm and solid that was biting
into the flesh. My hands were jammed up against what felt like
hot and cold water pipes. My body was dangling, my legs were
crumpled under me, not actually taking any of my weight.

Before I could test whether it was possible to shift my
weight to my feet without making a noise, the voice started
yammering again. "Look, it's your responsibility. She's got to
be dealt with, and now. She's seen the videos, for God's sake.
You might want to spend the next ten years being buggered by
some Neanderthal in the nick, but I don't." He paused. "Fine.
You better be here, that's all, or I'll be right on the phone to
Colin. And if you want another wage packet like today's, you
won't want me doing that." I heard the sound of a phone being
slammed down. The jangling crash cut through my head like a
blunt axe, snapping my eyes open.

I closed them to a slit at once, eager to look like I was still
out for the count. If I had any chance of getting clear of this place
before the hit man arrived, it was by playing dead and hoping
my captor would leave me alone. Through my lashes, I could
see I was in the kitchen, the fluorescent light a stab behind the
eyes. At the far end of the room, the man who'd been using the

wall-mounted phone turned towards me. He was tall and slim, his gingerish hair tousled from sleep. He had a neat, full moustache that jutted out like a ledge above thin lips and a sharp chin. The bleary eyes he focused on me narrowed vindictively. "Bitch," he said, savagely tightening the belt of his towelling dressing gown.

I knew him. Not his name, or anything like that, but I knew him. I'd seen him around, in the local shops, and in Manto's café bar on one of the handful of occasions I'd been in there waiting for Richard. We were on nodding terms, talking about the weather in the corner-shop terms. It was hard to get my head round the idea of being trussed up by someone I knew. I've never had the slightest desire to explore S&M, and I sure as hell didn't want to start now.

He turned away from me and picked up the kettle. He filled it up and switched it on. While he was waiting for it to boil he came over to me. I let my eyelids sink shut and tried to ignore the cramps that were sending spasms of agony from my lower back muscles through my shoulders and down into my triceps. I let my body hang limp. I was just fine till he kicked me in the ribs.

I think I passed out again for a moment, for the next time I cracked my eyes open he was pouring boiling water into a teapot. I had a funny feeling that he wasn't going to offer me a cup. I took the opportunity of his back being turned to check out my position.

I was handcuffed to water pipes, each about an inch in diameter. What was holding me up was the brackets that were screwed into the wall to keep the pipes in place. What worried me most of all was that I wasn't wearing my jacket or my cotton sweater. I was stripped down to my sports bra, and the entire length of my arms was covered in temporary tattoos. No wonder I was feeling out of it. The gratuitous kick had given me a vague feeling that I ought to be really, really angry, but I couldn't seem to get worked up. However, I was a long way from being totally stoned. Maybe the lack of circulation in my arms and hands had slowed down the process of absorption. Just how long had the tattoos been in place, and how long did I have before I became a silly giggling maniac?

While I worried about this, Moustache was brewing his tea. He poured himself a mug, gave me a last glance and walked out of the room. Judging by the shuffle of his slippers, he'd only gone as far as the living room.

I knew I didn't have a lot of time. The hit man was on his way, and I needed to be free and clear by then. Taking a deep breath, I shifted round so the soles of my feet were on the floor. Gradually, I allowed my legs to take the weight off my shoulders. For a moment, the pain in my shoulders vanished like magic. Then the pins and needles set in. From my hands to my shoulders, I twitched with a million stabs of irritation. I bit my lip to gag the whimpers that I couldn't stop escaping.

Slowly, inch by cautious inch, I straightened my legs, relieving all the strain on my arms and shoulders. It seemed to take forever, especially since I had to do it all in silence and the pounding in my head seemed to be growing rather than subsiding. When I was upright, I took stock again. The pipes looked pretty strong, but there were a couple of bends in them which might indicate weak points. The downside was that my arms were weak, my muscles twitching with pain. On the other hand, I had nothing to lose since the hit man was already on his way.

I took a deep breath and raised one leg, placing the sole of my foot against the wall, on a level with my hips. Then, gritting my teeth, I leaned back, taking my weight on my arms again, and swung my other leg up, bracing it against the wall on the other side of the pipe. With all my strength, I straightened my legs, pulling back against the handcuffs as hard as I could, my weight lending maximum force to my efforts.

At first, nothing happened. The cuffs dug into my hands, thankfully in a different place to the weals from my earlier suspension, but nothing moved. Then, suddenly, one of the brackets popped out of the walls like the pearl stud on a tight cowboy shirt. Another bracket followed it almost at once, and the pipe came away from the wall, bowing dramatically towards me. I bent my legs slightly, then prepared for a final, all-out effort. With a grunt that Monica Seles would have been proud of, I straightened my legs and hauled with everything I had. Just when I thought I would dislocate my shoulders, the pipe snapped about five feet from the ground and I crashed to the floor.

The roar of gushing water mingled with the roar of anger from behind me. I dragged myself upright and hauled my hands over the broken ends of the pipes, fast as I could. Even so, Moustache was on me as I swivelled round to face him. He'd grabbed the first thing to hand, which was the kettle, swinging it at my battered head. I did a staggering sidestep, as much to get away from the scalding blast of the hot pipe as to avoid the kettle. Moustache got the hot water straight in the face as the momentum of his running blow carried him past me and into the wall.

His scream would have been music to my ears if my head hadn't been splitting. Instead, all I wanted to do was shut him up. I aimed a Thai boxing kick at the crook of his knee. It was a pretty feeble kick, but he was off balance anyway. He dropped to his knees like a sack of spuds and I brought my clenched hands, complete with nasty sticking-out bits of handcuffs, down hard on the back of his neck. With a groan like an abandoned harmonium, he slumped against the wall and slithered down into the growing pool of water like something out of a Tom and Jerry cartoon.

I leaned against the sink, trying to catch my breath. I looked at the inert body crumpled at my feet and realized that all I had to do was walk away to get my own back for that gratuitous boot in the ribs. Given the rate the water was pouring into the kitchen, it wouldn't be long before Moustache said good night, Vienna.

Call me a wimp, but I couldn't do it. I crouched down, grabbed his hair and hauled his poleaxed head out of the water. I yanked him on to his back and propped him in a sitting position between the wall and the sink unit. I'm too nice for my own good.

Keeping one eye on him, I backed across the kitchen to the phone. Using both hands, I picked up the receiver and tucked it into my left shoulder. I punched in a familiar number and listened to it ring out. I was starting to panic when it reached the thirteenth ring: it's not easy being patient when you know someone's on their way to send you to the crematorium.

Just as I was about to abandon the phone and leg it, the ringing stopped and a blurred voice muttered, "'lo?"

"Della? It's Kate. This is an emergency. Are you awake?"

There was a grunt, then Della said, "Getting there. What is it?"

"Della, there's a guy on his way to kill me. It'll take too long to explain it all now, but he's the hit man who killed Cherie Roberts, the single mum who got blown away this afternoon? He's coming after me!" I could hear the hysteria rising in my voice, and I was overwhelmed by the urge to giggle.

"Kate? Are you pissed?" Della asked incredulously.

"No, but I think I've been drugged," I said. "I swear this isn't a wind-up, Della. I know it's not your beat, but you've got to get a posse out here right away, double urgent. This guy's a paid killer. And he's after me!" Even to me, my voice sounded like Minnie Mouse.

"OK, calm down. Where exactly are you?"

"I'm in a house on the corner of Oliver Tambo Close, near the Apollo. The house is full of kiddy porn. They've been drugging the kids to get them to perform," I gabbled.

"Later, Kate, later," Della interrupted. "I'm going to hang up now and get the local lads to send the area car round there pronto. And I'll be there myself as soon as I can. But I want you to get out of there right now. Don't hang about. Just get out. Go back to your house and I'll meet you there."

I snorted with insane laughter. I was beginning to feel really silly. "I can't go there," I giggled. "He knows where I live. He's already blown my door away." Before she could make another suggestion, the line went dead. Not the way it goes when someone hangs up on you. This was dead, hollow, a void. Suddenly, I didn't feel like giggling any more. Somewhere outside the house was the man who had been sent to kill me. And his automatic first action was to cut the lines of communication.

I checked my pockets for the van keys, but they weren't there. Wildly, I looked around the kitchen. I spotted them on one of the worktops, along with my wallet. I paddled through the water and picked them up, stuffing my wallet in my trouser pocket. In the kitchen doorway, I hesitated, water flowing like a spring stream round my ankles, trying to decide whether the assassin would approach from the front or the rear.

I didn't wonder for long. With a crash that reverberated round my skull, the back door slammed against the wall. I didn't even wait to look. I whirled round to the front door. The gods were on my side, for the key was in the lock. I turned the key, pulled it out of the lock and yanked the door open. I was through it and had it closed in the time it took the hit man to travel the length of the hall. I shoved the key in the lock and turned it. Then I stumbled and weaved down the path, my breath coming in ragged sobs.

I'd reached the pavement when the night exploded in a pair of catastrophic bangs. I turned to look back at the house. The door was hanging drunkenly on one of its hinges, and the silhouette of a man was pushing it aside. In his right hand, he carried a sawn-off shotgun. I drew in my breath in a horrified moan and ran for my life.

Now I was swerving madly by design as I approached the van. I pressed the burglar alarm remote-control button, which unlocks the doors as well as deactivating the alarm. I was barely at the back of the van, and I could hear him gaining on me. Then, suddenly, the sound of his footsteps stopped. I knew he was taking aim. Desperately, I threw myself into a rolling somersault round the rear of the van to the passenger side, putting the van between him and me.

Weeping with fear, sweating in spite of the cold night air on my freshly grazed skin, I scrambled to my feet and staggered along the side of the van to the passenger door. I grabbed the door handle like a lifeline and pulled myself into the cab. I had the presence of mind to lock the doors behind me. I fumbled the key into the ignition at the second attempt.

I was still cuffed, so driving wasn't going to be easy. I swivelled round to shift the gear stick into first, then released the handbrake. Movement at the edge of my peripheral vision made me swing round to look out of the driver's window. The shock of what I saw nearly had me stalling the engine. As it was, I let the clutch out way too fast and the van bucked forward in a series of jumps like a kangaroo on acid.

In my wing mirror, I saw him step back involuntarily to avoid having his feet run over by the van's rear wheels. Crazy Eddy Roberts, locked somewhere on the slopes of Mount Tumbledown, clutching his gun like mothers clutch frightened children. A man who'd lost touch with human feelings to the point where there was nothing difficult about taking a damn sight more than thirty pieces of silver to kill the mother of his children.

For a fraction of a second, our eyes locked. The engine was screaming a protest at still being in first, so I took my hands off the steering wheel to change up into second. When I looked in my mirror again, the twin barrels of the gun gleamed dully in the distant streetlights as Eddy swung it up towards me. I put my foot down and grabbed the steering wheel. I could feel the van fishtailing as I tried to wrench the wheel round to clear the oncoming corner.

I heard the boom of the gun as the window shattered. I'd lost control of the van almost simultaneously. I hit the kerb at speed and clipped a lamppost. As the van toppled over on its side, the last thing I saw was a pair of flashing blue lights.

# 25

I couldn't believe how blue the sea was. It glittered under Mediterranean sunlight like one of those crystal beds that New Age fanatics have lying around their living rooms. I propped myself up on one elbow and watched the lumbering half-tracked harvesters further down the beach, gathering and refining the spice that had caused the planet wars that had ravaged Dune for a generation. Suddenly, the sand shifted, only feet away from my leg, and the head of a huge, carnivorous sandworm reared up. The ferocious jaws opened, to reveal Moustache's face.

I swam up the levels to consciousness, passing from dreaming to awareness via that state where you know that you've just been dreaming, but you're not quite awake. My head felt like an oversized block of stone, though there didn't seem to be as much pain as I remembered enduring before the accident. The accident!

My eyes snapped open. I was in a small room, dimly illumined by lights glowing through frosted glass from the corridor outside. I tried to lift my head, but it was too much of an effort. Instead, I shifted my feet to check I was still functioning below the neck. You put your left leg in, you put your left leg out . . . Yeah, the lower limbs all did the hokey cokey. I breathed deeply. There was a bit of pain from my ribs and chest, but nothing felt broken, which was pretty miraculous given that I hadn't been wearing my seat belt when I crashed the van. I raised my right arm, which seemed fine, apart from the puffy bruises that ran round hand and wrist like designer bangles by the Marquis de Sade. My left arm had no watch on it, only grazes from shoulder to wrist, and a drip running into the back of my hand, which was more than a little disconcerting.

I moved my head to one side, trying to see if there was a clock anywhere. To my surprise, Della was fast asleep on a plastic bucket chair next to my bed. I felt mildly outraged. Someone had tried to kill me tonight, and she should have been down the police station, going through the hoops of the Police and Criminal Evidence Act to make sure Crazy Eddy spent the foreseeable future living at the taxpayers' expense in a room with a bucket to piss in and bars on the windows. Then a horrible thought struck me. What if Eddy Roberts had managed to give the plod a body swerve? What if Della was Greater Manchester Police's idea of a bodyguard? What if Crazy Eddy was still out there with his pump-action double-barrelled shotgun packed with cartridges with my name on?

I opened my mouth. My brain said, "Della?" but my mouth was too dry to play along. All I managed was a sort of strangulated croak.

She must only have been catnapping, for her eyes opened at once. Momentarily, she had the startled look of someone who has lost track of where she is. Then her conscious mind checked in and she sat bolt upright, staring at me with undisguised relief. "Kate?" she said softly. "Can you hear me?"

I tried to nod, but it wasn't in my repertoire yet. I waved my arm in the direction of the locker, where there was a jug of water and a bottle of orange juice. "Drink?" I mouthed.

Della jumped up and poured a glass of water. She leaned over me and tipped the glass to my lips. Most of the water went down my cheeks and on to the pillow, but I didn't care. All I was concerned about was getting some in my parched mouth.

The water was warm and stale and blissful. I didn't want to swallow, just hold it there in my mouth. Della gave me a concerned, anxious look as I waved her away.

Finally, I let the water trickle down my throat. "Thanks," I said in something approaching my normal voice. "What are you doing here? Shouldn't you be down the cells beating a confession out of that mad bastard with the shotgun?" She gave me an odd look. "You did *catch* him, didn't you," I demanded, panic gripping my chest and turning my stomach over.

"We caught him," Della said grimly. "The officers from Longsight got slightly over-enthusiastic with their truncheons when they realized he had a gun. Your assailant has a broken collar bone and a shattered wrist, you'll be sorry to hear."

"Is that why you're here and not down the nick taking a statement?" I asked.

Della looked awkward. "Actually, no," she said, shifting in her seat. "Kate, this isn't the same day," she said in a rush.

I frowned. "Not the same day? What do you mean?"

"You called me in the early hours of Wednesday morning." She glanced at her watch. "It's now four forty-seven a.m. on Thursday. You've been out cold for over a day."

"Over a day?" I echoed foolishly. I couldn't take it in. I had no sense of having lost a day of my life. I felt like I'd woken up from a strange dream after a brief spell of unconsciousness. Did people feel like this when they came out of comas that lasted weeks or years? No wonder they felt dislocated. I'd only lost a day and I felt like I'd stumbled into an episode of *The Twilight Zone*. I managed a twisted grin. "You know it's a bad case when the only way you can catch up on your sleep is to get unconscious."

"I'm glad you can joke about it. We were starting to get really worried. The doctors gave you a brain scan and said there seemed to be no damage, but they couldn't say how long you'd be out."

"Does Richard know?" I asked.

"I discussed it with Bill and Ruth, and we decided not to tell him before this morning's hearing. It seemed the best solution."

"Yeah," I sighed. "He couldn't have done anything, and they wouldn't have let him out unless I was really at death's door. It would only have had him climbing the walls. The last thing he needs right now is to be charged with assaulting a police officer." The only good thing I could see about having lost an entire day was that I wouldn't have to wait so long to see Richard again. With luck, he'd be out on bail by lunch time.

"How are you feeling?" Della asked.

"Took your time asking, didn't you?" I teased.

Della looked hurt for a few seconds, before it sank in that I was at the wind-up. "Listen, Brannigan," she said, pretending to be stern, "I don't have to be here. I'm not on duty. I'm here out of the goodness of my heart, you know."

"Thanks," I said, meaning it. "I'm impressed. I've never known you go this long without a cigarette voluntarily. Actually, I don't feel too bad. A bit woozy, that's all. And my head's throbbing. And now I'm awake, they'll probably give me something for that. At least I know I'll be out of here in a few days. How's Crazy Eddy handling it, being locked up in a cell?"

Della stiffened to attention again. Her face shifted from concerned friend to alert copper. "You *know* who this guy is?"

"Why? Don't you?"

She looked faintly embarrassed. "As it happens, we don't. He won't say a word. He had nothing on him that would identify him, and his prints don't seem to be on record. Who is he?"

"His name's Eddy Roberts. He's an ex-Para. He got invalided out a couple of years after the Falklands War because he was out to lunch and not coming back. He's supposedly been working all over the globe as a mercenary. He's been back in Manchester since Easter. Apparently working as a hired gun. Among other things." I stopped, suddenly exhausted.

"Kate, I know you've been through it, and I'm sorry to have to keep on at you. This isn't the time to take a formal statement, but this is really important information. How do you know all this? Have you been chasing him?" She had the good grace to look ashamed of herself.

I gave one of those laughs that turns into a cough halfway through. "No, Della. He was chasing me, remember. The reason I know so much about Crazy Eddy is because his wife and kids told me. Eddy Roberts used to be married to Cherie Roberts. The woman he blew away outside the post office on Tuesday."

That was revelation enough to shatter Della's official cool. "You mean, that wasn't a professional hit job? It was a domestic?"

"It was a hit job all right. Cherie had found out about the child porn racket. And I expect she threatened that she'd spill the beans to me. The fact that Eddy used to be married to her was, I suspect, totally irrelevant. If anything, it probably made it more exciting."

"And that's how you got involved? Through Cherie?"

I was growing wearier by the second, but I forced a smile. "I thought you weren't taking a statement?" Della started to apologize but I waved it aside. "Only joking, honest. No, I got involved because Davy came home stoned out of his mind." I gave Della the thirty-second version of events around Oliver Tambo Close. I'd just got to the bit about interviewing Wayne and Daniel when we were interrupted.

She was only in her mid-twenties, but the night sister was fierce. "Is the patient awake?" she demanded. "Chief Inspector, I gave you strict instructions to ring for a nurse if the patient showed signs of coming round. You've got no right to interrogate her on my ward without my permission."

"It's my fault," I butted in. "I wanted to know what had happened."

The sister busied herself with my pulse. "You're in no fit state to discuss it," she said firmly. "Chief Inspector, I'm going to have to ask you to leave. You can come back after Mr Rocco has seen the patient and if he decides she's fit to be interviewed."

Della got to her feet meekly and winked. "See you soon, Kate," she said.

"I hope so," I sighed. "Oh, Della—before you go . . . Sister, can I ask the officer one question?"

The sister smiled, unexpectedly. "If you must. But keep it short," she added, frowning pointedly at Della.

"The van. What sort of state is it in?"

"Amazingly enough, it's just superficial damage. You'll be relieved to hear it's not a write-off, according to Bill last night." She edged towards the door. "Thanks for your help, Kate."

I watched her retreating back while the sister bustled about doing sisterly things to my reflexes. She asked me who the Prime Minister was, and I told her about the pain, so she gave me some pills once she'd finished her neurological observations. The last thing I remembered as I drifted into sleep was being grateful that I hadn't written off the Little Rascal. It was only seven months since another homicidal nutter had sent my last company car to the great scrap yard in the sky. Any more of that, and the insurance premiums were going to be higher than the price of a new set of wheels.

⋘✦⋙

The next time my eyes flickered open, I thought I was hallucinating. There, sitting on the uncomfortable chair, brown hair flopping across his forehead, eyes intent behind his glasses, was Richard. Seeing me waken, a slow, joyful smile spread across his face. I'd never seen a more welcome sight. "Hiya, Brannigan," he said. "You're not fit to be let out on your own, are you?" He stretched out an arm and gripped my right hand tightly. The bruises sent out a protest bulletin on all frequencies, but I didn't care.

"You're a fine one to talk," I said. "This is all your fault anyway."

"I had a funny feeling it was going to be," he said, grinning, "I see the blow to your head hasn't improved your grasp of logic. They tell me you've not got brain damage, but I told the consultant different. He said there was nothing they could do about the state you were in before the accident. So I'm just going to have to live with it."

"Did you get bail, or was it Group 4 that escorted you to court this morning?"

"The police withdrew their objections to bail, and they let me go without conditions. Ruth says they'll drop charges once they've nailed the real guys in the black hats and cleared me. I came straight here, you know. I didn't even go home for fresh clothes and a joint. You did a great job, Brannigan." He released my hand and dropped to his knees, hands clenched in supplication. "How can I ever repay you?"

"I'll think of something," I said. "You can start by giving me a kiss."

He jumped to his feet. "I'll have to close my eyes," he said, mock-seriously.

"I look that bad?" I demanded, suddenly discovering a new anxiety. I put my hand up to my head, discovering a thick turban of bandage that extended halfway down my forehead.

"Two lovely black eyes, two lovely black eyes," he sang. "And a whopping great bruise on your jaw. Linda Evangelista won't be worrying about you taking her place on the catwalk for a while." Before I could say anything more, he stooped over me and kissed me gently on the lips.

"Call that a kiss?" I snarled.

It got better after that.

When he finally came up for air, he said softly, "I love you, Brannigan."

"Don't go getting soft on me," I murmured. "You're only saying that because I got you out of jail."

"And you took care of my kid. I've heard all about what went on. Bill came to court this morning and told me how you'd ended up in here."

"Speaking of which," I interrupted before he got hopelessly sentimental in the way that only cynical journos can. "Where is Davy?"

"Alexis took the day off to look after him. They've gone off to some fun palace this morning. She told Bill she'd meet me here . . ." He glanced at his watch. "In about ten minutes, actually."

"God, you'd better not let him in here if I'm as much of a sight as you seem to think I am. He'll have nightmares for weeks."

"Brannigan, you're talking about a kid who thought *Dracula* was a fun movie. I don't think a couple of bruises and a heavy-duty headscarf are going to freak him out. He knows you were in a car crash. The only thing I'm worried about is what he's going to tell his mother."

# EPILOGUE

On the first day of Davy's summer holidays, the three of us giggled our way along Blackpool Prom on the open top deck of a tram. I was wearing a baseball cap that said "Kiss me slow." Tacky, I know, but it covered the uneven hair growth. At least it wasn't stubble any more. I'd been less than thrilled to discover I had a bald patch where they'd had to shave me when they stitched up the hole that Moustache's tripod had made in the back of my head. The hair seems to be coming back just fine over the scar, but it's knackered my attempts at growing my hair. I'm back to short and spiky. *Passé*, sure, but I hadn't had a lot of choice. And I didn't look too much like a punk now the deep bruising had finally faded.

Davy had insisted on coming back north for part of the summer because he'd had such a good time at half-term. I can only presume he gave his mother a highly edited version of events, since she made no objection. We'd spent most of the day at the Pleasure Beach, only giving up on the white-knuckle rides when Richard dumped his lunch down the drain after a spectacular trip round the Grand National.

Now we were heading for the tower. Richard had decided that physically being on top of the world was the best way to symbolize the fact that as of tomorrow he'd officially be a free man. "I can't wait," he said as we queued for the lift.

"I didn't think you were into views," I said.

"No, for tomorrow, stupid. I can't wait to hear the prosecuting solicitor saying they're dropping all the charges against me."

I squeezed his hand. "Me too." It had been an interesting few weeks. In spite of his misgivings about my information, Geoff Turnbull had put full surveillance on Terry Fitz, Jammy James and the chemical kitchen. They'd swooped in the early hours of Friday morning. They'd actually caught Terry Fitz red-handed in a stolen Mazda MX-5 halfway down the M40 with trade plates and five kilos of crack in the boot. A dozen bodies had been remanded in custody at Saturday morning's Magistrates' Court. According to Ruth, nothing had come up in the interviews that even remotely implicated Richard or me. The police had even managed to establish that James and his team of dealers still had no idea who had driven off in a "stolen" car with a boot full of crack. Best of all, the police seemed to think they wouldn't need me to testify in court, which I reckoned significantly increased my chances of celebrating my thirtieth birthday. After all, Crazy Eddy wasn't the only hit man in Greater Manchester.

Speaking of Crazy Eddy, he'd been charged with murdering Cherie and attempting to murder me. According to Della, it looked like he was also going to be charged with a couple of other street shootings in Moss Side just after Easter. He was still doing the Trappist monk routine with all of the coppers who'd done their brains in trying to interview him. He hadn't even asked for a solicitor. Interestingly, it turned out that Terry Fitz had been in the Paras with Crazy Eddy, which was how Eddy had got involved as spotter for the car stealing racket. The police also suspected that Jammy James's outfit was responsible for recommending him to the child porn merchants as a hit man.

There was another connection between the two teams. It turned out that James's mob were supplying the designer drugs for the kids to the child porn gang in exchange for videos they could sell on through their own network. Or, in the case of one of Terry Fitz's cronies, hang on to for their own sick purposes. Which explained the mysterious Polaroid that had slipped down the side of the seat in the Gemini coupé.

The house in Oliver Tambo Close had been a proper little gold mine for the Vice Squad. Not only had they put a stop to the racket, they'd found the porn makers' mailing list, investigation of which was currently causing marital difficulties from Land's End to John O'Groats; or rather, from an executive housing estate in Penzance to a croft on the Shetland Isles. Served them right too. The only bleak piece of news was that the two middle-aged bastards who'd made most of the profits from the sleazy trade had legged it at the first sign of trouble. The word is they're somewhere on the Algarve, playing golf.

And the police had finally released Andrew Broderick's Leo Gemini turbo super coupé. In his shoes, I'd have been less than thrilled at being deprived of one of my company's flagship motors for so long, but Andrew was a happy man. More than two months had passed since Richard and I had started doing the groundwork to expose the fiddle that the car dealerships were up to. And not a single one of the cars we'd purchased had been reported sold to his finance company. Which meant Andrew had been absolutely right about the scam, and with every day that passed without the cars being notified, he had more ammo to fight the war for his new distribution system.

Not only that, but the vague hunch I'd had had paid off in spades. With all the aggro there had been the day after the bank holiday, I'd completely forgotten Julia was supposed to be sending me a fax. When I finally got out of hospital, it was sitting in my in-tray, buried in a pile of correspondence that Shelley had been carefully nurturing for me.

What I'd asked Julia for was a company check on both Richmond Credit Finance and the chain of car dealerships that had been the main target of our investigation. It wasn't difficult to come by the information. The only reason we don't have it on-line ourselves is that it's more cost-effective for us to get the info from Josh than to subscribe to the appropriate database. Anyway, when I'd been able to get my eyes to focus properly, I'd compared the two sets of directors. Surprise, surprise. The managing director and principal shareholder of Richmond Credit Finance was the wife of the managing director and principal shareholder of the garages, an interesting coincidence that is currently occupying some of the working hours of Detective Chief Inspector Della Prentice.

So, instead of trying to bully us into cutting our bill, Andrew was keen to make sure we felt Mortensen and Brannigan were properly rewarded for our efforts. I wasn't about to argue with him.

After the tower, there was nothing for it but fish and chips. I suggested beating the traffic by going back to Harry Ramsden's in Manchester, and the idea was supported by two votes to one. To take Davy's mind off his disappointment, we challenged him to a race back to the car. We let him win, of course. He looked much more appealing than the Rolls-Royce silver lady sitting on the bonnet of my slightly shop soiled, midnight blue Leo Gemini turbo super coupé GLXi. Some days you eat the bear.

# CLEAN BREAK

*To Chelsea fans everywhere,*
*in deepest sympathy;*
*God knows, you need something to*
*cheer you up.*

# ACKNOWLEDGEMENTS

The usual gang all let me pick their brains to make this a better and more accurate book than it would otherwise have been—Coop, Uncle Lee, BB, Paula, Jai, Brother Brian, Lisanne and Jane, and Julia. I also scrounged assistance from Frankie Hegarty, Fairy Baillie and Diana Muir. Don't blame them if you spot any mistake. To anyone who recognizes where we went on our holidays—my heartfelt sympathies.

# 1

I don't know much about art, but I know what I don't like. I don't like paintings that go walkabout after I've set up the security system. I especially don't like them when I've packed my business partner off to the Antipodes for two months with the calm assurance that I can handle things while he's gone.

The painting in question was a small Monet. When I say small, I mean in size, not in value. It would barely cover the hole my lover Richard punched in the wall of his living room in a moment of drunken ecstasy when Eric Cantona clinched the double for Manchester United, but it was worth a good dozen times as much as both our adjoining bungalows put together. Which, incidentally, they never will be. The painting depicted an apple tree in blossom and not a lot else. You could tell it was an apple tree; according to our office manager Shelley, that's because it was painted quite early on in Monet's career, before his eyesight began to go and his whole world started to look like an Impressionist painting. Imagine, a whole artistic movement emanating from one bloke's duff eyesight. Amazing what you can learn from the Open University. Shelley started a degree course last year, and what she doesn't know about the history of art I'm certainly not qualified to uncover. It's not one of the course options in Teach Yourself Private Dicking.

The Monet in question, called, imaginatively enough, *Apple Trees in Blossom*, belonged to Henry Naismith, Lord of the Manor of Birchfield with Polver. Henry to his friends, and, thanks to John Major's classless society, to mere tradespeople like me. There were no airs and graces with Henry, but that didn't mean he didn't hide his thoughts and feelings behind his charming façade. That's how I knew it was serious when I picked up the phone to his perfect vowels that September morning. "Kate? Henry Naismith," he started. I leaned back in my chair, expecting the usual cheery chat about his recent exploits before we got down to the nuts and bolts. Not today. "Can you come over to the house?" he asked.

I straightened up. This sounded like the kind of start to a Monday morning that makes me wish I'd stayed in bed. "When did you have in mind, Henry?"

"As soon as you can. We ah . . . we had a burglary in the night and a chap from the police is popping round for more details. He'll want to know things about the security system that I probably won't be able to answer, and I'd be awfully grateful if you could take a run over." All this barely pausing for breath, never mind giving me the opportunity to ask questions.

I didn't have to check the diary to know that I had nothing more pressing than routine inquiries into the whereabouts of a company chairman whose directors were rather eager to ask him some questions about the balance sheet. "No problem," I said. "What's missing?" I prayed it was going to be the TV and the video.

No such luck. There was silence on the end of the phone. I thought I could hear Henry drawing in a deep breath. "The Monet," he said tersely.

My stomach clenched. Birchfield Place was the first security system I'd designed and watched installed. My partner Bill Mortensen is the security expert, and he'd checked my work, but it was still down to me. "I'm leaving now," I said.

I drove out through the southern suburbs to the motorway on automatic pilot. Even the inevitable, ubiquitous roadworks didn't impinge. I was too busy reviewing Mortensen and Brannigan's involvement with Henry Naismith. When I'd seen his original appointment in the office diary, I'd thought Shelley was at the wind-up, especially since I'd been having one of my periodic anti-monarchy rants only the day before, triggered by the heir to the throne asserting that what was wrong with the country was not enough Shakespeare and smacking of small children. Once I realized the appointment was for real, I'd expected some chinless wonder with the sort of inbred stupidity that's only found among the aristocracy and the population of isolated mountain villages. I couldn't have been more wrong, on both counts.

Henry Naismith was in his late twenties, built like an Australian lifeguard with the blond hair to match and with more than enough chin to provide a boxer with a target. According to *Who's Who*, his only listed recreations were sailing and ocean yacht racing, something I could have guessed for myself the first time I saw him. He had sailor's eyes, always looking beyond me to some distant horizon only he could see. His face was burnished a ruddy brown by wind and sun, apart from the white creases round those dark blue eyes. He'd been educated at Marlborough and New College, Oxford. Even though I'd grown up there, I didn't think his city of dreaming spires and mine of car factories would give us much in common to reminisce about. He had the same clipped accent as Prince Charles, but in spite of that and everything else, I liked him. I liked anybody who was prepared to get off their backsides and graft. And Henry could graft, no messing. Anyone who tells you yacht racing is a holiday doesn't know an anchor from a wanker.

The newspaper archive database that we use had coloured in the outline. Henry had inherited his title, a black and white Tudor manor house in Cheshire, a clutch of valuable paintings and not a lot of readies a couple of years before when his parents had been caught in an avalanche in some chic Alpine resort. Henry had been sailing in the Caribbean at the time. Life's a bitch, and then you marry one. Only Henry hadn't. Married, that is. He was right up there in the gossip columnists' lists of eligible bachelors. Maybe not in the top twenty, on account of the lack of dosh, but the good looks and the tasty gaff put him in the running nevertheless.

Henry had come to us precisely because of the serious deficiencies in the cash flow area. Because his father hadn't anticipated dying at the age of forty-seven, he hadn't got round to the sort of arrangements the landed gentry usually make to avoid the Exchequer getting their mitts on the widow's mite. Having done his sums, Henry realized the only way he was going to be able to hang on to the house and the art collection and still spend half the year at the helm of a racing yacht was to bite the bullet and open Birchfield Place to the day-trippers.

The great British public are notoriously sticky-fingered on the stately home circuit. You wouldn't think it to look at the coachloads of little old ladies that roll up on bank holidays, but they'll walk off with anything that isn't actually nailed down, and one or two things that are. This makes insurance companies even more twitchy than usual when it comes to providing cover, which in turn makes the security business a nice little earner for private investigation agencies like us. These days, security makes up about a quarter of our annual turnover, which is why Bill and I had decided I needed to learn that side of the business.

It's impossible to make any building impregnable, unless you brick up the doors and windows, which makes it hard to get a decent light to do your petit point. The best you can do is make it obvious that you've made it as hard as possible to get in, so the prospective burglar goes away discouraged and turns over the next manor down the road. To make sure I got it right, as well as picking Bill's brains I'd consulted my old friend Dennis, himself a recovering burglar. "You know the one deterrent, Brannigan?" Dennis had demanded.

"Heat-seeking thermonuclear missiles?" I'd hazarded.

"A dog. You get a big Alsatian, give him the run of the place and your professional thief doesn't want to know. When I was at it, there wasn't an alarm system in the world that I wouldn't have a pop at. But dogs? Forget it."

Unfortunately, clients aren't too keen on having Rottweilers running around on their priceless Oriental carpets. They're too worried about finding dog hairs—or worse—on the Hepplewhite. So Birchfield Place had relied, like most stately homes, on a state-of-the-art mix of hard-wired detectors on doors and windows, passive infrared detectors at all key points and pressure-activated alert pads in front of any items of significance. Given the fail-safes I'd put in place, I couldn't for the life of me see how anyone could have got through my system undetected without setting off enough bells to drive Quasimodo completely round the twist.

I turned off the motorway and headed into the depths of the leafy Cheshire stockbroker, soap star and football player belt. As usual, I almost missed the gap in the tall hedgerow that marked the end of Birchfield Place's drive. The trippers' entrance was round the back, but I had no intention of parking in a field half a mile from the house. I yanked the wheel round just in time and turned on to an arrow ribbon of road curling between fields where placid sheep didn't even glance up from their chewing as I passed. I always feel slightly edgy out in the country; I don't know the names of anything and very quickly develop anxiety about where my next meal is coming from. Give me an urban landscape where no sensible sheep would think for even a fleeting moment it might safely graze. The field gave way to thick coppices of assorted trees that looked like they'd been on the planet longer than my Granny Brannigan. Then, suddenly, the drive took a sharp right-hand bend and I shot out of the trees to a full frontal view of Birchfield Place.

Built by some distant Naismith who had done some unmen-
tionable service to his monarch, the house looked as if it should
be on a postcard or a jigsaw. The passage of time had skewed
its black beams and white panels just enough to make sure no
self-respecting building society would grant you a mortgage on
it. It never looked real to me.

I pulled up beside an anonymous Ford which I assumed
belonged to the police on account of the radio. A peacock
screamed in the distance, more shattering to my composure
than any amount of midnight sirens. I only knew it was a peacock because Henry had told me the first time one had made me
jump out of my skin. Before I could reach out for the ancient
bell-pull, the door swung open and Henry smiled apologetically
at me. "I really appreciate this, Kate," he said.

"All part of the service," I said reassuringly. "The police
here?"

"An Inspector Mellor from the Art Squad," Henry said
as he led the way across the inner courtyard to the Great Hall,
where the Impressionist paintings hung incongruously. "He
doesn't say much."

We passed through the Hall Porch, whose solid oak door
looked like it had taken a few blows from a heavy sledgehammer.
At the door of the Great Hall, I put out a hand to delay Henry.
"So what exactly happened?"

Henry rubbed his jaw. "The alarm woke me. Just before
three, according to the clock. I checked the main panel. It said
Hall Porch, Great Hall door, Great Hall and pressure pads. I
phoned the police to confirm it wasn't a false alarm, and ran
downstairs. When I got to the hall, there was nobody in sight
and the Monet was gone. They must have been in and out again
in less than five minutes." He sighed. "They obviously knew
what they were looking for."

"Didn't the beeper on the courtyard security lights waken
you?" I asked, puzzled.

Henry looked sheepish. "I turned the beeper off. We've been having a bit of a problem with foxes, and I got fed up with being wakened up night after night." I said nothing. I hoped the look on my face said it for me. "I know, I know," Henry said. "I don't think Inspector Mellor's overly impressed either. Shall we?"

I followed him into the hall. It was a surprisingly bright room for the period. It was two storeys high, with a whitewashed vaulted roof and gallery for Blondel unplugged. The wall that gave on to the inner courtyard had a couple of feet of wood panelling above floor level, then it was hundreds of tiny leaded panes of glass to a height of about eight feet. The outer wall's panelling was about four feet high before it gave way to more windows. I didn't envy the window cleaner. At the far end was a raised dais where Henry's distant ancestors had sat and lorded it over the plebs and railed against the iniquities of the window tax. It was around the dais that the paintings hung. A tall, thin man was stooped like a crane over the space where the Monet used to be. As we entered, he turned towards us and fixed me with a glum stare.

Henry performed the introductions while Inspector Mellor and I weighed each other up. He looked more patrician than Henry, with a high forehead over a beaky nose and a small, cupid's bow mouth. At his request, I ran him through the security arrangements. He nodded noncommittally as he listened, then said, "Not a lot more you could have done, short of having CCTV."

"Professional job, yeah?" I said.

"No doubt about it. They obviously chose their target, cased the place thoroughly, then did a quick in and out. No identifiable forensic traces, according to my colleagues who turned up after the event." Mellor looked as depressed as I felt.

"Does it put you in mind of anyone in particular?" I asked.

Mellor shrugged. "I've seen jobs like this, but we haven't managed an arrest on any of them yet."

Henry closed his eyes and sighed. "Is there any chance of getting my Monet back?" he asked wearily.

"If I'm honest, sir, not a lot. Thieves like this only take what they've already got a market for," Mellor said. "Sooner or later, we'll get a lucky break and we'll nail them. It could be on this case. What I'd like to do is send a couple of my lads over when your staff are next in. These thieves will have been round the house more than once. It's just possible one of your attendants noticed repeat visitors."

"They'll be in at half past nine on Thursday," Henry said. "The house is closed to the public on Mondays, Tuesdays and Wednesdays, excepting bank holidays."

Mellor turned away and spent a few minutes studying the Boudin, the Renoir and the two Pissarros that flanked the space where the Monet had been. "Personally," he said softly, "I'd have gone for the Boudin."

Not me. The Monet would have looked much better with my colour scheme. But maybe Inspector Mellor's living room was blue-based rather than green, cream and peach. While Henry escorted Mellor off the premises, I mooched around the hall, wondering what to do next. Mellor's plan to interrogate the staff had disposed of the only idea I had for pursuing any kind of investigation. I slumped in the attendant's chair by the door and stared down the hall at the wires sticking out of the ancient panelling where the Monet had been attached to the alarm system and the wall. Inspiration failed to strike; but then, nothing does in this country any more.

When Henry came back, I forced myself upright and said brightly, "Well, Henry, Mellor didn't sound too optimistic about what the forces of law and order can achieve. Looks like it's down to me to get your Monet back."

Henry tugged at the lobe of his ear and looked uncomfortable. "Is there much point, Kate?" he asked. "I mean, if the specialists don't know where to start looking, how can you expect to succeed?"

"People have a tendency to tell me things they don't necessarily want to share with the police. And that includes insurance companies. I also have more unorthodox sources of information. I'm sure I can develop leads the police will never encounter." It was all true. Well, all except the last sentence.

"I don't know, Kate. These are professional thieves. Looking at the state of the porch door, they're clearly quite comfortable with a considerable degree of violence. I'm not sure I'm entirely happy about you pursuing them," he said dubiously.

"Henry, I might only be five foot three, but I can look after myself," I said, trying not to think about the last occasion where I'd told the men in my life the same damn lie. The scar on my head was just a distant twinge when I brushed my hair now, but the scar inside went a lot deeper. I hadn't exactly lost my bottle; I'd just acquired an overdose of wariness.

"Besides," I carried on, seeing his look of frank disbelief, "you're entitled to the first thirty hours of my time for free, according to your contract."

"Ah. Yes. Of course." His reserve was nailed firmly in place again, the eyes locked on the middle distance.

"Apart from anything else, me nosing around will convince your insurance company that you're not trying it on," I added.

His eyes narrowed, like a man who's seen a bloody great wave heading straight for his bows. "Why should they think that?" he said sharply.

"It wouldn't be the first time somebody's set up their own burglary for the insurance," I said. "It happens all the time round where I live." A frown flickered across Henry's face. "There's nothing you want to tell me, Henry, is there?" I added apprehensively.

"There's no earthly reason why I should arrange this," he said stiffly. "The police and the insurance company are welcome to check the books. We're making a profit here. House admissions are up on last year, the gift shop has increased its turnover by twenty-five per cent and the Great Hall is booked for banquets almost every Saturday between now and February. The only thing I'm concerned about is that I'm due to leave for Australia in three weeks and I'd like the matter resolved by then."

"I'd better get weaving, in that case," I said mildly.

I drove back to Manchester with a lot on my mind. I don't like secrets. It's one of the reasons I became a private eye in the first place. I especially don't like them when they're ones my client is keeping from me.

# 2

The atrium of Fortissimus Insurance told me all I needed to know about where Henry's massive premiums were going. The company had relocated in Manchester from the City, doubtless tempted by the wodges of cash being handed out by various inner city initiative programmes. They'd opted for a site five minutes' walk down Oxford Road from the rather less palatial offices of Mortensen and Brannigan. Handy, we'd thought, if they ever needed any freelance investigating, though if they had done, it hadn't been our door they'd come knocking on. They probably preferred firms with the same steel-and-glass taste in interior decor, and prices to match.

Like a lot of new office complexes in Manchester, Fortissimus had smacked a brand new modern building behind a grandiose Victorian façade. In their case, they'd acquired the front of what had been a rather grand hotel, its marble and granite buffed to a shine more sparkling than its native century had ever seen. The entrance hall retained some of the original character, but the glassed-in atrium beyond the security desk was one hundred per cent *fin de* quite another *siècle*. The pair of receptionists had clearly absorbed their customer care course. Their grooming was immaculate, their smiles would have made a crocodile proud, and the mid-Atlantic twang in their "Good

morning, how may I help you?" stopped short of making my ears
bleed. Needless to say, they were as misleading as the building's
façade. After I'd given them my card, asked for Michael Haroun
and told them his department, I still had to kick my heels for
ten minutes while they ran their debriefing on the weekend's
romantic encounters, rang Mr Haroun, filled out a visitor's pass
and told me Mr Haroun would be waiting for me at the lift.

I emerged on the fifth floor to find they'd been economical
with the truth. There was no Mr Haroun, and no one behind
the desk marked "Claims Inquiries" either. Before I could decide
which direction to head in, a door down the hallway opened
and someone backed out, saying, "And I want to compare those
other cases. Karen, dig out the files, there's a love."

He swivelled round on the balls of his feet and *déjà vu*
swept over me. Confused, I just stood and stared as he walked
towards me. When he got closer, he held out his hand and said,
"Ms Brannigan? Michael Haroun."

For a moment, I was speechless and paralysed. I must have
been gawping like a starving goldfish, for he frowned and said,
"You are Ms Brannigan?" Then, suspicion appeared in his liquid
sloe eyes. "What's the matter? Am I not what you expected? I
can assure you, I am head of the claims division."

Power returned to my muscles and I hurriedly reached out
and shook his hand. "Sorry," I stammered. "Yes, I . . . Sorry,
you're the spitting image of . . . somebody," I stumbled on. "I
was just taken aback, that's all."

He gave me a look that told me he'd already decided I was
either a racist pig or I didn't have all my chairs at home. His smile
was strained as he said, "I didn't realize I had a doppelgänger.
Shall we go through to my office and talk?"

Wordlessly, I nodded and followed his broad shoulders
back down the hall. He moved like a man who played a lot of
sport. It wasn't hard to imagine him in the same role as I'd first
seen his likeness.

When I was about fourteen, we'd gone on a school trip to the British Museum. I'd been so engrossed in the Rosetta Stone, I'd got separated from the rest of the group and wandered round for ages looking for them. That's how I stumbled on the Assyrian bas-reliefs. As soon as I saw them, I understood for the first time in my life that it wasn't entirely bullshit when critics said that great art speaks directly to us. These enormous carvings of the lion hunt didn't so much speak as resonate inside my chest like the bass note of an organ. I fell in love with the archers and the charioteers, their shoulder-length hair curled as tight as poodle fur, their profiles keen as sparrowhawks. I must have spent an hour there that day. Every time I went to London on shopping trips after that, I always found an excuse to slip away from my mates as they trawled Oxford Street so I could nip to the museum for a quick tryst with King Ashurbanipal. If Aslan had come along and breathed life into the carving of the Assyrian king, he would have walked off the wall looking just like Michael Haroun, his glowing skin the colour of perfect roast potatoes. OK, so he'd swapped the tunic for a Paul Smith shirt, Italian silk tie and chinos, but you don't make much progress up the corporate ladder wearing a mini-skirt unless you're a woman. Just one look at Michael Haroun and I was an adoring adolescent all over again, Richard a distant memory.

I followed Haroun meekly into his office. The opulence of the atrium hadn't quite made it this high. The furniture was functional rather than designed to impress. At least he overlooked the recently renovated Rochdale Canal (European funding), though the view of the Canal Café must have been a depressing reminder of the rest of the world enjoying itself while he was working. We settled down on the L-shaped sofa at right angles to each other, my adolescent urge to jump on him held in check by the low coffee table between us. Haroun dumped the file he'd been carrying on the table. "I hear good things about your agency, Ms Brannigan," he said. From his tone, I gathered he couldn't quite square what he'd heard with my moonstruck gaze.

I forced myself to get a grip and remember I was twice the age of that romantic teenager. "You've obviously been talking to the clients who haven't been burgled," I said in something approaching my normal voice.

"No security system is burglar-proof," he said gloomily.

"But some are better than others. And ours are better than most."

"That's certainly how it looked when we first agreed the premium. It's one of the factors we consider when we set the rate. That and how high-risk the area is."

"You don't have to tell me. My postcode is M13," I complained.

He pulled a face and sucked his breath in sharply, the way plumbers are trained to do when they look at your central heating system. "And I thought you security consultants made a good living."

"It's not all a hellhole," I said sharply.

He held his hands up and grinned. I felt the years slide away again and struggled to stay in the present. "Henry Naismith called to say you'd be coming in. He faxed me a preliminary claim," he said.

"I'm investigating the theft on Henry's behalf, and he thought it might be helpful if we had a chat," I said briskly.

"My pleasure," he said. "Of course, one of our staff investigators will also be looking into it, but I see no reason why we can't talk to you as well. Can you run it past me?"

I went through everything I'd learned from Henry and Inspector Mellor. Haroun took notes. "Just as a matter of interest," I finished up, "Inspector Mellor mentioned they'd had other burglaries with a similar style. Were any of them insured with you?"

Haroun nodded. "Yes, unfortunately. Off the top of my head, I'd say three others in the last nine months. And that's where we have a problem."

"We as in you and me, or we as in Fortissimus?"

"We as in Mr Naismith and Fortissimus."

"Does that mean you're not going to tell me about it?"

Haroun stared down at the file. "Client confidentiality. You should understand that."

"I wouldn't be here if Henry didn't trust me. Why don't you give him a call and confirm that you can tell me anything you would tell him? That way, I get it from the horse's mouth rather than via Chinese whispers."

His straight brows twitched. "Even if he agreed, it wouldn't be fair of me to have the conversation with you before I have it with him."

"So get Henry over. I don't mind waiting." As long as I can keep looking at you, I added mentally.

Haroun inclined his head, conceding. "I'll call him," he said.

He was gone for the best part of ten minutes. Instead of fishing a computer magazine out of my shoulder bag, or dictating a report into my microcassette recorder, I daydreamed. What about is nobody's business but mine.

When Haroun came back, he looked serious. "I've explained the situation to Mr Naismith, and he was quite insistent that I should discuss the ramifications with you."

I was too well brought up to say, "I told you so," but according to Richard I've cornered the market in smug smiles. I hoped I wasn't displaying one of them right then. "So, tell me about it," I said, locking eyes.

Haroun held my gaze for a long few seconds before turning back to his file. "As I said, we've had other incidents very similar to this. These thefts have all been from similar properties— medium-sized period properties that are open to the public. In each case, the thieves have broken in as near to the target as they could get. In a couple of cases, they've smashed through a window, but in a property like Birchfield Place, that obviously wasn't appropriate. They ignore the alarms, go straight to the object they're after, whip it off the wall or out of its case and get out. We estimate the longest they've been inside a property is five minutes. In most cases, that's barely enough time to alert the police or the security guards, never mind get anyone to the site."

"Very professional," I commented. "And?"

"We're very unhappy about it. It's costing us a lot of money. Normally, we'd simply have to bite the bullet and increase premiums accordingly."

"I hear the sound of a 'but' straining at the leash," I said.

"You have very acute hearing, Ms Brannigan."

"Kate," I smiled.

"Well, Kate," he said, echoing the smile, "here comes the 'but.' The first of our clients to be robbed in this way was targeted again three months later. Following that, my bosses took a policy decision that in future, after stately homes had been robbed once, we would refuse to reinsure unless and until their security was increased to an acceptable level."

He might have looked like an ancient Assyrian, but Michael Haroun sounded exactly like a twentieth-century insurance man. We won't make a drama out of a crisis; we'll make a full-scale tragic grand opera. Pay your spiralling premiums for ten years good as gold, and then when you really need us, we'll be gone like thieves in the night. Nothing like it for killing adolescent fantasies stone dead. "And what exactly is your definition of 'an acceptable level'?" I asked, hoping he was receiving the cold sarcasm I was sending.

"Obviously, it varies from case to case."

"In Henry's case then?"

Haroun shrugged. "I'd have to get one of our assessors out there to make an accurate judgement."

"Go on, stick your neck out. I know that comes as easy to an insurance man as it does to an ostrich, but give it a go." I kept my voice light with an effort. This was my security system he was damning.

He scowled, obviously needled. "Based on past experience, I would suggest a security guard on a 24-hour basis in the rooms where the most valuable items are sited."

I shook my head in disbelief. "You really believe in getting shut of clients who have the temerity to get robbed, don't you?"

"On the contrary. We want to ensure that neither we nor our clients are exposed to unacceptable losses," he said defensively.

"The cost of that kind of security could make the difference between profit and loss to an operation the size of Henry's. You must know that."

Haroun spread his hands out and shrugged. "He can always put up the admission charges if it's that crucial to the economics of running the place."

"So you're saying that as of now Birchfield Place is uninsured?"

"No, no, you misunderstand me. But we will retain a portion of the payout on the stolen property until the security levels are rendered acceptable. Kate, we do care about our clients, but we have a business to run too, you must see that." His eyes pleaded, and my fury melted. This was bad for my business, so I forced myself to my feet.

"We'll keep in touch," I said.

"I'd like that," he said, getting to his feet and nailing me with the sincerity in his voice.

As we walked back to the lift, my brain checked in again. "One more thing," I said. "How come I haven't been reading about these raids in the papers?"

Haroun smiled the thin smile of a lizard. "We like to keep things like this as low profile as possible," he said. "It does our clients' business no good at all if the public gain the impression that the choicest exhibits in their collections are no longer there. The thefts have been quite widely scattered, and the policy has been only to release the information to local press, and even then to keep it very low key. You know the sort of thing: 'Thieves broke in to Bloggs Manor last night, but were disturbed before they could remove the Manor's priceless collection of bottle tops.'"

"You just omit to mention that they had it away on their toes with the Constable," I said cynically.

"Something like that," he agreed. The lift pinged and I stepped inside as the doors opened. "Nice talking to you, Kate."

"We must do it again some time," I said before the doors cut him off from me. The day was looking up. Not only had I met Michael Haroun, but I knew where to go next.

I'm convinced that the security staff at the *Manchester Evening Chronicle* think I work there. Maybe it's because I know the door combination. Or maybe it's because I'm in and out of the building with a confident wave several times a week. Either way, it's handy to be able to stroll in and out at will. Their canteen is cheap and cheerful, a convenient place to refuel when I'm at the opposite end of town from the office. That day, though, I wasn't after a bacon butty and a mug of tea. My target was Alexis Lee, the *Chronicle*'s crime correspondent and my best buddy.

I walked briskly down the newsroom, no one paying any attention. I could probably walk off with the entire computer network before anyone would notice or try to stop me. Mind you, if I'd laid a finger on the newsdesk TV, I'd have been lynched before I'd got five yards.

I knew Alexis was at her desk. I couldn't actually see her through the wall of luxuriant foliage that surrounds her corner of the office. But the spiral of smoke climbing towards the air-conditioning vent was a clear indicator that she was there. When they installed the computer terminals at the *Chronicle*, the management tried to make the newsroom a no-smoking zone. The policy lasted about five minutes. Separating journalists from nicotine is about as easy as separating a philandering government minister from his job.

I stuck my head round the screen of variegated green stuff. Alexis was leaning back in her seat, feet propped up on the rim of her wastepaper bin, dabbing her cigarette vaguely at her mouth as she frowned at her terminal. I checked out her anarchic black hair. Its degree of chaos is a fairly accurate barometer of her stress levels. The more uptight she gets, the more she runs her hands through it. Today, it looked like I could risk interrupting her without getting a rich gobful of Scouse abuse.

"I thought they paid you to work," I said, moving through the gap in the leaves into her jungle cubbyhole.

She swung round and grinned. "All right, KB?" she rasped in her whisky-and-cigarettes voice.

"I think I'm in love, but apart from that, I'm fine." I pulled up the other chair.

Alexis snorted and went into Marlene Dietrich growl. *"Falling in love again, never wanted to,"* she groaned. *"Though I'm ninety-two, I can't help it.* I've told you before, it's about time you got shut of the wimp." She and Richard maintain this pretence of hostility. He's always giving her a bad time for being a siren chaser, and she pretends to despise him for devoting his life to the trivia of rock journalism. But underneath, I know there's a lot of affection and respect.

"Who said anything about Richard?" I asked innocently.

"And there's me thinking you two were getting things sorted out between you," she sighed. "So who's the lucky man? I mean, I'm assuming that you haven't seen the light, and it is a fella."

"His name's Michael Haroun. But don't worry, it's only lust. It'll pass as soon as I have a cold shower."

"So what does he do, this sex object?"

I pulled a face. "You're going to laugh," I said.

"Probably," Alexis agreed. "So you might as well get it over with."

"He's in insurance."

I'd been right. She did laugh, a deep, throaty guffaw that shook the leaves. I half expected an Amazonian parrot to fly out from among the undergrowth and join in. "You really know how to pick them, don't you?" Alexis wheezed.

"You don't pick sex objects, they just happen," I said frostily. "Anyway, nothing's going to happen, so it's all academic anyway. Things between me and Richard might have seen better days, but it's nothing we can't fix."

"So you don't want me to call Chris and get her to build a brick wall across the conservatory?"

Alexis's girlfriend Chris is the architect who designed the conservatory that runs along the back of the two houses Richard and I live in, linking them yet allowing us our own space. It had been the perfect solution for two people who want to be together but whose lifestyles are about as compatible as Burton and Taylor. "Restrain yourself, Alexis. I'm not about to let my hormones club my brain into submission."

"Is that it, then? You come in here, interrupting the creative process, just to tell me nothing's happening?"

"No, I only gave you the gossip so you wouldn't complain that I was only here to exploit you," I said.

Alexis blew out a cloud of smoke and a sigh. "All right, what do you want to know?"

"Is that any way to speak to a valued contact who's brought you a story?" I asked innocently.

Alexis tipped forward in her seat and crushed out her cigarette in an already brimming ashtray. "Why do I have the feeling that this is the kind of gift that takes more assembling than an Airfix kit?"

# 3

I left Alexis to hassle the police of six counties in search of the story we both knew was lurking somewhere and headed back to Mortensen and Brannigan. Shelley was busy on the phone, so I went straight through to my office. I stopped in my tracks on the threshold. I heard Shelley finish her call and swung round to glare at her. "What exactly is that?" I demanded.

She didn't look up from the note she was writing. "What does it look like? It's a weeping fig."

"It's fake," I said through gritted teeth.

"Silk," she corrected me absently.

"And that makes it OK?"

Shelley finally looked up. "Every six weeks you buy a healthy, thriving, living plant. Five weeks later, it looks like locust heaven. The weeping fig will have paid for itself within six months, and even you can't kill a silk plant," she said in matter-of-fact tones that made my fingers itch to get round her throat.

"If I wanted a schneid plant, I'd have bought one," I said.

"You sound . . ."

"'Like one of my kids,'" I finished, mimicking her calm voice. "You don't understand, do you? It's the challenge. One day, I'm going to find a plant that runs riot for me."

"By which time the planet will be a desert," Shelley said, tossing her head so that the beads she had plaited into her hair jangled like a bag of marbles.

I didn't dignify that with a reply. I simply marched into my office, picked up the weeping fig and dropped it next to her desk. "You like it so much, you live with it," I said, stomping back to my office. If she was going to treat me like one of her teenage kids, I might as well enjoy the tantrum. I pulled the brownish remains of the asparagus fern out of the bin and defiantly dumped it on the windowsill.

Before I could do anything more, my phone rang. "What now?" I barked at Shelley.

"Call for you. A gentleman who refuses to give his name."

"Did you tell him we don't do matrimonials?"

"Of course I did. I'm not the one who's premenstrual."

I bit back a snarl as Shelley put the call through. "Kate Brannigan," I said. "How can I help you?"

"I need your help, Ms Brannigan. It's an extremely confidential matter. Brian Chalmers from PharmAce recommended you."

"We're noted for our client confidentiality," I reeled off. "As you doubtless know if you've spoken to Brian. But I do need to know who I'm talking to."

There was a moment's hesitation, long enough for me to hear sufficient background noise to realize my caller was speaking from a bar. "My name's Trevor Kerr. I think the company I run is being blackmailed, and I need to talk to you about it."

"Fine," I said. "Why don't I come round to your office this afternoon and have a chat about it?"

"Christ, no," Kerr said, clearly alarmed. "The last thing I want is for the blackmailers to find out I'm talking to a private detective."

One of the ones that watches too many movies. That was all I needed to make my day. "No problem. You come to me."

"I don't think that's a good idea. You see, I think they're watching me."

Just when you thought it was safe to pick up the phone . . . "I know how disturbing threats can be when you're not accustomed to being on the receiving end," I tried. "Perhaps we could meet on neutral ground. Say in the lounge of the Midland?"

The reassuring tone hadn't worked. "No," Kerr said urgently. "Not in public. It's got to look completely normal. Have you got a boyfriend, Ms Brannigan?"

I should have put the phone down then and there, I realized four hours later as I tried to explain to Richard that a crumpled cream linen suit might be fine for going on the razz with Mick Hucknall, but there was no way it would help him to pass as a member of the Round Table. "Bloody hell, Brannigan," he grumbled. "I'm old enough to dress myself."

I ignored him and raked through his wardrobe, coming up with a fairly sober double-breasted Italian suit in dark navy. "This is more like it," I said.

Richard scowled. "I only wear that to funerals."

I threw it on the bed. "Not true. You wore it to your cousin's wedding."

"You forgotten her husband already? Anyway, I don't see why you're making me get dressed up like a tailor's dummy. After the last time I helped you out, you swore you'd never let me near your work again," he whinged as he shrugged out of the linen jacket.

"Believe me, if Bill wasn't out of the country, I wouldn't be asking you," I said grimly. "Besides, not even you can turn a Round Table treasure hunt and potluck supper into a life-threatening situation."

Richard froze. "That's a bit below the belt, Brannigan," he said bitterly.

"Yeah, well, I'm going next door to find something suitably naff in my own wardrobe. Come through when you're ready."

I walked down Richard's hall and cut through his living room to the conservatory. Back in my own house, I allowed myself a few moments of deep breathing to regain my equilibrium. A few months before, I had enlisted Richard's help in what should have been a straightforward case of car fraud. Only, as they say in all the worst police dramas, it all went pear-shaped. Spectacularly so. Richard ended up behind bars, his life in jeopardy, and I nearly got myself killed tracking down the real villains. As if that hadn't been enough, I'd also been landed with looking after his eight-year-old son Davy. And me with the maternal instincts of a Liquorice Allsort.

The physical scars had healed pretty quickly, but the real damage was to our relationship. You'd think he'd have been grateful that I sorted everything out. Instead, he'd been distant, sarcastic and out a lot. It hadn't been grim all the time, of course. If it had been, I'd have knocked it on the head weeks earlier. We still managed to have fun together, and sometimes for nearly a week things would be just like they used to be: lots of laughs, a few nights out, communal Chinese takeaways and spectacular sex. Then the clouds would descend, usually when I was up to the eyeballs in some demanding job.

This was the first time since our run-in with the drug warlords that I'd asked Richard to do anything connected with work. I'd argued with Trevor Kerr that there must be a less complicated way for us to meet, but Clever Trevor was convinced that he was right to take precautions. I nearly asked him why he was hiring a dog and still barking himself, but I bit my tongue. Business hadn't been so great lately that I could afford to antagonize new clients before they were actually signed up.

With a sigh, I walked into my own bedroom and considered the options. Richard says I don't have a wardrobe, just a collection of disguises. Looking at the array of clothes in front of me, I was tempted to agree with him. I pulled out a simple tailored dress in rough russet silk with a matching bolero jacket. I'd bought it while I'd been bodyguarding a Hollywood actress who was over here for a week to record an episode in a Granada drama series. She'd taken one look at the little black number I'd turned up in on the first evening and silently written me a cheque for five hundred pounds to go and buy "something a little more chic, hon." I'm not proud; I took the money and shopped. Alexis and I hadn't had so much fun in years.

I stepped into the dress and reached round to zip it up. Richard got there before me. He leaned forward and kissed me behind the ear. I turned to gooseflesh and shivered. "Sorry," he said. "Bad day. Let's go and see how the other half lives."

The address Trevor Kerr had given me was in Whitefield, a suburb of mostly semis just beyond the perennial roadworks on the M62. It's an area that's largely a colony of the upwardly mobile but not strictly Orthodox Jews who make up a significant proportion of Manchester's population. Beyond the streets of identical between-the-wars semis lay our destination, one of a handful of architect-designed developments where the serious money has gravitated. My plumber got the contract for one of them, and he told me about a conversation with one of his customers. My plumber thought the architect had made a mistake, because the plans showed plumbing for four dishwashers—two in the kitchen and two in the utility room. When he queried it, the customer looked at him as if he was thick as a yard of four-by-two and said, "We keep kosher and we entertain a lot." There's nothing you can say to that.

The house I'd been directed to looked more Frankenstein than Frank Lloyd Wright. It had more turrets and crenellations than Windsor Castle, all in bright red Accrington brick. "Sometimes it's nice to be potless," Richard remarked as we parked. It had a triple garage and hard-standing for half a dozen cars, but tonight was clearly party night. Richard's hot pink Volkswagen Beetle convertible looked as out of place as Cinderella at a minute past midnight. When the hostess opened the door, I smiled. "Good evening," I said. "We're with Trevor Kerr," I added.

The frosting on her immaculate coiffure spilled over on to the hostess's smile. "Do come in," she said.

The man who'd been hovering in the hall behind her stepped forward and said, "I'm Trevor Kerr." He signalled with his eyebrows towards the stairs and we followed him up into a den that looked like it had been bought clock, stock and panel from a country house. The only incongruity was the computer and fax machine smack in the middle of the desk. "We won't be disturbed here," he said. "It'll be at least half an hour before the host distributes the clues and we move off. Perhaps your friend would like to go downstairs and help himself to the buffet?"

I could hear Richard's hackles rising. "Mr Barclay is a valued associate of Mortensen and Brannigan. Anything you say is safe with him," I said stiffly. I dreaded to think how many people Richard could upset at a Round Table potluck buffet.

"That's right," he drawled. "I'm not just scenery."

Kerr looked uncomfortable but he wasn't really in a position to argue. As he settled himself in an armchair, we studied each other. Not even a hand-stitched suit could hide a body gone ruinously to seed. I was tempted to offer some fashion advice, but I didn't think he'd welcome the news that this year bellies are being worn inside the trousers. He couldn't have been much more than forty, but his eyes would have been the envy of any self-respecting bloodhound and his jowls would have set a bulldog a-quiver. The only attractive feature the man possessed was a head of thick, wavy brown hair with a faint silvering at the temples.

"Well, Mr Kerr?" I said.

He cleared his throat and said, "I run Kerrchem. You probably haven't heard of us, but we're quite a large concern. We've got a big plant out at Farnworth. We manufacture industrial cleaning materials, and we do one or two domestic products for supermarket own-brands. We pride ourselves on being a family business. Anyway, about a month ago, I got a letter in the post at home. As far as I can remember, it said I could avoid

Kerrchem ending up with the same reputation as Tylenol for a very modest sum of money."

"Product tampering," Richard said sagely.

Kerr nodded. "That's what I took it to mean."

"You said: 'as far as I can remember,'" I remarked. "Does that mean you haven't got the note?"

Kerr scowled. "That's right. I thought it was some crank. It looked ridiculous, all those letters cut out of a newspaper and Sellotaped down. I binned it. You can't blame me for that," he whined.

"No one's blaming you, Mr Kerr. It's just a pity you didn't keep the note. Has something happened since then to make you think they were serious?"

Kerr looked away and pulled a fat cigar from his inside pocket. As he went through the performance of lighting it, Richard leaned forward in his seat. "A man has died since then, hasn't he, Mr Kerr?" I was impressed. I didn't know what the hell he was talking about, but I was impressed.

A plume of acrid blue smoke obscured Kerr's eyes as he said, "Technically, yes. But there's no evidence that there's any connection."

"A man dies after opening a sealed container of your products, you've had a blackmail note and you don't believe there's a connection?" Richard asked, with only mild incredulity.

I could see mischief dancing behind his glasses, so I thought I'd better head this off at the pass. Any minute now, Richard would decide to start enjoying himself, completely oblivious to the fact that not everyone has the blithe disregard for human life that characterizes journalists. "Suppose you give me your version of events, Mr Kerr?"

He puffed on the cigar and I tried not to cough. "Like I said, I thought this note was some crank. Then, last week, we had a phone call from the police. They said a publican had dropped down dead at work. It seemed he'd just opened a fresh container of KerrSter. That's a universal cleanser that we produce. One of our biggest sellers to the trade. Anyway, according to the postmortem, this man had died from breathing in cyanide, which is ridiculous, because cyanide doesn't go anywhere near the KerrSter process. Nobody at our place could work out how him dying could have had anything to do with the KerrSter," he said defensively. "We weren't looking forward to the inquest, I'll be honest, but we didn't see how we could be held to blame."

"And?" I prompted him.

Kerr shifted in his seat, moving his weight from one buttock to the other in a movement I hadn't seen since *Dumbo*. "I swear I never connected it with the note I'd had. It'd completely slipped my mind. And then this morning, this came." His pudgy hand slid into his inside pocket again and emerged with a folded sheet of paper. He held it out towards me.

"Has anyone apart from you touched this?" I asked, not reaching for it.

He shook his head. "No. It came to the house, just like the other one."

"Put it down on the desk," I said, raking in my bag for a pen and my Swiss Army knife. I took the eyebrow tweezers out of their compartment on the knife and gingerly unfolded the note. It was a sheet from a glue-top A4 pad, hole-punched, narrow feint and margin. Across it, in straggling newsprint letters Sellotaped down, I read, "Bet you wish you'd done what you were told. We'll be in touch. No cops. We're watching you." The letters were a mixture of upper and lower case, and I recognized the familiar fonts of the *Manchester Evening Chronicle*. Well, that narrowed it down to a few million bodies.

I looked up and sighed. "On the face of it, it looks like your correspondent carried out his threat. Why haven't you taken this to the police, Mr Kerr? Murder and blackmail, that's what they're there for."

Kerr looked uncomfortable. "I didn't think they'd believe me," he said awkwardly. "Look at it from their point of view. My company's products have been implicated in a major tampering scandal. A man's dead. Can you imagine how much it's going to cost me to get out from under the lawsuits that are going to be flying around? There's nothing to show I didn't cobble this together myself to try and get off the hook. I bet mine are the only fingerprints on that note, and you can bet your bottom dollar that the police aren't going to waste their time hunting for industrial saboteurs they won't even believe exist. Anyway, the note says 'No cops.'"

"So you want me to find your saboteurs for you?" I asked resignedly.

"Can you?" Kerr asked eagerly.

I shrugged. "I can try."

Before we could discuss it further, there was a knock at the door and our hostess's head appeared. "Sorry to interrupt, Trevor, but we're about to distribute the treasure-hunt clues, and I know you'd hate to start at a disadvantage." She didn't invite us to join in, I noticed. Clearly my suit didn't come up to scratch.

"Be right with you, Charmian," Trevor said, hauling himself out of his chair. "My office, half past eight tomorrow morning?" he asked.

I had a lot more questions for Trevor Kerr, but they could wait. "I thought you were worried about me coming to the office?" I reminded him.

He barely paused on his way out the door. "I'll tell my secretary you're from the Health and Safety Executive," he said. "Those nosey bastards are always poking around where they're not wanted."

I shook my head in despair as he departed. Some clients are like that. Before you've agreed to work for them, they're practically on their knees. Soon as you come on board, they treat you like something nasty on their Gucci loafers. "And I thought heavy metal bands were arseholes," Richard mused.

"They are," I said. "And while we're on the subject, how come you knew about the KerrSter death?"

Richard winked and produced one of those smiles that got me tangled up with him in the first place. "Not much point in having the *Chronicle* delivered if you don't bother reading it, is there?" he asked sweetly.

"Some of us have more important things to do than laze around smoking joints and reading the papers," I snarled.

Richard pretended to look huffed. At least, I think he was pretending. "Oh well, if that's the way things are, you won't be wanting me to take you to dinner, will you?" he said airily.

"Try me," I said. There are few things in life that don't look better after aromatic crispy duck. How was I to know Trevor Kerr would be one of them?

# 4

As I waited for the security guard in charge of the barrier at Kerrchem's car park to check that I wasn't some devious industrial spy trying to sneak in to steal their secrets, I stared across at the sprawling factory, its red brick smudged black by years of industrial pollution. Somewhere inside there I'd find the end of the ball of string that would unravel to reveal a killer.

Eventually, he let me in and directed me to the administration offices. Trevor Kerr's secretary was already at her desk when I walked in at twenty-five past eight. Unfortunately, her boss wasn't. I introduced myself. "Mr Kerr's expecting me," I added.

She'd clearly been hired for her efficiency rather than her charm. "Health and Safety Executive," she said in the same tone of voice I'd have used for the VAT inspector. "Take a seat. Mr Kerr will be here soon." She returned to her word processor, attacking the keys with the ferocity of someone playing *Mortal Kombat*.

I looked around. Neither of the two chairs looked as if it had been chosen for comfort. The only available reading material was some trade journal that I wouldn't have picked up even on a twelve-hour flight with a Sylvester Stallone film as the in-flight movie. "Maybe I could make a start on the documents I need to see?" I said. "To save wasting time."

"Only Mr Kerr can authorize the release of company information to a third party," she said coldly. "He knows you're coming. I'm sure he won't keep you waiting for long."

I wished I shared her conviction. I tried to make myself comfortable and used the time to review the limited information I'd gleaned so far. After Richard and I had stuffed ourselves in a small Chinese restaurant in Whitefield, where we'd both felt seriously overdressed, I'd sat down with the previous weeks' papers and brought myself up to speed. Richard, meanwhile, had changed and gone off to some dive in Longsight to hear a local techno band who'd just landed a record deal. Frankly, I felt I'd got the best end of the bargain.

On my way through the stuttering early rush-hour traffic, I'd stopped by the office to fax my local friendly financial services expert. I needed some background on Trevor Kerr and his company, and if there was dirt to be dug, Josh Gilbert was the man. Josh and I have an arrangement: he supplies me with financial information and I buy him expensive dinners. The fact that Josh wouldn't know a scruple if it took him out to the Savoy is fine by me; I don't have to think about that, just reap the rewards.

The financial data would fill one gap in my knowledge. I hoped it would be more comprehensive than the newspaper accounts. When Joey Morton died, the media responded with ghoulish swiftness. For once, there were no government scandals to divert them, and all the papers had given the Stockport publican's death a good show. At first, I couldn't figure out how I'd missed the hue and cry, till I remembered that on the day in question I'd been out all day tracking down a key defence witness for Ruth Hunter, my favourite criminal solicitor. I'd barely had time for a sandwich on the hoof, never mind a browse through the dailies.

Joey Morton was thirty-eight, a former Third Division footballer turned publican. He and his wife Gail ran the Cob and Pen pub on the banks of the infant Mersey. Joey had gone down to the cellar to clean the beer pipes, taking a new container of KerrSter. Joey was proud of his real ale, and he never let anyone else near the cellarage. When he hadn't reappeared by opening time, Gail had sent one of the bar staff down to fetch him. The barman found his boss in a crumpled heap on the floor, the KerrSter sitting open beside him. The police had revealed that the postmortem indicated Joey had died as a result of inhaling hydrogen cyanide gas.

The pathologist's job had been made easier by the barman, who reported he'd smelt bitter almonds as soon as he'd entered the cramped cellar. Kerrchem had immediately denied that their product could possibly have caused the death, and the police had informed a waiting world that they were treating Joey's death as suspicious. Since then, the story seemed to have died, as always happens when there's a dearth of shocking revelations.

It didn't seem likely that Joey Morton could have died as a result of some ghastly error inside the Kerrchem factory. The obvious conclusion was industrial sabotage. The key questions were when and by whom. Was it an inside job? Was it a disgruntled former employee? Was it an outsider looking for blackmail money? Or was it a rival trying to annex Trevor Kerr's market? Killing people seemed a bit extreme, but as I know from bitter experience, the trouble with hiring outside help to do your dirty work is that things often get dangerously out of hand.

It was ten to nine when Trevor Kerr barged in. His eyes looked like the only treasure he'd found the night before had been in the bottom of a bottle. "You Miss Brannigan, then?" he greeted me. If he was harbouring dreams of an acting career, I could only hope that Kerrchem wasn't going to fold. I followed him into his office, catching an unappealing whiff of Scotch revisited blended with Polo before we moved into the aroma

of stale cigars and lemon furniture polish. Clearly, the Spartan
motif didn't extend beyond the outer office. Trevor Kerr had
spared no expense to make his office comfortable. That is, if
you find gentlemen's clubs comfortable. Leather wing armchairs
surrounded a low table buffed to a mirror sheen. Trevor's desk
was repro, but what it lacked in class, it made up for in size.
All they'd need to stage the world snooker championships on
it would be a bit of green baize. That and clear the clutter. The
walls were hung with old golfing prints. If his bulk was anything
to go by, golf was something Trevor Kerr honoured more in the
breach than the observance.

He dumped his briefcase by the desk and settled in behind
it. I chose the armchair nearest him. I figured if I waited till I
was invited, I'd be past my sell-by date. "So, what do you need
from me?" he demanded.

Before I could reply, the secretary came in with a steaming
mug of coffee. The mug said "World's Greatest Bullshitter." I
wasn't about to disagree. I wouldn't have minded a cup myself,
but clearly the hired help around Kerrchem wasn't deemed worthy of that. If I'd really been from the HSE, the lack of courtesy
would have had me sharpening my knives for Trevor Kerr's
well-cushioned ribs. I waited for the secretary to withdraw, then
I said, "Have you recalled the rest of the batch?"

He nodded impatiently. "Of course. We got on to all the
wholesalers, and we've placed an ad in the national press as well
as the trade. We've already had a load of stuff back, and there's
more due in today."

"Good," I said. "I'll want to see that, as well as the dispatch
paperwork relating to that batch. I take it that won't be a problem?"

"No problem. I'll get Sheila to sort it out for you." He made
a note on a pad on his desk. "Next?"

"Do you use cyanide in any of your processes?"

"No way," he said belligerently. "It has industrial uses,
but mainly in the plastics industry and electroplating. There's
nothing we produce that we'd need it for."

"OK. Going back to the original blackmail note. Did it include any instructions about the amount of money they were after, or how you were to contact them?"

He took a cigar out of a humidor the size of a small green-house and rolled it between his fingers. "They didn't put a figure on it, no. There was a phone number, and the note said it was the number of one of the public phones at Piccadilly Station. I was supposed to be there at nine o'clock on the Friday night. I didn't go, of course."

"Pity you didn't call us then," I said.

"I told you, I thought it was a crank. Some nutter trying to wind me up. No way was I going to give him the satisfaction."

"Or her," I added. "The thing that bothers me, Mr Kerr, is that killing people is a pretty extreme thing for a blackmailer to do. The usual analysis of blackmailers is that they are on the cowardly side. The crimes they commit are at arm's length, and usually don't put life at risk. I would have expected the black-mailer in this case to have done something a lot more low key, certainly initially. You know, dumped caustic soda in washing-up liquid, that sort of thing."

"Maybe they didn't intend to kill anybody, just to give people a nasty turn," he said. He lit the cigar, exhaling a cloud of smoke that gave me a nasty turn so early in the day.

I shrugged. "In that case, cyanide's a strange choice. The fatal dose is pretty small. Also, you couldn't just stick it in the drum and wait for someone to open it up. There must have been some kind of device rigged up inside it. To produce the lethal gas, cyanide pellets need to react with something else. So they'd have had to be released into the liquid somehow. That's a lot of trouble to go to when you could achieve an unpleas-ant warning with dozens of other chemical mixtures. If it was me, I'd have filled a few drums either with something that smelled disgusting, or something that would destroy surfaces rather than clean them, just to persuade you that they were capable of making your life hell. Then, I'd have followed it up with a second note saying something like: 'Next time, it'll be cyanide.'"

"So maybe we're dealing with a complete nutter," he said bitterly. "Great."

"Or maybe it's someone who wants to destroy you rather than blackmail you," I said simply.

Kerr took his cigar out of his mouth, which remained in a perfect O. Finally, he said, "You've got to be kidding."

"It's something you should consider. In relation to both your professional and your personal life." He was having a lot of trouble getting his head round the idea, I could see. If he'd been a bit nicer to me, I'd have been gentler. But I figure you shouldn't dish it out unless you can take it. "What about business rivals? Is anybody snapping at your heels? Is anybody going under because you've brought out new products or developed new sales strategies?"

"You don't murder people in business," he protested. "Not in my line of business, you don't."

"Murder might not have been what was planned," I told him flatly. "If they wanted to sabotage you and stay at arm's length, they might have hired someone to do the dirty. And they in turn might have hired someone else. And somewhere along the line, the Chinese whispers took over. So is there any other firm that might have a particular reason for wanting Kerrchem to go down the tubes?"

He frowned. "The last few years have been tough, there's no denying that. Firms go bust, so there's not as much industrial cleaning to be done. Businesses cut their cleaners down from five days to three, so the commercial cleaners cut back on their purchases. We've kept our heads above water, but it's been a struggle. We've had a couple of rounds of redundancies, we've been a bit slower bringing in some new processes, and we've had to market ourselves more aggressively, but that's the story across the industry. One of our main competitors went bust about nine months ago, but that wasn't because we were squeezing them. It was more because they were based in Basingstoke and they had higher labour costs than us. I haven't heard that anybody else is on the edge, and it's a small world. To be honest, we're one of the smaller fishes. Most of our rivals are big multinationals. If they wanted to take us out, they'd come to the family and make us an offer we couldn't refuse."

That disposed of the easy option. Time to move on. "Has anybody left under a cloud? Any unfair dismissal claims pending?"

He shook his head. "Not that I know of. As far as I know, and believe me, I would know, the only people who have gone are the ones we cleared out under the redundancy deals. I suppose some of them might have been a bit disgruntled, but if any of them had made any threats, I would have heard about it. Like I said, we pride ourselves on being a family firm, and the department head and production foremen all know not to keep problems to themselves."

We were going nowhere fast, which only left the sticky bit. "OK," I said. "I don't want you to take this the wrong way, Mr Kerr, but I have to ask these things. You've said that Kerrchem is a family firm. Is there any possibility that another member of the family wants to discredit you? To make it look like the company's not safe in your hands?"

Suddenly I was looking at Trevor Kerr's future. Written all over his scarlet face was the not-so-distant early warning of the heart attack that was lurking in his silted arteries. His mouth opened and closed a couple of times, then he roared, "Bollocks. Pure, absolute bollocks."

"Think about it," I said, smiling sweetly. That'll teach him to deprive me of a caffeine fix. "The other thing is more personal, I'm afraid. Are you married, Mr Kerr?"

"'Course I am. Three children." He jerked his thumb towards a photograph frame on the desk. I leaned forward and turned it round. Standard studio shot of a woman groomed to within an inch of her life, two sulky-looking boys with their father's features, and a girl who'd had the dental work but still looked disturbingly like a rabbit. "Been married to the same woman for sixteen years."

"So there're no ex-wives or ex-girlfriends lurking around with an axe to grind?" I asked.

His eyes drifted away from mine to a point elsewhere on the far wall. "Don't be ridiculous," he said abruptly. Then, in an effort to win me round, he gave a bark of laughter and said, "Bloody hell, Kate, it's me that hired you, not the wife."

So now I knew he had, or had had, a mistress. That was the long shot I'd have to keep in the back of my mind. Before I could explore this avenue further, the intercom on his desk buzzed. He pressed a button and said, "What is it, Sheila?"

"Reg Unsworth is here, Mr Kerr. He say she needs to talk to you."

"I'm in a meeting, Sheila," he said irritably.

There were muffled sounds of conversation, then Sheila said, "He says it's urgent, Mr Kerr. He says you'll want to know immediately. It's to do with the recalled product, he says."

"Why didn't you say so? Send him in."

A burly man in a brown warehouseman's coat with a head bald as a boiled egg and approximately the same shape walked in. "Sorry to bother you, Mr Kerr. It's about the KerrSter recall."

"Well, Reg, spit it out," Kerr said impatiently.

Unsworth gave me a worried look. "It's a bit confidential, like."

"It's all right. Miss Brannigan here's from the Health and Safety Executive. She's here to help us sort this mess out."

Unsworth still looked uncertain. "I checked the records before the returns started coming in. We sent out a total of four hundred and eighty-three gallon containers with the same batch number as the one that there was the problem with. Only . . . so far, we've had six hundred and twenty-seven back."

# 5

Kerr looked gobsmacked. "You must have made a mistake," he blustered.

"I double-checked," Unsworth said. His jaw set in a line as obstinate as his boss's. "Then I went back down to production and checked again. There's no doubt about it. We've had back one hundred and forty-four containers more than we sent out. And that's not even taking into account the one that the dead man opened, or ones that have already been used, or people who haven't even heard about the recall yet."

"There's got to be some mistake," Kerr repeated. "What about the batch coding machine? Has anybody checked that it's working OK?"

"I checked with the line foreman myself," Unsworth said. "They've had no problems with it, and I've seen quality control's sheets. There's no two ways about it. We only sent out four hundred and eighty-three. There's a gross of gallon drums of KerrSter that we can't account for sitting in the loading bay. Come and see for yourself if you don't believe me," he added in an aggrieved tone.

"Let's do just that," Kerr said, heaving himself to his feet. "Come on, Miss Brannigan. Come and see how the workers earn a living."

I followed Kerr out of the room. Unsworth hung back, holding the door open and falling in beside me as we strode down the covered walkway that linked the administration offices with the factory. "It's a real mystery," he offered.

I had my own ideas about what was going on, but for the time being I decided to keep them to myself. "The drums that have been returned," I said, "are they all sealed, or have some of them already been opened?"

"Some of them have been started on," he said. "The batch went out into the warehouse the Tuesday before last. They'll probably have started taking it out on the Thursday or Friday, going by our normal stockpile levels, so there's been plenty of time for people to use them."

"And no one else has reported any adverse effect?"

Unsworth looked uncomfortable. "Not as such," he said.

Kerr half turned to catch my reply. "But?" I asked.

Unsworth glanced at Kerr, who nodded impatiently. "Well, a couple of the wholesalers and one or two of the reps had already had containers from that batch returned," Unsworth admitted.

"Do you know why that was?" I asked.

"Customers complained the goods weren't up to us usual standard," he said grudgingly.

"What sort of complaints?" Kerr demanded indignantly. "Why wasn't I told about this?"

"It's only just come to light, Mr Kerr. They said the KerrSter wasn't right. One of them claimed it had stripped the finish off the flooring in his office toilets."

Kerr snorted. "He should tell his bloody workforce to stick with Boddingtons. They'll have been pissing that foreign lager all over the bloody tiles."

"Have you had the chance to analyse any of the containers that have come back?" I butted in.

Unsworth nodded. "The lads in the lab worked through the night on samples from some of the drums. There wasn't a trace of cyanide in any of them."

Kerr shouldered open a pair of double doors. As I caught one on the backswing, the smell hit me. It was a curious amalgam of pine, lemon and soap suds, but pervaded throughout with sharp chemical smells that bit my nose and throat. It was a bit like driving past the chemical works at Ellesmere Port with one of those ersatz air fresheners in the car. The ones that make you feel that a rotting polecat under the driver's seat would be preferable. Right after the smell came the noise of machinery, overlaid with the bubbling and gurgling of liquid. Kerr climbed a flight of narrow iron stairs, and I followed him along a high-level walkway that travelled the length of the factory floor. It was unpleasantly humid. I felt like a damp wash that's just been dumped in the tumble dryer.

Beneath us, vats seethed, nozzles squirted liquid into plastic containers, and surprisingly few people moved around. "Not many bodies," I said loudly over my shoulder to Unsworth.

"Computer controlled," he said succinctly.

Another avenue to pursue. If the sabotage was internal, perhaps the culprit was simply sending the wrong instructions to the plant. I'd thought this was going to be a straightforward case of industrial sabotage, but my head was beginning to hurt with the permutations it was throwing up.

A couple of hundred yards along the walkway, we descended and cut through a heavy door into a warehouse. Now I know how the Finns feel when they walk into the snow from the sauna. I could feel my pores snapping shut in shock. Here, the air smelled of oil and diesel. The only sound came from fork-lift trucks shunting pallets on and off shelves. "This is the warehouse," Kerr said. I'd never have worked that one out all by myself. "The full containers go through from the factory to packing, where the machines label them, stamp them with batch numbers and seal-wrap them in dozens. Then they come through here on conveyor belts and they're shelved or loaded." He turned to Unsworth. "Where have you stacked the recalls?"

Before Unsworth could reply, my mobile started ringing. "Excuse me," I said, moving away a few yards and pulling the phone out. "Kate Brannigan," I announced.

"Tell me," an amused voice said. "Is Alexis Lee a real person, or is it just your pen name?"

I recognized the voice at once. I moved further away from Kerr's curious stare and turned my back so he couldn't see that my ears had gone bright red. "She's real all right, Mr Haroun," I said. "Why do you ask?"

"Oh, I think it had better be Michael. Otherwise I'd start to suspect you were being unfriendly. I've just been handed the early edition of the *Evening Chronicle*."

"And what does it say?"

"Do you really need me to tell you?" he asked, still sounding amused.

"I forgot to bring my crystal ball with me. If you want to hang on, I'll see if I can find a chicken to disembowel so I can check out the entrails."

He laughed. It was a sound I could easily get used to. "It'd be a lot simpler to pop into a newsagent."

"You're not going to tell me?"

"Oh no, I'd hate to spoil the surprise. Tell me, Kate . . . Do you fancy dinner some evening?"

"Michael, it may not look like it, but I fancy dinner every evening." I couldn't believe myself—I'd read better lines than that in teenage romances.

Bless him, he laughed again. I like a man who doesn't seize on the first sign of weakness. "Are you free this evening?"

I pretended to think. Let's face it, I'd have turned down Mel Gibson, Sean Bean, Linford Christie and Daniel Day-Lewis for dinner with Michael Haroun. I didn't pretend for too long, in case he lost interest. "I can be. As long as it's after seven."

"Great. Shall I pick you up?"

That was a harder decision. I didn't want to let myself forget that this was a business dinner. On the other hand, it wouldn't hurt to give Richard something to think about. I gave Michael the address and we agreed on half past seven. Unlike everybody on TV who uses a mobile phone, I hit the "end" button with a flourish, then turned back to a scowling Trevor Kerr.

"Sorry about that," I lied. "Somebody I've been trying to get hold of on another investigation. Now, Mr Unsworth, you were going to show us these recalled containers."

The next half-hour was one of the more boring ones in my life, made doubly so by the fact that I was itching to get my hands on the *Chronicle*. I finally escaped at half past eleven, leaving Trevor Kerr with the suggestion that his chemists should analyse the contents of a random sample of the containers. Only this time, they wouldn't just be looking for cyanide. They'd be checking to see whether the KerrSter in the drums was the real thing. Or something quite different and a whole lot nastier.

By the third newsagent's, I'd confirmed what I'd always suspected about Farnworth. It's a depressing little dump that civilization forgot. Nobody had the *Chronicle*. They wouldn't have it till some time in the afternoon. They all looked deeply offended and incredulous when I explained that no, the *Bolton Evening News* just wouldn't be the same. I had to possess my soul in patience till I hit the East Lancs. Road. I sat on a garage forecourt reading the results of Alexis's research. She'd done me proud.

## CULTURAL HERITAGE VANISHES

**A series of spectacular robberies has been hushed up by police and stately home owners.**

Now fears are growing that a gang of professional thieves are stripping Britain of valuable art works that form a key part of the nation's heritage. Among the stolen pieces are paintings by French Impressionists Monet and Cézanne, and a bronze bust by the Italian Baroque master Bernini. Also missing is a collection of Elizabethan miniature paintings by Nicholas Hilliard. Together, the thieves' haul is estimated at nearly £10 million.

The cover-up campaign was a joint decision made by several police forces and the owners of the stately homes in question. Police did not want publicity because they were following up leads and did not want the thieves to know that they had realized one gang was behind the thefts.

And the owners were reluctant to admit the jewels of their collections had gone missing in case public attendance figures at their homes dropped off as a result.

Some owners have even resorted to hanging replicas of the missing masterpieces in a bid to fool the public.

The latest victim of the audacious robbers is the owner of a Cheshire manor house. Police have refused to reveal his identity, but will only say that a nineteenth-century French painting has been stolen.

The cheeky thieves have adopted the techniques of the pair who caused outrage at the Lillehammer Olympics when they stole Edvard Munch's *The Scream*.

They break in through the nearest door or window, go straight to the one item they have selected and make their getaway. Often they are in the house or gallery for no more than a minute.

A police source said last night, "There's no doubt that we are dealing with professionals who may well steal to order. There are obviously a limited number of outlets for their loot, and we are making inquiries in the art world."

One of the robbed aristos, who was only prepared to talk anonymously, said, "It's not just the heritage of this country that is at stake. It's our businesses. We employ a lot of people and if the public stop coming because our most famous exhibits have gone, it will have repercussions.

"We do our best to maintain tight security, but you can never keep the professional out."

There was some more whingeing in the same vein, but nothing startling. Call me nit-picking, but I've never understood how the art of several European cultures has come to be a key part of our British heritage, unless it symbolizes the brigand spirit that made the Empire great. That aside, I reckoned Alexis's story would achieve what I hoped for. With a bit of luck, the nationals would pick the story up the next morning, and the jungle drums would start beating. Soon it would be time for a chat with my friend Dennis. If he ever decides to go completely straight, he could make a living as a journalist. I've never known anybody absorb or disseminate so much criminal intelligence. I'm just grateful some of it comes my way when I need it.

For the time being, I headed back to the office, stopping to pick up a couple of pizzas on the way. I knew Shelley would be waiting behind the door with a pile of paperwork that would cause more concussion than a rolling pin. At least a pizza offering might reduce the aggro to a minimum.

I was halfway through the painful process of signing cheques when Josh arrived. I pretended astonishment. "Josh!" I exclaimed. "It's between the hours of one and three and you're not in a restaurant! What's happened? Has the stock market collapsed?"

His sharp blue eyes crinkled in the smile that he's practised to maximize his resemblance to Robert Redford. Frankly, I'm surprised the light brown hair hasn't been bleached to perfect it, since Josh is a man whose energies are devoted to only two things—making lots of money and women. His track record with the latter is dismal; luckily he's a lot more successful with the former, which is how he's ended up as the senior partner of one of the city's most successful master brokerages. Shelley developed a theory about Josh and women after she did her A level psychology. She reckons that behind the confident façade there lurks a well of low self-esteem. So when it comes to women, his subconscious decides that any woman with half a brain and a shred of personality wouldn't spend more than five minutes with him. The logical extension of that is that any woman who sticks around for more than six weeks must by definition be a boring bimbo, and thus he shouldn't be seen dead with her.

Me, I think he just likes having fun. He swears he plans to retire when he turns forty, and that's early enough to think about settling down. I like him because he's always treated me as an equal, never as a potential conquest. I'm glad about that; I'd hate to lose my fast track into the bowels of the financial world. Believe me, the Nikkei Index doesn't burp without Josh knowing exactly what it had for dinner.

Josh flicked an imaginary speck of dust off one of the clients' chairs and sat down, crossing his elegantly suited legs. "Things are changing in the big bad world of money, you know," he said. "The days of the three-hour lunch are over. Except when it's you that's buying, of course." He tossed a file on to my desk.

"You've stopped doing lunch?" I waited for the world to stop turning.

"Today, I had a Marks and Spencer prawn sandwich in the office of one of my principal clients. Washed down with a rather piquant sparkling mineral water from the Welsh valleys. An interesting diversification from coal mining, don't you think?"

I picked up the file. "Kerrchem?"

"The same. Want the gossip since I'm here?"

I gave him my best suspicious frown. "Is this going to cost me?"

He pouted. "Maybe an extra glass of XO?"

"It's worth it," I decided. "Tell me about it."

"OK. Kerrchem is a family firm. Started in 1934 by Josiah Kerr, the grandfather of the present chairman, chief executive and managing director Trevor Kerr. They made soap. They were no Lever Brothers, though they've always provided a reasonable living for the family. Trevor's father Hartley was a clever chap, by all accounts, had a chemistry degree, and he made certain they spent enough on R & D to keep ahead of the game. He moved them into the industrial cleaning market." All this off the top of his head. One of the secrets of Josh's success is a virtually photographic memory for facts and figures. Figures of the balance sheet variety, that is.

"Hartley Kerr was an only child," he continued. "He had three kids: Trevor, Margaret and Elizabeth. Trevor, although the youngest, owns forty-nine per cent of the shares, Margaret and Elizabeth own twenty per cent each. The remaining eleven per cent is held by Hartley Kerr's widow, Elaine Kerr. Elaine is in her early seventies, in full possession of her marbles, lives in Bermuda, and takes little part in things except for voting against Trevor at every opportunity. Trevor's sons are still at school, but he has three nephews who work at Kerrchem. John Hardy works in R & D, his brother Paul is in accounts and Margaret's son Will Tomasiuk is in sales. Trevor is by all accounts a complete and utter shit, but against all the odds, he appears to run the company well. Never been a history of industrial problems. Financially and fiscally all seems above board. Frankly, Kate, if Kerrchem were going public, they're exactly the kind of company I'd advise you to put your money in if you wanted to keep it unspectacularly safe. Before people started dying, that is."

"I suppose that rules out an insurance job, then. Is everybody in the family happy with Trevor's stewardship? No young bucks snapping at his heels?"

Josh shook his head. "That's not the word on the exchange floor. The old lady only votes against Trevor because she thinks he's not a patch on his old man and she wants to make a point. And the nephews have all learned the business from the bottom up, but they're climbing the greasy pole at an impressive rate. So, no, that kite won't fly, Kate." He glanced at a watch so slim it looked anorexic and uncrossed his legs.

"You're a star, Josh. I owe you a meal."

"Fix up a date with Julia, would you? I don't have my diary with me." He stood up and I came round the desk to swap kisses on both cheeks. I watched five hundred pounds' worth of immaculate tailoring walk out the door. Not even that amount of dosh to spend on clothes could make me spend my days talking about pension funds and unit trusts.

On the other hand, all it took to get me salivating at the thought of an evening's conversation about insurance was a profile from an ancient carving. Maybe I wasn't such a smart cookie after all.

# 6

I'd almost forgotten there are restaurants that don't serve dim sum. For as long as I've known Richard, he's maintained that if you don't use chopsticks on it, it ain't food. And Josh has recently taken to extracting his payment in kind in Manchester's clutch of excellent Thai restaurants. I'm not sure if that's down to the food or the subservient waitresses. Either way, I'd entirely lost touch with anything that didn't come out of a wok. Which made Michael Haroun a refreshing change in more ways than one.

He'd arrived promptly at twenty-nine minutes past seven. I'd grown so used to Richard's flexible idea of time that I was still applying eye pencil when the doorbell rang. I nearly poked my eye out in shock, and had to answer the door with a tissue covering the damage. Eat your heart out, Cindy Crawford. Michael lounged against the door frame, looking drop-dead gorgeous in blue jeans, navy silk blouson and an off-white collarless linen shirt that sure as hell hadn't come from Marks and Spencer. My stomach churned, and I don't think it was hunger. "Long John Silver, I presume," he said.

"Watch it, or I'll set the parrot on you," I replied, stepping back and waving him in.

He shrugged away from the door and followed me down the hall. I gestured towards the living room and said, "Give me a minute."

Back in the bathroom, I repaired the damage and surveyed myself in the full-length mirror. Navy linen trousers, russet knitted silk T-shirt, navy silk tweed jacket. I looked like I'd taken a bit of trouble, without actually departing from the businesslike image. Michael wasn't to know this was my newest, smartest outfit. Besides, I'd told Richard my evening engagement was a business meeting, and I wasn't entirely ready for him to get any other ideas if he saw me leave.

I rubbed a smudge of gel over my fingers and thrust them through my hair, which I'd kept fairly short since I was shorn without consultation earlier in the year. My right eye still looked a bit red, but this was as good as it was going to get. A quick squirt of Richard's Eternity by Calvin Klein and I was ready.

I walked down the hall and stood in the doorway. Michael obviously hadn't heard me. He was deep in a computer gaming magazine. Bonus points for the boy. I cleared my throat. "Ready when you are," I said.

He looked up and smiled appreciatively. "I don't want to sound disablist," he said, "but I have to admit I prefer the two-eyed look." He closed the magazine and stood up. "Shall we go?"

He drove a top-of-the-range Citroën. "Company car?" I asked, looking forward to the prospect of being driven for a change.

"Yeah, but they let me choose. I've always had a soft spot for Citroën. I think the DS was one of the most beautiful cars ever built," he said as he did a neat three-point turn to get out of the parking area outside my bungalow. "My father always used to drive one."

That told me Michael Haroun hadn't grown up on a council estate with the arse hanging out of his trousers. "Lucky you," I said with feeling. "My dad works for Rover, so my childhood was spent in the back of a Mini. That's how I ended up only five foot three. The British equivalent of binding the feet."

Michael laughed as he hit a button on the CD player and Bonnie Raitt filled the car. Richard would have giggled helplessly at something so middle of the road. Me, I was just glad of something that didn't feature crashing guitars or that insistent zippy beat that sounds just like a fly hitting an incinerator. We turned out of the small "single professionals" development where I live and into the council estate. To my surprise, instead of heading down Upper Brook Street towards town, he turned left. As we headed down Stockport Road, my heart sank. I prayed this wasn't going to be one of those twenty-mile drives to some pretentious bistro in the sticks with compulsory spinach pancakes and only one choice of vodka.

"You into computer games, then?" I asked. Time to check out just how much I had in common with this breathtaking profile.

"I have a 486 multi-media system in my spare room. Does that answer the question?"

"It's not what you've got, it's what you do with it that counts," I replied. As soon as I'd spoken, I wished I was on a five-second delay loop, like radio phone-ins.

He grinned and listed his current favourites. We were still arguing the relative merits of submarine simulations when he pulled up outside a snooker supplies shop in an unpromising part of Stockport Road. A short walk down the pavement brought us to That Café, an unpretentious restaurant done out in Thirties style. I'd heard plenty of good reports about it, but I'd never quite made it across the door before. The locale had put me off for one thing. Call me fussy, but I like to be sure that my car's still going to be waiting for me after I've finished dinner.

The interior looked like flea market meets Irish country pub, but the menu had me salivating. The waitress, dressed in jeans, a Deacon Blue T-shirt, big fuck-off Doc Marten boots and a long white French waiter's apron, showed us to a quiet corner table next to a blazing fire. OK, they only had one vodka, but at least it wasn't some locally distilled garbage with a phoney Russian name.

As our starters arrived, I said ruefully, "I wish finding Henry Naismith's Monet was as easy as a computer game."

"Yeah. At least with games, there's always a bulletin board you can access for hints. I suppose you're out on your own with this," Michael said.

"Not entirely on my own," I corrected him. "I do have one or two contacts."

He swallowed his mouthful of food and looked slightly pained. "Is that why you agreed to have dinner with me?" he asked.

"Only partly."

"What was the other part?" he asked, obviously fishing.

"I enjoy a good scoff, and I like interesting conversation with it." I was back in control of myself, the adolescent firmly stuffed back into the box marked "not wanted on voyage."

"And you thought I'd be an interesting conversationalist, did you?"

"Bound to be," I said sweetly. "You're an insurance man, and right now insurance claims are one of my principal interests."

We ate in silence for a few moments, then he said, "I take it you were behind the story in the *Chronicle*?"

I shrugged. "I like to stir the pot. That way, the scum rises to the surface."

"You certainly stirred things around our office," Michael said drily.

"The people have a right to know," I said, self-righteously quoting Alexis.

"Cheers," Michael said, clinking his glass against mine. "Here's to a profitable relationship."

"Oh, you mean Fortissimus are going to hire Mortensen and Brannigan?" I asked innocently.

He grinned again. "I think I'll pass on that one. I simply meant that with luck, you might track down Henry Naismith's Monet."

"Speaking of which," I said, "I spoke to Henry this afternoon. He says your assessor was there this afternoon."

"That's right," Michael said cagily.

"Henry says your man put a very interesting suggestion to him. Purely in confidence. Now, would that be the kind of confidence you're already privy to?"

Michael carefully placed his fork and knife together on the plate and mopped his lips with the napkin. "It might be," he said cautiously. "But if it were, I wouldn't be inclined to discuss it with someone who has a hotline to the front page of the *Chronicle*."

"Not even if I promised it would go no further?"

"You expect me to believe that after today's performance?" he demanded.

I smiled. "There's a crucial difference. I was acting in my client's best interests by setting the cat among the pigeons with Alexis's story. I didn't breach my client's confidentiality, and I didn't tell Alexis anything that wasn't already in the public domain. She just put the bits together. However, if Henry acted on your colleague's suggestion and I leaked that to the press, it would seriously damage his business. And I don't do that to the people who pay my mortgage. Trust me, Michael. It won't go any further."

The arrival of the waitress gave him a moment's breathing space. She removed the debris. "So this would be strictly off the record?"

"Information only," I agreed.

The waitress returned with a cheerful smile and two huge plates. I stared down at mine, where enough rabbit to account for half the population of Watership Down sat in a pool of creamy sauce. "*Nouvelle cuisine* obviously passed this place by," I said faintly.

"I suspect we Mancunians are too canny to pay half a week's wages for a sliver of meat surrounded by three baby carrots, two mangetouts, one baby sweetcorn and an artistically carved radish," he said wryly.

"And is it that Mancunian canniness that underlies your assessor's underhand suggestion?" I asked innocently.

"Nothing regional about it," Michael said. "You have to have a degree in bloody-minded caution before you get the job."

"So you think it's OK to ask your clients to hang fakes on the wall?"

"It's a very effective safety precaution," he said carefully.

"That's what your assessor told Henry. He said you'd be prepared not to increase his premium by the equivalent of the gross national product of a small African nation if he had copies made of his remaining masterpieces and hung them on the walls instead of the real thing," I said conversationally.

"That's about the size of it," Michael admitted. At least he had the decency to look uncomfortable about it.

"And is this a general policy these days?"

Slicing up his vegetables gave Michael an excuse for not meeting my eyes. "Quite a few of our clients have opted for it as a solution to their security problems," he said. "It makes sense, Kate. We agreed this morning that there isn't a security system that can't be breached. If having a guard physically on site twenty-four hours a day isn't practical because of the expense or because the policyholder doesn't want that sort of presence in what is, after all, his home, then it avoids sky-high premiums."

"It's not just about money, though," I protested. "It's like Henry says. He knows those paintings. He's lived with them most of his life. You get a buzz from the real thing that a fake just doesn't provide."

"Not one member of the public has noticed the substitutions," Michael said.

"Maybe not so far," I conceded. "But according to my understanding, the trouble with fakes is that they don't stand the test of time." Thanking Shelley silently for my art tutorial that afternoon, I launched myself into my spiel. "Look at van Meegeren's fake Vermeers. At the time, all the experts were convinced they were the real thing. But you look at them now, and they wouldn't even fool a philistine like me. The difference between schneid and kosher is that fakes date, but the really great paintings don't. They're timeless."

He frowned. "Even if you're right, which I don't concede for a moment, that's not a bridge that our clients will have to cross for a long time yet."

I wasn't about to give up that easily. "Even so, don't you think it's a bit of a con to pull on the public? A bit of a swizz to spend your bank holiday Monday in a traffic jam just so you can ogle a Constable that's more phoney than a plastic Rolex? Aren't you in danger of breaching the Trades Descriptions Act?" I asked.

"Our clients may be," Michael said carelessly. "We're not."

The brazen effrontery of it gobsmacked me. "I can't believe I'm hearing this," I said. "You work in a business that must spend hundreds of thousands a year trying to catch its customers out in fraud, and yet you're happily suggesting to another bunch of clients that they go off and commit a fraud?"

"That's not how we see it," he said stiffly. "Besides, it works," he said. "In at least two cases that I know about personally, customers who have been burgled have only lost copies. Surely that proves it's worthwhile."

In spite of the blazing fire, I felt a chill on the back of my neck. Only a man with no personal knowledge of the strung-out world of crime could have made that pronouncement with such self-satisfaction. It doesn't take much imagination to picture the scene when an overwrought burglar turns up at his fence's gaff with something he thinks is an old master, only to be told it's Rembrandt by numbers. Scenario number one is that the burglar thinks the fence is trying to have him over so he takes the appropriate steps. Scenario number two is that the fence thinks the burglar is trying to have him over, and takes the appropriate steps. Either way, somebody ends up in casualty. And that's looking on the bright side. Doubtless law-abiding citizens like Michael think they've got what they deserve, but even villains have wives and kids who don't want to spend their spare time visiting hospital beds or graves.

My silence clearly spelled out defeat to Michael, since he leaned over and squeezed my hand. "Trust me, Kate. Our way, everybody's happy," he said.

I pretended to push my chair back and look frantically for the door. "I'm out of here," I said. "Soon as an insurance man says 'trust me,' you know you should be in the next county."

He grinned. "I promise I'll never try to sell you insurance."

"OK. But I won't promise I'll never try to pitch you into using Mortensen and Brannigan."

"Speaking of which, how did you get into the private eye business?" Michael said.

I couldn't decide whether it was an attempt to change the subject or a deliberate shift away from the professional towards the personal. Either way, I was happy to go along with him. I didn't think I was going to get any more useful information out of him, and I only had to look across the table to remember that when I'd agreed to this dinner, my motives hadn't been entirely selfless. By the time we'd moved on to coffee and Armagnac, he knew all about my aborted law degree, abandoned after two years because the part-time job I'd got doing bread-and-butter process serving for Bill Mortensen was a damn sight more interesting than the finer points of jurisprudence.

"So tell me about your most interesting case," he coaxed me.

"Maybe later," I said. "It's your turn now. How did you get into insurance?"

"It's the family business," he said, looking faintly embarrassed.

"So you followed in Daddy's footsteps," I said. I felt disappointed. I couldn't put my finger on why, exactly. Maybe I expected him to live up to that profile with a suitably buccaneering past.

"Eventually," he said. "I read Arabic at university, then I worked for the BBC World Service for a while. But the money was dire and there were no prospects. My father had the sense to see that sales had never interested me, but he persuaded me to take a shot at working in claims." Michael raised his shoulders and held out his hands in an expressive shrug. "What can I say? I really enjoy it."

All of a sudden, I remembered one of the key reasons I like being with Richard. He lives an interesting life: music journalist, football fan and Sunday morning player, part-time father. I was sure if I hung around with Michael Haroun, I'd learn a lot of invaluable stuff. But not even the most brilliant raconteur can make insurance interesting forever. With Richard, no two days are the same. With Michael, I suspected variety might not be the spice of life.

Now I'd established that I didn't want to spend the rest of my life with the man, I felt a sense of release. I could take what I needed from the encounter, and that would be that. My life wasn't about to be turned on its head because I'd fallen in love with a profile when I was fourteen.

With that comforting thought in the front of my mind, I had no hesitation about inviting him back for more coffee. The fact that I'd forgotten to mention Richard to him somehow didn't seem too important at the time.

# 7

Richard's car wasn't home when we got there. I wasn't sure whether to be pleased or not. On the one hand, I wanted him to see me with Michael Haroun. If it took a bit of the green-eyed monster to make Richard start thinking about where our relationship was headed, so be it. On the other hand, the last thing I wanted was for him to throw a jealous wobbler in front of someone who was potentially a useful source, if not a prospective client.

"You live alone, then?" Michael asked casually as we walked up the path.

"Yes and no," I said. "I have a relationship with the man next door, but we don't actually live together." I unlocked the door, switched off the burglar alarm and led him through the living room into the conservatory that links both houses. "This is the common ground," I said. "We each reserve the right to lock the door into the conservatory." I wasn't sure why I was telling Michael all this. Maybe there was still a smidgen of lust running through my hormones.

Michael followed me back into the living room, closing the patio doors behind him. "Coffee?" I asked. "Or would you prefer a drink?"

He smiled mischievously. "That depends."

"Oh, you'll be driving," I told him. Even if I'd been young, free and single, he'd have been driving, I told myself firmly.

He pulled a rueful face and said, "It had better be coffee then."

I'd just finished grinding the beans when I heard the clattering of Richard's engine. I glanced out of the window and watched the hot pink, customized Volkswagen Beetle convertible nose into the space between Michael's car and my Leo Gemini turbo super coupé, a trophy from the case which had put our relationship on the line in the first place. I kept meaning to trade it in for something more suited to surveillance work, the coupé being about as unobtrusive as Chatsworth on a council estate. But it was such a pleasure to drive, I hadn't got round to it yet.

Back in the living room, Michael clearly wasn't brooding on his rebuff. He was absorbed in the computer games reviews again. "Coffee won't be long," I said.

He closed the magazine and replaced it in the rack. Either he had very good manners, or he was as obsessively tidy as I was. Richard calls it anal retentive, but I don't see why you have to live in a tip just to prove you're laid back. Before we could get back into computer games, I heard the patio doors on the far side of the conservatory open. Richard's yell of greeting penetrated even my closed doors. "Brannigan, I'm home," he called.

Seconds later, he appeared at my doors, brandishing the unmistakable carrier bag of a Chinese takeaway. He pulled the door back, took in Michael and grinned. "Hi," he said expansively. I estimated three joints. "You two still working?"

"We finished ages ago," I said. "Michael came back for coffee."

"Right," said Richard, oblivious to the implication I was thrusting under his nose. "You won't mind if I join you then?"

Without waiting for an answer, he plonked himself down on the sofa opposite Michael and unpacked his takeaway. "I'm Richard Barclay, by the way," he said, extending a hand across the table to Michael. "You wait for Brannigan to remember her manners, you could be dead."

"Michael Haroun," he said, shaking Richard's hand. "Pleased to meet you." Yes, an insurance man born and bred. Only an estate agent could have lied more convincingly.

Richard jumped to his feet and headed for the door. "Chopsticks and bowls for three?" he asked. "Sorry, Mike, I wasn't expecting company, but there's probably enough to go around."

"We've just had dinner, Richard," I said. "I did leave you a message."

"Yeah, I know," he grinned. "But I've never known you refuse a salt and pepper rib, Brannigan."

"Sorry about that," I said as he left.

Michael winked. "Gives me a chance to suss out the competition."

I didn't like the idea that I was some kind of prize, even if it was gratifying to know that he was interested in more than recovering Henry Naismith's Monet. And he didn't even have the excuse of a previous encounter in the British Museum. "What makes you think there's a competition?" I asked sweetly.

Michael leaned back against the sofa and stretched his legs out. "I thought you were the detective? Kate, if you two were as happy as pigs, you'd have left me sitting in the car wondering where exactly I'd made the wrong move."

Before I could reply, Richard was back. "I'll get the coffee," I said, annoyed with myself for my transparency. By the time I got back, Richard and Michael were getting to know each other. And they say women are bitches.

"So, what do you do when you're not chipping a oner off people's car theft claims because your assessor spoke to the next-door neighbour who revealed that the ashtray was full?" Richard asked through a mouthful of shiu mai.

As I sat down next to him, Michael smiled at me and said, "I play computer games. Like Kate."

I poured the coffee in silence and let the boys play. "All a bit sedentary," Richard remarked, loading his bowl with fried rice and what looked like a chicken hoi nam.

"Oh, I work out down the gym," Michael said. I believed him. I could feel the hard muscles in the arm pressed against mine.

Richard nodded, as if confirming a guess. "Thought as much," he said. "Bit too pointless for me, all that humping metal around. I prefer something a bit more social for keeping in shape. But then, I suppose it can't be easy finding people who want to play with you when you're an insurance claims manager," he added, almost as an afterthought. "Bit like being a VAT man."

"I've never had any problems finding people to play with," Michael drawled. I had no trouble believing that. "What exactly is it that you do to keep fit, Richard? Squash? Real tennis? Polo? Or do you prefer raves?"

Richard almost choked on his food. Neither of us rushed to perform the Heimlich manoeuvre. Recovering, he swallowed hard and said, "I'm a footie man myself. Local league. Every Sunday morning, never mind the weather."

Michael smiled. Remember that poem? "The Assyrian came down like the wolf on the fold"?

"I've never been much into mud myself," he said.

"Had a good evening?" I chipped in before things got out of hand.

Richard nodded. "Been down the Academy listening to East European grunge bands. Some good sounds." He gave me one of his perfect smiles. "How's your workload progressing?"

I shrugged. "Slowly," I said. "Michael's been giving me some background on the art front, and I've got Alexis to chuck a few bricks into the pond. It's a question of waiting to see what floats to the surface."

"And we all know what floats," Richard said drily, glancing at Michael.

Michael decided enough was enough. He drained his mug and put it down on the coffee table. "I'd better be on my way," he said. "Busy day tomorrow."

We both stood up. "I'll see you out," I said.

"Nice to meet you, Richard," Michael said politely on his way out the door.

"Feeling's entirely mutual," Richard said ironically.

On the doorstep, I thanked Michael for dinner. "It was a pleasant change," I said.

"I can see that," Michael said. "Maybe we could do it again some time."

I only hesitated for a moment. "That'd be nice," I admitted.

"Let me know how your investigation progresses," he said. "Stay in touch." He leaned forward and brushed my cheek with his lips. He smelled of warm, clean animal, the last traces of his aftershave lingering muskily underneath. The hairs on the back of my neck stood on end as my body tingled.

I turned my head and met his lips in a swift, breathless kiss. Before it could turn into anything more, I stepped back. "Drive safely," I said.

I watched him walk to his car, enjoying the light bounce of his step. Then I took a deep breath and walked back indoors.

After Michael had gone, Richard polished off the remains of his Chinese, making no comment on my choice of company for the evening. He asked if I wanted to see a movie the following evening and we bickered companionably about what we'd go to see, me holding out for *Blade Runner: The Director's Cut*, revisiting the Cornerhouse for the umpteenth time. "No way," Richard had said emphatically. "I'm not going to the Cornerhouse. I'm getting too old for art houses. They're full of politically correct wankers trying to pretend they understand the articles in the *Modern Review*. You can't move for people rabbiting about semiotics and Foucault and deconstruction." He paused, then got to the real reason. "Besides, they don't sell popcorn or Häagen-Dazs. You can't call that a night out at the movies."

I gave in gracefully. Satisfied that I'd made the concession, Richard announced he had to write an article about the post-Communist rockers for some American West Coast magazine, and he wanted to get it written and faxed before he went to bed. He swept the remains of his takeaway into the carrier bag and gave me a swift hug. "I love you, Brannigan," he muttered gruffly into my ear.

I fell asleep with the words of Dean Friedman's "Love Is Not Enough" swirling round my head like a mantra. I woke up alone the next morning, and not particularly surprised by that. I felt strangely deflated, as if something I'd been anticipating hadn't happened. I wasn't sure if that was to do with Michael or Richard. Either way, I didn't like the feeling that my state of mind was dependent on anyone else. I stood in the shower for a long time, letting the water pour down. A friend of mine who's into all that New Age stuff reckons a shower cleanses your aura. I don't know about that, but it always helps me put things into perspective.

By the time I walked through the office door, I was feeling in control of my life again. That might have had something to do with the miracle of finding a parking meter that was nearer the office than my house. Parking in this city gets worse by the day. I've been seriously wondering how much it would cost to bribe the security men at the BBC building across the road to let me park my car inside their compound. Probably more than I earn.

Shelley was on the phone, so I headed straight for the coffee maker, a shiny chrome cappuccino machine that my partner, the gadget king of the Northwest, bought us for a treat after a grateful client gave us a bonus because we'd done the job faster than Speedy Gonzales. Somehow, I couldn't see either of our current employers rewarding my swiftness. I was beginning to feel like I was wading through cement on both cases.

Before I could fill the scoop with coffee, I heard Shelley say, "Hang on, she's just walked in."

I turned to see her waving the phone at me. "Alexis," Shelley said.

I headed for my office. "Coffee?" It was a try-on, I admit it. Mortensen and Brannigan adopts a firm "you want it, you make it" policy on coffee. But every now and again, Shelley takes pity on me.

I guess I didn't look needy enough, for there were no signs of her crossing the office after she'd switched the call through. I sighed and picked up the phone. "'Morning," I said.

"Don't sound so enthusiastic," the familiar Liverpudlian voice rasped. "Here am I, bringing you tidings from the front line and you greet me with all the eager anticipation of a woman expecting bad news from her dentist."

"It's your own fault. Never come between a woman and her cappuccino," I retorted crisply.

I heard the sound of smoke being inhaled, then a husky chuckle. "Some of us don't need coffee this late in the day. Some of us have already done half a day's work, KB."

"Self-righteousness doesn't become you," I snarled. "Did you call for a reason, or did you just want to be told there's something clever about having a job that starts in the middle of the night?"

"There's gratitude for you," Alexis said cheerfully. "I call you up to pass on vital information, and what thanks do I get?"

I took a deep breath. "Thank you, O bountiful one," I grovelled. "So what's this vital piece of information?"

"What have you got to swap for it?"

I thought for a moment. "You can borrow my leather jacket for a week."

"Too tight under the armpits. What's the matter, KB? Got no gossip to trade? What's happening with the insurance man?"

If the *Chronicle*'s editor ever decides he needs to pacify the anti-smoking lobby and fire Alexis, she'll never starve. She could set up tomorrow in a booth on Blackpool pier. She wouldn't even have to change her name. Gypsy Alexis Lee sounds just fine to me. "We had dinner last night," I said abruptly.

"And?"

"And nothing. Dinner at That Café, he came in for coffee, Richard barged in waving a Chinese, they squabbled like two dogs over a bone, he went home."

"Alone?"

"Of course alone, what do you take me for? On second thoughts, don't answer that. Trust me, Alexis, nothing's happening with the insurance man. You'll be the first to know if and when there is. Now, cut the crap and tell me what you rang for."

"OK. The jungle drums have obviously been beating after that piece I did yesterday on the robberies."

Nothing warms the cockles of the heart like the smug self-satisfaction of being right. "So what's the word on the street?"

"I don't know about the street. I'm working the stately home circuit these days," Alexis replied disdainfully. "I've just come off the blower with a punter called Lord Ballantrae."

"Who's he?"

"I'm not entirely sure of all the titles, since I've not looked him up in Debrett yet, but he's some sort of Scotch baron."

"You mean he's in the whisky trade?"

"No, soft girl, he's a baron and he comes from Scotland, though you'd never know to hear him talk."

"So has he been burgled too?"

"Yeah, but that's not why he rang. Apparently, after he got turned over, he had a chat with some of his blue-blood buddies and found there was a lot of it about, so they got together in a sort of semi-informal network to pool their info and help other rich bastards to avoid the same happening to them. One of them spotted the story I did and told him about it, so he rang me for a chat. I'm doing a news feature on him and his gang, about how they're banding together to foil the robbers. And get this. They call themselves the Nottingham Group." She paused, expectantly.

I took the bait. It was a small price to pay to keep the wheels of friendship oiled. "Go on, tell me. I know you're dying to. Why the Nottingham Group?"

"After the Sheriff of Nottingham. On account of their goal is to stop these robbin' hoods from ripping off their wealth for redistribution to the selected poor."

"Nice one," I said. "You going to give me his number?" I copied down Alexis's information and stuck the Post-it note on my phone. "Thanks."

"Is that it? What about 'I owe you one'?"

Nobody's ever accused Alexis of being a shrinking violet. "I don't. You're paying me back for your exclusive last night."

"OK. You free for lunch?"

"Doubt it, somehow. What about tonight? Richard and I are going to the multi-screen. Do you two want to join us?"

"Sorry, we've already booked for *Blade Runner* at the Cornerhouse."

Typical. "Don't forget your Foucault," I said.

I was halfway out of my chair, destination coffee machine, when the phone rang again. Suppressing a growl, I grabbed it and injected a bit of warmth into my voice. "Good morning, Kate Brannigan speaking."

"It's Trevor Kerr here."

I wished I hadn't bothered with the warmth. "Hello, Mr Kerr. What news?"

"I could ask you the same thing, since I'm paying you to investigate this business," he grumbled. "I'm ringing to let you know that my lab people have come up with some results from the analysis I asked them to carry out."

Not a man to give credit where it's due, our Mr Kerr. I stifled a sigh and said, "What did they discover?"

"A bloody nightmare, that's what. About half the samples they tested aren't bloody KerrSter."

"Cyanide?" I asked, suddenly anxious.

"No, nothing like that. Just a mixture of chemicals that wouldn't clean anything. Not only would they not clean things, there are certain surfaces they'd ruin. Anything with a sealed finish like floor tiles or worktops. Bastards!" Kerr spat.

"Are these common chemicals, or what?"

"Ever heard of caustic soda? That's how bloody common we're talking here."

"So cheap as well as common?" I asked.

"A lot bloody cheaper than what we put in KerrSter, let me tell you. So what are you going to do about it?" he demanded pugnaciously.

"Your killer's a counterfeiter," I said, ignoring his belligerence. "Either they're trying to wreck your business or else they're simply after a quick buck."

"Even I'd got that far," he said sarcastically. "What I want you to do is find these buggers while I've still got a business left. You hear what I'm saying, Miss Brannigan? Find these bastards, or there won't be a pot left to pay you out of."

# 8

Sometimes I wonder how clients managed to go to the bathroom before they hired us. Trevor Kerr was clearly one of those who think once they've hired you, you're responsible for everything up to and including emptying the wastepaper bins at night. He was adamant that it was down to me to go and see the detectives investigating the death of Joey Morton, the Stockport publican, to inform them that the person who was sabotaging Kerrchem's products was probably the one they should be beating up with rubber hoses. Incidentally, never believe the politicians and top coppers who tell you that sort of thing can't happen now all interviews are tape recorded. There are no tape recorders in police cars or vans, and I've heard of cases where it's taken three hours for a police car to travel two inner city miles.

I wasn't relishing telling some overworked and overstressed police officer how to run an inquiry. If there's one thing your average cop hates more than becoming the middle man in a domestic, it's being put on the right track by a private eye. I was even less thrilled when Kerr told me who the investigating officer was. Detective Inspector Cliff Jackson and I were old sparring partners. The first time one of my cases ended in murder, he was running the show. He hadn't exactly covered himself in glory, twice arresting the wrong person before the real killer had eventually ended up behind bars, largely as a result of some judicious tampering by Mortensen and Brannigan. You'd think he'd have been grateful. Think again.

I drove out to the incident room in Stockport. The one time I'd have welcomed being stuck in traffic, I cruised down Stockport Road without encountering a single red light. My luck was still out to lunch when I arrived at the police station. Jackson was in. I didn't even have to kick my heels while he pretended to be too busy to slot me in right away.

He didn't get up when I was shown into his office. He hadn't changed much: still slim, hair still dark and barbered to within an inch of its life, eyes still hidden behind a pair of tinted prescription lenses. His dress sense hadn't improved any. He wore a white shirt with a heavy emerald green stripe, the sleeves rolled up over his bony elbows. His tie was shiny polyester, in a shade of green that screamed for mercy against the shirt. "I wasn't expecting to see you again," he greeted me ungraciously.

"Nice to see you too, Inspector," I said pleasantly. "But let's not waste our time on pleasantries. I wanted to talk to you about Joey Morton's death."

"I see," he said. "Go on, then, talk."

I told him all he needed to know. "So you see," I concluded, "it looks like someone had got it in for Kerrchem, and Joey Morton just got in the way."

He rubbed the bridge of his nose in a familiar gesture. It didn't erase the frown he'd had since I first walked through the door. "Very interesting, Miss Brannigan," he said. "I take it you're planning to pursue your own inquiries along these lines?"

"It's what I'm paid to do," I said.

"This is a possible murder inquiry," he said sententiously. "There's no place for you poking around in it."

"Inspector, in case you've forgotten, it was me that came to you. I'm trying to be helpful," I said, forcing my jaw to unclench.

"And your 'help' is duly noted," he said. "It's our job now. If you interfere with this investigation like you did the last time, I'll have no hesitation in arresting you. Is that clear?"

I stood up. I know five foot three isn't exactly intimidating, but it made me feel better. "I'll do my job, Inspector. And when I've done it, I'll tell you where you can find your killer."

I tried to slam the door behind me, but it had one of those hydraulic arms. Instead of a satisfying crash, I ended up with a twisted wrist. I was still fizzing when I got back to the car, so I decided to kill two birds with one stone. Down the Thai boxing gym I could work out my rage and frustration and, with a bit of luck, acquire some information too.

I like the gym. It's a no-frills establishment, which means I tend not to run into clients there. As well as the boxing gym, it's got a weights room and basic changing facilities. The only drawback is that there are never enough showers at busy times. Judging by the number of open lockers, that wasn't going to be a problem today. I emerged from the women's changing room in the breeze-block drill hall to find my mate Dennis O'Brien lounging in a director's chair in his sweats. He was reading the *Chronicle*, his mobile phone, cigarettes and a mug of tea strategically placed on the floor by his feet. Dennis used to be a serious burglar, the kind who turn over the vulgar suburban houses of the nouveau riche. But it all came on top for him when a young lad he'd brought in to help him with a big job managed to drop the safe on Dennis's leg as they were making their getaway. He left Dennis lying on the drive with a broken ankle. By the time the cops arrived, he'd crawled half a mile. When he got out of prison three years later, he swore he was never going to do anything that would get him taken away from his kids again. As far as I know, he's kept his word, with one exception. The lad who abandoned him still walks with a limp.

It was Dennis who got me into Thai boxing. He believes all women should have self-defence skills, and when he discovered I'd been relying on nothing more than charm and a reasonable turn of speed, he'd dragged me down to the gym. His daughter's been a finalist in the national championships for the last three years running, and he lets her beat me up on a regular basis, just to remind me that there are people out there who could cause me serious damage. As if I need reminding after some of the crap I've been through in recent years.

Now he's out of major-league villainy and into "a bit of this, a bit of that, a bit of ducking and diving," Dennis has taken to using the gym as his corporate headquarters. I don't suppose the management mind. All the locals know Dennis's Draconian views on drugs so his presence keeps the gym clear of steroid abuse. And there are never any fights outside the ring. He's not known in South Manchester as Dennis the Menace for nothing.

I checked out a couple of black lads working the heavy bags at the far end of the room. They were too far away to overhear. "Your backside will start looking like Richard's car if you carry on like that," I said, smiling over the top of his paper.

"At last, someone worth sparring with," Dennis said, bouncing to his feet. "How's it hanging, kid?"

"By a fingernail," I said, bending over to start my warm-up exercises. "What do you know?" I glanced over at Dennis, who was mirroring my movements.

He looked glum. "Tell you the truth, Kate, I'm in the shit," he said.

"Want to tell me about it?"

"Remember that nice little earner I told you about a while back? My crime prevention scheme?"

How could I forget? Dennis's latest scam involved parting villains from large wads of money by persuading them they were buying a truckload of stolen merchandise from him. Dennis would show them a sample of the goods (bought or shoplifted from one of the dozens of wholesalers down Strangeways) and arrange a handover the following day in a motorway service area. Only, once the punters had swapped their stash for the keys to the alleged wagonload and Dennis's car was a distant puff of exhaust, the crooks would discover that the keys he'd handed them didn't open a single truck on the lorry park. Crime prevention? Well, if Dennis was taking their money off them, they wouldn't be inciting anyone else to steal something for them to buy, now would they?

"Somebody catch up with you?" I gasped between sit-ups.

"Worse than that," he said gloomily. "I set up a meet at Anderton Services on the 61. Ten grand for a wagon of Levis. Everything's going sweet as a Sunday morning shag when it all comes on top. All of a sudden, there's more bizzies than you get on crowd control at a United/City match. I legged it over the footbridge and dived into the ladies' toilet. Sat there for two hours. I went back over just in time to see the Dibble loading my Audi on to a tow truck. I couldn't fucking believe it, could I?" Dennis grunted as he did a handful of squat thrusts.

"Somebody tip them off about you?" I asked, fastening a body protector over my front.

"You kidding me? This wasn't regular Old Bill, this was the Drugs Squad. They'd only been staking the place out because they'd had a tip a big crack deal was going down. They see somebody handing over a wad of cash, and they jump to the wrong conclusion."

"So what's happening?" I asked, pulling the ropes apart and climbing into the ring.

Dennis followed me and we began to circle each other cautiously. "They lifted my punter and accused him of being a drug baron." He snorted. "That pillock couldn't deal a hand of poker, never mind a key of crack. Any road, he's so desperate to get out of the shit he's drowning in that he coughs the lot. Next morning, they're round my house mob-handed. The wife was mortified."

"They charging you?" I asked, swinging a swift kick in towards Dennis's knee.

He sidestepped and twisted round, catching me over the right hip. "Got to, haven't they? Otherwise they come away from their big stakeout empty-handed. Theft, and obtaining by deception."

I didn't say anything. I didn't need to. Dennis might have been clean as far as the law is concerned for half a dozen years now, but with his record, he was looking at doing time. I feinted left and pivoted on the ball of my foot to bring my right leg up in a fast arc that caught Dennis in the ribs.

"Nice one, Kate," he wheezed as he bounced back off the ropes.

"Bit of luck, your punters might decide it would be bad for their reputations if they weigh in as witnesses when it comes to court." It wasn't much consolation but it was all I could think of.

"Never mind their reputation, it wouldn't be too good for their health," he said darkly. "Anyway, I've got one or two things on the boil. Just a bit of insurance in case I do go down. Make sure Debbie and the kids don't go without if I'm away."

I didn't ask what kind of insurance. I knew better. We worked out in silence for a while. I was upset at the thought of only seeing Dennis with a visiting order for the next couple of years, but there was nothing I could do to help him out, and he knew that as well as I did. Even though we have more attitudes in common than seems likely on the surface, there are areas of each other's lives we take care to avoid. Mostly they're to do with knowledge that either of us would feel uncomfortable about keeping to ourselves. I don't tell him when I'm about to drop people in it who he knows, and he doesn't tell me things I'd feel impelled to pass on to the cops.

After fifteen minutes of dodging each other round the ring, we were both sweating. I lost concentration for a moment, which was all it took. Next thing I knew, I was on my back staring at the strip lights.

"Sloppy," Dennis remarked.

I scrambled up to find him leaning on the ropes. I could have knocked the wind out of him with one kick. Or maybe not. I've come into contact with that rock-hard diaphragm before. "Got a lot on my mind," I said.

"Anything I can help with?" he asked. Typical Dennis. Didn't matter how much crap of his own he had to sort out, he was still determined to stay in the buddy role.

"Maybe," I said, slipping between the ropes and heading for the neat stack of scruffy towels on a shelf.

Dennis followed me, and we sat companionably on a bench while we talked. I gave him a brief outline of the Kerrchem case. "You know anybody who's doing schneid cleaning fluid?" I ended up.

He shook his head. "I don't know anybody that stupid," he said scornfully. "There's not nearly enough margin in it, is there? And it's bulky. Costs you a lot to shift it around, and you can't exactly set up a street-corner pitch with it, can you? There was a team from Liverpool tried schneid washing powder a couple of years back. They'd done a raid on a chemical firm, nicked one of their vans to do the getaway. There were a couple of drums of chemicals in the back, and they decided not to waste it so they printed up some boxes and flogged it on the markets. Nasty stuff. Took the skin off your fingers if you tried hand-washing. Mind you, there weren't any of them 'difficult' stains left. That's because there wasn't a lot of clothes left."

"So you don't reckon it's any of the usual faces?"

Dennis shook his head. "Like I said, you'd have to be stupid to go for that when there's plenty of hooky gear around with bigger profits and a lot less risk. I reckon you're looking closer to home on this one. This is a grudge match."

"An ex-employee? A competitor?" Even though it's a long way removed from his world, it's always worth bouncing ideas off Dennis.

Dennis shrugged. "You're the corporate expert. Is this the kind of stunt big business pulls these days? I'd heard things were getting a bit tough out there, but bumping people off is a bit heavy for a takeover bid."

"So an ex-employee, you reckon?"

"That's where I'd put my money. Stands to reason—they're the ones with a real grudge, and there's no comeback. And what about them thingumabobs . . . what do they call it? When they give you the bullet and make you sign a bit of paper saying you can't go off and sell their secrets to the opposition?"

"Golden handcuffs," I said ruefully. I was slipping. That should have been one of the first half-dozen questions I asked Trevor Kerr.

"Yeah well, nobody likes being stuck in a pair of handcuffs, don't matter whether they're gold or steel," Dennis said with feeling. "It was me, I'd feel pretty cheesed. Specially if I was one of them boffins whose expertise goes out of date faster than a Marks and Spencer ready meal."

I stretched an arm round his muscular shoulders and hugged him. "You're a pal, Dennis."

"I haven't done anything," he said. "That it? You consulted the oracle?"

"That's it. Unless you know an international gang of art thieves."

"Art thieves?" he asked, sounding interested.

"They've been working all over the country, turning over stately homes. They go for one item and crash in through the nearest door or window. No finesse, just sledgehammers. Straight in and out. Obviously very professional. Sound like anybody you know?"

Dennis pulled a face. "I'm well out of touch with that scene," he said, getting to his feet. "I'm off for a shower. Will you still be here when I'm done?"

I glanced at my watch. "No, got to run." Whatever else happened today, I couldn't leave Richard standing around at the multi-screen.

"See you around, kid," Dennis said, walking off.

"Yeah. And Dennis . . ."

He looked over his shoulder, the changing room door half open.

"If there's anything I can do . . ."

Dennis's smile was as crooked as his business. "You'll know," he said.

Back at the car, I hit the phone. Sheila the Dragon Queen tried to tell me Trevor Kerr was in a meeting, but she was no match for my civil servant impersonation. I had good teachers; I once devoted most of my spare time for six months to screwing housing benefit out of a succession of bloody-minded officials.

"Trevor Kerr," the phone barked at me.

"Kate Brannigan here. I've spoken to the police, who were very interested in what I had to tell them about the fake KerrSter," I said. "They said they would investigate that angle."

"You pulled me out of a production meeting to tell me that?" he demanded.

"Not only that," I said mildly. It was an effort. If he carried on like this, I reckoned there was going to be a five per cent surliness surcharge on Trevor Kerr's bill.

"What, then?"

"You mentioned you'd had a round of redundancies," I said.

"So?"

"I wondered if anyone who'd gone out the door had been subject to a golden handcuffs deal."

There was a moment's silence. "There must have been a few," he admitted grudgingly. "It's standard practice for anybody working in research or in key production jobs."

"I'll need a list."

"You'll have one," he said.

"Have it faxed to my office," I replied. "The number's on the card." I cut the connection. That's the great thing with mobile phones. There are so many black holes around that nobody dares accuse you of hanging up on them any more.

I took out my notebook and rang the number Alexis had given me earlier. The voice that answered the phone didn't sound like Lord Ballantrae. Not unless he'd had an unfortunate accident. "I'm looking for Lord Ballantrae," I said.

"This is his wife," she said. "Who's calling?"

"My name is Kate Brannigan. I'm a private investigator in Manchester. I understand Lord Ballantrae is the coordinator of a group of stately home owners who have been burgled recently. One of my clients has had a Monet stolen, and I wondered if Lord Ballantrae could spare me some time to discuss it."

"I'm sure he'd be happy to do so. Bear with me a moment, I'll check the diary." I hung on for an expensive minute. Then she was back. "How does tomorrow at ten sound?"

"No problem," I said.

"Now, if you're coming from Manchester, the easiest way is to come straight up the M6, then take the A7 at Carlisle as far as Hawick, then the A698 through Kelso. About six miles past Kelso, you'll see a couple of stone gateposts on the left with pineapples on top of them. You can't miss them. That's us. Castle Dumdivie. Did you get all that?"

"Yes, thank you," I said weakly. I'd got it, all right. A good three to four hours' driving.

"We'll look forward to seeing you then," Lady Ballantrae said. She sounded remarkably cheerful. It was nice to know one of us was.

# 9

Richard didn't even stir when the alarm cut through my dreams at ten to six like a hot wire through cheese. I staggered to the shower, feeling like my eyes had closed only ten minutes before. Until I started this job, I didn't even know there were two six o'clocks in the same day. Richard still doesn't. I suppose that's why he suggested a club after the latest Steven Spielberg, enough popcorn to feed Bosnia and burgers and beer at Starvin' Marvin's authentic American diner. We'd been having fun together, and I didn't want it to end on a sour note, so I'd agreed with the proviso that I could be a party pooper at one. It goes without saying that we were still dancing at two.

Even a ten-minute power shower couldn't convince my body and my brain that I'd had more than three hours' sleep. Sometimes I wish I hadn't jacked in the law degree after two years, so I could have become a nine-to-five crown prosecutor. I put a pot of strong coffee on to brew while I dressed. Just what do you wear for a Scottish baron that won't look like a limp dishrag after four hours behind the wheel? I ended up with navy leggings, a cream cotton Aran jumper and a military-style navy wool blouson that I inherited from Alexis. I'd told her in the shop that it made her look too heavy in the hips, but would she listen?

By the third cup of coffee, I felt like I could be trusted to drive without causing a major pile-up. Not that there was a lot of traffic around to test my conviction. For once, it was sheer pleasure to motor down the East Lancs. Road. No boy racers wanting to get into a traffic-lights grand prix with my coupé, no little old men with porkpie hats and pipes dithering between lanes, no macho reps waving their mobile phones like battle honours. Just blissful open road spread out before me and Deacon Blue's greatest hits. Since I was going to Scotland, I thought I'd better opt for the native sound. When I left the motorway at Carlisle, it was just after eight. I promised myself breakfast at the first greasy spoon I passed, forgetting what roads in the Scottish borders are like. There was nothing for the best part of an hour, and then it was Hawick. I ended up with a bacon and egg roll from a bakery washed down with a carton of milky industrial effluent that they claimed was coffee.

At a quarter to ten, I spotted the gateposts. When Lady Ballantrae had said pineapples, I was expecting some discreet little stone ornaments. What I got were two squat pillars topped with carved monstrosities the size of telephone kiosks. She'd been right when she said I couldn't miss them. I turned into a narrow corridor between two beech hedges taller than my house. The road curved round in a gentle arc. Abruptly the trees stopped and I found myself in a grassy clearing dominated by Lord Ballantrae's house. I use the term "house" loosely. At one end of the sprawling building was a massive square stone tower with a sharply pitched roof. Extending out from it, built in the same forbidding grey stone, was the main house. The basic shape was rectangular, but it was dotted with so many turrets, buttresses and assorted excrescences that it was hard to grasp at first. The whole thing was surmounted by an incongruous white belvedere with a green roof. One of Ballantrae's ancestors either had a hell of a sense of humour or a few bricks short of a wall.

I pulled up on the gravel between a Range Rover and a top-of-the-range BMW. What they call in Manchester a

"Break My Windows." Like Henry, Lord Ballantrae clearly kept the trippers' coaches well away from the house. By the time I'd got out of the car, I had a spectator. At the top of a short flight of steps like a giant's mounting block a tall man stood staring at me, a hand shielding his eyes from the sun. I walked towards him, taking in the tweed jacket with leather shooting patches, cavalry twills, mustard waistcoat and tattersall check shirt. He was even wearing a tweed cap that matched the jacket. As soon as I was in hailing distance, he called, "Miss Brannigan, is it?"

"The same. Lord Ballantrae?"

The man dropped his hand and looked amused. "No, ma'am, I'm his lordship's estate manager. Barry Adamson. Come away in, he's expecting you."

I followed Adamson's burly back into a comfortable dining kitchen. Judging by the microwave and food processor on the pine worktops, this wasn't part of the castle's historical tour. Beyond the kitchen, we entered a narrow passage that turned into a splendid baronial hall. I don't know much about weapons, but judging by the amount of military hardware in the room, I'd stumbled upon Bonnie Prince Charlie's secret armoury. "Through here," Adamson said, opening a heavy oak door. I followed him through the arched doorway into an office that looked nearly as high tech as Bill's.

A dark-haired man in his early forties was frowning into a PC screen. Without looking up, he said, "With you in two shakes." He hit a couple of keys and the frown cleared. Then he pushed his chair back and jumped to his feet. "You must be Kate Brannigan," he said, coming round the desk and thrusting his hand towards me. "James Ballantrae." The handshake was cool and dry, but surprisingly limp. "Pull up a seat," he said, waving at a couple of typist's chairs that sat in front of a desk top that ran the length of one wall. "Barry, Ellen's in the tack room. Can you give her a shout and ask her to bring us some coffee?" he added as he dragged his own chair round the desk. "How was your journey?" he asked. "Bitch of a drive, isn't it? I sometimes wish I could ship this place stone by stone to somewhere approximating civilization, but they'd never let me get away with it. It's Grade Two listed, which means we couldn't even have satellite TV installed without some bod from the Department of the Environment making a meal out of it."

Whatever I'd been expecting, it wasn't this. Lord Ballantrae was wearing faded jeans and a Scottish rugby shirt that matched sparkling navy blue eyes. His wavy hair fell over his collar at the back, its coal black a startling contrast to his milky skin. There was an air of suppressed energy about him. He looked more like a computer-game writer than a major land owner. He sat down, stretching long legs in front of him, and lit a cigarette. "So, Henry Naismith tells me you're looking for his Monet?" he said.

I tried to hide my surprise. "You know Henry?" I asked. Let's face it, they both spoke the same language. Their voices were virtually indistinguishable. How in God's name do Sloanes know who's calling when they pick up the phone?

He grinned. "We met once on a friend's boat. When my wife told me about your call yesterday, I put two and two together. I'd already spoken to a reporter on the Manchester evening paper about these art robberies and when she mentioned a Monet going missing in Cheshire, I could only think of the Naismith collection. So I gave Henry a ring."

"The reporter you spoke to is a friend of mine," I said. "She passed your number on to me."

"Old girls' network. I like it," he exclaimed with delight. "She did the right thing. God, listen to me. My wife tells me that arrogance runs in the family. All I mean is that I'm probably the only person who has an overview of the situation. The downside of having locally accountable police forces is that crime gets compartmentalized. Sussex don't talk to Strathclyde, Derbyshire don't talk to Devon. It was us who brought to the police's attention the fact that there had been something of a spate of these robberies, all with the same pattern of forced entry, complete disregard for the alarm system and single targets."

"How did you find out about the connections?" I asked.

"A group of us who open our places to the public get together informally . . ." I heard the door open behind me and turned to see a thirty-something redhead with matching freckles stick her head through the gap.

"Coffee all round?" she said.

"My wife, Ellen," Ballantrae said. "Ellen, this is Kate Brannigan, the private eye from Manchester."

The redhead grinned. "Pleased to meet you. Be right back," she said, disappearing from sight, leaving the door ajar.

"Where was I? Oh yes, we get together a couple of times a year for a few sherbets, swap ideas and tips, that sort of thing. Last time we met was a couple of weeks after I'd had a Raeburn portrait lifted, so of course it was uppermost in my mind. Three others immediately chipped in with identical tales—a Gainsborough, a Canaletto and a Ruisdael. In every case, it was one of the two or three best pieces they had," he added ruefully.

"And that's when you realized there was something organized going on?" I asked.

"Correct."

"I'm amazed you managed to keep these thefts out of the papers," I said.

"It's not the sort of thing you boast about," he said drily. "We've all become dependent on the income that comes through the doors from the heritage junkies. The police were happy to go along with that, since they never like high-profile cases where they don't catch anyone."

"What did you do then?"

"Well, I offered to act as coordinator, and I spoke to all the police forces concerned. I also wrote to as many other stately home owners as I could track down and asked if they'd had similar experiences."

"How many?" I asked.

"Including Henry Naismith's Monet, thirteen in the last nine months."

I took a deep breath. At this rate, the stately homes of Britain would soon have nothing left but the seven hundred and thirty-six beds Good Queen Bess slept in. "That's a lot of art," I said. "Has anything been recovered?"

"Coffee," Ellen Ballantrae announced, walking in with a tray. She was wearing baggy khaki cords and a shapeless bottle green chenille sweater. When she moved, it was obvious she was hiding a slim figure underneath, but on first sight I'd have taken her for the cleaner.

I fell on the mug like a deprived waif. "You've probably saved my life," I told her. "My system's still recovering from what they call coffee in Hawick."

Both Ballantraes grinned. "Don't tell me," Ellen said. "Warm milk, globules floating on top and all the flavour of rainwater."

"It wasn't that good," I said with feeling.

"Don't let me interrupt you," she said, giving her husband's hair an affectionate tousle as she perched on the table. "He was about to tell you about the Canaletto they got back."

Ballantrae reached out absently and laid his hand on her thigh. "Absolutely right. Nothing to do with the diligence of the police, however. There was a multiple pile-up on a German autobahn about a fortnight after Gerald Brockleston-Camber lost his Canaletto. One of the dead was an antique dealer from Leyden in Holland, Kees van der Rohe. His car was shunted at both ends, the boot flew open, throwing a suitcase clear of the wreckage. The case burst open, revealing the Canaletto behind a false lid. Luckily the painting was undamaged."

"Not so lucky for Mr van der Rohe," I remarked. "What leads did they come up with?"

"Not a one," Ballantrae said. "They couldn't find anything about the Canaletto in his records. He conducted his business from home, and the neighbours said there were sometimes cars there with foreign plates, but no one had bothered to take a note of registrations." He shrugged. "Why should they? There was no indication as to his destination, apart from the fact that he had a couple of hundred pounds' worth of lire in the front pocket of the suitcase. Unfortunately, van der Rohe's body was badly burned, along with his diary and his wallet. Frustrating, but at least Gerald got his painting back."

Frustrating was right. This was turning into one of those cases where I was sucking up information like a demented Hoover, but none of it was taking me anywhere. The only thing I could think of doing now was getting in touch with a Dutch private eye and asking him or her to check out Kees van der Rohe, to see if he could come up with something the police had missed. "Any indication of a foreign connection in the other cases?" I asked.

"Not really," Ballantrae said. "We suspect that individual pieces are being stolen to order. If anything, I'd hazard a guess that if they're for a private collector, we're looking at someone English. A lot of the items that have been stolen have quite a narrow appeal—the Hilliard miniatures, for example. And my Raeburn too, I suppose. They wouldn't exactly set the international art world ablaze."

"Maybe that's part of the plan," I mused.

"How do you mean?" Ellen Ballantrae leaned forward, frowning.

"If they went for really big stuff like the thieves who stole the Munch painting in Norway, there would be a huge hue and cry, Interpol alerted, round up the usual suspects, that sort of thing. But by going for less valuable pieces, maybe they're relying on there being less of a fuss, especially if they're moving their loot across international borders," I explained.

Ballantrae nodded appreciatively. "Good thinking, that woman. You could have something there. The only thefts that fall outside that are the Bernini bust and Henry's Monet, but even those two aren't the absolutely prime examples of their creators' works."

"Can you think of any collectors whose particular interests are covered by the thefts?" I asked.

"Do you know, I hadn't thought about that. I don't know personally, but I have a couple of chums in the gallery business. I could ask them to ask around and see what they come up with. That's a really constructive idea," Ballantrae enthused.

I basked in the glow of his praise. It made a refreshing change from Trevor Kerr's charmlessness. "What's the geographical spread like?" I asked.

"We were the most northerly victims. But there doesn't seem to be any real pattern. They go from Northumberland to Cornwall north to south, and from Lincolnshire to Anglesey east to west. I can let you have a print-out," he added, jumping to his feet and walking behind his computer. He hit a few keys, and the printer behind me cranked itself into life.

I twirled the chair round and took the sheet of paper out of the machine. Reading down it, I saw the glimmer of an idea. "Have you got a map of the UK I can look at?" I asked.

Ballantrae nodded. "I've got a data disk with various maps on it. Want a look?"

I came round behind his desk and waited for him to load the disk. He called up a map of the UK with major cities and the road network. "Can you import this map and manipulate it in a graphics file?" I asked.

"Sure," he said. And promptly did it. He gave me a quick tutorial on how to use his software, and I started fiddling with it. First, I marked the approximate locations of the burglaries, with a little help from Ballantrae in identifying locations. I looked at the array.

"I wish we had one of those programs that crime pattern analysts use," I muttered. I'd recently spent a day at a seminar run by the Association of British Investigators where an academic had shown us how sophisticated computer programs were helping police to predict where repeat offenders might strike next. It had been impressive, though not a lot of use to the likes of me.

"I never imagined I'd have any use for one of those," Ballantrae said drily.

Ellen laughed. "No doubt the software king will have one by next week," she said.

Using the mouse, I drew a line connecting the outermost burglaries. There were eight in that group, scattered round the fringes of England and Wales. Then I repeated the exercise with the remainder. The outer line was a rough oval, with a kink over Cornwall. It looked like a cartoon speech balloon, containing the immortal words of the Scilly Isles. The inner line was more jagged. I disconnected Henry Naismith's robbery and another outside Burnley. Now, the inner line was more like a trapezium, narrower at the top, spreading at the bottom. Finally, I linked Henry and the Burnley job with a pair of semi-circles. "See anything?" I asked.

"Greater Manchester," Ballantrae breathed. "How fascinating. Well, Ms Brannigan, you're clearly the right woman for the job."

I was glad somebody thought so. "Have there been any clues at all in any of the cases?" I asked.

Ballantrae walked over to a shelf that held his computer software boxes and manuals. "I don't know if you'd call it a clue, exactly. But one of the properties that was burgled had just installed closed-circuit TV and they have a video of the robbery. But it's not actually a lot of help, since the thieves were very sensibly wearing ski masks." He took a video down from the shelf. "Would you like to see it?"

"Why not?" I'd schlepped all the way up here. I wasn't going home before I'd extracted every last drop of info out of Lord Ballantrae.

"We'll have to go through to the den," he said.

As I followed him back across the hall, Ellen said affectionately, "Some days I think he's auditioning for *Crimewatch*."

We retraced my steps back towards the kitchen, turning into a room only twice the size of my living room. The view was spectacular, if you like that sort of thing, looking out across a swathe of grass, a river and not very distant hills. Me, I'm happy with my garden fence. As Ballantrae crossed to the video, I gave the room the once-over. It wasn't a bit like a stately home. The mismatched collection of sofas and armchairs was modern, looking comfortable if a bit dog-haired and dog-eared. Shelves along one wall held a selection of board games, jigsaws, console games and video tapes. A coffee table was strewn with comics and magazines. In one corner there was a huge Nicam stereo TV and video with a Nintendo console lying in front of it. The only picture on the walls was a framed photograph of James and Ellen with a young boy and girl, sitting round a picnic table in skiing clothes. They all looked as if the world was their oyster. Come to think of it, it probably was.

"Sorry about the mess," Ellen said in the offhand tone that told me she didn't give a shit about tidiness. "The children make it and I can't be bothered unmaking it. Have a seat."

She walked over to the windows and pulled one of the curtains across, cutting down the brightness so we could see the video more clearly. I sat down opposite the TV, where daytime TV's best actors played out their roles as a happily married couple telling the rest of us how to beat cellulite. Ballantrae slumped down beside me and hit the "play" button. "This is Morton Grange in Humberside," he said. "Home of Lord Andrew Cumberbatch. His was the Ruisdael."

The screen showed an empty room lined with paintings. Suddenly, from the bottom left-hand corner, the burglars appeared. The staccato movements of the time-lapse photography made them look like puppets in an amateur performance.

Both men were wearing ski masks with holes for eyes and mouth only, and the kind of overalls you can pick up for next to nothing in any army surplus store. One of them ran across to the painting, pulled out a power screwdriver and unscrewed the clips that held the frame to the wall. The other, holding a sledgehammer, hung back. Then he turned towards the camera and took a couple of steps forward.

Recognition hit me like a punch to the stomach.

# 10

One of the mysteries of the universe is how I got out of Castle Dumdivie without confessing that I knew exactly who had had it away on his toes with Lord Andrew Cumberbatch's nice little Ruisdael. I was only grateful that James Ballantrae was sitting next to me and couldn't see my face.

After the first seconds of shock, I tried to tell myself I was imagining things. But the longer I watched, the more convinced I was that I was right. I knew those shoulders, those light, bouncing steps. God knows I'd watched that footwork often enough, trying to gauge where the next kick was coming from. I forced myself to sit motionless to the bitter end. Then I said, "I see what you mean. Even their own mothers wouldn't recognize them from that."

"Their lovers might," Ellen said shrewdly. "Don't they say a person's walk is the one thing they can never disguise?"

She was bang on the button, of course. "The video makes it look too jerky for that, I'd have thought," I said.

"I don't know." Ballantrae lit another cigarette and inhaled deeply. "Body language and gesture are pretty individual. Look at the number of crimimals who get caught by the videos they show on *Crimewatch*."

"Told you," Ellen said fondly. "He's dying to go on and talk about his art robberies. The only thing that's holding him back is that all his cronies are terrified about what the publicity might do to their admissions."

"Yes, but now the cat's out of the bag with that newspaper story in Manchester, there's no point in holding back," Ballantrae said. "Maybe I should give them a ring . . ."

"Any chance you could let me have a copy of the tape?" I asked. "I'd like to show it to Henry Naismith's staff while everything's still fresh in their memories. Perhaps, as Ellen suggests, there might be something in the way these men move that triggers something off. The police reckon they will have gone round the house a couple of times as regular punters, sussing it out, so we might just get lucky if one of Henry's staff has a photographic memory."

Ballantrae got up and took the video out of the machine. "Take this one," he said. "I can easily get Andrew to run me off another copy."

I took the tape and stood up. "I really appreciate your help on this," I said. "If anything else should come to mind that might be useful, please give me a ring." I fished a business card out of my bag.

"What will you do now?" Ballantrae asked.

"Like I said, show the vid to Henry's staff. I'm also hopeful that the story in the *Chronicle* might stir the pot a bit. The chances are that it's not just the robbers themselves who know who they are. Maybe you should think about getting together with your insurance companies and offering a reward. It would make a good follow-up story for the paper and it might just be what we need to lever the lid off things." I was starting to gabble, I noticed. Time for a sharp exit. I ostentatiously looked at my watch. "I'd better be heading back to the wicked city," I said.

"You're sure you've got to go?" Ballantrae asked with the pathetic eagerness of a small boy who sees his legitimate diversion from homework disappearing over a distant horizon. "I could show you round the house. You could see for yourself where they broke in."

Amused, Ellen said, "I'm sure Ms Brannigan's seen one or two windows in her time." Turning to me, she added, "You're very welcome to stay for lunch, but if you have to get back, don't feel the need to apologize for turning down the guided tour of Dumdivie's loot."

"Thanks for the offer, but I need to hit the road," I said. "This isn't the only case we've got on right now, and my partner's out of the country." I really was wittering now. I took a step towards the door. "I'll keep you posted."

I drove back to Manchester on automatic pilot, my thoughts whirling. Shelley phoned at one point, but I'm damned if I know what we talked about. When I hit the city, I didn't go to the office. I didn't want any witnesses to the conversation I was planning. I drove straight home, glad for once to find Richard was out.

My stomach was churning, so I brewed some coffee and made myself a sandwich of ciabatta, tuna, olives and plum tomatoes. It was only when I tried to eat it and found I had no appetite that I realized it was anxiety rather than hunger that was responsible for the awesome rumblings. Sighing, I wrapped the sandwich in clingfilm and tossed it in the fridge. I picked up the phone. Some money-grabbing computer took ten pence off me for the privilege of telling me Dennis's mobile was switched off.

Next, I rang the gym. Don, the manager, told me Dennis had been in earlier, but had gone off a couple of hours ago suited up. "If he comes back, tell him I've been visiting the gentry and he needs to see me, double urgent. I'll be at home," I said grimly.

That left his home. His wife Debbie answered on the third ring. She's got a heart of gold, but she could have provided the model for the dumb blonde stereotype. I'd always reckoned that if a brain tumour were to find its way inside her skull it would bounce around for days looking for a place to settle. However, I wasn't planning on challenging her intellect. I just asked if Dennis was there, and she said she hadn't seen him since breakfast. "Do you know where he is?" I asked.

She snorted incredulously. "I gave up asking him stuff like that fifteen years ago," she said. Maybe she wasn't as thick as I'd always thought. "To be honest, I'd rather not know what he's up to most of the time. Long as he gives me money for the kids and the house and he stays out of jail, I ask no questions. That way, when the Old Bill comes knocking, there's nothing I can tell them. He knows I'm a crap liar," she giggled.

"When are you expecting him back?"

"When I see him, love. Have you tried his mobile?"

"Switched off."

"He won't have it turned off for long," Debbie reassured me. "If he comes home before you catch him, do you want me to get him to give you a bell?"

"No. I want him to come round the house. Tell him it's urgent, would you?"

"You're not in any trouble, are you, Kate?" Debbie asked anxiously. "Only, if you need somebody in a hurry, I could get one of the lads to come round."

Like I said, heart of gold. "Don't worry, Debbie, I'm fine. I've got something I need to show Dennis, that's all. Just ask him to come round soon as."

We chatted for a bit about the kids, then I rang off. I knew I should go into the office and pick up Trevor Kerr's list of former employees, but I knew I wouldn't be able to concentrate on it. I switched on the computer and loaded up *Epic Pinball*. I thrashed the ball round the bumpers and ramps a few times, but I couldn't get into it. My scores would have shamed an arthritic octogenarian. I decided I needed something more violent, so I started playing *Doom*, the ultimate shoot-'em-up, at maximum danger level. After I got killed for the tenth time, I gave up and switched the machine off. I know it's as bad as it can get when I can't lose myself in a computer game.

I ended up cleaning the house. The trouble with modern bungalows is that it doesn't take nearly long enough to bottom them when you want a really good angst-letting. By the time the doorbell rang, I'd moved on to purging my wardrobe of all those garments I hadn't worn for two years but had cost too much for me to dump in my normal frame of mind. A disastrous pair of leggings that looked like stretch chintz curtains were saved by the bell.

Dennis stood on the doorstep, grinning cheerily. I wanted to smack him, but good sense prevailed over desire. It seemed to have been doing that a lot lately. "Hiya. Debbie says you've got something for me," he greeted me, leaning forward to kiss my cheek.

I backed off, letting him teeter. "Something to show you," I corrected him, marching through into my living room. Without waiting for him to sit down, I smacked the tape into the video, turned on the TV and pressed "play." I kept my back to him while the robbery replayed itself before our eyes. As the two burglars disappeared from sight, I switched off the TV and turned to face him.

Dennis's expression revealed nothing. I might as well have shown him a blank screen for all the reaction I was getting. "Nice one, Dennis," I said bitterly. "Thanks for marking my card."

He thrust his hands into the trouser pockets of his immaculate, pearl grey, double-breasted suit. "What did you expect me to do? Put my hands up when you told me what you was looking into?" he said quietly.

"Never mind what I expected," I said. "What you did do has dropped me right in it."

Dennis frowned. "What is this?" he demanded angrily. "You know the kind of thing I do for a living. I'm not some snow-white straight man. I'm a thief, Kate, a fucking criminal. I steal things, I have people over, I pull scams. How else do you think I put food in my kids' mouths and clothes on their backs? It's not like I've been keeping it a big fucking secret, is it?"

"No, but . . ."

"What's wrong? You're quick enough to come to me for help because I can go places and get people to talk that you can't. You think I could do that if I wasn't as bent as the bastards you chase? What is it, Kate? You can't handle the fact that one of your mates is a crook now you're faced with the evidence?"

I found myself subsiding on to a sofa. He was right, of course. I've always known in the abstract that Dennis was a villain, but I'd never had to confront it directly. "I thought you weren't doing this kind of thing any more," I said weakly. "You always said you wouldn't do stuff that would get you a long stretch again."

Dennis threw himself on to the sofa opposite me. A grim smile flashed across his face. "That was the plan. Then everything came on top, like I told you. Kate, I could get five for that. My kids shouldn't have to suffer because I'm a villain, should they? I don't want my kids not being able to go to university because their old man's inside and there's no money. I don't want my family living in some bed-and-breakfast doss house because the mortgage hasn't been paid and the house has been repo'ed. Now, the only way I know to make sure that doesn't happen is to salt away some insurance money. And the only way I know to get money is robbing."

"So you've been doing these art robberies," I said.

"That's right. Listen, if I'd known that you'd done the security on Birchfield Place, I wouldn't have gone near the gaff. You're my mate, I don't want to embarrass you."

I shook my head. "If I recognized you, Dennis, chances are someone else might, especially if they put the tape on the box."

He sighed. "So do what you have to do, Kate." He met my eyes, not in a challenge, but in a kind of agreement.

"You don't think I'm going to shop you, do you?" I blurted out indignantly.

"It's your job," he said simply.

I shook my head. "No, it's not. My job is to get my clients' property back. It's the police that arrest villains, not me."

"You've turned people over to the Dibble before," Dennis pointed out. "You got principles, you should stick to them. It's OK, Kate, I won't hold it against you. It's an occupational hazard. You work with asbestos, sometimes you get lung cancer. You go robbing for a living, sometimes you get a nicking. There's nothing personal in it."

"Will you get it into your thick head that I am not going to grass you up?" I said belligerently. "The only thing I'm interested in is getting Henry Naismith's Monet back. Anyway, you're only a small fish. If I want anybody, I want the whale."

Dennis's lips tightened to a thin line. "OK, I hear you," he said grimly. I didn't expect him to fall to his knees in gratitude. Nobody likes being placed under the kind of obligation I'd just laid on him.

"So cough," I said.

He cleared his throat. "It's not that simple," he said, taking his time over pulling out his cigarettes and lighting up. "I haven't got it any more."

"That was quick," I said, disappointed. From what Dennis had told me about his previous exploits in the field of executive burglary, it often takes some time to shift the proceeds, fences being notoriously twitchy about taking responsibility for stolen goods that are still so hot they risk meltdown.

Dennis leaned back in his seat, unbuttoning his jacket. "A ready market. That's one of the reasons I got into this in the first place. See, what happened was when I realized this court case wasn't going to go away, I put the word out that I was looking for a nice little earner. A couple of weeks later, I get a call from this bloke I know in Leeds. I fenced a couple of choice antique items with him in the old days when I was pursuing my former career. Anyway, he says he's heard about my bit of bother, and he's got a contact for me. He gives me this mobile phone number, and tells me to ring this bloke.

"So I ring the number and mention my contact's name and this bloke says to me he's in the market for serious art. He says he has a client for top-flight gear, flat fee of ten grand a pop for pieces agreed in advance. I go, 'How do I know I can trust you?' And he goes, 'You don't part with the gear till you see the colour of my money.' I go, 'How does it work?' And he goes, 'You decide on something you think you can get away with, and you ring me and ask me if I want it. I ring you back the next day with a yes or a no.'"

"So you embark on your new career as an art robber," I said. "Simple, really."

"You wouldn't be so sarcastic if you knew what a nause it is shifting stuff like that on the open market," Dennis said with feeling.

"How did you know what to go for? And where to go for it?" I demanded. I'd never had Dennis pegged as a paid-up member of the National Trust.

"My mate Frankie came out a while back," he said. I didn't think he meant that Frankie had revealed he was a raging queen. "He's been doing an eight stretch for armed robbery, and he did an Open University degree while he was inside. He did a couple of courses in history of art. He reckoned it would come in useful on the outside," he added drily.

"I don't think that's quite what the government had in mind when they set up the OU," I said.

Dennis grinned. "Get an education, get on in life. Anyway, we spent a couple of months schlepping round these country houses, sussing out what was where, what was worth nicking and what the security was like. Pathetic, most of it."

I had a sudden thought. "Dennis, these robberies have been going on for nine months now. You only got nicked a few weeks ago. You didn't start doing this for insurance money, you started doing this out of sheer badness," I accused him.

He shrugged, looking slightly shamefaced. "So I lied. I'm sorry, Kate, I can't change the habit of a lifetime. This was just too good to miss. And watertight. We don't touch places with security guards so nobody gets hurt or upset. We're in and out so fast there's no way we're going to get caught."

"I caught you," I pointed out.

"Yeah, but you're a special case," Dennis said. "Besides, the CCTV wasn't there when we cased the place. They must have only just put it in."

"So who is this guy who's giving you peanuts for these masterpieces?"

Dennis smiled wryly. "It's not peanuts, Kate. It's good money and no hassle."

"It's a tiny fraction of what they're worth," I said.

"Define worth. What an insurance company pays out? What you could get at auction? Worth is what somebody's prepared to pay. I reckon ten grand for a night's work is not bad going."

"A grand for every year if they catch you. You'd get a better rate of pay working in a sweatshop making schneid T-shirts. So who's the buyer? Some private collector or what?"

"I don't know," Dennis said. "I don't even know who the fence is."

I snorted incredulously. "Come on, Dennis, you've done more than a dozen deals with this guy, you must know who he is."

"I've never met him before this run of jobs," Dennis said. "All I've got is the number for his mobile."

"You're kidding," I said. "You've done over a hundred grand's worth of work for some punter whose name you don't even know?"

"'S right," he said easily. "My business isn't like yours, Kate, I don't take out credit references on the people I do business with. Look, what happens is, every few weeks I ring the guy up with one of Frankie's suggestions. He gives me the nod, we go out and do the job, and I give him a bell. We meet on the motorway services, we show him the goods, he counts the dosh in front of us, and we all go home happy boys."

"What about the fakes?"

There was a deathly silence. He ground out his cigarette viciously in the ashtray. "How did you find out about them?" Dennis asked warily. "There's been nothing in the papers or anything about that."

"What happens when it turns out you've nicked a copy?" I asked, ignoring him.

Dennis shifted in his seat, leaning forward with his elbows on his knees. "You setting me up, or what?" he asked. "You saying that Monet wasn't kosher?"

"It was kosher," I said. "But they haven't all been, have they?"

Dennis lit his cigarette like an actor in a Pinter play filling one of the gaps with a complicated bit of business. "Three of them were bent as a nine-bob note," he said. "First I knew about it was about a week after we'd done the handover when the geezer bells me and tells me. I said I never knew anything about it, and he goes, 'I'm sure you were acting in good faith, but the problem is that so was my client. He reckons you owe him ten grand. And he has very efficient debt collectors. But he's a fair man. He'll cancel the debt if you provide another painting for free.' So we to and fro a bit, and eventually he agrees that he'll pay us a grand for expenses for the next kosher one we bring him, and we're all square. So we go and do another one, and bugger me if it isn't bent as well." He shook his head in wonderment.

"Talk about a scam," he said. "These bastards with their country houses really know how to pull a con job on the punters. Anyway, we end up having to do a third job, this time for fuck all, just to get ourselves square. I mean, he's obviously dealing with the kind of money that can buy a lot of very vicious muscle. You don't mess with that."

"But everything's hunky-dory now, is it?"

He nodded, eating smoke. "Sweet."

"Great," I said. "Then you won't mind putting the two of us together, will you, Dennis?"

# 11

Once upon a time I had a fling with a Telecom engineer. It didn't end happily ever after, but he taught me more than I'll ever need to know about crossed lines. Along the way, before I accepted that great sex wasn't a long-term compensation for the conversational skills of Bonzo the chimpanzee, I met some very useful people. I met some bloody boring ones too, and unfortunately the crossover between the two groups was disturbingly large. Even more unfortunately, I was going to have to talk to one of them.

After I'd finally convinced Dennis that I wasn't going to back off and that the price of his liberty was putting me together with his fence, it hadn't taken me long to squeeze out of him the phone number of the contact. He'd left, grumbling that I was getting in over my head and I needn't come running to him when the roof fell in. Naturally, we both knew that in the event of such an architectural disaster, the combined emergency services of six counties wouldn't keep him away.

I watched his car drive away, not entirely certain I was doing the right thing. But I knew I couldn't turn Dennis over to the cops. It wasn't just about friendship, though that had been the key factor in my decision, no doubt about it. But I hadn't been lying when I said I wanted the people behind the whole shooting match. Without them, the robberies wouldn't end. They'd just find another Dennis to do the dirty work and carry the can. Besides, I wanted Henry's Monet back, and Dennis didn't have it any more.

After Dennis had gone, I rediscovered my appetite and wolfed the sandwich from the fridge before settling down to the thankless task of calling Gizmo. Gizmo works for Telecom as a systems engineer, which suits him down to the ground since he's the ultimate computer nerd. The first time I met him, he was even wearing an anorak. In a nightclub. I later discovered it was rare as hen's teeth to catch Gizmo out on the town. Normally the only thing that will prize him away from his computer screen is the promise of a secret password that will allow him to penetrate to the heart of some company's as yet virgin network. He's only ever happy when his modem's skittering round the world's bulletin boards. Gizmo would much rather be wandering round the Internet than the streets of Manchester. I thought Bill and I were pretty nifty movers round the intangible world of computer communications till I met Gizmo. Then I realized our joint hacking skills were the equivalent of comparing a ten-year-old's "What I did on my holidays" essay with Jan Morris on just about anywhere.

I looked Gizmo up in my Filofax. There were several points of contact listed there. I tried his phone, but it was engaged. What a surprise. I booted up my computer, loaded up my comms software and logged on to the electronic mail network that Mortensen and Brannigan subscribe to. I typed a message asking Gizmo to call me urgently and sent it to his mailbox.

The phone rang five minutes later. I'd specifically asked him to call me person to person. The last thing I wanted was to relay my request to him over the Net. You never know who's looking in, no matter how secure you think you are. That's one of the first things Gizmo taught me. "Kate?" he said suspiciously. Gizmo doesn't like talking; he prefers people to know only the constructed personality he releases over the computer network.

"Hi, Gizmo. How's life?" Silly question, really. Gizmo and life are barely on speaking terms.

"Just got myself a state-of-the-art rig," he said. "She's so fast, it's beautiful. So, what's going down with you?"

"Busy, busy. You know how it is. Gizmo, I need some help. Usual terms." Fifty quid in used notes in a brown envelope through his letter box. He comes so cheap because he loves poking around other people's computers in the same way that some men like blondes with long legs.

"Speak, it's your dime," he said. I took that for agreement.

"I've got a mobile number here that I need a name and address for."

"Is that all?" He sounded disappointed. I gave him the number. "Fine," he said. "I should be back to you later today."

"You're a star, Giz. If I'm not here, leave a message on the machine. The answering machine. OK?"

"OK."

The next call was to Lord Ballantrae. "I think I've got a lead," I told him. "To the fence, not the principal behind the robberies. But I need some help."

"That's quick work," he said. "Fire away. If I can do, I will do."

"I need something to sell him. Not a painting, something fairly small but very valuable. Not small as in brooch, but maybe a small statuette, a gold goblet, that kind of thing. Now, I know that some of your associates have taken to displaying copies rather than the real thing. One of those dummies would be ideal, provided that it would pass muster on reasonably close scrutiny. You think you can come up with something like that?" I asked.

"Hmm," he mused. "Leave it with me. I'll get back to you."

Two down, one to go. I dialled a number from memory and said, "Mr Abercrombie, please. It's Kate Brannigan." The electronic chirrup of the "Cuckoo Waltz" assaulted my eardrums as I waited for whatever length of time Clive Abercrombie deemed necessary to put me firmly in my place. Clive is a partner in one of the city's prestige jewellers. He would say *the* prestige jewellers. That's the kind of pretentious wally he is. We pulled Clive's nuts out of the fire on a major counterfeiting scam a couple of years back, and I know that deep down he's eternally grateful, though he'd die before he'd reveal it to a mere tradesperson like me. His gratitude had turned into a mixed blessing, however. It was thanks to Clive's recommendation that we'd got the case that had put Richard behind bars and me at risk of parting company with my life. By my reckoning, that meant he still owed me.

We were on the third chorus when he deigned to come on the line. "Kate," he said cautiously. Obviously I wasn't important enough to merit solicitous inquiries about my health. Not a stupid man, Clive. He's clearly sussed out that Richard and I are not in the market for a diamond solitaire.

"Good afternoon, Clive," I said sweetly. "I find myself in need of a good jeweller, and I can't think of anyone who fits the bill better than you."

"You flatter me," he said, flattered.

"I'm like you, Clive. When I need a job doing, I come to the experts."

"A job?" he echoed.

"A little bit of tinkering," I said soothingly. "Tomorrow, probably. Will one of your master craftspeople have a little time to spare for me then?"

"That depends on what we're talking about," he said warily. "I hope you're not suggesting something illegal, Kate."

"Would I?" I said, trying to sound outraged.

"Quite possibly," he said drily. "What exactly did you have in mind?"

"I don't have all the details yet, but it would involve . . . a slight addition to an existing piece."

He sighed. "Come round tomorrow morning after eleven. I'll discuss it with you then."

"Thank you, Clive," I said to dead air.

I checked my watch. Half past four. Just time to nip round to the office and collect Trevor Kerr's list of former staff. I swapped the smart clothes for a pair of leggings and a sweat shirt and took my bike. It would be quicker than the car this time of day, and besides, I wanted the exercise. I found Shelley in the throes of preparing the quarterly VAT return. "Kate," she said grimly. "Just the person I wanted to see." She waved a small bundle of crumpled receipts at me. "I know it's really unreasonable of me, but do you suppose you could enlighten me as to what precisely these bills are for? Only, by my calculations, we're due a VAT inspection some time within the next six months, and I don't think they're going to be thrilled by your idea of keeping records. 'Miscellaneous petty cash' isn't good enough, you know."

I groaned. "Can't you just make it up?" I wheedled, picking up the top receipt. "This is from the electrical wholesalers; just call it batteries or light bulbs or cassette tapes. Use your imagination. We don't often let you do that," I added with a smile.

Shelley curled her lip. "I don't have an imagination. I've never found it necessary. You're not leaving here till you've told me what's what. And if *you* make it up, I can blame you when the VAT inspector doesn't believe me."

It didn't take me as long as I feared. Imagination is not something I've ever lacked. What I couldn't remember, I invented. There wasn't a VAT person in the land who'd dare question what I needed thirty-five metres of speaker wire for. Having mollified the real boss at Mortensen and Brannigan, I grabbed my fax and headed out the door before she could think of something else that would keep me from my work.

In the short interval that I'd been out, both Gizmo and Ballantrae had been back to me. The name and address attached to the phone didn't fill me with confidence. Cradaco International, 679A Otley Road, Leeds. On an impulse, I grabbed the phone and rang Josh's office. The man himself was in a meeting, but Julia, his personal assistant, was free. I pitched her into hitting the database right away and finding out whatever details Cradaco International had filed at Companies House. I hung on while she looked. Now that everything's on-line, information it used to take days to dig out of dusty files is available at the touch of a fingertip.

She didn't keep me waiting long. "Kate? As you thought, it's an off-the-shelf company. Share capital of one pound. Managing director James Connery. Company Secretary Sean Bond. Uh-oh. Does something smell a bit fishy to you, Kate?"

I groaned. "Any other directors?"

"Have a guess?"

"Miss Moneypenny? M?" I said, resignedly.

"Nearly. Miss Penny Cash."

I sighed. "You'd better give me the addresses, just in case." I copied down three addresses in Leeds. At least they were all in the same city. One trip would check out the directors and the company. "You're a pal, Julia," I said.

"Don't mention it. You could do me a small favour in return," she said.

"Try me."

"Could you ask Richard if there's any chance he could get me a bootleg tape of the Streisand Wembley concert?" she asked.

I'd never have put cut-glass, upper-middle-class Julia down as a Streisand fan, but there's no accounting for taste. "It's a bit off his beat, but I'll see what I can do," I promised.

Time to get back to Ballantrae. He answered on the first ring. "I think I've got the very thing for you," he said. "How does an Anglo-Saxon belt buckle sound?"

"Useful if you've got an Anglo-Saxon belt," I said.

He chuckled. "It's a ceremonial buckle, worn by chieftains and buried with them. It's about five inches by two inches. The original is made of solid gold, chased with Celtic designs and studded with semi-precious stones. There are only two known to be in existence. One's in the British Museum, the other's in a private collection in High Hammerton Hall near Whitby."

"Sounds perfect," I said. "Have you spoken to the owner?"

"I have. He's been displaying a replica for the last five months, but I've managed to persuade him to lend it to you. We were at school together," he added in explanation.

"What's it made of?" I asked.

"The replica's made of lead and plastic, with a thin coating of gold leaf. He says it would fool someone who wasn't an expert, even close up. He says if you sit the two of them side by side, it's almost impossible to tell them apart."

"Sounds perfect," I said. "When can I get it?"

"He's sending it to you by overnight courier. It will be at your office by ten tomorrow morning."

"Lord Ballantrae, you are a star," I said, meaning it. So much for the inbred stupidity of the aristocracy. This guy was more on the ball than ninety-five per cent of the people I have to deal with.

"No problem. I want to get these people as badly as you do. Probably more so. Then we can all get back to the business of doing what we do best."

Speaking of which, I finally got down to doing something about Trevor Kerr's case. I felt guilty for ignoring the material he'd sent me, but the art-theft case was far more absorbing. I felt it was something I could get to the bottom of single-handed, unlike the Kerrchem case. I found myself inclined to agree with Jackson. This was a case for the cops, if only because they had the staffing resources to cover all the bases that it would take me weeks to get round. Then the little voice in my head kicked in with the real reason. "You can't stand Trevor Kerr so you don't want to put yourself out for him. And you're desperate to impress that Michael Haroun."

"Bollocks," I muttered out loud, seizing the sheets of fax paper with fresh energy. Someone—the indomitable Sheila, I suspected—had conveniently included the job titles as well as the names and addresses of those made redundant. I reckoned I could exclude anyone who worked on the factory floor or in the warehouse. They would have neither the chemical know-how nor the access to sales and distribution information that would allow them to pull a sabotage scheme as complex as this. That left thirty-seven people in clerical, managerial and scientific posts who had all been given what looked like a tin handshake to quit their jobs at Kerrchem.

By nine, I felt like the phone was welded to my ear. I was using a labour-market research pitch, which seemed to be working reasonably well. I claimed to be working for the EC Regional Fund, doing research to see what sort of skills were not being catered for by current job vacancies. I told my victims that I was calling people who had been made redundant over the previous year to discover whether they had found alternative employment. A depressingly low number of Kerrchem's junked staff fell into that category, and they were mostly low-grade clerical staff. Not one of the ten middle managers had found new jobs, and to a man they were bitter as hell about it. Of the chemists, two out of the three lab technicians were working in less skilled but better paid jobs. The four research lab staff who had been laid off were bound by their contracts and the terms of their redundancies not to work for direct competitors. One had taken a job as an analyst on a North Sea oil rig, two of the other three were kicking their heels and hating it, and one was no longer at the address the company had for him. It looked like I had no shortage of suspects.

I stood up and stretched. Richard still hadn't come home, so there was nothing to divert me from work. I couldn't move on with the Kerrchem stuff tonight, but I wasn't quite stalled on the other investigation. The sensible part of me knew I should go to bed and catch up on last night's missed sleep, but I'd had enough of being sensible for one week. I went through to the kitchen, cut open the other half of the ciabatta and loaded it with mozzarella, taramasalata and some sun dried tomatoes. I wrapped it in clingfilm, and took a small bottle of mineral water out of the fridge. Fifteen minutes later, I was cruising

down the M62, singing along cheerfully to a new compilation
of Dusty Springfield's greatest hits that I'd found lying around
in Richard's half of the conservatory. Never mind the mascara,
check out that voice.

I was in Leeds before ten, nervously navigating my way
through the subterranean tunnels of the inner ring road, emerging somewhere near the white monolith of the university. The
roads were quiet out through Headingley, but every now and
again, a beam of light split the night from on high as the police
helicopter quartered the skies, trying to protect the homes of the
more prosperous residents from the attentions of the burglars.
Burglary has reached epidemic proportions in Leeds these days;
I know someone whose house was turned over seven times in
six months. Every time they came home with a new stereo, so
did the burglars. Now, their house is more secure than Armley
jail and their insurance premiums are nearly as much as the
mortgage.

I slowed as I approached the Weetwood roundabout, scanning houses for their numbers. 679A looked like it might be one
of an arcade of shops, so I parked up and stretched my legs. I
can't say I was surprised to find there was no 679A. There was a
679, though, a small newsagent's squeezed between a bakery and
a hairdresser. I walked round the back of the shops, checking to
see if the flats above had entrances at the rear. A couple did, but
679 wasn't one of them. I walked back to the car, with plenty to
think about. Whoever Dennis's fence was, he was determined to
cover his tracks. Using an accommodation address for his phone
bills was about as careful as you could get without actually being
sectioned for paranoia.

I decided to check out the directors' addresses while I was
in the city, but I held out little hope of finding any of them at
home. James Connery's alleged residence was nearest, back in
Headingley proper. It was number thirty-nine in a street of ten
houses. On to Chapel Allerton, where Sean Bond apparently
lived in a hostel for the visually handicapped. Penny Cash was

even worse off. According to Companies House, she was living on a piece of waste ground in Burmantofts. I doubled back through the city centre, passing the new Health Ministry building up on Quarry Hill, spotlit to look like a set from Fritz Lang's *Metropolis*. Apparently, the place contains a full-size swimming pool, Jacuzzi and multi-gym. Nice to know our hard-earned taxes are being spent on the health of the nation, isn't it?

It was nearly midnight when I got home. Richard's car was parked outside, though I didn't need that clue to know he was home as soon as I touched the front door. It was vibrating with the pulse of the bass coming through the bricks from next door. As I shoved my key in the lock, I could feel exhaustion flow through me, settling in a painful knot at the base of my skull.

I walked through the house to the conservatory. Richard's patio doors were open, revealing half a dozen bodies in varying states of consciousness draped over the furniture. Techno dance music drilled through my head like a tribe of termites who have just discovered a log cabin. The man himself was nowhere to be seen. I picked a path to the kitchen, where I found him taking a tray of spring rolls out of the oven. "Hi," he said. His eyes were as stoned as the woman taken in adultery.

"Any chance of the volume coming down? I need some sleep," I said.

"That's cool," he said, a lazy smile spreading across his face. "Want some company?"

"You've already got some."

"They can be out of here in ten minutes," he said. "Then I'm all yours."

He was as good as his word. Eleven minutes later, he crawled into my blissfully silent bed. Unfortunately, I'm not into necrophilia.

# 12

The buckle got to the office before I did, which gave Shelley something to puzzle over. I arrived to find her using it as a paperweight. "OK," she said. "I give in."

I don't often find myself one up on Shelley, so I decided to drag it out a bit. "If you can guess, I'll buy lunch," I said.

"What makes you think you're going to have time for lunch?" she asked sweetly. "Besides, I told you yesterday, I don't do imagination. You want me to learn how, you're going to have to pay me a lot more."

I should know better. The woman is the mother of two teenagers. What chance do I have? "It's a replica of an Anglo-Saxon ceremonial belt buckle," I said. "Also known as a honey pot." Mustering what was left of my dignity, I scooped up the buckle and marched through to my office.

This time Dennis's mobile was switched on. "I want you to set up a meet for me with your man," I said. "Tell him you vouch for me, and that I've got something really special for him."

"I'm not sure if he'll go for it," Dennis tried. "Like I told you, we have to wait for a yes or a no before we lift stuff. He's very picky, and he likes to be in control."

"Tell him there's only two in the world. I've got one and the British Museum's got the other one. Tell him it's from the collection at High Hammerton Hall. And it's gold. He should be able to work it out himself from that. Believe me, Dennis, he'll want this."

"All right," he said grudgingly. "But I'm coming with you on the meet."

"No, you're not," I told him firmly. "You're in enough trouble as it is. This is not going to be heavy, Dennis. I can handle one man in a car park. You should know, you train me."

"I still think you're crazy, chasing this," he said. "Your client's going to be better off with the insurance company's readies in his bank account than he is with a poxy picture on the wall."

"Call it professional pride."

"Call it pig-headedness," he said. "I'll get back to you."

I went through to Bill's office and opened the cupboard where we keep our stock of technological wizardry. I found what I was looking for in a cardboard box at the back of the top shelf. It's not something we use very often, reeking as it does of *The Man from U.N.C.L.E.*, but given that Dennis's fence seemed to be an aficionado of James Bond, it seemed entirely appropriate to use a directional bug. If that conjures up images of chunky metal boxes stuck to the bottom of cars, forget it. Thanks to modern miniaturization technology, the bugs we've got are about the size of an indigestion tablet. The transmission batteries last about a week, and allow the bug to send a signal to a base unit. The range is about fifteen kilometres, provided large mountains don't get in the way, and the screen gives a read-out of direction and distance. Perfect for tracking the buckle back to source, so long as the fence was going to get rid of it sharpish.

Next stop, Clive Abercrombie, with a brief detour via the terraced streets of Whalley Range to stuff Gizmo's used tenners through his letter box. When I got to the shop, Clive was hovering behind a counter, ostentatiously leaving the waiting-on to the lesser mortals he employs to be polite to the rich. When I walked in, he shot forward and had me through the door to the back of the shop so fast my feet didn't even leave tracks in the shag pile. Obviously, he doesn't want proles like me hanging around making the place look like Ratners. "In a hurry, Clive?" I asked innocently.

"I thought *you* would be. You usually are," he replied acidly. "Now, what was it you wanted?"

I took the buckle out of my handbag. In spite of himself, Clive drew his breath in sharply. "Where did you get that?" he demanded, extending one finger to point dramatically at the twinkling gold lump.

"Don't worry, my life of crime runs to solving it, not committing it," I soothed. "It's not the real thing. It's a copy."

If anything, he looked even more disturbed. "Why are you walking around with it in your *handbag*?" he demanded, giving Lady Bracknell a run for her money.

Knowing Clive's weakness for anything reeking of snobbery, I said, "I'm doing a job for the Nottingham Group."

"Should I know the name?" he asked snottily.

"Probably not, Clive. It's a consortium of the landed gentry, headed by Lord Ballantrae of Dumdivie. Art thefts. Very hush-hush. I'm very close to Mr Big, and this is a ploy to smoke him out." I pulled the bug out of my pocket. "What I need is for one of your craftsmen to incorporate this in the piece. Preferably on the outside. I'd thought under one of the stones." I handed the bug and the buckle to Clive, who already had his loupe out.

He took a few minutes to scrutinize the buckle, which was heavy enough to make a useful weapon, especially if it was attached to a belt. "Nice piece of work," he commented. "If you hadn't told me it was a fake, I'd have had my work cut out to spot it." Praise indeed, coming from Clive. He unscrewed the loupe from his eye socket and said, "It'll take a few hours. And it will cost."

"Now there's a surprise," I said. "Just send us an invoice. Give me a bell when it's ready." I turned to go back through the shop, but Clive gripped my elbow and steered me further into the nether regions.

"Easier if you pop out the back door," he said. Half a minute later, I was in the street. I reckoned I deserved a cappuccino made by someone other than me, so I decided to take the scenic route back to the office. For a brief moment, I toyed with the idea of ringing Michael Haroun and suggesting he play truant for half an hour, but I told myself severely that it wouldn't help my pursuit of the art thieves to involve the insurers at this stage. They'd only start muttering about doing things by the book and informing the police. I smacked my hormones firmly on the wrist and drove the length of Deansgate to the Atlas Café, where they claim to make the best coffee outside Italy. I wasn't going to argue. I dumped the car on a yellow line down by the canal basin and walked back up to the chic glass-and-wood interior. I sat by the window, sipping the kind of cappuccino that acts like intravenous caffeine, and pulled the Kerrchem papers out of my bag. Time for a file review.

I didn't know exactly what I was looking for. All I knew was that I wanted to find something, anything that would legitimately allow me to postpone or short-circuit the tedious process of doing background checks into all of the redundant staff that I hadn't been able to eliminate on the phone. On the second read-through, I found exactly what I was looking for.

Joey Morton's supply of KerrSter came from the local branch of a national chain of trade wholesalers, Filbert Brown. His wife couldn't remember which of them had actually made the trip to the cash-and-carry when the fatal drum of KerrSter had been bought, but there was no doubt that that was the original source of the tainted cleanser.

It wasn't much to go on, but it was a place to start. One of the dozens of pieces of normally useless information cluttering up my dustbin brain was the fact that Filbert Brown were a Manchester-based company. I knew this because I passed their head office and flagship cash-and-carry every time I drove from my house to North Manchester. Suddenly energized, I abandoned the hedonism of the Atlas and trotted down the steps to the car.

It didn't take long to skirt the city centre. It took longer to get through to the customers' car park at Filbert Brown. They occupied an old factory building just off Ancoats Street. The area was in the middle of that chaotic upheaval known as urban renewal. East Manchester is supposedly coming up in the world; home of the new Commonwealth Games stadium, spiffy new housing developments and sports facilities. Oh, and roads, of course. Lots of them. Virgin territory for the traffic cones and temporary traffic lights that have become an epidemic on the roads of the Northwest. My political friends reckon it's the government's revenge because most of us up here didn't vote for them.

Considering it was the middle of the morning when all of us small business people are supposed to have our noses firmly to the grindstone, Filbert Brown was surprisingly busy. I walked in without challenge and found myself in a glorified warehouse. It reminded me of those cheap and cheerless back-to-basics supermarkets that we've imported from Europe in recent years. Anyone who did their shopping in Netto or Aldi would have been right at home in Filbert Brown. Me, I always find it incredibly cheap to shop there—they never stock anything I'd want to buy. The same went for Filbert Brown. I know Richard thinks I have an unhealthy obsession with cleanliness, but even I couldn't get turned on by cases of dishwasher powder, drums of worktop bactericide and cartons of paper towels. I was clearly in a minority, judging by the number of people who were happily filling up their trolleys.

I wandered up and down the aisles for a few minutes, getting a feel for the place. One of the things that struck me was how prominent KerrSter was among the cleansers. It occupied the whole width of a shelf at eye level, the key position in shifting merchandise. Compared with the other Kerrchem products, which seemed to be doing just about OK compared with their competitors, KerrSter was king of the castle.

What I needed now was a pretext. Thoughtfully, I wandered back to the car. I always keep a fold-over clipboard in the boot for those occasions when I need to pretend to be a market researcher. You'd be amazed at what people will tell you if you've got a clipboard. I gave my clothes the once-over. I was wearing tan jodhpur-style leggings, a cream linen collarless shirt and a chocolate brown jacket with a mandarin collar. The jacket was too smart for the pitch, so I folded it up and left it in the boot. In the shirt and leggings, I could just about pass. Freeze, maybe, but pass.

I walked briskly into Filbert Brown and strode up to the customer service counter. I say counter, but it was more of a hole in the wall. Customers here clearly weren't encouraged to complain. The woman behind the counter looked as if she'd been hired because of her resemblance to a bulldog. "Yes?" she demanded, teeth snapping.

"I'm sorry to trouble you," I said brightly. "I'm doing an MBA at Manchester Business School and I'm doing some research into sales and marketing. I wonder if I could perhaps have a word with your stock controller?"

"You got an appointment?"

"I'm afraid not."

She looked triumphant. "You'd need an appointment."

I looked disappointed. "It's a bit of an emergency. I had arranged to see someone at one of the big DIY stores, but she's come down with a bug and she had to cancel and I really need to get the initial research done this week. It won't take more than half an hour. Can't you just ring through and see if it would be possible for me to see someone?"

"We're a bit busy just now," she said. "We" was inaccurate; "they" would have been nearer the mark, judging by the queues at the tills.

"Please?" I tried for the about-to-burst-into-tears look.
She cast her eyes heavenwards. "It's a waste of time, you
know."

"If they're busy, I could make an appointment for later,"
I said firmly.

With a deep sigh, she picked up the phone, consulted a list
taped to the wall of her booth and dialled a number. "Sandra?
It's Maureen at customer services. There's a student here says she
wants to talk to you . . . Some project or other . . ." She looked
me up and down disparagingly. Then her eyebrows shot up.
"You will?" she said incredulously. "All right, I'll tell her." She
dropped the phone as if it had bitten her and said, "Miss Bates
will be with you in a moment."

I leaned against the wall and waited. A couple of minutes passed, then a woman approached through the checkouts.
Her outfit was in the same colours as the rest of the staff, but
where they wore red and cream overalls, she wore a red skirt
and a blouse in the red and cream material. She smiled as she
approached, which explained why she'd never get the job in
customer services. "I'm Sandra Bates," she greeted me. "How
can I help you?"

I gave her the same spiel. "What I need is a few minutes
of your time so you can run through your shelf-allocation principles," I finished.

She nodded. "No problem. Come along to my office; I'll
take you through it."

I fell into step beside her. "I really appreciate this," I said.
"I know how busy you must be."

"You're not kidding," she said. "But this business needs
more women who can give the boys a run for their money.
When I was doing my business studies degree at the poly, it was
almost impossible to get any of them to spare any of their precious time," she added grimly. Thank God for the sisterhood.

She ushered me into an office that was marginally bigger
than the room off my office that doubles as a darkroom and

the ladies' loo. Most of the floor space was taken up by a desk dominated by a PC. The desk surface and the floor around it were stacked with files and papers. Sandra Bates picked her way through the piles and sat in her chair. "Give me a second," she said, staring at the monitor.

I used the time to check her out. She looked to be in her late twenties, about my height, her jaw-length light brown hair expertly highlighted with blonde streaks. She was attractive in a china doll sort of way, pink and white complexion, unexceptional blue eyes and a slightly uptilted nose. Her determined mouth was the only contrasting feature, indicating an inner strength that might just give the boys a run for their money in the promotion stakes.

"Right," she said, looking up and grinning at me. "What do you want to know?"

"How you decide what goes where on the shelves?" I said. I don't know why I wanted to know that, but it seemed a good place to start if I wanted to get round to KerrSter.

"The general order of the products in the aisles is ordained from above, based on market research and psychological analysis, would you believe," she said. "It's the same way that supermarkets decide you get the fruit and veg first and the booze last. I mean, those of us who actually do the shopping know that your grapes get crushed by the six packs of lager, but I suppose they work on the principle that by the time you've cruised the aisles, you feel like you need a drink."

My turn to grin. "So what decisions do you actually make on the shop floor?"

"What we decide is what goes where within each section. The received wisdom is that items placed at eye level sell better than those you have to reach up for or bend down to. Now, all the checkouts are computerized, and I can access all the product figures from this terminal here. That way, I can see what stock is moving fast, and make sure we reorder at the right time so that we neither run out nor end up with huge stockpiles. When a particular line starts to outstrip rival products, it automatically goes into the best shelf position so that those sales are maintained or increased. With me so far?"

I nodded. It was all terribly logical. "Are there any exceptions?"

Sandra nodded approvingly. "Oh, yes. Lots. For example, when a company brings out a new product, they will often arrange to pay us a premium in return for our displaying it in the most advantageous shelf position. Or if a company's product has been ousted from its top selling position by a rival, they'll offer us a loss-leader price on the product for a limited period in exchange for them getting their old shelf site back so they can try to re-establish their old supremacy."

"Is that what Kerrchem have done with KerrSter?" I asked.

Sandra blinked. "I'm sorry?" she asked, sounding startled.

"I was having a browse round before I asked to see you, and I couldn't help noticing how prominent the KerrSter was. And with that guy dying after he opened it, I'd have thought sales would have gone through the floor," I said innocently.

"Yes, well, it's always been a popular seller, KerrSter," Sandra gabbled. "I suppose our customers haven't seen the stories."

"I'd have thought Kerrchem would have recalled it," I went on. For some reason, talk of KerrSter was making Sandra Bates twitchy. Rule number one of interrogation: when you've got them on the run, keep chasing.

"They recalled one batch," she said, regaining her composure.

"Still, I wouldn't buy it," I said. "I'm surprised one of their competitors hasn't tried to exploit the situation. In fact, I'm surprised a small company like them outsells the opposition so comprehensively."

"Yes, well, there's no accounting for customer preferences. Now, if there's nothing more you'd like to know about the shelf-stacking, I have got a lot on my plate," Sandra said, getting to her feet and waving vaguely at the paperwork on her desk.

I was back on the street inside a minute. Being hustled twice in one morning was bad for the ego. Clive Abercrombie I could understand. But the mere mention of KerrSter had shifted Sandra Bates from cooperative sisterhood to the verge of hostility. Something was going on that I didn't understand. And if there's one thing I hate, it's things I don't understand.

# 13

I'm no cyberpunk, but I'm knowledgeable enough about hacking to know that I couldn't have penetrated Filbert Brown's computer network on my own. I was sure they had to have a central computer that dealt with all their individual branches. Via that it should be possible to crawl back inside Sandra Bates's data. Way back in the mists of time—say, around 1991—I could probably have reached first base. Bill has a program that dials consecutive phone numbers till his modem connects with another computer. I could have set that to run through all the numbers on the same exchange as Filbert Brown's head office. It would probably have taken all night to run, but it would have got me there in the end.

However, the powers that be have decided that darkside hackers like us need to be cracked down on, so now they've got their own sophisticated equipment that picks up on sequential dialling like that and traces it. Then the Dibble comes and knocks on your door in a very user-unfriendly way. Besides, getting the computer's number was only the start. I'd need a login to get through the front door, and a password to get any further. Ideally, I needed the password of the sysman—the system manager. Most people who are authorized users of a network system have logins which allow them only limited access to the part of the system they need to work with. The sysman is what computerspeak calls a super user, which means he or she can wander unimpeded throughout the system, checking out each and every little nook and cranny. With Bill's help, I might just have managed to achieve sysman status on the Filbert Brown network. But Bill was on the other side of the world.

That only left Gizmo. I tried his number, and got lucky. "Wozzat?" a voice grunted.

"Gizmo?"

"Yeah?"

"Kate. Did I wake you?"

He cleared his throat noisily. "Yeah. Been up all night. What d'you want?"

I told him. He whistled. "Can't do that one for the usual," he said.

"But can you do it?"

"Sure, I can *do* it," he said confidently. "Getting in shouldn't be a problem. But if you want sysman status, that'll cost you."

"How much?" I sighed.

"One and a half."

Trevor Kerr could stand another hundred and fifty quid, I decided. "Done deal," I told Gizmo. "How soon?"

He sniffed. Probably on account of the whizz he'd have snorted to keep him awake all night. "Few hours," he said.

"Sooner the better."

Back in the office, routine awaited. A stack of background information had arrived in the post that morning. I'd been waiting for it so that I could complete a report for a client on the three candidates they'd short-listed for the head of their international marketing division. One of them looked like he'd have a promising career writing fiction. The candidate's degree from Oxford turned out to have been a two-year vocational course at the former poly. His credit rating was worse than the average Third World country's. And one of his previous employers seemed to think that his financial skills were focused more in the direction of his bank account than theirs. All of which would make the selection panel's job a bit easier.

It was just after four when Clive Abercrombie rang to tell me the buckle was ready and waiting. I worked for another hour, then collected it on the way home. Clive's jeweller had done a good job. I was looking for the bug, and I couldn't see it. No way would the fence spot it in the middle of a motorway service station. Back in the car, I checked the receiver was picking it up. Loud and clear.

When I got in, there was a message from Gizmo on my machine. "Hi. I've got your order ready. I think you should collect it in person. I'll expect you." I sighed and got back in the car. Just because you're paranoid doesn't mean they're not out to get you. In Gizmo's case, I thought it was a small miracle the hacker crackers hadn't already kicked his door in. In his shoes, I wouldn't trust the phone lines either.

I hit the cash machine on the way, taking myself up to my daily limit. I parked round the corner from his house, just in case he really was under surveillance, and wishing I'd remembered to do the same on my earlier drop. I rang the bell and waited. Nearly a minute passed before the door cracked open on the chain. "It's me, Giz," I said patiently. "Alone."

He handed me a piece of paper. I handed him the cash. "See you around," he said and closed the door.

Back in the car, I unfolded the paper. There was a telephone number, FB7792JS (the login), and CONAN (the sysman's password). I'd bet it was Conan the Barbarian the sysman had in mind, not the creator of the world's first PI. Yet another wimpy computer nerd with delusions of grandeur. I drove home via Rusholme, where I picked up a selection of samosas, onion bhajis, chicken pakora and saag aloo bhajis. I had the feeling it was going to be a long night, and I didn't know if I could rely on Richard to come home with a Chinese.

I brought the coffee machine through to my study and sat down at the computer with the Indian snacks and the coffee to hand. I booted up and loaded my comms program. Dialling the number on the paper brought me a short pause, then the monitor said, "Welcome to FB. Login?" I typed the digits Gizmo had given me. "Password?" the monitor asked. "Conan," I typed. "As in Doyle," I said firmly.

The screen cleared and offered me a set of options. The first thing I had to do was to familiarize myself with the system. I needed to know how the different areas were arranged, how the directory trees were laid out, and how to move around to remote terminals. Somehow, I didn't think I'd be having an early night.

By nine, I'd got the basic layout clear in my mind. My mind and a sheaf of scribbled maps and diagrams that strewed my desk top. Now all I had to do was find Sandra Bates's terminal and start sifting her data. Doesn't sound much, does it? Imagine trying to find a single street in Manchester with only the motorway map as a guide. I took a screen break in the shower, brewed another pot of coffee and settled down to do battle with Filbert Brown's computer.

When the phone rang, I jumped a clear inch off my chair. I grabbed it and barked, "Hello?"

"It's me," Dennis's voice announced. "Sorted." Dennis is another one who doesn't like confiding in the phone system.

"Great. When?"

"Tomorrow. Half past three, eastbound at Hartshead Services."

"How will I know him?"

"He drives a metallic green Mercedes. He's about forty, five ten, bald on top. Anyway, I told him to look for a tarty-looking little blonde." Dennis couldn't keep the triumph out of his voice.

"You did what?"

"I didn't think you'd want to go looking like yourself," he said defensively. "Kate, these are not people you want coming after you with a clear picture. Wear a blonde wig, stick on the stilettos and the short skirt. And don't drive that poncy coupé. It sticks out like a prick in a brothel."

"Thank you very much, Dennis," I said.

Impervious to my sarcasm, he said, "My pleasure. Be careful out there now, you hear? Let me know how you go on."

"OK."

"Be lucky."

If only it was as simple as that. With a groan, I turned back to the computer. Just after eleven, I made it into Sandra Bates's data. Interestingly, it looked like Sandra had overall supervisory responsibility for about half of the Filbert Brown warehouses in the Northwest, as well as her day-to-day charge of the Ancoats cash-and-carry. She hadn't mentioned that in our brief encounter. I decided to concentrate on Manchester for the time being. The first thing I went for was the purchase orders for Kerrchem. When I reached those files, I printed the lot out. Analysis could wait until a time when I wasn't wandering round someone else's system like an illegal alien. After a bit of searching, I found the till data, sorted product by product. I scrolled through till I found KerrSter and printed that lot out too. Finally, I made myself at home in the invoices section of Sandra's files. That was the first indication I had that there was something going on. As a matter of course, I'd been checking for hidden files as I went along. When I added up the sizes of the individual files in the invoices subdirectory, it came to less than the amount of space the terminal told me the subdirectory occupied. The difference was about the size of one biggish file.

What Sandra Bates had done was clever. She could have made the file a password file, but anyone from head office trying to get into it would have become immediately suspicious. With a hidden file, there was no way of knowing it was there unless you were looking for precisely that, and nothing to trigger off suspicions in a routine trawl. I copied the hidden file on to my own hard disk, not wanting to interfere with it in Sandra's environment, and also copied the visible Kerrchem invoice file. I couldn't think of anything else I needed right then, so I made my way out of the system. If what I already had suggested fresh avenues of inquiry, I could always go back in. I didn't think I'd left any footprints obvious enough for the sysman to notice and do anything panicky like change his password.

The last thing I did was to open up the hidden file and print out the contents of it and the other invoice file. Then, clutching my pile of papers, I staggered off to bed. Richard hadn't appeared, which meant he was probably out on the razz with a bunch of musicians. When he finally came home, he'd collapse into his own bed rather than waken me. Just one of the advantages of our semi-detached lifestyle.

I woke up just before eight, the light still on, the papers strewn all over the duvet and the floor. I hadn't got past page one before sleep had overwhelmed me. I picked up the papers and shuffled them together. I showered, sliced a banana into a bowl of muesli and took breakfast and coffee out into the conservatory. As I ate, I started to read the paperwork. The purchase order for KerrSter showed a sudden hike about two months previously, virtually tripling overnight. Interestingly, they weren't big orders. According to this print-out, Sandra hadn't increased the amount of KerrSter on each order. It was the number of orders that had shot up. That seemed a pretty inefficient way of doing business to me.

I checked back with the till receipts to see when the sudden surge in sales of KerrSter had started. I knew then that I was on to something. If what Sandra Bates had told me was the truth, the increased orders should have been sales-led. But what I was seeing was something very different. The till receipts for KerrSter didn't start to pick up until a few days after the orders increased dramatically. It looked as if the product had been given its starry position before the sales justified it. I was sure Trevor Kerr hadn't been paying them a premium to improve the profile of his product; I couldn't imagine him parting with his company's cash in a deal like that. Trevor struck me as a man who liked his profits, and wouldn't cede them to anyone.

By now, I was gripped by the paper trail. Time for the invoices. First, I went through the accessible KerrSter invoice file. That was when the alarm bells started ringing. The product orders might have tripled, but the invoices hadn't. I double-checked, but there was no mistake. Filbert Brown were still paying Kerrchem for the same amount of cleaning fluid as they had been before the order hike.

That left the contents of the hidden file. It contained the invoices for the remaining two thirds of the KerrSter. There was one crucial difference. The bank account where the electronic fund transfer was sending the money for the extra KerrSter wasn't the same as the bank account on the other, upfront invoices. Whoever Sandra Bates was paying for the KerrSter, it wasn't Kerrchem.

That left me two possibilities. Either somebody at Kerrchem was creaming off a tidy back-door profit for themselves, or Sandra Bates was dealing with the chemical merchants who were peddling phoney KerrSter with such disastrous results. I knew which theory looked most likely to me.

I checked the clock. Ten to nine. Chances were that management staff at Filbert Brown didn't start work until nine. If I was quick, I could be in and out of their computer before their sysman logged in to find someone else using his ID. To be on the safe side, I should have waited until the evening, but I was behind the door when they were handing out patience.

Two minutes later, I was in the system again. This time, I wasn't looking for Sandra Bates's terminal. I wanted her personnel file. I got into personnel at three minutes to nine. A minute took me to staff personnel files. Once I was there, I downloaded Sandra Bates's file to my own hard disk. I was back out of Filbert Brown by one minute past nine. A couple of minutes later, I was looking at Sandra Bates's CV.

She'd been to school in Ashton-under-Lyne, a once separate town now attached to East Manchester by a string of down-at-heel suburbs. She'd done a degree in business studies at what was then Manchester Poly and is now Manchester Metropolitan

University. You'd think when they got their university status that someone would have noticed their new initials translate only too readily to Mickey Mouse University, endorsing the snooty opinions of those who attended "real" universities. After her degree, Sandra had gone to work for one of the big chains of DIY stores, havens for suburbanites on Sundays and bank holidays. She'd stayed there for a couple of years before joining Filbert Brown three years previously. She'd had one promotion since then and was pulling down just over twenty grand. The item that really interested me was her address: 37 Alder Way, Burnage. I needed to check out her house at some point today while she was at work. I would probably have to stake her out or do a little bit of illegal bugging to discover who her phoney KerrSter supplier was, and to do that, I needed to get a picture of the set-up in Alder Way.

Before I could do any of that, I had to get dressed and stop by the office. I had plenty of time before the meet with Dennis's fence, so I could at least put off the tart's disguise till later. I grabbed a clean pair of jeans, my Reeboks and denim-look cotton sweater. If I was going to spend the afternoon teetering on stilettos, I could at least spend the morning in comfort.

Shelley was catching up on the filing when I walked in, a clear sign that she was bored. "Going part-time now, are we?" she asked acidly.

"I've been doing some work on the computer at home," I said defensively. Shelley has the unerring knack of making me feel fifteen and guilty again.

"A report would be nice now and then," she said. "I know I'm only the office manager, but it does help when clients phone if I know where we're up to."

"Sorry," I said contritely. "It's just that most of the things I've been doing for the last couple of days are the kind of things I don't want the clients to know I'm up to. I'll get something down on tape for you by the end of today, promise." I smiled ingratiatingly. "Would you like a cappuccino?"

"How much is it going to cost me?" Shelley asked suspiciously. Abe Lincoln wouldn't have said you can fool all the people some of the time if he'd ever met Shelley.

"Can I borrow you and your car this afternoon?" I asked. "I've got a meet with the fence who's been handling these stolen art works, and I'm going to need to tail him afterwards. He's going to have clocked the coupé, and it's too obvious a car to follow him in. I want you to come out there with me and after the meet, we can swap cars. I go off in your motor, you come back in the coupé."

"You saying my Rover's common?" Shelley asked.

"Only in a numerical sense. Please?"

"How do I know you'll bring it back in one piece?"

She had a point. In the past eighteen months I'd written off one car and done serious damage to the Little Rascal, the van we've got fitted out with full surveillance gear. Neither incident had been my fault, but it still made me the butt of all office jokes about drivers. "I'll bring it back in one piece," I said through gritted teeth.

"What about the Little Rascal?" Shelley demanded. "You could tail him in that. All you have to do is make sure he doesn't see you getting out of it. Just be there early, out of the car, waiting for him."

I pulled a face. "The guy drives a Merc. I suspect I'd lose him on the motorway. Besides, he's no dummy. He's probably going to wait till he sees me drive off before he takes off himself."

"So if you drive off, how are we going to swap cars?"

"Trust me. I'll show you when we get there."

"I get the coupé overnight?" she bargained.

"But of course. I might as well take your car now, since I've got to look unobtrusive in Burnage."

We swapped keys and I headed off in her four-year-old Rover to Burnage. My first stop was the local library, where I checked the electoral roll. Sandra Bates was the only resident listed at 37. Alder Way was a quiet street of 1930s semis, each with a small garden. I marched boldly up the path of 37 and knocked on the door. There was no reply. There was an empty carport at the side of the house, and I walked cautiously through it and opened the wrought iron gate leading into the back garden. Sandra was obviously as efficient at home as she was at work. There was a line of washing pegged out, drying in the watery sunlight. Whatever the electoral roll said, Sandra didn't live alone. Hanging beside her underwear were boxer shorts and socks. Flapping in the breeze like a phantom among the shirts and blouses were two pairs of overalls. Maybe I wouldn't have to look so far for the mystery chemist after all.

# 14

I rang the doorbell of 35 Alder Way. I was about to give up when the door opened. I realized why it had taken so long. The harassed-looking young woman who stood in the doorway had identical toddlers clinging on to each leg of her jeans. As a handicapping system, it beat anything the Jockey Club has ever come up with. The twins stared up at me and conducted a conversation with each other in what sounded like some East European language, all sibilants and diphthongs. "Yes?" the woman said. At least she spoke Mancunian.

"Sorry to bother you," I said. "I'm looking for a guy called Richard Barclay. The address I've got for him is next door at number thirty-seven. But there doesn't seem to be anybody in."

She shook her head. "There's nobody by that name next door," she said with an air of finality, her hand rising to close the door.

"Are you sure?" I said, looking puzzled and referring to the piece of paper in my hand where I'd just written my lover's name and Sandra Bates's address. I waved it at her. "I was supposed to meet him here. About a job."

She took the paper and frowned. "There must be some mistake. The bloke next door's called Simon. Simon Morley."

I sighed. "I don't suppose he's the one taking people on, then? I mean, I've not got the right address and the wrong name?"

One of the twins detached itself from the woman's jeans and lurched towards me. Without looking down, she stuck her leg out and stopped its progress. "I shouldn't think so, love," she said. "Simon got made redundant about six months ago. He's only started working himself a couple of months back, and judging from the overalls he goes in and out in, he's not hiring and firing."

I did the disappointed look, but it was wasted on the hassled woman. The pitch of the twins' dialogue had risen to a level she couldn't ignore. "Sorry," she said, closing the door firmly in my face.

"Don't be sorry," I said softly as I walked back to the Rover. "Lady, you just made my day." Simon Morley's name had rung so many bells my head felt like the cathedral belfry.

❧

By three o'clock, everything was in place. Shelley and I had driven across the Pennines on the M62, to the Bradford exit, the first past Hartshead Services. We'd turned off on the Halifax Road, where I remembered there was a lay-by just after the motorway roundabout. I left Shelley there in her Rover while I zoomed back down the motorway, doubling back so I ended up on the correct side of the sprawling service area. I parked away from the main body of cars and teetered up the car park on the white stilettos I keep in the bottom of the wardrobe for days like these.

I went to the ladies' room to check that I still looked like a tarty blonde. I don't often go in for disguises that involve wigs, but a couple of years before, I'd needed a radical appearance change, so I'd spent a substantial chunk of Mortensen and Brannigan's petty cash on a really good wig. It was a reddish blonde, which meant it didn't look too odd against my skin, which is the typically yellow-based freckle-face that goes with auburn hair. Coupled with a much heavier make-up than I'd normally be seen dead in, the image that peered out of the mirror at me was credible, if a bit on the dodgy side. I'd dressed to emphasize that impression, in a black Lycra mini-skirt and a cream scoop-necked vest under my well-worn brown leather blouson. My own mother would have thrown me out of the house.

I touched up the scarlet lipstick and gave myself a toothy grin. "Show time, Brannigan," I muttered as I walked back across the car park and leaned against the door of my coupé.

He was right on time. At precisely 3.30, a metallic green Mercedes appeared at the entrance to the car park. He cruised round slowly, before purring to a halt next to my car. The driver was indeed fortyish, though calling him bald on top seemed to be a euphemistic description for someone well on the way to the billiard-ball look. I opened the passenger door and sank into the leather seat. "Pleased to meet you," I said.

"Dennis tells me you have something I might be interested in," he said without preamble. His voice was nasal, the kind that gets on my nerves after about five minutes. "I don't normally deal with people on a freelance basis," he added, glancing at me for the first time.

"I know. Dennis explained how you like to work. But I thought that if I showed you what I can do, you might put some work my way," I said, trying to sound hard-bitten.

"Let's see what you've got, then." He turned in his seat towards me. His eyes were grey and cold, slightly narrowed. When he spoke, his mouth moved asymmetrically, as if he were gripping an imaginary cigarette in one corner.

"What about the colour of your money?" I demanded.

He leaned across. For a wild moment, I thought his hand was heading for my legs, but he carried on to the glove box. It fell open to reveal bundles of notes. I could see they were fifties, banded into packs of a thousand. There were ten of them.

He picked one up and riffled it in my face, so I could see it was fifties all the way through. Then he slammed the glove box shut again. "Satisfied?"

"You will be," I said, reaching into my bag. I took out the buckle, wrapped in an ordinary yellow duster. I opened it up and displayed the buckle. "Anglo-Saxon," I said. "From High Hammerton Hall."

"I know where it's from," he said brusquely, taking a loupe out of his pocket and picking up the buckle. I hoped he couldn't hear the pounding of the blood in my ears as he examined it. I could feel a prickle of sweat under the foundation on my upper lip. "Is this the real thing or is it a fake?" he asked.

I pointed to the twenty-grand car sitting next to us. "Is that a real Leo Gemini turbo super coupé or is it a fake? Behave. It's the business," I said aggressively.

"There's been nothing in the papers," he said.

"I can't help that, can I? What do you want me to do, issue a press release?"

A half-smile twitched at the corners of his mouth. "You done much of this sort of thing?" he asked.

"What d'you want, a fucking CV? Listen, all you need to know is that I can deliver the goods, and I haven't got a record, which makes me a damn sight better bet than Dennis and Frankie. D'you want this or not?" I held my hand out for the buckle.

"Oh, I think my clients will be happy with this," he said, pocketing the buckle and the loupe. "Help yourself." He gestured towards the glove box, at the same time taking a card out of his inside pocket. I grabbed the money and stuffed it in my bag.

"Cheers," I said.

He handed me the card. It was one of those ones you get made up on those instant print machines at railway stations and motorway services. I'd passed one minutes before. All it had on it was his mobile number. "Next time, phone me before you do the job and I'll tell you whether we want the piece or not."

"No sweat," I said, opening the door. "I like a man who knows what he wants." I closed the door with a soft click and got behind the wheel of the coupé. The fence showed no sign of moving, so I started the engine and drove off. As I joined the motorway, I clocked him a few cars behind me. I stayed in the inside lane, and he made no move to catch me up, never mind overtake me. I left the motorway at the next junction, going round the roundabout twice to make certain he wasn't following me, then I turned down the Halifax Road. Shelley got out of the Rover as I pulled in behind her. I jumped out of the coupé and raced for the Rover, pulling off my jacket as I ran. Shelley had left the engine running, as I'd asked her to.

"Speak to you later," I shouted as I put the car in gear, did an illegal U-turn at the first opportunity and tore back to the motorway. The receiver for the bug beeped reassuringly. He was already five kilometres away from me, and climbing. I floored the accelerator as I rejoined the M62. The car seemed sluggish after the coupé, but it didn't take long to push it up to ninety. I pulled off the wig and ran a hand through my hair. I'd left a packet of moist tissues on the passenger seat of the Rover, and I used a handful of them to scrub the make-up off my face.

According to the tracer screen, the fence's direction had changed slightly. As I'd expected, he'd turned off on the M621 for Leeds. I followed, noting that I'd narrowed the distance between us. He was only 2.7 kilometres ahead of me now. I really needed to be a lot closer before he turned off and lost me in a maze of city streets. Luckily, the M621 runs downhill, and he was sticking to a speed that wouldn't get him picked up by the speed cameras. By the time we came to the Wetherby and Harrogate slip road, I was close enough to glimpse his pale green roof leave the motorway. Fortunately, there was a fair bit of traffic, so I was able to keep a couple of cars between us. In the queue at the Armley roundabout, I pulled on my denim shirt over the vest, completing the transformation from the waist up.

I had a momentary panic when he entered the tunnels of the inner city ring road and the signal disappeared from the receiver. But as soon as we emerged into daylight, the beep came back. I kept him in sight as we approached the complex confluence of roads at Sheepscar, one car behind as he swung right into Roundhay Road. I reckoned he had no idea that he was being followed, since he wasn't doing any of the things you do when you think you've got a tail; no jumping red lights, no sudden turns off the main road, no lane switching.

He stayed on Roundhay Road, then, just by the park, he turned left and drove up Princes Avenue, through the manicured green of playing fields and enough grass to walk all the dogs of Leeds simultaneously. Where the avenue shaded into Street Lane, he turned right into a drive. I cruised past with a sidelong glance that revealed the Merc pulling into a double garage, then found a place to park round the corner. I kicked off the stilettos and pulled on the leggings I'd left in the car. I wriggled out of the Lycra mini and got out of the car, stuffing my feet into my Reeboks. Then I strolled back along Princes Avenue. Clearly, being a fence was a lot more lucrative than being a private eye. Baldy's house was set back from the road, a big detached job in stone blackened with a century and a half of industrial pollution. Not much change out of a quarter of a million for that one, by my reckoning. Probably the most popular man in the street too; they say good fences make good neighbours! I carried on down the road and bought an ice-cream from one of the vans by the park gates. I sat on a wall and ate my cornet, keeping an eye on Baldy's house all the while.

Five minutes later, an Audi convertible pulled in to the drive. A blonde woman got out, followed by two girls in the kind of posh school uniform that has straw boaters in the summer term. From where I was sitting, the girls looked to be in their early teens. The woman left the car on the drive and followed the girls into the house. I finished my ice-cream and walked back to the car. I drove around for a few minutes, trying to find

a suitable place for a stakeout. Eventually, I parked just round
the bend on the forecourt of a row of shops. I couldn't see the
whole house from there, but I could see the door and the drive,
and I hoped that by not parking outside anyone else's house, I'd
escape the worst excesses of the neighbourhood watch. If I was
going to have to come back tomorrow, I'd ring the local police
and tell them I was in the area on a surveillance to do with a
non-criminal matter. What's a few white lies between friends?

I took out the phone and rang the local library and asked
them to check the address on the electoral roll. They told me
the residents listed at that address were Nicholas and Michelle
Turner. At last, I had a name that hadn't come from the pages
of Ian Fleming.

Just after six, the woman came out again with the girls,
each carrying a holdall. They drove off, passing me without a
glance. They came back after eight, all with damp hair. I deduced
they'd been indulging in some sporting activity. That's why I'm
a detective. At half past eight, I phoned the Flying Pizza, a few
hundred yards up the road, and ordered myself a takeaway pizza.
Ten minutes later, I walked up and collected it, using their loo
at the same time. I ate the pizza in the car, taking care not to
drop my olives on Shelley's immaculate carpet and upholstery.
At nine, my phone rang. "Kate? It's Michael Haroun," the voice
on the other end announced.

I jerked upright, ran a hand through my hair and smiled.
As if he could see me. Pathetic, really. "Hello, Michael," I said.
"What can I do for you?"

"I wondered if you were free for a drink this evening? You
could give me a progress report."

"No, and no. I'm working, and you're not my client. Not
that that means we can't have a friendly drink together," I added
hastily, in case he thought I was being unfriendly.

"You can't blame me for trying," he said. "I do have an
interest."

"In the case or in me?" I asked tartly.

"Both, of course. When are you going to finish work?"

"Not for a while yet, and I'm over in Leeds." I hoped the regret I felt was being transmitted through the ether.

"In Leeds? What are you doing there?"

"Just checking out an anonymous tip-off."

"So you're making progress? Great!"

"I never said I was working on Henry's case," I said. "We do have more than one client, you know."

"OK, OK, I get the message. Keep your nose out, Haroun. I'm sorry you can't make it tonight. Maybe we could get together soon?"

"Why don't you give me a ring tomorrow? I might have a clearer idea what my commitments are then."

"I'll do that. Nice to talk to you, Kate."

"Ditto." After that little interlude, my surveillance seemed even more unbearably tedious. When the radio told me it was time for a book at bedtime, I decided to call it a day. It didn't look like Nicholas Turner or my buckle were going anywhere tonight.

When I got home, I picked up the Kerrchem file I'd left there when I'd got changed earlier. I skimmed the list of former employees, and one name jumped straight out at me. I hadn't been mistaken about Simon Morley. He'd been a lab technician at Kerrchem, made redundant with golden handcuffs six months before. He'd been the one I hadn't been able to contact because he'd moved. At least I knew where he was now. And I had a funny feeling that I knew just what he was doing in his overalls.

# 15

I pulled up on the forecourt of the shops in Street Lane at five to seven in Bill's Saab turbo convertible. One of the first rules of surveillance is to vary the vehicle you're sitting around in. Luckily, when Bill had gone off to Australia, he'd left me with a set of keys for his house and the car. I'd left Shelley's Rover in Bill's garage, with a message on the office answering machine telling her to hang on to the coupé for the time being. I felt sure this was a hardship she'd be able to bear, always supposing she didn't leap to the conclusion that the reason I wasn't back with her Rover was that her beloved heap was in some garage being restored to its former glory.

It had been a toss-up whose house I was going to sit outside this morning. On the one hand, if I didn't keep close tabs on Nicholas Turner, having the buckle bugged would have been a complete waste of time. On the other hand, Simon Morley's little adventures in cleaning had already cost a man his life. I'd lain awake, tossing and turning to the point where Richard, who normally sleeps like a man in persistent vegetative state, had sat up in bed and demanded to know what was going on. He'd eventually persuaded me to talk the dilemma over with him, something I always used to do but had been avoiding since his involvement in the car fraud case caused us both so much grief.

"You've got to go after the fence," he finally said.

"Why?"

"Because if you lose him this time, you'll never get a second bite of the cherry. Sooner or later, someone's going to spot that your buckle isn't just a fake but a bugged fake, and then you're going to be on someone's most wanted list. And if this Simon Morley really has killed some bloke accidentally, he's going to be a damn sight more careful what he puts in his chemical soup in future. I'd be surprised if he's still at it. Maybe I should give him a bell; if he's such a shit hot chemist, I know some people who'd be delighted to have him on the payroll."

I smacked his shoulder. "I've told you before about the people you hang out with."

He grinned. "Only joking. You know I'm allergic to anything stronger than draw. Anyway, Brannigan, you should go for the fence."

"You sure?" I asked, still doubtful.

"I'm sure."

"And what about the ten grand?"

Richard shrugged. "Hang on to it for now. We all need walking-around money."

"It's a lot to be walking around with. Shouldn't I be paying it back to the insurance company, or somebody?"

"They don't know you've got it, they're not going to miss it. Maybe you should just look on it as an early Christmas bonus for Mortensen and Brannigan."

"I don't know . . ."

"Trust me. I'm not a doctor," he said, wrapping his arms around me and nuzzling the back of my neck. Instant goose-flesh. You can't fight your gonads. I hadn't even wanted to try. Michael who?

The Turner household came to life around half past seven. The curtains in the master bedroom opened, and I caught a glimpse of Nicholas in his dressing gown. This time I'd come fully equipped for surveillance. I had a video camera in the well of the passenger seat, cunningly hidden in a bag made of one-way fabric which allowed the camera to see out but prevented anyone seeing in. I had a pair of high-powered binoculars in my bag, and my Nikon with a long lens attached sitting on the passenger seat. And five hundred quid of walking-around money in the inside pocket of my jacket. I'd left the other nine and a half grand with Richard, who had strict instructions to pay it into a building society account which I hold in a false name for those odd bits and pieces of money that it's sometimes advisable to lose for a while.

At quarter past eight, Mrs Turner and her two daughters emerged, the girls in the same smart school uniform. The Audi drove off. Two hours later, the Audi came back. Mrs Turner staggered indoors with enough Tesco carrier bags to stock a corner shop. Then nothing for two more hours. At a quarter to one, Mrs T came out, got into the Audi and drove off. She came back at ten past two, when I was halfway through my Flying Pizza special. If something didn't happen soon, I was either going to die of boredom or go home. Apart from anything else, Radio 4 loses its marbles between three and four in the afternoon, and I didn't think I could bear to listen to an hour of the opinions of those who are proof positive that care in the community isn't working.

Half an hour later, the front door opened, and Nicholas Turner came out. He was carrying a briefcase and a suit carrier. He opened the garage, dumped the suit carrier in the boot and reversed out into the road. "Geronimo," I muttered, starting my engine. Within seconds, the screen told me that he had the buckle with him. I eased out into the traffic and followed him back through the park.

The traffic was pretty much nose to tail as we came down the hill towards the city centre so it wasn't hard to stay in touch with the Mercedes. I kept a couple of cars between us, which meant I got snagged up a couple of times at red lights, but there wasn't enough free road for him to make much headway. I realized pretty soon he was heading for the motorways, which took some of the pressure off. I caught up with him just before he hit the junction where he had to choose between the M621 towards Manchester and the M1 for the south and east. He ignored the first slip road and roared off down the M1. In the Saab, it was easy to keep pace with him, which was another good reason for having swapped the Rover. I kept about half a mile behind to begin with, since I didn't want to lose him at the M62 junction. Sure enough, he turned off, heading east towards Hull.

We hammered down the motorway, the speedo never varying much either side of eighty-five. He'd obviously heard the same rumour I had about that being the speed cameras' trigger point. When we hit Hull, he followed the signs for the ferry port. I followed, with sinking heart. At the port, he parked and went into the booking office. I got into the queue in time to hear him book the car and himself on to that night's ferry. I didn't have any choice. I had to do the same thing.

By the time I emerged, he'd disappeared. I ran to the car, and saw that the buckle was moving away from the ferry port. He was either going to dispose of it now, or it was going on the ferry with him. Either way, I needed to try and follow him. I drove off in the direction the receiver indicated, grabbing my phone as I went and punching in Richard's number. The dashboard clock told me it was five past four. I prayed. He answered on the third ring. "Yo, Richard Barclay," he said.

"I need a mega favour," I said.

"Lovely to hear your voice too, Brannigan," he said.

"It's an emergency. I'm in Hull."

"That sounds like an emergency to me."

"I've got to be on the half past six ferry to Holland. My passport's in the top drawer of my desk. Can you get it, and get here by then?"

"In my car? You've got to be kidding."

I could have wept. He was right, of course. Even though it's pretty souped up, his Volkswagen just couldn't do the distance

in the time. Then I remembered the coupé. "Shelley's got the
Gemini," I told him. "I'll get her to meet you outside the office
in five minutes with it. Can you do it?"

"I'll be there," he promised.

I rang the office, one eye on the monitor, one eye on the
road. I was probably the most dangerous thing on the streets of
Hull. We seemed to be heading east, further down the Humber
estuary. Shelley answered brightly.

"Don't ask questions, it's an emergency," I said.

"You've been arrested," she replied resignedly.

"I have not been arrested. I'm hot on the trail of a team
of international art thieves. Some people would be proud to
work with me."

"OK, it's an emergency. What's it got to do with me?"

"Hang on, I think I'm losing someone . . ." We'd cleared
the suburbs of Hull, and the receiver was registering a sharp
change in direction. Sure enough, about a kilometre up the
road, there was a right turn. Cautiously, I drove into the narrow road then pulled up. The distance between us remained
constant. He'd stopped.

And the phone was squawking in my ear. "Sorry, Shelley.
OK, what I need is for you to meet Richard downstairs in five
minutes with the Gemini. He'll leave you his car so you won't
be without wheels," I added weakly.

"You expect me to drive *that?*"

"It'll do wonders for your street cred," I said, ending the
call. I was in no mood for banter or argument. I put the car in
gear and moved slowly down the lane, keeping an eye open for
Turner's car. The tarmac ended a few hundred yards later in the
car park of a pub overlooking the wide estuary. There were only
two cars apart from Turner's Merc. There was no way I was
going in there, even if he was offering the buckle to the highest
bidder. With so few customers, I'd be painfully obvious. All I
could do was head back to the main road and pray that Turner
would still have the buckle with him.

I fretted for an hour, then the screen revealed signs of activity. The buckle was moving back towards me. Moments later, Turner's car emerged from the side road and headed back into Hull. "There is a God," I said, pulling out behind him. We got back to the ferry port at half past five. Turner joined the queue of cars waiting to board, but I stayed over by the booking office. The last thing I wanted was for him to clock me and the Saab at this stage in the game.

Richard skidded to a halt beside me at five to six. He gave me a thumbs-up sign as he got out. He picked up my emergency overnight bag from the passenger seat and came over to the Saab. He tossed the bag into the back and settled into my passenger seat. "Well done," I said, leaning across to give him a smacking kiss on the cheek.

"You'll have to stand on for any speeders I picked up," he said. "It really is a flying machine, that coupé."

"You brought the passport?"

Richard pulled out two passports from his inside pocket. Mine and his. "I thought I'd come along for the ride," he said. "I've got nothing pressing for the next couple of days, and it's about time we had a jaunt."

I shook my head. "No way. This isn't a jaunt. It's work. I've got enough to worry about without having to think about whether you're having a nice time. I really appreciate you doing this, but you're not coming with me."

Richard scowled. "I don't suppose you know where this guy's going?"

"I've no idea. But where he goes, I follow."

"You might need some protective colouring," he pointed out. "I've heard you say that sometimes there are situations where a woman on her own stands out where a couple don't. I think I should come along. I could share the driving."

"No. And no. And no again. You don't expect me to interview spotty adolescent wannabe rock stars, and I don't expect you to play detectives. Go home, Richard. Please?"

He sighed, looking mutinous. "All right," he said, sounding exactly like his nine-year-old son Davy when I drag him off the computer and tell him ten is not an unreasonable bedtime. He flung open the door and got out, turning back to say, "Just don't expect me to feed the cat."

"I haven't got a cat," I said, grinning at his olive branch.

"You could have by the time you get back. Take care, Brannigan."

I waved as I drove off, keeping an eye on him in my rear-view mirror. As I took my place in the slowly moving queue, I saw him get in the car and drive off. Half an hour later, I was standing in the stern of the ship, watching the quay recede inch by inch as we slowly moved away from the dock and out towards the choppy, steel grey waters of the North Sea.

I spent almost all of the trip closeted in my cabin with a spy thriller I'd found stuffed into the door pocket of Bill's car. The only time I went out was for dinner, which comes included in the fare. I left it to the last possible moment, hoping Turner would have eaten and gone by then. I'd made the right decision; there was no sign of him in the restaurant, so I was able to enjoy my meal without having to worry about him clocking me. I was certain he wouldn't recognize me as the tart with the buckle, but if this surveillance lasted any length of time, the chances were that he'd see me somewhere along the line. I didn't want him connecting me back to the ferry crossing.

On the way back to the cabin, I changed some money: fifty pounds each of guilders, Belgian francs, deutschemarks, French francs, Swiss francs and lire. Nothing like hedging your bets. The sea was calm enough for me to get a decent night's sleep, and when we docked at Rotterdam, I felt refreshed enough to drive all day if I had to. From where I was placed on the car deck, I couldn't actually see Turner, and the steel hull of the ship didn't do a lot of favours for the reception on the tracking monitor.

Once I was clear of the ship, however, the signal came back strong and clear. For once, Bill's mongrel European ancestry worked to my advantage. He makes so many trips to the Continent to visit family that he has serious road maps and city street plans for most of northern Europe neatly arranged in a box in his boot. I'd shifted the box to the back seat and unfolded a map of Holland and Belgium on the passenger seat. Comparing the map to the monitor, I reckoned that Turner was heading for Eindhoven. As soon as I got on the motorway, I stepped on the gas, pushing my speed up towards a ton, trying to close the distance between us.

Within half an hour, I had Turner in my sights again. He was cruising along just under ninety, and there was enough traffic on the road for me to stay in reasonably close touch without actually sitting on his bumper. He stayed on the motorway past Eindhoven. The next possible stop was Antwerp. From my point of view, there couldn't be a better destination. Bill's mother grew up in the city and he still has a tribe of relations there. I've been over with him on weekend trips a couple of times, and I fell in love with the city at first sight. Now, I feel like I know it with the intimacy of a lover.

It was my lucky day. He swung off the E34 at the Antwerp turn-off and headed straight for the city centre. He seemed to know where he was going, which made following him a lot easier than if he'd kept pulling over to consult a map or ask a passer-by for his destination. Me, I was just enjoying being back in Antwerp. I don't know how it manages it, but it still manages to be a charming city even though it's the economic heartbeat of Belgium. You don't normally associate culture with huge docks, a bustling financial centre and the major petrochemical industries. Not forgetting Pelikaanstraat, second only to Wall Street in the roll of the richest streets in the world. Come to think of it, what better reason could a fence have for coming to Antwerp than to do a deal in Pelikaanstraat, since its diamonds are the most portable form of hard currency in the world?

It began to look as if that was Turner's destination. We actually drove along the street itself, diamond merchants lining one side, the railway line the other. But he carried on up to the corner by Central Station and turned left into the Keyserlei. He slipped into a parking space just past De Keyser, the city centre's most expensive hotel, took his briefcase and suit carrier out of the car and walked inside. Cursing, I made a quick circuit of the block till I found a parking garage a couple of hundred metres away. I chose one of the several bars and restaurants opposite the hotel and settled down with a coffee and a Belgian waffle. I was just in time to see a liveried flunkey drive off in Turner's car, presumably taking it to the hotel garage.

I was on my third coffee when Turner re-emerged. I left the cup, threw some money on the table and went after him. He crossed over to the square by the station and walked towards the row of tram stops on Carnotstraat. He joined the bunch of people waiting for a tram. I dodged into a nearby tobacconist and bought a book of tram tickets, praying he'd still be there when I came out.

He was, but only just. He was stepping forward to board a tram that was pulling up at the stop. I ran across the street and leapt on to the second of the two carriages just before the doors hissed shut. Turner was sitting near the front, his back to me. He got off near the Melkmarkt, and I had no trouble following him past the cathedral and into the twisting medieval streets of the old town. He was strolling rather than striding, and he didn't look like he had the slightest notion that he might be followed. That was more than I could say for myself. I kept getting a prickling sensation in the back of my neck, as if I were aware at some subconscious level of being watched. I kept glancing over my shoulder, but I saw nothing to alarm me.

Eventually, we ended up in the Vrijdagmarkt. Since it was too late for the twice-weekly secondhand auction, I could only assume Turner was heading for the Plantin-Moretus Museum. I'd tracked him all the way round Antwerp just so we could go round a printing museum? I hung back while he bought a ticket, then I followed him in. While it was no hardship to me to revisit one of my favourite museums, I couldn't see how it was taking me any nearer my art-racket mastermind.

The Plantin-Moretus house and its furnishings are just as they were when Christophe Plantin was Europe's boss printer back in the sixteenth century. But Nicholas Turner didn't seem too interested in soaking up the paintings, tapestries, manuscripts and antique furniture. He was moving swiftly through the rooms. Then I realized he was heading straight for the enclosed garden at the heart of the rectangular house. Rather than follow him out into the open air, I stayed put on the first floor where I could see what was going on.

Turner sat down on a bench, appearing to be simply enjoying the air. After about five minutes, another man joined him. They said nothing, but when the stranger moved on a few minutes later, he left his newspaper beside Turner's briefcase. Another few minutes went by, then Turner picked up the paper, placed it in his briefcase and started for the exit. The man had definitely been watching too many James Bond films.

I hurried back through the rooms I'd already visited and made it into the street in time to see Turner hail a cab. I ran up the square after him, but there wasn't another cab in sight. I ran all the way up to the Grote Markt before I could get a cab to stop for me.

Luck was still running my way. As we turned into the Keyserlei, Turner was walking into the hotel. I paid off the cab and chose another bar to watch from. I'd eaten a bucket of mussels and drunk three more coffees before I saw any action. This time, he walked round the corner into the Pelikaanstraat. A couple of hundred yards down the street, he turned into a diamond merchant's. I wasn't too happy about staking the place out; it's an area where people are understandably suspicious of idle loitering. I'd noticed a slightly seedy-looking hotel on the way down the street, so I doubled back and walked into the foyer. It seemed as handy a place as any to spend the night, so I booked a room. I settled down on a sofa near the door and waited.

I was beginning to think Turner had gone off in the other direction when he finally walked past just before six. This time, I followed him into the hotel, where he headed for reception to pick up his key. I picked up a brochure about daily excursions to Bruges, managing to get close enough to hear him book a table for one in the restaurant at seven and an early-morning call at six. It sounded like he wasn't planning on anything more exciting than an early night. It sounded like a good idea to me.

I had one or two things to see to before I could crash out, but by half past seven, I was sorted. I'd used the hotel phone to check in with Shelley, since my mobile isn't configured to work with the continental system. She was singularly unimpressed with where I was, what I was doing and Richard's car. She was even less impressed when I confessed that her own car was less than a couple of miles from her house, locked safely inside Bill's garage, since I had the keys for the garage lurking somewhere at the bottom of my bag.

Thanks to the wonders of car hire, I was better off than she was. I had my very own Mercedes stashed in the parking garage round the corner. The Saab was safely parked behind a high fence at the Hertz office, and I'd dined on a giant slab of steak with a pile of crisp chips and thick mayo. I hadn't eaten so well on a job for years.

By nine, I was watching CNN in my hotel room, a large vodka and grapefruit juice sweating on the bedside table next to me. I was just about to get up and run a bath when I heard the unmistakable sound of a key fumbling into the lock of my bedroom door.

# 16

I was off the bed in seconds and in through the open door of the bathroom, hitting the light switches on the way. Whoever was outside the door would have to pass me on their way into the room itself, with only the flickering light of the television screen to guide them. The scrabbling stopped, and an arc of light from the hallway spilled across the carpet as the door opened. A shadow crossed the light, then the arc narrowed and disappeared as the door closed. I tensed, ready to come out kicking.

A hand groped along the far wall, followed by a shoulder. I leapt through the doorway, pivoted on one foot and put all my weight behind a straight kick at stomach level, yelling as loudly as I could to multiply the fear and surprise. My foot made contact with flesh and the body staggered back against the door with a heavy crash, the air shooting out of him in a groaning rush as he crumpled on the floor. I stepped back, keeping my weight on the balls of my feet, and reached for the lights.

Richard was doubled up on the carpet, arms folded defensively over his guts. For once, I was lost for words. I relaxed my fighting stance and stood staring at him.

"Fucking hell," he gasped. "Was that some traditional Belgian greeting, or what?"

"It's a traditional private eye's greeting for uninvited visitors," I snarled. "What the hell are you doing here?"

Richard struggled to his feet, still clutching his stomach. "Nice to see you too, Brannigan." He pushed past me and stumbled on to the bed, where he curled into a ball. "Oh shit, I think you've relocated my stomach somewhere around my left shoulder blade."

"Serves you right," I said heartlessly. "You scared me shitless."

"That why you were in the bathroom?" he said innocently.

"What was wrong with the phone? Was it too much for you to handle, a foreign phone system? Besides, how did you get here? How did you find me? Did Shelley tell you where I was?"

Richard stopped rubbing his stomach and eased up into a sitting position. "I thought I'd surprise you. I don't know, call yourself a detective? I've been tailing you ever since you got off the ferry, and you didn't even notice," he said proudly.

I moved across the room to the only chair and sat down heavily. "You've been tailing *me*?"

"Piece of piss," he said.

He had me worried now. If I'd been so busy watching Nicholas Turner that I hadn't spotted a car as obvious as a snazzy UK-registered coupé on my own tail, it was time I gave up detective work and settled for something like social work where I could get away with a complete lack of observational skills. "I don't believe you," I said. "Shelley told you where I was and you got a flight over here."

He grinned. For once, it made me want to hit him, not kiss him. "Sorry, Brannigan. I did it all by myself."

"No way. I couldn't have missed seeing the coupé on the ferry," I said, positive now. The Saab had been one of the last cars to board. He simply couldn't have got the coupé on board without me spotting it.

"That's what I thought too," he said complacently. "That's why I left it at Hull. I travelled as a foot passenger, which meant I got off the ferry before you. I hired a Merc at the ferry terminal and picked you up as you came off. Then I followed you here. I thought I'd lost you when you got on the tram, but I managed to get a taxi and he followed the tram. Just like the movies, really. I waited outside while you were in that museum, and I hung about just inside the station when you came in here first time around."

I shook my head in bewildered amazement. "So how did you get a key for the room?"

His grin was beginning to infuriate me. "I had a word with the desk clerk. Told him my girlfriend was here on business and I'd come to surprise her. It cost me two thousand francs. Most I've ever paid for a good kicking."

Forty quid. I was impressed. "I suppose you're potless now, are you?" I said sternly.

He looked sheepish. "Not as such. I forgot to go to the building society with the nine and a half grand, so I brought it with me."

I didn't know whether to be furious or impressed. There was no doubt the money would come in handy, at the rate I was spending, but I didn't want Richard around on the chase. I had enough to worry about keeping tabs on Turner without having to be constantly aware of what Richard was up to. "Thanks," I said. "I was wondering what to do when I ran out of cash. You can leave it with me when you go home tomorrow."

He looked crestfallen. "I thought you'd be pleased to see me," he said.

I got up and sat down beside him on the bed. "Of course I'm pleased to see you. I just don't need to have to worry about you while I'm trying to do my job."

"What's to worry about?" he demanded. "I'm not a kid, Kate. Look, these are heavy people you're after, there's no two ways about it. You could use an extra pair of eyes. Not to mention an extra set of wheels. If he's going on a long haul, you can't use the same car all the way, and you could lose him while you're swapping over at some car-hire place. If I stay, we can rent a couple of mobile phones and that way one of us can stay with him while the other one does things like fill up with petrol or stop for a piss."

The most irritating thing was that he was right. I'd been worrying about that very thing myself. "I don't know," I said. I wanted to say, 'This is my territory, my skill area, my speciality and you're just an amateur.' But I didn't want to throw that down on the bed for both of us to look at. The thing that worried me most was that after the debacle when he'd last tried to help me out, Richard felt he had something to prove. And there's nothing more dangerous on a job that needs patience than someone with something to prove.

At quarter past six the following morning, I was sitting in the dark in my rented Mercedes on Pelikaanstraat. Richard was on the Keyserlei, a couple of hundred yards up from the hotel. Whichever way Turner went, one of us would pick him up. I checked the equipment on the passenger seat one more time. Richard hadn't been strictly honest with me the previous evening. Once I'd reluctantly agreed to let him tag along, he confessed that he'd already hired a pair of mobile phones, so convinced was he that I'd see what he called sense.

We'd already agreed on a modus operandi. I would use the bugging equipment to keep tabs on Turner. Richard would sit tucked in behind me. If I wanted to stop to change cars, fill up with petrol or go to the loo, I'd phone him and he'd overtake me. Then, when he had Turner in sight, he'd call me and I'd go and do whatever I needed to. Once I was back on track, Richard would fall back behind me again. That was the theory. I'd put money on it working like a wind-up toy with a broken spring.

I sipped the carton of coffee I'd bought from the vending machine in the station and watched the screen. The buckle wasn't moving yet. I ate one of the waffles I'd bought the evening before. I could feel my blood sugar rising with every mouthful. The combination of sugar and caffeine had me feeling almost human by the time the phone rang at five to seven. "Yes?" I said.

"Z-Victor One to BD," Richard said. "Target on move. I've just pulled out in front of him. Heading for the traffic lights. He's staying in the left-hand lane. Roger and out."

If he carried on like this all day, I might just kill him by dinner time, I decided. I stepped on the accelerator and swung round the corner. I was just in time to see the two cars turn left at the traffic lights. No way was I going to catch them, so I settled for watching the screen. I caught up with them about a mile from the motorway. It looked like we were heading southeast, towards Germany.

Once we hit the motorway, I called Richard and told him to fall back behind me. I kept a steady two kilometres behind Turner, which was far enough at a hundred and forty kph, and five minutes later Richard appeared in front of me, slowing down enough to slide into my slipstream with a cheery wave. By nine, we'd sailed past Maastricht and Aachen, the bug had seen us safely through the maze of autobahns round Köln, and Bonn was fast approaching on the port bow as we rolled on to the west of the Rhine. The boring flat land of Belgium was a distant memory now as the motorway swept us inexorably through rolling hills and woodland. Somehow, the motorways in Europe seem to be much more attractively landscaped than ours do. Maybe it's just the indefinably foreign quality of the scenery, but I suspect it's more to do with the fact that the Germans in particular have had to take Green politics seriously for a few years longer than we have.

Just before eleven, we crossed the Rhine north of Karls-
ruhe, with no sign of slowing up. I rang Richard and told him
to overtake me and get on Turner's back bumper again. The
motorway split just south of the city, the A5 carrying on south
and the A8 cutting off east. Unlike in Köln, there was no quick
way to double back if we made the wrong decision. A few minutes later, he called telling me to stay on the A5. We carried on
down the river valley, the wooded hills on the left starting to
become mountains, the occasional rocky peak flashing in and
out of sight for seconds at a time.

A few kilometres before the Swiss border, the blip on the
screen started moving towards me. It looked like Turner had
stopped. Judging by the state of my fuel gauge, he was probably buying petrol. I rang Richard and told him to pull off at
the approaching services while I carried on across the border.
I stopped as soon as I could after waving my passport at Swiss
customs and poured petrol into my tank till I couldn't squeeze
another drop in. I bought a couple of sandwiches, bars of yummy
Swiss chocolate and cans of mineral water, then rushed back to
the car. The buckle was still behind me, but closing fast. I rang
Richard.

"We both filled up with petrol," he reported. "I waited till
he'd cleared the shop before I went in to pay, then I followed
him through the border. Where are you?"

"In the service area you're about to pass," I told him. "You
can let Turner get away from you now. If you drive into the
services, you can fall in behind me again." I couldn't believe it
was all going so well. I kept waiting for the other shoe to drop.

We carried on past Basel and on to Zürich. By now, we
were properly into the Alps, mountains towering above us on
all sides. If I hadn't been concentrating so hard on staying in
touch with Turner and the buckle, I'd have been enjoying the
drive. As it was, I felt as stressed as if I'd been sitting in city
rush-hour traffic for the five and a half hours it had taken us
to get this far.

We skirted the outskirts of the city and drove on down the side of Lake Zürich. About halfway down the lake, the blip on the screen suddenly swung off to the right. "Oh shit," I muttered. I stepped on the accelerator, checking in my mirror that Richard was still with me. The motorway exit was only seconds away, and I swung off on a road that led into the mountains. I grabbed the phone, punched the memory redial that linked me to Richard and said, "Wait here. Turn round to face the motorway so you can pick him up if he heads back."

"Roger Wilco," Richard said. "Call me if you need back-up."

I carried on, checking the blip on the screen against the road map. Cursing the fact that I didn't have a more detailed map of Switzerland, I swung the car through the bends of what was rapidly becoming a mountain road. A couple of miles further on, I realized that staying on the main road had been the wrong decision, as the buckle was moving further away from me at an angle. Swearing so fluently my mother would have disowned me, I nearly caused a small pile-up with a U-turn that took a thousand miles off the tyres and hammered back down the road and on to a narrow, twisting side road. About a kilometre away from the main drag, the screen suddenly went blank.

I panicked. My first thought was that Turner had met someone or picked someone up who had taken one look at the buckle, spotted the bug and disabled it. Then logic kicked in and told me that was impossible in so short a time. As I swung round yet another bend with a sheer rock wall on one side and a vertiginous drop on the other, I twigged. The mountains were so high and so dense that the radio signal was blocked.

I raced the car round the bends as fast as I could, tyres screaming on every one, wrists starting to feel it in spite of the power steering. I was concentrating so hard on not ending up as a sheet of scrap metal on the valley floor that I nearly missed Turner. With the suddenness of daylight at the end of a tunnel, the road emerged on to a wide plateau about halfway up the mountain. In the middle of an Alpine meadow complete with cows that tinkled like bass wind chimes stood an inn, as pretty as a picture postcard, as Swiss as a Chalet School novel. On the edge of the crowded car park, Turner's pale green Mercedes was parked. And the screen flashed back into life.

Heaving a huge sigh of relief, I drove to the far end of the car park and tried to ring Richard and let him know everything was OK. No joy. I supposed the mountain was in the way again. I got out of the car, took a black beret and a pair of granny glasses with clear lenses out of my stakeout-disguises holdall and walked into the inn. Inside, it was the traditional Swiss chalet: wood everywhere, walls decorated with huge posters of Alpine scenery, a blazing fire in a central stone fireplace. The room was crammed with tables, most of them occupied. A quick scan showed me Turner sitting alone at a table for two, studying the menu. A waitress dressed in traditional costume bustled up to me and said something in German. I shrugged and tried out my school French, saying I wanted to eat, one alone, and did they have a telephone?

She smiled and showed me to a table near the fire and pointed out the phone. I got change from the cashier and gave Richard a quick call. For some reason, he was less than thrilled that I was sitting down to some Tyrolean speciality while he was stuck on the verge of the road with nothing in sight but the motorway and a field of the inevitable cows. "Go and get some sandwiches or something," I instructed him. "I'll let you know when we set off."

I went back to my table. Out of the corner of my eye, I could see Turner tucking into a steaming bowl of soup, a stein of beer beside him, so I figured I'd have time to eat something. I ordered Tiroler Gröstl, a mixture of potatoes, onions and ham with a fried egg on top. It looked like the nearest thing to fast food on the menu. I was right. My meal was in front of me in under five minutes. I was halfway through it before Turner's main course arrived. Judging by the pile of chips that was all I could identify, he was eating for two. Frankly, I could see why he'd made the detour. The food was more than worth it, if my plateful was anything to go by. Definitely one to cut out and keep for next time we were passing Zürich.

By the time I'd finished and lingered over a cup of coffee, Turner had also demolished a huge wedge of lemon meringue pie. If I'd scoffed that much in the middle of the day, I'd have been asleep at the wheel ten miles down the road. I hoped he had a more lively metabolism. When he called for the bill, I took mine to the cashier, rang Richard to warn him we were on the move, and headed back to the car. Minutes later, Turner was heading back down the road, with me a couple of bends behind him.

As we hit the motorway, I had another panic. Where I'd expected to see Richard in his Mercedes, there was a black BMW. As I sailed past, I glanced across and saw the familiar grin behind the thumbs-up sign. Moments later, as he swung in behind me, the phone rang. "Sierra Forty-nine to Sierra Oscar," he said. "Surprise, surprise. I nipped back to Zürich and swapped the cars. I thought it was about time for a change."

"Nice one," I conceded. Maybe he wasn't the liability I'd feared he'd be after all. And there was me thinking that he was as subtle as Jean Paul Gaultier. This wasn't the time to reassess the capabilities of the man in my life, but I filed the thought away for future scrutiny.

I figured we must be heading for Liechtenstein, haven for tax dodgers, fraudsters and stamp-collecting anoraks. No such luck. We carried on south, deep into the Alps. Richard was in front of me again, keeping tabs on Turner. The bug kept cutting out because of the mountains, and I was determined that we weren't going to lose him after coming this far. Now Richard was in another car, I felt happy about him staying in fairly close touch.

A few miles down the road, my bottle started twitching. There was no getting away from it. We were heading for the San Bernardino tunnel. Ten kilometres in that dark tube, aware of the millions of tons of rock just sitting above my head, waiting to crush me thin as a postage stamp. Just the thought of it forced a groan from my lips. I'm terrified of tunnels. Not a lot of people know that. It doesn't sit well with the fearless, feisty image. I've even been known to drive thirty miles out of my way to avoid going through the tunnels under the Mersey.

With every minute that passed, that gaping hole in the hillside was getting closer and my heart was pounding faster. Desperately, I rattled through the handful of cassettes I'd grabbed when I'd picked up Bill's car. Not a soothing one among them. No Enya, no Mary Coughlan, not even Everything but the Girl. Plenty of Pet Shop Boys, Eurythmics and R.E.M. I settled for Crowded House turned up loud to keep the eerie boom of the tunnel traffic at bay and tried to concentrate on their harmonies.

Two minutes into the tunnel and the sweat was clammy on my back. Three minutes in and my upper lip was damp. Four minutes in and my forehead was slimy as a sewer wall. Six minutes in and my knuckles were white on the steering wheel. The walls looked as if they were closing in. I tried telling myself it was only imagination, and Crowded House promised they could ease my pain. They were lying. Ten minutes and I could feel a scream bubbling in my throat. I was on the point of tears when a doughnut of light appeared around the cars in front of me.

As soon as I burst out again into daylight, my phone started ringing. "Yeah?" I gasped.

"You OK?" Richard asked. He knows all about me and tunnels.

"I'll live." I swallowed hard. "Thanks for asking."

"You're a hero, Brannigan," he said.

"Never mind that," I said gruffly. "You still with Turner?"

"Tight as Jagger's jeans. He's got his foot down. Looks like we're heading for *la bella Italia*."

At least I'd be somewhere I could speak the language, I thought with relief. I'd been worried all the way down Germany and Switzerland that Turner was going to end up in a close encounter that I couldn't understand a word of. But my Italian was fluent, a hangover from the summer before university, when I'd worked in the kitchens of Oxford's most select trattoria. It was learn the language or take a vow of silence. I'd prevented it from getting too rusty by holidaying in Italy whenever I could.

I drove cheerfully down the mountain, glad to be out in the open air again, relieved that we were gradually leaving the mountains behind us. We worked our way round Milan just after five, Richard back behind me, and by seven we were skirting Genoa. This was turning into one hell of a drive. My shoulders were locked, my backside numb, my hips stiff in spite of regular squirming. If they ever start making private eyes work with tachographs, I'm going to be as much use to my clients as a cardboard chip pan. I shuddered to think what this overtime was going to look like on Henry's bill. He'd run out of buckshee hours a while back.

At Genoa we turned east again on the A12, another one of those autostradas carved out of the side of a mountain. I kept telling myself the little tunnels were just like driving under big bridges, but it didn't help a lot, especially since the receiver kept cutting out, giving me panic attacks every time.

Three quarters of an hour past Genoa, the screen told me Turner was moving off to one side. First, he went right, then crossed back left. I nearly missed the exit, I was concentrating so hard on the screen, but I managed to get off with Richard on my tail. We were on the outskirts of some town called Sestri Levante, but according to my screen, Turner was heading away from it. Praying I was going the right way, I swung left and found myself driving along a river valley, the road lined with shops and houses. Sestri Levante shaded into Casarza Ligure, then we were out into open country, wooded hills on either side of the valley. We hit a small village called Bargonasco just as the direction changed on the receiver. A couple of kilometres further up, there was a turning on the left. It was a narrow, asphalt road, with a sign saying "Villa San Pietro." The blip on the screen stayed steady. A kilometre away, straight up the Villa San Pietro's drive.

Journey's end.

# 17

"What now, Sam Spade?" Richard asked as we both bent and stretched in vain attempts to restore our bodies to something like their normal configuration.

"You go back to the village and find us somewhere to stay for the night, then you sit outside in the car in case Turner comes back down the valley," I told him.

"And what are you doing while I'm doing that?" Richard asked.

"I'm going to take a look at the Villa San Pietro," I told him.

He looked at me as if I'd gone stark staring mad. "You can't just drive up there like the milkman," he said.

"Correct. I'm going to walk up, like a tourist. And you're going to take the receiver with you, just in case the buckle's going anywhere Turner isn't."

"You're not going up there on your own," Richard said firmly.

"Of course I am," I stated even more firmly. "You are waiting down here with a car, a phone and a bug receiver. If we both go and Turner comes driving back down with the buckle while we're ten minutes away from the cars, he could be outside the range of the receiver in any direction before we get mobile.

I'm not trekking all the way across Europe only to lose the guy because you want to play macho man."

Richard shook his head in exasperation. "I hate it when you find a logical explanation for what you intend to do regardless," he muttered, throwing himself back into the driver's seat of the BMW. "See you later."

I waved him off, then moved the Merc up the road a few hundred yards. I scuffed some dust over my trainers, put on a pair of sunglasses even though dusk was already gathering, hung my camera round my neck and trudged off up the drive.

There was a three-foot ditch on one side of the twisting road, which appeared to have been carved out of the rough scrub and stunted trees of the hillside. Ten minutes' brisk climbing brought me to the edge of a clearing. I hung back in the shelter of a couple of gnarled olive trees and took a good look. The ground had been cleared for about a hundred metres up to a wall. Painted pinkish brown, it was a good six feet high and extended for about thirty metres either side of a wrought iron gate. Above the wall, I could see an extensive roof in the traditional terracotta pantiles. Through the gates, I could just about make out the villa itself, a two-storey white stucco building with shutters over the upper-storey windows. It looked like serious money to me.

I would have been tempted to go in for a closer look, except that a closed-circuit video camera was mounted by the gate, doing a continuous 180-degree sweep of the road and the clearing. Not just serious money, but serious paranoia too.

Staying inside the cover of the trees and the scrub, I circled the villa. By the time I got back to the drive, I had more scratches than Richard's record collection, and the certainty that Nicholas Turner was playing with the big boys. There were video cameras mounted on each corner of the compound, all programmed to carry out regular sweeps. If I'd had enough time and a computer, I could probably have worked out where and when the blind spots would occur, but anyone who's that serious about their perimeter security probably hasn't left the back door on the latch. This was one burglary that was well out of my league.

I found Richard sitting on the bonnet of his car on the forecourt of a building with all the grace and charm of a Sixties tower block. Green neon script along the front of the three-storey rectangle proclaimed Casa Nico. Below that, red neon told us this was a Ristorante-Bar-Pensione. The only other vehicles on the parking area were a couple of battered pickups and a clutch of elderly motor scooters. So much for Italian style.

"This is it?" I asked, my heart sinking.

"This is it," Richard confirmed gloomily. "Wait till you see the room."

I gathered my overnight bag, the video camera bag and my camera gear and followed Richard indoors. To get to the rooms, we had to go through the bar. In spite of the floor-to-ceiling windows along one wall, it somehow managed to be dark and gloomy. As soon as we walked through the bead curtain that separated the bar from the forecourt, the rumble of male voices stopped dead. In a silence cut only by the slushy Italian Muzak from the jukebox, we crossed the room. I smiled inanely round me at the half-dozen men sprawled around a couple of tables. I got as cheerful a welcome as a Trot at a Tory party conference. Not even the human bear leaning on the Gaggia coffee machine behind the bar acknowledged our existence. The minute we left by a door in the rear, the conversation started up again. So much for the friendly hospitality of the Italian people. Somehow, I didn't see myself managing to engage mine host in a bit of friendly gossip about the Villa San Pietro.

The third-floor room was big, with a spectacular view up the wooded river valley. That was all you could say for it. Painted a shade of yellow that I haven't seen since the last time I had food poisoning, it contained the sort of vast, heavy wooden furniture that could only have been built *in situ*, unless it was moved into the room before the walls went up. Above the double bed was a crucifix, and the view from the bed was a massive, sentimental print of Jesus displaying the Sacred Heart with all the dedication of an offal butcher.

"Bit of a turn-off, eh?" Richard said.

"I expect Jeffrey Dahmer would love it." I sat down on the bed, testing the mattress. Another mistake. I thought I was going to be swallowed whole. "How much is this costing us?" I asked.

"About the same as a night in the Gritti Palace. Mind you, that also includes dinner. Not that it'll be edible," he added pessimistically.

After we'd had a quick shower, I set the bug receiver to auto-alert, so that it would give a series of audible bleeps if the buckle moved more than half a kilometre from its current relative position. Then we went in search of food. Richard had been right about that too. We were the only two people in the cheerless dining room, which resembled a school dining room with tablecloths. The sole waitress, presumably the wife of Grizzly Adams behind the bar, looked as if she'd last laughed somewhere around 1974 and hadn't enjoyed the experience enough to want to repeat it. We started with a platter of mixed meats, most of which looked and tasted like they'd made their getaway from the local cobbler. The pasta that followed was *al dente* enough to be a threat to dentistry. The sauce was so sparing that the only way we could identify it as pesto was by the colour.

Richard and I ate in virtual silence. "What was that you said about it being time we had a bit of a jaunt?" I said at one point.

He prodded one of the overcooked lamb chops that looked small enough to have come from a rabbit and scowled. "Next time, I won't be so bloody helpful," he muttered. "This is hell. I haven't had proper food for two days and I'd kill for a joint."

"Not many Chinese restaurants in Italy," I remarked. "It's on account of them inventing one of the world's great cuisines." Richard took one look at my deadpan face and we both burst out laughing. "One day," I gasped, "we'll look back at this and laugh."

"Don't bet on it," he said darkly.

We passed on pudding. We both have too much respect for our digestive tracts. At least the coffee was good. So good we ordered a second cup and took it upstairs with us. The one good thing about the bed was the trough in the middle that forced us into each other's arms. After the day we'd had, it was more than time to remind each other that the world isn't all grief.

My eyelids unstuck themselves ten hours later. The bleeding heart on the wall wasn't a great sight to wake up to, so I rolled over and checked the receiver sitting on the bedside table. No movement. By nine, we were both showered, dressed and back in the dining room. Breakfast was a pleasant surprise. Freshly baked focaccia, three different cheeses and a choice of jam. "What's the game plan for today?" Richard asked through a mouthful of Gorgonzola and bread.

"We stick with the buckle," I said. "If it moves, we follow. If it stays put and Turner moves, we stay put too and follow Plan B."

"What's Plan B?"

"I don't know yet."

After breakfast, Richard took his BMW up the valley past the drive. I'd told him to park facing up the valley and to follow anything that came down the drive, unless I called him and told him different. I sat on a bench on the forecourt of Casa Nico, reading Bill's thriller, the receiver in my open bag next to me. I hoped that anyone passing would take me for a tourist making the most of the watery autumn sunshine. I only had thirty pages to go when the receiver bleeped so loudly I nearly fell off my seat.

I picked it up and stared at the read-out. The buckle was moving steadily towards me. I leapt to my feet and jumped into the car, gunning the engine into life. Still the buckle was drawing nearer. There was a sudden change of direction, which I guessed was the turn from the drive on to the main road. I edged forward, ready to pull out after the target vehicle had passed, one eye on the screen. Seconds later, a stretch Mercedes limo cruised past me, followed in short order by Richard in the BMW.

I slotted into place behind him, and our little cavalcade made its way back down the valley and into Sestri Levante. The outskirts of the town were typical of northern Italy—dusty, slightly shabby, somehow old-fashioned. The centre was much smarter, a trim holiday resort all stucco in assorted pastel shades, green shuttered windows on big hotels and small *pensiones*, expensive shops, grass and palm trees. We skirted the wide crescent of the main beach and headed along the isthmus to the harbour. As the limo turned on to a quay, I dumped the car in an illegal parking space and watched Richard do the same. I ran up to join him, linked arms and together we strolled up the quay, our faces pointing towards the sea and the floating gin palaces lined up at the pontoons. The great thing about wrap-round sunglasses is the way you can look in one direction while your head is pointing in the other.

From the corner of my eye, I saw the stretch limo glide to a halt at the foot of a gangway. The boat at the end of it was bigger than my house, and probably worth as much as Henry's Monet. The driver's door opened and a gorilla in uniform got out. Even from that distance, I could see muscles so developed they made him look round-shouldered. He wore sunglasses and a heavy moustache and looked around him with the economical watchfulness of a good bodyguard. Martin Scorsese would have swooned.

Satisfied that there was no one on the quay more dangerous than a couple of goggling tourists, he opened the back door. By now, we were close enough for me to get a good look at the presumed owner of the Villa San Pietro. He wasn't much more than my own five feet and three inches, but he looked a hell of a lot harder than me. He was handsome in the way that birds of prey are handsome, all hooked nose and hooded eyes. His perfectly groomed black hair had a wing of silver over each temple. He was wearing immaculately pressed cream yachting ducks, a full-cut, canary yellow silk shirt with a navy guernsey thrown over his shoulders. He carried a slim briefcase. He stood for a moment on the quayside, shaking the crease straight on his trouser legs, then headed up the gangplank without waiting for Turner, who scrambled out of the car behind him.

I pulled Richard into a tight embrace as Turner and the bodyguard went on board, just in case Turner was looking. When they'd disappeared below, we carried on strolling past the *Petronella Azura III*. I can't say I was surprised to see that the expensive motor cruiser was registered out of Palermo.

"Fucking hell," Richard murmured as we passed the boat. "It's the Mafia. Brannigan, this is no place for us to be," he said, casting a nervous look back over his shoulder.

"They don't know we're here," I pointed out. "Let's keep it that way, huh?" At the end of the quay, we stared out to sea for a few minutes.

"We're going to pull out now, aren't we?" Richard demanded. "I mean, it's time to bring in the big battalions, isn't it?"

"Who did you have in mind?" I asked pointedly. "This isn't Manchester. I don't know the good cops from the bad cops. From what I've heard of Italian corruption, I could walk into the nearest police station and find myself talking to this mob's tame copper. Can you think of a better short cut to a concrete bathing suit?"

Richard looked hurt. "I was only trying to be helpful," he said.

"Well, don't. When I want help, I'll ask for it." I can't help myself. The more scared I get, the more I bite lumps out of the nearest body. Besides, I didn't figure I was obliged to feel guilty. As far as I was concerned, Richard had drawn the short straw from choice.

I got to my feet and started to stroll back down the quay. After a moment, Richard caught up with me. We were just in time to see the chauffeur and a young lad in shorts and a striped T-shirt trot down the gangplank and start unloading suitcases from the boot of the limo. They ferried half a dozen bags on board, not even giving us a second glance. We walked back to my car and stared at the receiver in a moody silence neither of us felt like breaking.

After about half an hour, Turner and the bodyguard came off the yacht and got in the car. "You want to follow them?" I asked Richard. "I'll stay here and watch the boat."

"No heroics," he bargained.

"No heroics," I agreed.

He just caught the lights at the end of the road where the limo had turned right. It looked like the chauffeur was taking Turner back to the villa. And judging by the screen, the buckle was now aboard the yacht. One of two things was going to happen now. Either the yacht was going to take off, complete with buckle, or some third party was going to come to the yacht and get the buckle. My money was on the former, but I felt duty-bound to sit it out. The phone rang about twenty minutes later. "They're back at the villa," Richard reported. "Do you want me to wait and see if Turner takes off?"

"Please," I said. "Thanks, Richard. Sorry I bit your head off earlier."

"So you should be. You're lucky to have me." He ended the call before I could find a retort.

Suddenly the receiver screen went blank. I sat bolt upright. I pulled the connector out of the cigarette-lighter socket where I'd been recharging the batteries and slid the power compartment cover off. I broke one of my nails getting the batteries out in a hurry, and stuffed replacements in. But when I switched on again, the screen was still blank. Given that it wasn't the batteries and the yacht hadn't moved out of range, there was only one possible reason why my screen was blank. Someone had discovered the bug and put it out of action. I took a deep breath and thanked my lucky stars that my name wasn't Nicholas Turner.

Ten minutes later, the lad in the shorts was back on the quayside, casting off. Within twenty minutes, the *Petronella Azura III* had disappeared round the point. Pondering my next step, I drove back up the valley and found Richard sitting in the BMW a couple of hundred yards up the road from the turn-off to the drive. I parked my Merc at Casa Nico and walked up to join him. I filled him in on the latest turn of events. It didn't take long.

"So do we go home now?" he asked plaintively.

"I suppose so," I said reluctantly. "I'd like to get inside that villa, though."

"You said yourself it was impregnable," he pointed out.

"I know, but I never could resist a challenge."

Richard took a deep breath. "Brannigan, you know I never try to come between you and your job. But this time, you've got to back off. Go home, tell the police what you've got so far. They can pick up Turner and they can talk to the good cops over here and get them to look at the villa and the boat. There's nothing more you can do here. Besides, you've got another investigation you're supposed to be working on, in case you'd forgotten."

Part of me knew he was right. But there is another part of me that responds to being told what to do by doing just the opposite. It overrides all my common sense, and it's one of the reasons why I prefer to work alone. Besides, I knew that all we had was an address and the name of a boat. That wouldn't necessarily take the authorities anywhere at all. I wanted more. But I didn't want to get into that right then. "Let's book in at Casa Nico for another night," I said. "We might as well get an early start tomorrow and shoot straight back to Antwerp in a oner," I said. "We don't have to eat there," I added hastily. "Sestri Levante looked like it might have a few decent restaurants."

Richard scowled. "So why don't we go the whole hog and book in at a decent hotel too?"

"I'd like to stay up here, keep an eye on the place, see if there are any more comings and goings," I told him. "You can go down to Sestri and potter round the shops if you want."

The scowl deepened. "I'm not some bloody bimbo," he complained. "If you're waiting here, I'll keep you company."

It was a long afternoon. I finished the thriller and Richard started it. We played I-Spy. We played Bonaparte. We played "I went to the doctor's with . . ." right through the alphabet. The only break was when I nipped back to the Casa Nico to book us a room for the night. I was about to give in to Richard's pleas to call it a day when there was movement. An Alfa Romeo sports saloon shot out of the drive heading up the valley. Even at the speed it was travelling, I recognized the bodyguard behind the wheel. "Move it," I told Richard. He pulled the BMW round in a tight arc and shot after the Alfa.

We didn't have far to go. A few miles up the road was a bar whose owner could have taught Nico a thing or two. Even from our slow cruise past, it was obvious that Bar Bargonasco made Nico's look like a funeral parlour. The music was loud and cheerful, the car park didn't look like an apprentice scrap yard and there were more than six people in there. "Pull up round the corner," I said.

When the car stopped, I opened the door. "Where are you going?" Richard said, panic in his eyes.

"I'm going to get into that villa one way or another. If I can't do it Dennis O'Brien style, I'm going to do it Kate Brannigan style. I'm going to chat up the bodyguard." I shut the door and took off the shirt I was wearing over the cotton vest that was tucked into my jeans. As I was stuffing the shirt into my handbag, Richard jumped out of the driver's seat.

"You're out of your mind," he yelled at me. "Have you seen the size of that guy?"

"That's the whole point. He's obviously been hired for his size, not his brains. He probably keeps them in his trousers, which gives me a head start."

"You'll never get his keys off him," Richard exploded. "For fuck's sake, Kate. This is madness."

"I'm not planning on getting his keys off him. I'm planning on getting him to take me home with him," I said, starting off towards the bar.

Richard caught up with me two steps further on and grabbed my arm. "No way," he shouted.

Mistake, really. In one short, sharp move, I freed myself and left Richard white-faced and clutching his wrist. "Never, never grab me like that," I said softly. "You don't own me, Richard, and you don't tell me what to do."

For a long moment we stood in a silent standoff. "I love you, you silly bitch," Richard finally said. "If you want to go off and get yourself killed, you'll have to knock me out first."

"I'll do it if I have to. You better believe me. This is my job, Richard. I know what I'm doing."

"You'd fuck that gorilla because you think it'll help you nail some mafioso?"

I snorted. "Is that what this is about? Sexual jealousy? What do you think I am, Richard? A tart? I never said I was going to fuck the guy. If he thinks that's on the agenda, that'll be his first mistake."

"You think you can sort out a fucking monster like that with a bit of Thai boxing? Brannigan, you're off your head!" Richard was scarlet by now, his hands bunched into fists by his side.

I was inches away from completely losing control, but I had enough sense left not to flatten him. That would be one move that our relationship wouldn't survive. "Trust me, Richard," I said quietly. "I know what I'm doing."

He laughed bitterly. "Fine," he spat at me. "Treat me like an idiot. I'm used to it, after all. That's what you all think I am anyway, isn't it? Richard the wimp, Richard the pillock, Richard the doormat, Richard the wanker, Richard who lets Kate do his thinking for him, Richard the limp dick who can't be trusted to do the simplest of jobs without ending up in the nick," he ranted.

"Nobody thinks you're a wimp. I don't think you're a wanker, or any of the other things," I shouted back at him. "What happened to you with the car could have happened just as easily to me."

"Oh no, it couldn't," he screamed back at me. "Clever clogs Brannigan would have phoned the police as soon as she found the car. Clever clogs Brannigan would have checked the car to see if there was anything in it there shouldn't have been. Clever clogs Brannigan and the girls would never have got themselves banged up. Because the girls are smart, and I'm just a fucking stupid arsehole *man* who gets put up with because he's marginally more fun than a vibrator." He stopped suddenly, out of steam.

"I love you, Richard," I said quietly. It's not an expression I'm given to, but extreme circumstances demand extreme responses.

"Bollocks," he shouted. "I'm a fucking convenience. You don't know what love is. You never let anyone close enough. It's all a fucking game to you, Brannigan. Like your fucking job. It's all a game. Nothing ever gets you in here," he added, thumping his chest like an opera buffa tenor.

He looked so ridiculous, I couldn't help a smile twitching at the corners of my mouth. "This isn't the time for this," I said, trying to make my amusement look like conciliation. "I'd no idea you felt this bad about what happened, and it's important that we sort it out. But we're both tired, we're both under a lot of pressure. Let's leave it till we get home, OK? Now, let me do what I've got to do. I'll see you back at Casa Nico later, OK?"

Richard shook his head. "You really are a piece of work, Brannigan. You think you can just sweep all this aside like that? Forget it. You can go back to Casa fucking Nico if you want. But I won't be there."

He turned on his heel and stormed back to the car. As he opened the door, he said, "You coming?"

I shook my head. He slammed the car door behind him, swung the car round and headed back down the valley. I watched him go, my stomach feeling hollow, my eyes suddenly swimming with tears. Impatiently, I blinked them away. I tried to convince myself that Richard would be back at Casa Nico once he'd calmed down.

In the meantime, I had work to do. Besides, now I needed a lift back down the valley.

# 18

No woman is a heroine to her dentist. Along with my phobia about tunnels goes my paralysing fear of needles and drills. As a result, I knew I wasn't going to have to rely on anything as crude as physical strength to beat the bodyguard. If Richard hadn't pissed me off so much, I'd have explained it to him. But Watsons who scream at their Holmeses don't get the inside track on methodology.

Picking up the bodyguard was a doddle. Any man who spends as much time as he obviously did on keeping his body in peak condition has to have a streak of vanity a mile wide. He fully expected that if an attractive foreign woman walked into a bar where he was drinking, he'd be the one she'd inevitably be drawn to. And in a country where the native women are so sexually constrained by religion, it's equally inevitable that foreign women who walk into bars alone and with bare shoulders must be whores. My target thought it was his lucky night as soon as I settled on the bar stool next to him and smiled as I ordered a Peroni.

On the short walk to the bar, I'd come up with the cover story that I was a professional photographer, in Italy to take pictures for a coffee-table book of Italian church bell towers. Gianni the bodyguard and his drinking companions fell for it hook, line and sinker, with much nudging in the ribs about women who liked big ones. I suppose they thought my Italian wasn't up to mucky innuendo. By the time I'd finished my first beer, they were competing over who was going to buy the next one. By the time I'd finished my second, his heavy, muscular arm was draped over my naked shoulders and his equally heavy cologne had invaded my nostrils. The hardest part of the whole production number was hiding my revulsion. If there's one thing I hate it's hairy men, and this guy was covered like a shag pile carpet. Just the thought of his shoulders was enough to make me feel queasy.

I was on my fourth beer when I casually let slip that I was staying at Casa Nico and that I'd left my car down there while I walked up the valley. Immediately, Gianni volunteered to drive me back down. Then, of course, he suddenly remembered how terrible the cooking was at Casa Nico. Cue for nods of agreement from his buddies, coupled with nudges and winks acknowledging the cleverness of Gianni's moves. Why, he asked innocently, didn't I come back to the villa with him for some genuine Italian home cooking. His boss was away, and he was a dab hand with the spaghetti sauce. We could eat on the terrace like the rich folks do, and then, later, he could run me back down to the *pensione*.

I looked up adoringly at him and said how delightful it was to meet such hospitable people. We left a couple of minutes later, accompanied by whoops and grunts from his cronies. In the car, he put a proprietary paw on my knee between gear changes. I fought the urge to lean over and grip his balls so tight his eyes would pop from their sockets like shelled peas. He was the driver, after all, and I didn't want to end up on the river bed looking like spaghetti sauce.

As we approached the villa, he pulled a little black electronic box out of his tight jeans and punched a button. The gates swung open, the Alfa shot through and I got my first full frontal view of the Villa San Pietro. It was magnificent. A modern villa in the style of the traditional houses that front every fashionable resort in Italy. Immaculate pink stucco, green louvred shutters. And a satellite dish the size of a kid's paddling pool. "*Molto elegante*," I said softly.

"Good, huh?" Gianni said proudly, as if it were all his. The drive swung round the side of the house, past a tennis court and swimming pool and over to a separate, single-storey building. As we drew near, Gianni hit the button on the box again and an up-and-over garage door opened before us. Inside the garage was the stretch limo, Turner's Merc and a small green Fiat van. At the sight of Turner's car, I started to get a bad feeling in the pit of my stomach. Gianni had said we'd have the place to ourselves. But Turner had come back to the villa with him in the afternoon, and his car was still here as proof positive that he hadn't left. Maybe he'd nipped into Sestri for the evening in a taxi. Somehow, I didn't think so. For the first time since I'd started this crazy expedition, I allowed a trickle of fear to creep in. Maybe I should have listened to Richard after all.

We got out of the car and Gianni folded me into a bear hug, his tongue thrusting between my teeth. It felt like my tonsils were being raped. "What happened to dinner?" I asked as soon as I could get my mouth clear. "I don't know about you, but I can't think about having fun when I'm hungry."

Gianni chuckled. "OK, OK. First the food, then the fun." He leered and gestured with his thumb towards a door at the side of the garage. "That's my apartment over there. But we'll go over to the house to eat. My boss has better food and drink than me."

We walked over to the house, his arm heavy across my shoulders. We crossed a marble patio, complete with built-in barbecue and pizza oven, and entered the kitchen through tall French windows. It was like a temple to the culinary arts. There was a free-standing butcher's block in the middle of the floor, complete with a set of Sabatier knives in their slots. Above it hung a *batterie de cuisine*. On the blond wooden worktops, there was every conceivable kitchen machine from ice-cream maker to a full-sized Gaggia espresso machine. Bunches of dried herbs hung from the walls, while pots of fresh basil, coriander and parsley lined a deep windowsill to the side. "He likes to cook," Gianni said. "He likes me to cook too, when we have guests."

"Nice one," I said. "Where's the drink?"

He nodded towards a door. "Through there. There's a wet bar in the dining room. It's got everything. There's white wine in the fridge, and red wine in the cupboard here. Why don't you help yourself?" He moved towards me again and clutched me close, his huge hands cupping my buttocks. "Mmm, gorgeous," he growled.

I reached round and let my fingers stray up and down his back. That way I stopped myself thrusting my thumbs into his eyeballs. "Tell you what," I whispered, "I'll fix us some cocktails. I might not be much good in the kitchen, but I'm terrific with a cocktail shaker."

He released me and leered again. "I can't wait to experience your wrist action."

I giggled. "You won't be disappointed, I promise you."

I left him staring into a big larder fridge. He hadn't lied about the wet bar. It did have everything. The first thing I did was dredge my phial of Valium out of the bottom of my bag. I'm pretty hostile to pharmaceuticals in general, but without the Valium, I'd have blackened stumps where my teeth should be. I tipped the tablets out. There were six. I hoped that would be enough on an empty stomach to knock Gianni out before I had to test whether I really did have the skills to stop a man in his tracks. I spotted a sharp knife by a basket of lemons and oranges, and quickly crushed the tablets with the blade. Then I took a quick inventory of the bar. What I needed was a cocktail that was strong and bittersweet.

I found the measure and the shaker sitting on a shelf behind me. A small fridge contained a variety of fruit juices and a couple of bags of ice. I settled on a Florida. Into a cocktail shaker I put three measures of gin, six measures of grapefruit juice, three measures of Galliano, and one and a half measures of Campari. I tossed in a couple of ice cubes, closed the shaker and did a quick salsa round the bar with the shaker providing the beat. "Sounds good," Gianni shouted from the kitchen.

"Wait till you taste it," I called back. I chose a couple of tall glasses and scraped the Valium powder into one. I topped it up with about two thirds of the cocktail mixture and stirred it vigorously with a glass rod. I poured the rest into the other glass and topped it up with grapefruit juice and a dash of grenadine syrup to make the colours match. I swallowed hard, picked up both glasses and walked through to the kitchen. Gianni was chopping red onions with a wide-bladed chef's knife. "A very Italian cocktail," I announced, handing the drugged glass to him.

He took it from me and swigged a generous mouthful. He savoured it, swilling it round his mouth before swallowing it. "You're right. Bitter and sweet. Like love, huh?" The leer was back.

"Not too bitter, I hope," I giggled, moving behind him and hugging him from behind.

"Not with me, baby. With me, it'll be sweeter than sugar," he said arrogantly.

"I can hardly wait," I murmured. I wasn't exactly lying. I moved away and perched on a high stool, watching him cook. The onions went into a deep pan with olive oil and garlic. Next, he chopped a fennel bulb into thin slices and added them to the stewing onions. He took a punnet of wild mushrooms from the fridge, washed them under running water, patted them dry lovingly with paper towels and chopped them coarsely. Into the pan they went along with a torn handful of coriander leaves.

"It smells wonderful," I said.

"Wait till you taste it," he said. "There's only one thing tastes better." Time for another leer. The temperature was rising in more ways than one. The only good thing about that was the speed at which he was drinking his cocktail.

"No contest," I said, watching him measure out round grains of risotto rice. He tipped the rice into the pan, stirred it into the mixture for a couple of minutes, then took a carton out of the freezer.

"Chicken stock," he said, tossing the solid lump into the pan amidst much hissing and clouds of steam. He kept stirring till the stock had defrosted and the pan was bubbling gently. Then he put a lid on, set the timer for twelve minutes and drained his glass.

"How about a salad to go with it?" I asked hastily as he started to move towards me. "And I'll mix you another drink, OK?"

His eyes seemed to lose focus momentarily and he shook his head like a bull bothered by flies. He rubbed his hands over his face and mumbled, "OK." I'd reckoned about twenty minutes for the drugs to take effect, but maybe the amount he'd had to drink on an empty stomach was accelerating things.

I'd barely got the cap off the gin bottle when there was a sound like a tree falling in the kitchen. I tiptoed back to the doorway to see Gianni spread-eagled on the marble floor. For one terrible moment, I thought I'd killed him. Then he started to snore like a sawmill on overtime. I ran across to the butcher's block and picked up the knife. It took seconds to saw off the electric cable from a couple of the kitchen appliances. Tying him up took quite a bit longer, but the snoring didn't even change in note while I was doing it. I took the black box out of his pocket and tucked it in my bag.

I found the cellar door on the second try. A wide flight of stairs led down into the depths. One thing about marble floors is that they make shifting heavy loads a lot easier. I got down on my knees behind Gianni and shoved with all my strength. Foot by foot, we slid across the gleaming tiles to the doorway.

One last push sent him skidding over the first step, feet first. He bounced down the stairs like a sack of potatoes, still snoring. I staggered to my feet. For the first time, I was grateful that Gianni's boss was security conscious. The cellar door had bolts top and bottom as well as a lock on the door. I slid the bolts home and leaned against the door to get my breath back.

When the timer went off, I nearly jumped out of my skin. Automatically, I turned off the gas under the pan. Now the adrenaline surge was slipping away, I realized that I was in fact ravenous. I shrugged. The food was there, I might as well eat. I didn't think Gianni was going to be knocking at the door demanding his share in a hurry.

He might have been the world's worst lecher, but he was a fabulous cook. I shovelled the risotto down, savouring every delicious mouthful. Now I needed coffee. It was going to be a long night. I wished I hadn't chopped the lead off the Gaggia. A search of the cupboards eventually turned up a jar of instant and a Thermos jug. I brewed up and, armed with jug, mug and shoulder bag, I set off to explore.

Whatever Gianni's boss was, he wasn't short of a bob. The public rooms on the ground floor were all marble floored, with expensive Oriental rugs scattered around. The furniture was upmarket repro, all polished to a mirror finish. There was nothing in the dining room, drawing room, morning room or the TV lounge to indicate that this was anything other than the home of a successful businessman. Even the videos lined up in the cabinet by the oversized TV were completely innocuous.

Cautiously, I made my way up the stairs. It was always possible that Turner was a prisoner somewhere inside the villa rather than the victim of my worst imaginings. Six doors opened off the long landing. The first two were lavish guest bedrooms, complete with *en suite* bathrooms. If Gianni's boss ever set up in competition with Casa Nico, the *pensione* down the valley would go out of business within hours. The third door opened on what was clearly the master bedroom. The wardrobes were filled with designer suits and shirts, the drawers with silk underwear and the kind of leisure wear that has the labels on the outside. No trace of a woman in residence. No trace of any papers, either.

The fourth door opened on to a library. It was obviously a reader's library rather than one where the books had been bought by the yard. Modern hardbacks lined the shelves. I noticed a sizeable chunk of crime fiction, but most of the books were by authors I'd never heard of. There was also a whole section of legal textbooks, mostly covering commercial and international law. But again, there were no papers anywhere, unless some of the books were dummies. If they were, they'd be hanging on to their secrets. There was no way I had time to go through that lot book by book.

The fifth door was locked. I left it for a moment and tried the sixth. Another guest bedroom. That told me that either Turner was behind the locked door, or something significant was. Unfortunately, I didn't have my set of picklocks with me. I don't carry them routinely, and when I'd set off on my pursuit of Turner, I hadn't expected to be doing any burglaries. I could of course simply smash the lock with one of the dozens of marble statuettes that hung around in niches all over the place. But I didn't want the villa's owner to know the extent to which he'd been turned over if I could possibly help it.

I looked up at the door lintel. Gianni's boss was not much bigger than me, so the chances were that the key wasn't sitting up there. I went back to the master bedroom and began a proper search. I got lucky in the bathroom. I'd taken the contents of the bathroom cupboard off the shelves one by one, just to make sure there was nothing behind them. There were two aerosol cans of Polo shaving foam, and one was a lot lighter than the other. I looked more closely at the heavier of the two. Gripping it tightly, I twisted the bottom of the can. It unscrewed smoothly, revealing a compartment lined with Bubble Wrap. Inside was what looked like a handkerchief. I pulled it out and a bunch of keys tumbled to the floor. "Gotcha!" I murmured.

The longest of the keys opened the locked door. Inside was a starkly functional office, a sharp contrast to the luxurious appointments of the rest of the villa. I switched the light on, closed the shutters and took a good look around. A basic desk stood against one wall with a computer, a modem and a fax machine on it. To one side there was a photocopier and a laser printer. Automatically, I switched them on. I noticed a shredder under the desk as I sat down and hit the computer's power button. The machine booted up and I called up the directories. Ten minutes later, my jubilation had given way to depression. Every single data file I'd tried to access was password protected. I couldn't get in to read them. All it would let me do was print out a list of all files, which I duly did.

Muttering dark imprecations, I returned to the main directory. Time for some lateral thinking. In the years since I first started working at Mortensen and Brannigan and discovered the wonderful world of electronic mail, the Internet had grown from the home of academics and a handful of computer loonies like me to the world's bulletin board. The communications software that was running on this machine was a standard business package that I'd used dozens of times before. Even if the files were password protected, I reckoned that the communications program would still be able to transmit them intact to somewhere I could retrieve them later and pass them on to someone who could crack the passwording. All I needed was a local number for the Internet. If I was lucky, there would be one already loaded in the comms program. I started it running and called up the telephone directory screen.

It was my lucky night. Right at the top of the list was the number for the local Internet node—the e-mail equivalent of a postal sorting office. The way the Net works is simple. It's analogous to sending a letter rather than making a phone call. The network is connected by phone lines, and works on what they call a parcel switching system. What happens is you dial a local number and send your data to it. The computer there reads the address and shunts your data down the network, section by section, till it arrives at its destination. But unlike a letter, which takes days if you're lucky, this takes less time than it takes to describe the process.

I used the edit mode to discover Gianni's boss's login and password, then I instructed the computer to connect me to the Internet. Less than a minute later, we were in. I typed in the electronic mail address of the office, then I started sending the files one by one. An hour and a mug of coffee later, I'd sent a copy of every data file in the machine back to Manchester.

Breathing a deep sigh of relief, I switched off the machine. Now it was time for the desk drawers. I unlocked each drawer with the remaining keys on the bunch. The first drawer held stationery. The second held junk—rubber bands, spare computer disks, a couple of computer cables, a half-eaten chocolate bar and a box of Post-it notes. The bottom drawer looked more promising, with its collection of suspension files. No such luck. All the files held was the paperwork for the house: utility bills, receipts for furniture, building work, landscaping, pool maintenance. The only interesting thing was that everything was in the name of a company—Gruppo Leopardi. There was no clue as to who was behind Gruppo Leopardi. And I didn't have the time for the kind of thorough search that might reveal that. I'd already been there too long, and I was getting too tired to concentrate. It was time to make tracks.

I went back over to the window, to open the shutters again. I wanted to leave everything exactly as I'd found it. As I turned back, clumsy with exhaustion, I caught the Thermos jug with my elbow. It sailed off the desk and bounced off the panelled wall under the window. It landed on its side on the floor, apparently undamaged. Not so the wall. The wood panelling where the jug had hit had slowly swung away from the wall, revealing a safe. Eat your heart out, Enid Blyton. If preposterous coincidence is good enough for the Secret Seven, it's good enough for me.

# 19

If the Brannigans were posh enough to have a family motto, it would go something like, "What do you mean, I *can't?*" Just because I've never learned how to crack a safe didn't mean I was going to close the panel and walk away. I sat on the floor opposite the safe and studied it. There was a six-digit electronic display above a keypad with the letters of the alphabet and the numbers zero to nine. Beside the keypad were buttons that I translated as "enter code," "open," "random reset," "master." That didn't take me a whole lot further forward.

I checked my watch. Ten o'clock. Not too late to make a call. I took the mobile out of my bag and rang Dennis. It would have been cheaper to use the fax phone, but I'd already noticed that Gruppo Leopardi had itemized billing on their phone account and I didn't want to leave a trail straight back to Dennis, especially given that he already had connections with these people via Turner. Dennis answered his phone on the second ring. "Hi, Dennis," I said. "I'm looking at the outside of a safe and I want to be looking at the inside. Any ideas?"

"Kate, you're more of a villain than I am. You know I haven't touched a safe since Billy the Whip dropped one on my foot in 1983."

"This isn't the time for reminiscing. This call's costing me a week's wages."

He chuckled. "Then somebody else must be paying for it. What does this safe look like?"

I described it to him. "You're wasting your time, Kate. Beast like that, you've got no chance unless you know the combo," he said sorrowfully.

"You sure?"

"I'm sure. He might be a sloppy git, though, this guy you're having over. He might have gone for something really stupid like the last six digits of the phone number. Or the first six. Or his date of birth. Or his girlfriend's name. Or some set of letters and numbers he sees in his office every day."

I groaned. "Enough, already. You sure there's no other way?"

"That's why they call them safes," Dennis said. "Where are you, anyway?"

"You don't want to know. Believe me, you don't want to know. I'll be in touch. Thanks for your help."

I went back to the domestic files and tried various combinations of the phone number and any other number I could find, including the vehicle registrations. No joy. I sat in the boss's chair and looked around me. What would he see from here that would be a constant *aide-mémoire*? I got up and tried the model numbers of the fax machine, the modem and the photocopier. Nothing. I didn't know the boss's birthday, but I had a feeling that a man as security conscious as him wouldn't have gone for anything that obvious.

It was last resort time. What would *I* do if I wanted a code that was random enough for no one to guess, but accessible to me whenever I forgot it? Acting on pure instinct, I hit the power button on the computer again and watched the screen, looking for any six-digit combinations that came up during the boot process. I ended up with two. MB 4D33 was part of the operating system ident. And the CD-ROM drive's device model number was CR-563-X. The first string did nothing. But when I entered the second set of digits, the display changed from red to green. I couldn't believe it.

Holding my breath, I hit the "open" button. There was a soft click and the door catch released. "There is a God, and she likes me," I said softly. I opened the safe and stared in at the contents. There was a stack of papers about half an inch thick. On top of them sat a loose-leaf folder, slightly bigger than a Filofax. I took everything out of the safe and moved back to the desk. I started with the folder. First there was a list of names, with dates and figures next to it. Following that were half a dozen pages listing numbered locations. Some of them had ticks beside them, and a couple were crossed out. Castle Dumdivie was on the list, with a tick. So were a few other names I recognized. Next came a list of dates and places followed by a number and letter code—20CC, 34H, 50,000E, that sort of thing. The fourth column was a number. A little bit of crosschecking, and I realized that the numbers corresponded to ticked locations on the list, and, in the cases I knew about, the dates were all two to four weeks after the burglaries. Finally, there were several pages of names, addresses and phone numbers. Halfway down the third page, I spotted Turner. I wasn't sure what all of this meant, but I was beginning to have the glimmerings of an idea.

I opened the clasps of the folder and put the pages through the photocopier. While they were feeding through, I looked at the other papers. Some of them were legal contracts, and I couldn't make head nor tail of them. Others were handwritten notes which seemed to refer to meetings, but although I understood most of the words, I couldn't get a lot of sense out of them. There were a few business letters, mostly of the "thank you for your letter of the fifteenth, we can confirm the safe arrival of your consignment" type. The final bundle of papers were draft accounts of Gruppo Leopardi. I copied the lot.

Once I'd finished, I replaced everything in the safe, exactly as I'd found it. I had the papers, but I wanted a little bit of insurance, just in case anything happened on the way home to deprive me of my photocopies. The fax machine was the best source of that insurance, but I didn't want to send the stuff to my office number for the same reason I'd used the mobile to phone Dennis. It needed to go somewhere secure, but somewhere large enough for it not to be obvious who specifically it had gone to. Ideally, it also had to go somewhere that even the Mafia would think twice about storming mob-handed.

There was only one place and one person I could think of that fitted the bill. Detective Chief Inspector Della Prentice, top dog on the Regional Crime Squad's fraud task force. This wasn't her bailiwick, but Della's still the only copper I'd trust with anything that might put me at risk. I'd worked with Della a couple of times now since we'd first been introduced by Josh Gilbert. They'd been at Cambridge together, and although their fascination with finance high and low had taken them in radically different directions, they'd stayed close enough for Josh to recognize that Della and I are kindred spirits. Since our first encounter, we'd become close friends. I knew if I faxed this wodge of incomprehensible paperwork to Della, she'd tuck it away safely in her drawer till I turned up to explain its significance.

I took a sheet of paper out of the stationery drawer and scribbled a cover sheet. "Fax for the urgent and confidential attention of DCI Prentice, Regional Crime Squad. Dear Della, Vital evidence. Please keep safe until I can fill you in on the deep background. I'll call you as soon as I get back. Thanks. KB." That should do it, I thought, dialling her departmental fax machine. God knows what the duty CID would make of a hundred-page fax from Italy in the middle of the night.

By the time I'd finished, it was after two. I bundled up my photocopies, stuffed them in an envelope and tucked the lot into my bulging bag. Time to get the hell out of here, as far away as possible. I had a horrible feeling that I knew what had happened to Nicholas Turner, probably because of my bug, and I didn't want to end up the same way. There wasn't a trace of the guy in any of the spare bedrooms, which put paid to any comforting ideas about him having nipped into Sestri in a taxi for dinner.

I switched everything off and locked the desk drawers again. Satisfied that it all looked just as it had when I'd walked into the office, I got out, locking the door behind me. I replaced the keys in the dummy can, hoping that my memory of how the contents of the cabinet had been arranged was accurate. I trotted down the stairs and back to the kitchen. I put my ear to the cellar door. Silence. I had a momentary pang of conscience, wondering what would happen to the big man when he came round and found himself tied up in the dark for an indefinite period of time. Then I reminded myself that he was probably directly responsible for whatever had happened to Turner, and I stopped feeling guilty. Besides, judging by the pristine condition of the villa, I reckoned there must be a maid who came in every day to polish the floors, the furniture and the kitchen equipment. By the time she arrived, Gianni would probably be bellowing like a bull.

I let myself out of the French windows and stood on the patio, weighing up what to do next. I had the black box that would open the gates for me, but I didn't know where the security system was controlled from, and the cameras would still be rolling. I wasn't keen on finding myself the star of the Mafia equivalent of *Crimewatch*, so I decided to help myself to one of the vehicles, just to keep myself hidden from the all-seeing eyes by the gate. You can only do so much with computer enhancement, and I reckoned the combination of the darkness and the obscurity of being inside a car would make sure I couldn't be identified.

A quick sortie in the garage revealed that the keys for all the vehicles were hanging on the board where Gianni had deposited his set earlier. I settled on the van, on the basis that it was the least memorable of the three. I opened the door, threw my bag on the passenger seat and climbed behind the wheel. I was just about to stick the key in the ignition, when something stopped me.

I don't believe in sixth sense or second sight or seventh sons of seventh sons. But something was making the hair on the back of my neck stand up, and it wasn't love at first sight. I took a deep breath and looked over my shoulder into the back of the van.

At once I wished I hadn't. There's only one thing comes in a six-feet-long, heavy-duty black bag with a zipper up the front. It didn't take many of my detective skills to decide that I'd probably solved the mystery of Nicholas Turner's disappearance.

I was out of the van in seconds. I stood in the garage, leaning against the wall for support, my breath coming fast, clammy sweat in my armpits. The combination of shock and exhaustion was making my limbs tremble. I don't know how long I stood there like that, frozen in horror, incapable of movement, never mind decisive action. It's one thing to think somebody might be dead. It's another thing entirely to find yourself sitting in a van with their mortal remains. Especially when you're the one who's responsible for their present state.

It was only fear that got me moving again. Hanging around the Villa San Pietro was about as clever a move as a mouse going walkabout in a cattery. My first instinct was to dive into the Alfa and put as much distance between me and the villa as fast as I could. I was halfway across the garage when I realized that wasn't an answer I could live with. It was my bug and my fake that had got Nicholas Turner murdered. I couldn't just walk away and let the people who'd had him killed dispose of the body and wash their hands of the whole business. If I left him here, that's exactly what would happen. I couldn't just drive to the nearest police station and tell them what I knew. They might be on the villa's payroll, for a kickoff. And even if they weren't and I did get them to believe me, I couldn't think of a cover story that wouldn't leave me facing charges of false imprisonment, assault, deception, breaking and entering, and probably the murder of Aldo Moro.

I thought about waking Della and bringing her up to speed so we could do it through official channels, but by the time we'd got the wheels of justice rolling, there would be no evidence of murder at the villa, the body would be miles away, and even if it did eventually turn up, there would be nothing to connect it to Gianni and his boss.

Taking a deep breath, I opened the back of the van. Before I did anything else, I needed to be sure it really was Turner in the bag. Gingerly, I reached out for the tab of the zip and pushed it away from me. It wouldn't budge. I could feel my stomach begin to turn over as I gripped the slick, rubberized bag with one hand and forced the zip down. A few inches was all I needed. Nicholas Turner's eyes stared up at me out of a face grey in the stark fluorescent light of the garage. I gagged and whipped round just in time for the contents of my stomach to miss the van and hit the floor. I stood there, hands on my knees, throwing up till my stomach and throat were raw. Shaking and sweating, my fingers slippery on the body bag, I managed to pull up the zip. Turner's face showed no signs of how he had met his end, but I'd have been willing to bet it hadn't been a brain tumour.

I don't remember how I managed it, but somehow I got back behind the wheel and drove out of the garage. All I could think of was getting out of there and putting some distance between me and the Villa San Pietro. I hurtled down the drive, punching the steering wheel in frustration as the gates took their time opening. I shot down the track so fast I nearly lost it on one of the bends. The shock of that sobered me enough to slow me down to a more reasonable speed. As I hit the main road, I realized I'd have to move the Mercedes away from Casa Nico, since Gianni knew that was where I was staying, and I couldn't guarantee I'd get back to the car before he was released from his prison.

I left the van parked on the verge by the villa turn-off and jogged the couple of kilometres back to the *pensione*. There was no sign of the BMW. So much for expecting Richard to see

sense and come back. I drove the Merc back up the valley, past
the van, looking for somewhere to stash it. About a kilometre
further on, there was a cluster of houses and a mini-market. I
left the car just off the main road and half jogged, half staggered
back to the van. I didn't pass another car the whole hour.

I turned the van round and headed back towards Sestri
Levante. I reckoned I needed to leave the van somewhere no
one would notice if it was parked for a few days. I thought
about finding some remote forest track in the mountains, but I
vetoed that. It would be difficult to find the right place in the
dark, it would be impossible for me to remember where it was
with pinpoint accuracy, and it wouldn't be easy for me to make
my way back to the Merc. I didn't want to leave it parked on a
street, because I didn't know how long it was going to take to
get anyone to listen to my tale, and after a day or two in Italian
sunshine, the van wasn't going to smell too appetizing. What
I needed, ideally, was an underground car park where no one
would pay attention.

Either I needed a big city, or a swanky resort where people
left their cars in the hotel car park for a few days. The solution
popped out of my memory just as the autostrada junction hove
into sight. The picture postcard village of Portofino, star of
a thousand jigsaw puzzles, its harbour lined with picturesque
houses painted every colour of the ice-cream spectrum. I'd been
there a couple of years before with Richard, and remembered the
big car park, half underground, where tourists left their cars to
avoid completely choking the centre of the former fishing village.

I drove into Portofino just after 5.00 a.m. It's probably the
only time of day when there isn't a queue to get into the village.
I drove straight into the car park, taking a ticket at the automatic
barrier. I left the van on the lowest level and walked up the
stairs to the street. The pale light of dawn was just beginning
to brighten the eastern sky as I strolled down to the harbour.
There were a few boatmen around in the harbour, but I didn't
want to draw too much attention to myself by asking any of

them how soon I could get out of the place. I tried to look like an insomniac tourist enjoying the peace and quiet, and wandered down the quayside to where the pleasure boats departed. I was in luck. At nine, there was a boat that went to Sestri Levante and on to the Cinque Terre beyond.

I walked on round the harbour and found a bench that overlooked the bay. Using my bag as a pillow, I put my head down and managed to doze off. Strange dreams featuring Gianni's chef's knife and bodies that climbed out of bags and into passenger seats prevented it from being a restful sleep, but I was so exhausted that even the nightmares couldn't wake me up. The sound of a pleasure steamer's hooter jerked me into wakefulness just after eight, and I staggered back into the village, bought myself a couple of sandwiches and a cappuccino from a café and headed for the pleasure boat.

I don't remember much about the sail. I was too jittery from lack of sleep and the horrors of the night. I kept nodding off, and starting awake, nerves jangling and eyes staring in paranoia. I couldn't stop thinking about Turner's wife and those two daughters. Not only had they lost a husband and father, but they were going to find out about it in a blitz of police and media activity.

In spite of the fact that arriving on dry land brought me nearer to the enemy, I was glad to be off the boat. Somehow, I felt more in control. In Sestri, I found the tourist office and discovered where I could catch a bus up the valley. The next one left in twenty minutes, and I was first on it, complete with brand new sun hat. I sat at the back, slouched low in my seat. As Casa Nico approached, I put my sunglasses on and pulled the hat forward. The bus was so much higher off the road than a car would have been that I was able to look right down on Casa Nico. As the bus rounded the bend beyond the *pensione*, I looked back. Parked behind the building, where I wouldn't have been able to spot it in a car, was Gianni's Alfa.

I got off at the next stop and walked cautiously past the alley where I'd left the Merc. It was still there, and no one seemed to be watching it. I doubled back behind the houses and came up the alley from the far end. I crept into the car, not even slamming the door shut until I had the engine running. Then I shot out on to the main road and headed up the valley, away from Casa Nico and the Villa San Pietro, my foot hard on the accelerator, my eyes on the rear-view mirror. As I joined the autostrada, I wondered how long Gianni would stake out the *pensione*. It was worth the loss of my overnight bag not to have him on my tail.

Nigel Mansell couldn't have got to Milan airport faster than I did that day. I dumped the car with the local Hertz agent and headed for the terminal. I'd just missed a flight to Brussels, but there was one to Amsterdam an hour later. If I could only stay awake, I could pick up Bill's Saab in Antwerp, catch the night ferry from Zeebrugge and be home the following morning some time. Frankly, I couldn't wait to feel British soil under my feet.

I had half an hour to kill in the international departure lounge. I thought I'd better give Shelley a ring before she decided tracking me down was a job for Interpol. She answered on the first ring, and I could hear relief in her voice. I knew then it must be bad, since Shelley never lets on that anything's beyond her competence.

"Thank God it's you," she said. "Where are you? You've got to get back here. There's been another death."

# 20

I nearly dropped the phone. My first thought was, how the hell had Shelley found out about Nicholas Turner? Her voice cut through my panic. "Kate? Are you still there? I said there's been another death involving KerrSter." This time round, I heard the whole sentence.

"Oh fuck," I groaned.

"Where *are* you? Trevor Kerr is reading me the riot act every ten minutes. I've managed to stall him so far, but if you don't speak to him soon, he's threatening to sack us and go to the press saying the reason for the second death is your dereliction of duty," Shelley continued, her voice betraying an agitation I'd never heard from her before.

"I'm at Milan airport. On the way to Amsterdam, *en route* for Antwerp. I'll have to leave Bill's car in Belgium and get a flight straight back to the UK. When did this happen?"

"This morning. An office cleaner. They found her dead beside a new drum of KerrSter. It looks like another case of cyanide poisoning, according to Alexis. Incidentally, she wants to talk to you too."

I glanced over at the gate. They hadn't started boarding us yet. "Is Kerr still in his office?"

"He was five minutes ago," Shelley said. "He's had the Merseyside police all over his factory this afternoon."

"I'll call him and stall him," I said. "I'm sorry you've had all this shit to deal with on your own. If it's any consolation, this trip's been a nightmare. I've already had one close encounter with death today. I'm not sure if I'm up to another one."

"You're all right?" Shelley demanded anxiously.

"I wouldn't pitch it that high. I'm in one piece, which is more than I can say for Turner."

"Oh my God," she said, sounding stricken.

"Look, it's OK. Let me talk to Kerr. I'll call you from Amsterdam. There's a flight gets in to Manchester about half-seven tonight. See if you can get me a seat on it. I don't care if it's business class, club class or standing in the toilet, just get me on it."

"Will do. I'll hang on here till I hear from you," she promised. "For God's sake, be careful."

It was a bit late for me to take heed of that warning. I took a deep breath, bracing myself for battle, and rang Trevor Kerr. Not even my powers of imagination had prepared me for his onslaught. For two straight minutes he ranted at me, with a string of obscenities that would have won him admiration on the football terraces but didn't do a lot for me. I made a mental note to bump that surliness surcharge up to ten per cent. When he paused to regroup for a second outpouring, I cut in decisively. "I'm sorry you've had a difficult day, but you're not the only one," I said grimly. "I have been pursuing my inquiries into your problem as fast as I can. I've made a lot of progress, but I needed a crucial piece of information that I've not been able to get hold of yet. Now, I'm meeting someone in an hour's time who can tell me what I need to know," I continued, raising my voice to cut through his crap.

"Bullshit!" he hollered like a bear with its leg in a gin. "You've been doing fuck all. Give me one good reason why I shouldn't fire you this fucking minute."

"Because if you do, some other private eye with half my talent is going to have to start from square one because you'll have to sue me to get one single scrap of the information I've already uncovered."

That silenced him for all of ten seconds. "I'll tell the police you're withholding information," he blustered.

"Tell them. Inspector Jackson knows me well enough to realize that shoving me in a cell won't make a blind bit of difference to what I have to say for myself."

"You can't treat me like this," he howled, the ultimate spoilt bully.

"If you want us to discuss this like reasonable adults, you can meet me this evening in the bar of the Hilton at the airport at eight o'clock," I said. "Otherwise, I'm taking my bat and ball home, Mr Kerr." Out of the corner of my eye, I could see my fellow passengers disappearing through the gate. "It's up to you," I said, replacing the phone.

The flight to Amsterdam seemed never ending. I stared gloomily out of the window, feeling more guilty than a Catholic in bed with a married man. My meddling had cost Nicholas Turner his life. Meddling I'd done while I should have been nailing down my suspicions about the product-tampering racket. If I'd done that job properly, the culprits would be answering Inspector Jackson's questions now and maybe the woman who had died would still be alive. I should never have taken Trevor Kerr's case on when I was in the middle of another demanding investigation. But I had to be smart, prove to the world that I was twice as good as any reasonable private investigator needed to be. I'd been trying to show Bill that I was more than capable of being left to run the agency single-handed. All I'd done so far was get two people killed.

Not only that, but I'd fractured my relationship with Richard, perhaps beyond repair this time. All because I was determined to be the big shot, doing things my way. I began to wonder why I was bothering to go back. On my present form, the only people

I'd be keeping satisfied were the undertakers. I had the best part of nine grand in my bag, a car waiting at Antwerp. In all my working life, I've never been closer to running away.

When it came to the crunch, I couldn't do it. Call it duty, call it stubbornness, call it pure bloody-mindedness. Whatever it was, it propelled me off that plane and over to the check-in desk for the flight to Manchester. Shelley had come up trumps. I was booked on a seat in business class. I had ten minutes to give her a quick ring and tell her I was meeting Kerr at the airport hotel. Slightly reassured, she told me again to take care. She was warning the wrong person.

They had that evening's *Chronicle* on the plane. CLEANER'S MYSTERY DEATH hit me like a stab in the guts. Even though she'd died in Liverpool, Mary Halloran had made the front page in Manchester because of the KerrSter connection and because it gave the paper the chance to rehash the Joey Morton story. Feeling accused by every word, especially since they came under the by-line of Alexis Lee, I read on. Mrs Halloran, forty-three, a mother of two (oh God, another two kids I'd deprived of a parent . . .), had started her own commercial cleaning firm after she was made redundant by the city council. The business had grown into a real money-spinner, but Mrs Halloran liked to keep her hand in on the office floor, presumably to stay in touch with her roots. She had a regular stint three mornings a week in a local solicitor's office, where she started work at half past five. Normally, she worked with another woman, but her partner had been off sick that week. Mrs Halloran's body had been found outside the cleaning cupboard on the first floor by one of the solicitors who had come in just after seven to catch up on some work. She was slumped on the floor beside an open but full container of KerrSter. The police had revealed that the postmortem indicated Mrs Halloran had died as a result of inhaling hydrogen cyanide gas.

The pathologist must have been quick off the mark, I thought. Not to mention in possession of a nasty, suspicious mind. After Joey Morton's death I'd checked my reference shelves, which had confirmed what I'd already thought—death by cyanide's a real pig to diagnose. It happens almost instantaneously, and there's not much to see on the pathologist's slab. Maybe a trace of frothing round the mouth, possibly a few irregular pink patches on the skin like you get with people who suck too long on their car exhausts. If you get the body open quickly, there might be a faint trace of the smell of bitter almonds in the mouth, chest and abdominal cavity. But if you don't get your samples pdq, you're knackered because the cyanide metamorphoses into sulphocyanides, which you'd expect to find there anyway. The only reason they'd picked up on it right away in Joey's case was that the barman who discovered his body noticed the smell and happened to be a keen reader of detective fiction.

The Merseyside police were being pretty cautious, and there was a stonewalling quote from Jackson, but reading between the lines, you could see they were talking to each other already. Trevor Kerr was on the record as saying he was confident that there was no problem with the products leaving his factory and he was sure that any investigation would completely vindicate Kerrchem. Never one to miss the chance for a bit of speculation, Alexis had flown the kite of industrial sabotage, but she had no quotes to back her up. No wonder she wanted to talk to me. I wondered if Trevor Kerr had told her I was working for him as part of his attempt to get out from under.

By the time the plane landed, I could have done with a couple of lines of speed. I'd had a stressful couple of days with almost no sleep, and the coffee I'd been mainlining in the air was starting to give me the jitters rather than simply keeping me awake. I was just in the mood for Trevor Kerr.

I reclaimed my bags by ten to eight and pushed them through customs on a trolley, like a sleepwalker. Halfway down the customs hall, I felt a hand on my shoulder and heard a voice say, "Step this way, madam." I looked up blearily at the customs officer, inches away from tears. The last thing I needed right now was to explain my bizarre assortment of possessions, ranging from a box of maps to a wad of cash and a radio receiver.

"What's going on?" I asked.

"Just follow me, please," he said, leaving me no choice. We walked across the hall to a door on the far side. I was aware of several curious stares from my fellow passengers. The customs man showed me into a small office and closed the door behind me. Leaning against the wall, exhaling a mouthful of smoke, stood Detective Chief Inspector Della Prentice, a wry smile on her lips. Her chestnut hair was loose, hanging round her face in a shining fall. Her green eyes were clear, her skin glowing. She'd clearly had more than two hours' sleep in the last thirty-six. I hated her.

"You look like you had a rough flight," she said.

"The flight was fine," I told her, slumping into one of the room's plastic bucket chairs. "It's just the last two days that have been hell."

"Anything to do with the collected works that was waiting on my desk this morning?" she asked.

I groaned. "More than somewhat. I realize it won't have made a word of sense to you, but I needed to send it somewhere safe."

"Come on," Della said, shrugging away from the wall. "I'll drive you home and we'll talk."

"I'm meeting a client at the Hilton," I said, glancing at my watch. "Two minutes from now. On a totally unrelated matter," I added.

Della looked concerned. "You sure you're up to that?"

I laughed affectionately. "The copper in you never quite goes off duty, does it? I'm in a fit state for you to give me the third degree, but let me near a client? Oh no, I'm far too knackered for that."

Della gave me a playful punch on the shoulder. "I can't imagine that your client's planning to run you a hot bath laden with stimulating essential oils or to cook you a meal while you luxuriate with a stiff Stoli and grapefruit juice. And if he is, maybe I should call Richard and let him know the competition's hotting up."

My head fell into my hands. "Not one of your better ideas, Della," I sighed.

"Oh God, you've not been checking out the insurance man's endowments, have you?" she giggled.

"Thank you, Alexis," I said, getting wearily to my feet. "And thank you for your confidence in me, Della. Come on, then. You can give me a lift over to the Hilton so I can talk to the client. Then you can take me home and I'll tell you all about it."

One of the good things about having the cops meet you at the airport is that they get to park right outside the door without the traffic wardens turning their windscreens into scrapbooks. We drove across to the Hilton in blissful silence, and I left Della in reception with strict instructions to get me out of there in no more than ten minutes.

Trevor Kerr was planted in an armchair in the corner with a brandy glass in front of him. I sat down opposite him. He didn't offer me a drink. "So what have you got to say for yourself?" he demanded by way of greeting. "I've had a hell of a day thanks to your incompetence. The police have turned my bloody factory upside down, questioning everybody. God knows what today's production figures will be like."

"Somebody is making fake KerrSter. They're releasing it on to the market via a little scam they've got going with one of the major wholesale chains. I know how the scam works and I know who's pulling it. The only thing I don't yet know is where they're manufacturing the stuff," I said in an exhausted monotone. I just didn't have the energy to let Trevor Kerr wind me up.

His red face turned purple. "Who is it? Who's doing this to me?" he shouted, leaning forward and banging the table with his fist. Several distant drinkers turned towards us, curious. The

Hilton's bar isn't a place that's used to raised voices that early in the evening.

"It's a former employee, who clearly wasn't too impressed with the golden handcuffs you slapped on him," I said.

"I want a name," he demanded, his voice lower but his expression no less menacing. "And an address. I'm going to break every bone in his fucking body when I get my hands on him."

I shook my head, weary of his incontinent anger. "No way."

"What the hell do you think I'm paying you for, girl? Give me the name and address!"

"Mr Kerr, shut up and listen to me." I'd reached the end of my rope and I suspect it showed. Kerr fell back in his seat as if I'd hit him. "A client hires me to do a job, and I do that job. Sometimes I come up against things that make people want to take the law into their own hands. Part of my job is stopping them. If I give you that name and address, and you go round there and give this bloke a good seeing to, you won't thank me tomorrow when you're in a police cell and he's sitting in his hospital bed free and clear because there isn't a shred of tangible evidence to tie him to the fake KerrSter or these killings. Sure, he'll have a sticky couple of hours down the nick, but unless we find where this stuff is being made and connect him directly to it, all we have is a chain of circumstantial evidence." Kerr opened his mouth to speak, but I waved a finger at him and carried on. "And I have to tell you that because of the way I've collected some of that circumstantial evidence, we're not going to be able to produce it for the police. We can tell them where to look, but we can't show them all we've got. We *need* the factory. I'm not keeping the name from you out of bloody-mindedness. I'm doing the job you paid me for, and I intend to finish it before somebody else dies. Do you have a problem with any of that?" I challenged him.

"Your name will be mud in this town," he blustered.

"For what? Keeping my client out of jail? Mr Kerr, if I ever get the faintest whiff that you have bad-mouthed me to a living soul, our solicitors will slap a writ on you so fast it'll make your eyes water. If you want this case clearing up, and your good name restored, you'll give me till this time tomorrow to come up with the final piece of evidence that we need to hand this mess over to the police."

Before he could answer, the barman appeared at his shoulder. "Excuse me? Miss Brannigan?"

"That's me," I said wearily.

"Phone call for you. You can take it at the bar."

Thank you, Della. Without a word to Kerr, I got up and went to the phone. "Time to go," Della said.

"I'll be right with you." I replaced the phone and returned to the table. "I have to go now," I said. "Frankly, Mr Kerr, there are plenty more productive things for me to be doing than talking to you. I'll be in touch."

Della was as good as her word. While I soaked in a bath laced with refreshing essential oils, a cold drink sweating on the side, she knocked together a chicken and spinach curry from the contents of the freezer. Wrapped in my cuddly towelling dressing gown, I curled up in a corner of one of the sofas and tucked in. I hadn't been able to face food on the flight, and as soon as the first forkful hit my mouth, I realized I was absolutely ravenous. As we ate, I gave Della the rundown on the case. "And so I sent you the stuff from the safe," I ended up.

Della nodded. "I've been through it, as far as I could get with an Italian dictionary. What's your conclusion?"

"Drugs," I said. "They're swapping art for drugs. Those number and letter combinations—20CC, 34H, 50,000E. I make that twenty kilos crack cocaine, thirty-four kilos heroin, fifty thousand tabs of Ecstasy. Once you've taken a painting out of its frame, it's a lot more portable than the cash equivalent, and a lot easier to smuggle. It's costing them next to nothing to acquire the stolen art, and it's got a sizeable black-market value, so they can swap it for a much greater value in drugs than they've initially laid out to have it stolen."

Della nodded. "I think you're right. Kate, you know I'm going to have to pass all this on to other teams, don't you? It's not my field."

I sighed. "I know. And somebody's going to have to liaise with the Italians so they can send someone to pick up Nicholas Turner's body. But I can't handle going through all this with some sceptical stranger tonight."

"Of course you can't. And before you talk to any other coppers, you need to have Ruth with you. They're going to put a lot of pressure on you to come up with the original source that put you on to Turner in the first place. I've got a shrewd idea who that might be, but I don't see any need to pass my suspicions on."

I smiled gratefully. She was right about Ruth. I'd broken the law too many times in the previous couple of days to be prepared to talk to the police without a solicitor. And my buddy Ruth Hunter is the best criminal solicitor in Manchester. "Thanks, Della," I said. "Can you start the ball rolling tomorrow? I warn you now that I'm not going to be available for questioning till the day after. I've got something else to chase that I can't ignore."

Della looked doubtful. "I don't know if they'll want to wait that long."

"They'll have to. Watch my lips. I'm not going to be available. I won't be in the office, I won't be here, I won't be answering my mobile."

Della grinned. "I hear you. I'll leave a message on the machine." She gave me the copper's once-over look. "You need to sleep, Kate. Speak to me tomorrow, OK?"

After Della had gone, I went next door. No sign of the coupé, which wasn't surprising if Richard had chosen to drive back. He might have made tonight's ferry out of Rotterdam, or he might have decided to take the long way home. I was still furious with him, but something inside me didn't want it to end here. I climbed into his bed, drinking in the smell of him from his pillows.

Call me sentimental. On the other hand, if you've just handed the police a stack of information pointing straight to a Mafia-style drug-running operation, sleeping in your own bed might not seem to be the safest option.

# 21

Some mornings you wake up ready to take on the world, feeling invincible, immortal and potentially omniscient. This wasn't one of them. I'd set Richard's *Star Trek* alarm clock for seven, which meant I'd had a straight eight hours' sleep before Captain James T. Kirk intoned, "Landing party to *Enterprise*, beam us up, Scotty," but I was in no mood to boldly go. I felt rested, but the hangover you get from guilt is infinitely worse than the one that comes from drink.

I dragged myself next door, called a cab and dived into the shower. I dressed in the last clean pair of jeans, a dark blue shirt and the new navy blazer, and managed half a cup of instant before the taxi pulled up outside. I picked up Shelley's Rover from Bill's garage, making a mental note to ring Hertz in Antwerp and ask them to hang on to Bill's car till I could get back over to pick it up. I was parked at the end of Alder Way by eight.

For once, I didn't have long to wait. At ten past, Sandra Bates left the house with a tall, skinny bloke in overalls. She passed me without a glance in her little Vauxhall Corsa. Clearly her feminism didn't extend to boycotting products that indulge in blatantly sexist advertising. The man I took to be Simon Morley followed in a two-year-old Escort. I slipped into the traffic a couple of cars behind him.

When we reached Kingsway, he turned left, heading away from the city centre. I had no trouble staying in touch with him as we drove down the dual carriageway. We went out through Cheadle, past Heald Green, and on into Handforth. He turned left in the centre of the village, out past the station. We drove through a housing estate, then, just as we reached open country, he turned right. A couple of hundred yards down the road, there was a turning on the right, leading to a small industrial estate. I pulled up and watched as he parked outside a unit that wasn't much bigger than a double garage.

As he disappeared inside, I cruised into the estate and parked further down the road, outside a company that made garden sheds. Just after nine, a battered Transit van pulled up behind Morley's car. The two lads in overalls who got out looked as if they should still be in school. You know you're getting old when even the villains start looking young. I gave it another ten minutes, then I grabbed my clipboard and the bag containing the video camera, and headed for the unmarked warehouse.

I knocked on the door and marched straight in. At one end of the room were a couple of tall vats with taps on the bottom of them. On a platform behind them, one of the lads was empty-ing the contents of a white plastic five-gallon drum into a vat. The other lad was halfway down the room, pushing a trolley that held gallon drums identical to the ones Kerrchem used for KerrSter. Simon Morley had his back to me, doing something at a bench on the far wall. Compared to the high-tech world of Kerrchem, this was a medieval alchemist's cell.

The lad pushing the trolley looked over at me, and called, "Can I help you, love?"

At the sound of his voice, Simon Morley whirled round, consternation written all over his face. "Who are you?" he demanded, crossing the room towards me.

"Is this Qualcraft?" I asked, casually swinging my bag through a gentle arc, hoping the video was getting the full flavour of the premises. "Only, there's no name on the door, and I've got an order for Qualcraft, and I can't seem to find them."

By now, Simon Morley was feet away from me. He looked like the classroom swot twenty years on, gangling limbs, acne scars and glasses that were constantly slipping down his sharp nose. "You've come to the wrong place," he said nervously. "This isn't Qualcraft."

If I hadn't stepped backwards, he'd have trodden on my trainers. "Sorry," I said. "You don't know where Qualcraft is, do you?"

"No," he said.

I smiled. "Sorry to have bothered you." I carried on backing out the door. Morley closed it firmly behind me, and I heard a key turn in the lock.

I pressed my ear to the door and heard him say, "How many times have I told you to keep the door locked?" He said something more, but he was obviously moving back to his workbench, since I couldn't make out the words.

Back at the car, I checked the video on playback. The picture was slightly hazy, but the vats and the gallon drums were clearly discernible, along with a nice clear shot of Morley's face. I set the video camera upon the dashboard and waited. I rang Shelley and filled her in on what had happened to me in Italy and told her to call me as soon as she heard from Richard. "Don't worry if you get diverted to the message service," I added. "I'm trying to avoid the cops, so I won't actually be answering the phone." Wonderful thing, technology. If I don't want to take calls on my mobile, I can divert them to an answering machine. Then, when I want to pick the messages up, I simply dial a number and it plays them over to me.

By eleven, I'd had messages from Della, Mellor from the Art Squad, a superintendent from the Drugs Squad, Alexis and Michael Haroun. I didn't feel like talking to any of them, but I made myself ring Michael. I still had a client, after all, something I'd kind of lost sight of as I'd chased across Europe. And Henry needed insurance. If I could convince Michael Haroun that the art thieves' racket was over for the time being, maybe he'd be a little more flexible about Henry's premium.

Michael was in a meeting, but I made an appointment with his secretary for three o'clock. I figured I'd be through here by then. Next, I took out my microcassette recorder and dictated a full report on the KerrSter scam. I'd drop it off with Shelley on my way to meet Michael so I could hand the client a copy this evening. I'd also be dropping off a copy with Inspector Jackson, just so Clever Trevor couldn't go taking the law into his own hands.

There was movement at the warehouse just after noon. I hit the "record" button on the video and taped Simon Morley and the two lads loading up the van with pallets of schneid KerrSter. Simon went back indoors with one of the lads, and the van took off. I followed at a discreet distance. I needn't have bothered. If I'd just driven straight to Filbert Brown's Manchester HQ, I'd have been able to film them arriving just as easily.

I was gobsmacked at their sheer cheek. Two people had died because of their crazy product tampering, yet they were still milking the racket for all it was worth. The more I thought about it, the more disturbing I found that. Simon Morley might well be crazy enough to carry on putting people's lives at risk in his vendetta against Kerrchem. But Sandra Bates hadn't struck me as a woman who would go along with random murder. I know people do ridiculous things for love, but I couldn't get the scenario into a credible shape at all.

But if Sandra Bates and Simon Morley weren't bumping people off, who was? It went beyond the bounds of credibility to imagine two lots of blackmailing saboteurs. I know coincidences do happen, but this wasn't one I could buy into. I closed my eyes and groaned. All this time and effort and I had a horrible feeling I wasn't any nearer the killer than I had been at the start.

Michael looked delighted to see me, greeting me with an unprofessional kiss on the lips. The tingle factor was still firing on all
four cylinders, I noted as I moved away and sat demurely on
the opposite side of the table from him. "You've been keeping
a very low profile," he complained jocularly. "I've been trying
to reach you for days. Your secretary keeps telling me you're
unavailable. I was beginning to think you'd gone off me."

"She wasn't bullshitting," I said. "I genuinely have been
unavailable. I've been out of the country. The good news is that
you're not going to have any more trouble from this particular
gang of art thieves."

He leaned forward, his eyes surprised and interested.
"Really? They've been arrested?"

"Let's just say the market's collapsed," I replied. "Take it
from me, the racket's over and done with. So you can safely
reinsure Henry Naismith's property. They won't be back for a
second bite of the cherry."

Michael ran a hand through his dark hair and shook his
head. "This is incredible. What on earth have you been up to?
It all sounds very unorthodox."

"That's a word," I said.

"You're going to have to tell me more than that," Michael
said, his face and voice equally determined. "It's not that I don't
believe you. But I have to explain myself to higher powers, and
they're not going to be overly impressed if I tell them I've taken
a particular course of action on the say-so of a private eye who
isn't even our employee."

I was growing bored with this story already, and I was still
going to have to repeat it more times than the sole survivor of
an air crash. "Look, I can't go into great detail. I've still got
a lot of talking to do to the police, and there are going to be
arrests to come. The bare bones go like this. I got a tip-off
from a good source as to who was fencing the goods. I tracked
him back to an international criminal consortium who have
been using art works as payment in kind for drugs. The fence

is out of the game for good, and the police will be closing in on the rest of the syndicate. Without a guaranteed market, the thieves won't be doing any more robberies. I promise you, Michael, it's all over."

He looked up from the pad where he'd been taking notes. "You're sure? You don't think the fence is going to start up again once everything quietens down?"

I closed my eyes briefly. "Not unless you believe in communications from beyond the grave," I said.

Michael's mouth opened as he stared at me with new eyes. "He's dead?" His voice was incredulous.

"Very."

"You didn't . . . ? It wasn't . . . ?" A flicker of fear showed in his eyes.

I snorted with ironic laughter. "Please," I said. "I didn't kill him, Michael, I only set him up. And my payoff was getting to discover the body."

He looked faintly queasy. I can't say I blamed him. "Is there any chance of recovering any of the stolen paintings?" he asked.

I shrugged. "I shouldn't think so. I'm afraid you're going to have to bite the bullet and cough up. But like I said, you won't be having any repeat business from this team."

"What can I say?" He spread his hands. "I'm impressed. Look, I can't make any promises at this stage, but I'd be interested in working with you in future. On a more official basis."

"Fine by me. Anything you need sorting, give us a call and we'll talk." Normally, I'd have been punching the air in jubilation at landing a client as major as Fortissimus. Today, all I could muster was a moment's satisfaction. Fortissimus had been too expensive an acquisition.

I got to my feet. "And on a personal note," Michael added, his eyes crinkling in a smile, "when can I see you again?"

"Tomorrow night?" I suggested. "Meet me in the bar at the Cornerhouse at half past seven?"

"Fine. See you then."

I sketched a wave and moved towards the door. He bounded to his feet and caught up with me on the threshold. He tried to put his arms round me in a hug, but I backed off. "Not in business hours," I said defensively. "If we're going to work together, we need some ground rules. Rule one, no messing about on the company's time."

His mouth turned down ruefully. "Sorry. You're absolutely right. See you tomorrow. Stay lucky."

I stopped off at the Cigar Store café for a bite to eat and a cappuccino, then went back to the office to pick up the Kerrchem reports from Shelley. "Nice work," she remarked as she handed me two neatly bound copies.

"Yeah," I said, my lack of conviction obvious.

"So what's the problem?"

I told her my reservations about Sandra Bates and her boyfriend. At the end of my tale, Shelley nodded sympathetically. "I see what you mean," she said. "Are you going to front them up and see what they've got to say for themselves?"

"I hadn't planned on it," I said. "I was just going to hand over the reports to Trevor Kerr and the cops and let them get on with it. I can't pretend murder isn't police business, can I?"

"No, but if they're not the killers, maybe you should go and talk to them. They might have some useful ideas as to who actually is doing the killing."

She was right, of course. Before I blew their lives out of the water, I should at least talk to Sandra Bates and Simon Morley. "What if they leg it?" I protested weakly.

"If you drop off the reports with Kerr and Jackson and go straight round there, they won't have time to leg it, will they? This isn't a lead that Jackson's going to sit on till morning, is it?"

Half an hour later, I was walking up the path of 37 Alder Way. I'd sent Kerr's copy of the report round by motorbike courier, and I'd left Jackson's copy with his sergeant. I estimated I probably had a maximum of half an hour before the police came knocking.

Sandra Bates opened the door. Her first reaction was bemused bewilderment, then, clearly remembering what I'd been asking about, she tried to close the door. I stepped forward, shoving my shoulder between the door and jamb. "What's going on?" she demanded.

"Too slow, Sandra," I said. "An innocent woman would have spoken sooner. We need to talk."

"You're not a student," she accused me, eyes narrowing.

"Correct." I handed her one of my business cards. "I'm Kate Brannigan. I'm working for Kerrchem, and we need to talk."

"I've got nothing to say to you," she said desperately, her voice rising.

From inside the house, Simon Morley's voice joined in. "What's going on, Sandra?"

"Go *away*," she said to me, shoving the door harder.

"Sandra, would you rather talk to me about industrial sabotage or to the police about murder?" I replied, leaning back against the door. "You've got ten seconds to decide. I know all about the scam. There's no hiding place."

Simon's tall figure loomed behind Sandra in the hall. "What's . . . ? Wait a minute, you were at the factory this morning." He looked down at Sandra. "What the hell's going on?"

"She's a private detective," Sandra spat out.

"Simon, we need to talk," I said, struggling to maintain a responsible façade with my shoulder jammed painfully between two bits of wood. "I know about the fake KerrSter, I've got videos of your factory and your delivery run this morning, I know exactly how Sandra's working the fiddle at her end. You're already in the frame for product tampering and attempted blackmail. Do you really want two counts of murder adding to the list?"

"Let her in," Simon said dully. Sandra looked up pleadingly at him, but he simply nodded. "Do it, love," he said.

I followed them into a living room that came straight from Laura Ashley without any intervening application of taste. I chose an armchair upholstered in a mimsy floral chintz, and they sat down together on a matching sofa. Sandra's hand crept out and clutched Simon's. "There's no way you can wriggle out of the scam," I said brutally. "But I don't think murder was on the agenda."

"I haven't killed anybody," Simon said defiantly, pushing his glasses up his nose.

"It doesn't look that way," I said.

"Look, I admit I wanted to get my own back on Kerrchem," he said.

"The golden handcuffs?" I asked.

He nodded. "That was bad enough, but then I found out they were refusing to give me a proper reference."

I frowned. Nobody at Kerrchem had indicated that anyone had left under a cloud. "Why?" I said.

"It was my department head, Keith Murray. He screwed up on a research project I was working on with him and it ended up costing the company about twenty grand in wasted time and materials. It was just before the redundancies were going to be announced and everybody was twitchy about their jobs, and he blamed me for the cockup. Now, because of that, personnel say I can't have a good reference. So I've ended up totally shafted. Never mind waiting six months, I'll be waiting six years before anybody gives me a responsible research job again. Kerrchem owes me." The words spilled out angrily, tumbling out in the rush of a normally reticent man who's had enough.

"So you decided to take it out in blackmail?"

"Why not?" he asked defiantly.

"Apart from the fact that it's illegal, no reason at all," I said tartly. "What about the two people who died?"

"That's got nothing to do with us," Sandra butted in. "You've got to believe us!" She looked as if she was about to burst into tears.

"She's right," Simon said, patting Sandra's knee with his free hand. "The papers said they'd died from cyanide poisoning—that's right, isn't it?" I nodded. "Well, then," he said. "All the stuff I've been using is over-the-counter chemicals, mostly ones Sandra's picked up through work. I've got no access to cyanide. I've got none in the warehouse or here. You can search all you like, but you can't tie us in to any cyanide. Look, all we wanted was to get some money out of Trevor Kerr. Why would we kill people if that was what we were trying to do? It'd be daft. You pay off somebody who's wrecking your commercial operation, you do it quiet so the opposition don't get to hear about it. You don't go to the police. You don't pay off murderers. You can't hide murder."

"What about the note? The one that came after the first death? That implied there would be more if Kerrchem didn't pay up," I said.

This time, Sandra did start crying. "I said we shouldn't have sent that one," she sobbed, pulling her hand away from Simon and punching ineffectually at his chest.

Gently, Simon gripped her wrists, then pulled her into a tight hug. "You were right, I'm sorry," he told her. Then he turned back to me. "I thought if we pretended to be more ruthless than we were, Kerr might cough up. It was stupid, I see that now. But he got me so mad when he just ignored the first note and nobody seemed to notice what we were doing. I had to make him pay attention."

"So if you're not doing the killings, who is?" I demanded, finally getting round to the reason why I'd put myself through another harrowing encounter.

I was too late. Before Simon could answer, the doorbell rang, followed by a tattoo of knocking. "Police, open up," I heard someone shout from the other side of the door. I thought about making a run for it through the back door, but the way my luck had been running lately, I'd probably have been savaged by a police dog.

The pair on the sofa had the wide-eyed look of rabbits transfixed by car headlights. By the time they got it together to let the cops in, their front door was going to be matchwood. With a sigh, I got to my feet and prepared for another jolly chat with Detective Inspector Cliff Jackson.

# 22

My encounter with Jackson reminded me of the old radical slogan: help the police, beat yourself up. After listening to the usual rant about obstructing the police, withholding evidence and interfering with witnesses, I needed a drink. I was only a couple of miles away from the Cob and Pen, the pub where Joey Morton had breathed his last, which clinched the decision.

If they'd gone into mourning over the death of mine host, it hadn't been a prolonged period of grief. It was pub quiz night, and the place was packed. In the gaps between the packed bodies, I got the impression of a bar that had been done out in the brewery version of traditional country house: dark, William Morris-style wallpaper, hunting prints, and bookshelves containing all those 1930s best sellers that no one has read since 1941, not even in hospital out-patients' queues. No chance of anyone nicking them, that was for sure.

I bought myself a vodka and grapefruit juice and retreated into the furthest corner from the epicentre of the quiz. I squeezed on the end of a banquette, ignored by the other four people surrounding the nearby table. They were much too involved in arguing about the identity of the first Welsh footballer to play in the Italian league. There was no chance of engaging any of the bar staff in a bit of gossip, not even lubricated with the odd tenner. They were too busy pulling pints and popping the caps off bottles of Bud. I sipped my drink and waited for an interval in the incessant trivia questions. Eventually, they announced a fifteen-minute break.

The foursome round my table sat back in their seats. "John Charles," I said. They looked blankly at me. "The first Welshman to play in Italy. John Charles." Amazing the junk that invades your brain cells when you live with a football fan.

"Really?" the lad with the pen and the answer sheet said.
"Truly."

The one who'd been rooting for Charles against the other three grinned and clapped me on the back. "Told you so," he said. "Can I get you a drink?"

I shook my head. "I've got to get off. But thanks all the same. I'm surprised you didn't all know the answer. I'd have thought anybody who was a regular in Joey Morton's pub would have been shit hot on all the football questions."

They all looked momentarily embarrassed, as if they'd caught me swearing in front of their mothers. "Did you know Joey, then?" the pen-pusher said.

"We met a couple of times. My fella's a journalist. Bad business."

"You're not kidding," another said with feeling. "Now, if you'd said it was Mrs M. that took a breadknife to him, I wouldn't have been half as surprised. But dying like that, a casual bystander in somebody else's war, that's seriously bad news."

"You thought his wife had done it?" I asked, trying to keep my voice light and jokey.

They all snorted with laughter. "Gail? Get real," Pen-pusher said scornfully. "Like Tez said, if it had been a breadknife job, nobody would have been gobsmacked. Them two fighting behind the bar's the nearest thing you used to get to cabaret in here. But rigging up a drum of cleaning stuff with cyanide? Nah, Gail's too thick."

"When Gail writes the daily specials up on the board, there's more spelling mistakes than there are hot dinners," another added. "She probably thinks cyanide's a perfume by Elizabeth Taylor."

"Must have been a hell of a shock, then. I guess it hit her hard," I said.

The one I'd backed up gestured over his shoulder with his thumb towards the bar. "Looks like it, doesn't it?"

I looked across. "Which one's Gail? I never met her, just Joey."

"The bottle blonde with the cleavage," Penpusher said.

I didn't have to ask for more details. Gail Morton's tumbled blonde mane looked as natural as candy-floss, and the bra under her tight, V-necked T-shirt didn't so much lift and separate as point and aim. As I looked she served a customer, giving a laugh that revealed perfect teeth and healthy tonsils. "A bit of a merry widow," I remarked.

"Widow's weeds up until the funeral, then back to normal."

I began to wonder if my eager inquiries down the line of industrial sabotage had shunted Jackson off the right track. After all, it's one of the great truisms that when wives or husbands die of unnatural causes, the prime suspect is the spouse. I was going to have to eat more than my usual portion of humble pie with Jackson if Gail Morton turned out to be Joey's killer. But that didn't explain why Mary Halloran had died. Time to go and pick some more brains.

I made my excuses and left. I headed east out of Stockport, and soon I was on the edge of the Pennine moors. About a mile before I hit Charlesworth village, I turned right on to a narrow road whose blacktop had been laid so recently it still gleamed in my headlights. The road climbed round the side of a hill and emerged in what had originally been a quarry. In the huge horseshoe carved out of the side of the hill stood ten beautiful stone houses, each individually designed by Chris.

For as long as I'd known them, Chris and Alexis had cherished the dream of building their own home, designed by Chris to their own specifications. They'd joined a self-build scheme a few years back, and, after a few hiccups, the dream had finally become a reality. Chris had swapped her architectural skills for things like plumbing, bricklaying, carpentry and wiring, while Alexis had served as everybody's unskilled labourer. The site was perfect for people who get off on a spectacular view, looking out through a gap in the Pennines to the Cheshire Plain. There isn't a pub within three miles, the nearest decent restaurant is ten miles away, and if you run out of milk at half past nine at night, you're drinking black coffee. Me, I'd rather live in a luggage locker at Piccadilly Station.

The house wasn't quite ready to be inhabited yet. A small matter of connection to the main gas, electricity, telephone and sewage systems. So for the time being Alexis and Chris were living in an ugly little caravan parked in their drive. It must have been a bit like going out for dinner to the best restaurant in town with your jaw wired up.

The light was on in their van, so I knocked. Chris opened the door in her dressing gown, blonde hair in a damp, tousled halo round her head. Seeing me, a broad grin split her face. "Kate!" she exclaimed, then made a point of leaning out and scanning the area beyond me. "And you made it without a team of native bearers and Sherpa guides."

"Sarcasm doesn't become you," I muttered as I followed her into the claustrophobe's nightmare. The caravan was a four-berth job which might conceivably have contained a family for a fortnight's holiday. Right now, it was bursting at the seams with the worldly goods that Chris and Alexis simply couldn't do without. Once they'd packed in their work clothes, their casual clothes, a couple of shelves of books, a portable CD player with the accompanying music library, two wine racks, a drawing board for Chris and the files Alexis deemed too sensitive to trust to her office drawers, there wasn't a lot of room left for bodies.

Alexis was sprawled on the double bed watching the TV news in a pair of plaster- and paint-stained jogging pants and a ripped T-shirt, her unruly hair tied back in a ponytail with an elastic band. She greeted me with a languid wave and said, "Kettle's just boiled. Help yourself."

I made a cup of instant and joined the two of them on the bed. It wasn't that we were planning an orgy; there just wasn't anywhere else to sit. "So what brings you up here in the hours of darkness, girl?" Alexis asked, leaning across me to switch off the TV. "You finally decided to tell me why you've been doing a Cook's tour of the EC?"

"I bring greetings from civilization," I told her. "Cliff Jackson's just arrested two suspects in the Kerrchem product-tampering scam."

I had all her attention now. Alexis pushed herself into an upright position. "Really? He charging them with the murders?"

"I don't know. If he does, he'll be making a mistake," I said.

"So, spill," Alexis urged.

I gave her the bare bones of the tale, knowing she wouldn't be able to say much in the following day's paper because of the reporting restrictions that swing into place as soon as suspects are charged with an offence. But the details would be filed away in Alexis's prodigious memory, to be dragged out as deep background when the case finally came to court. And she wouldn't forget where the information came from.

"And you believe them when they say they had nothing to do with the two deaths?" Chris chipped in.

"Actually, I do," I said. "Breaks my heart to say so, but I don't think the job's finished yet, whatever Cliff Jackson decides to charge them with."

Alexis lit a cigarette. Chris pointedly cracked the window open an inch and moved out of the draught. "I know, I know,"

Alexis sighed. "But how can I possibly be a labourer without a fag hanging out of my mouth and a rolled-up copy of the *Sun* stuffed in my back pocket? Anyway, KB, I suppose this means that you're here for access to the Alexis Lee reference library?"

"You can see why she's an investigative reporter, can't you?" I said nonchalantly to Chris.

"So what do you want to know?" Alexis asked.

"Tell me about Joey Morton," I said. First rule of murder investigation, according to all the detective novels I've read: find out about the victim. Embarrassing that it had taken me so long to get there.

"Born and raised in Belfast. Came over here with a fanfare of trumpets that said he was going to be the next George Best. Unfortunately, the only thing Georgie and Joey had in common was their talent for pissing it all up against the wall. United took him on as an apprentice, but they didn't keep him on, and he never made it past the Third Division. Gail believed the publicity when she married him. She was expecting the days of wine and roses, and she never forgave him for not making the big time. So she gave him the days of bitter and thorns. They fought like cat and dog. When we were living in the Heatons, we used to pop into the Cob and Pen occasionally for a drink and the spectator sport of watching Joey and Gail tear lumps out of each other."

"So why didn't she leave him?" I asked.

Alexis shrugged. "Some people get addicted to rowing," Chris said. "You watch them at it and imagine how stressed it would make you to live like that, but then you realize they actually thrive on it. If they ever found themselves in agreement, the relationship would die on the spot."

"Also, where would she go? It's not a bad life, being the *grande dame* of a busy pub like the Cob," Alexis added. "Besides, Joey was a staunch Catholic. He'd never have stood on for a divorce."

"Now she's got it all," I said. "She's got her freedom, and presumably the brewery aren't going to chuck her out of the pub as long as it keeps making money."

"And the insurance," Alexis said. "Word is, Joey was worth a lot more dead than he ever was in the transfer market."

"All of which adds up to a tidy bit of motive for Mrs Morton," I said. "But if she's behind Joey's murder, how does Mary Halloran's death fit in?"

"Copycat?" Alexis suggested.

"Maybe, but cyanide isn't exactly a common household chemical. I wouldn't know how to get my hands on it. Would you?"

Alexis shrugged. "I've never wanted to kill her enough," she joked, grabbing Chris and hugging her. A sudden pang of envy took me by surprise. All too painfully, I could remember when Richard and I were as easy and warm together. It felt like a long time had passed since then. I wanted that back. I just didn't know any more if I could recover it with Richard or if I was going to have to start all over again on the wary process of love.

I must have shown something on my face, for Chris looked at me with a worried frown. "You all right, Kate?" she asked.

"Not really," I said. "Me and Richard have had a major falling out. We parted company in Italy a couple of days ago, and I've not heard from him since. I'm just not sure if we can fix it this time."

I could hardly bear the love and concern on their faces. Chris pulled free from Alexis and leaned over to hug me. "He'll be back," she said with more confidence than I felt.

"Yeah, but will he be back with a bricklayer to build a wall across the conservatory?" I asked bitterly.

"If Richard needed a brickie, he'd have to ask you where to find one," Alexis said. "You don't get rid of him that easy, girl."

"He's obviously not very happy," I told them. "He said he's pissed off with everybody treating him like he's a pillock."

"Maybe he should stop behaving like one, then," Alexis said. "Ever since he got himself arrested, he's been walking around like a dog waiting for the next kick. Wait till he comes back, girl, I'll take him out for a drink and put him right."

I couldn't help smiling. That was one encounter I'd pay for a video of. "Anyway, I don't want to talk about my troubles," I said briskly. "I've got too much to do trying to put right all the cockups I've made this week to worry about Richard. Did he have any dodgy contacts, this Joey Morton?"

"Not that I've heard. He hung out with one or two moody people, but that was probably for the so-called glamour as much as anything. He was probably into a few bits and pieces on the side, but he wasn't a player."

So I wasn't looking for some gangster that Joey had double-crossed on a deal over stolen Scotch. "What's the score with this Mary Halloran?" I asked.

"I haven't been over there myself, but I've still gorra few good contacts in Liverpool," she said, becoming more Scouse by the syllable. "This Mary Halloran, she was a real grafter. The only out-of-the-way thing about her was that her staff actually liked her. They said she was a great boss, good payer, dead fair. According to them, she lived for her kids and her old man, Desmond. Our Desmond is apparently devastated. My mate Mo went round to try for a talk for the *Post*, but the guy was too distraught. She said he just burst into tears, then one of the relatives did the Rottweiler and saw her off."

"This Desmond. Has he got a job?"

"He's got his own business too. Not as successful as Mary's by all accounts, but he does OK. He's a photographer. Does portraits mainly. Dead artistic, according to Mo. Specializes in unusual printing techniques and special effects stuff. Not your weddings and babies type. Charges about five hundred a shot, apparently. God knows where he gets clients. The only pictures I've ever seen of people in Liverpool with that kind of money are in police mugshots and wanted posters."

"And no connection between the Hallorans and the Mortons?"

"Nothing that's come up so far. The only thing they've got in common, except for the way they died, is that they've left their surviving partners a lot better off than they were before. Mo says the girls that worked for Mary Halloran reckoned she was well insured. Had to be. If anything happened to her, the business was bound to suffer a bit, because Mary was one of those who had to take charge of everything herself."

"Maybe they did a *Strangers on a Train*," Chris volunteered. "You know, I'll do your murder, you do mine." We both looked at her, gobsmacked. "It was only a suggestion," she said defensively.

"The only point in doing something like that is when the murder method's one where having an alibi puts you in the clear. Like a shooting or a stabbing," Alexis finally said. "A delayed-action thing like this, there wouldn't be any point."

"Nice idea, though," I mused. Suddenly, a huge yawn crept up on me and shook me by the scruff of my neck. "Oh God," I groaned. "I'm going to have to go, girls. If my overdraft was as big as my sleep deficit, the bailiffs would be kicking my door down."

I leaned over and hugged the pair of them. "You never know," Chris said. "He might be there when you get home."

It's just as well Chris is such a good architect. She'd never make a living as a fortune teller.

# 23

The answering machine was flashing like a sex offender. I played back the long chain of messages against my better judgement. I'd had enough coppers on the line to staff my very own Tactical Aid Group minibus. But the one message I really wanted wasn't there. I hated myself for letting Richard's childish behaviour get to me, but that didn't make it any easier to escape. I ignored the rest of the messages and crashed out in my own bed. Deep down, I knew the Mafia weren't after me. Sleeping in Richard's bed the night before had been nothing but a self-indulgence I wasn't about to allow myself again.

I woke up just after eight, my head muzzy with the novel experience of a proper night's sleep. The phone was ringing already, but I had no problem ignoring it. I took a long, leisurely bath, deciding on my plans for the day. I'd told Della I'd be prepared to talk to the Art Squad and the Drugs Squad, but I had other ideas now. A few hours' delay wasn't going to make a whole lot of difference to their investigation, and I was determined to press on with my inquiries into the KerrSter murders as fast as I could. The last thing I wanted was another head-to-head with Cliff Jackson, and the best way to avoid that was to move as fast as I could while he was still working out what to do with Sandra Bates and Simon Morley.

After breakfast, I filled the washing machine with the first load of dirty clothes. Glancing out of the kitchen window, I noticed an unfamiliar car parked in one of the residents' bays. I didn't have to be Manchester's answer to Nancy Drew to work out that an unmarked saloon with a radio aerial and two men in it was a police car. The only thing left to wonder was which squad it belonged to. I wasn't about to pop over and ask a policeman.

I pulled the blonde wig out of its bag and arranged it on my head, adding the granny glasses with the clear lenses and a pair of stilettos to give me a bit of extra height. Then I nipped through the conservatory into Richard's house and out his front door. The two bobbies gave me a cursory glance, but they were waiting for a petite redhead from next door. That told me Della wasn't responsible, even indirectly, for their presence; she'd have told them about the conservatory. Which left Jackson.

Of course, the car was in the clear, since I was still driving Shelley's Rover. She'd tried the previous afternoon to persuade me to swap it for Richard's Beetle, but I played the card of professional necessity and managed to hang on to hers for the time being. I headed out of town towards Stockport and got to the Cob and Pen while the cleaners were still doing their thing. The bar stank of stale tobacco and sour beer, somehow more noticeable when the place was empty. "I'm looking for Mrs Morton," I told one of them.

"You from the papers?" she asked.

I shook my head. "I'm representing Kerrchem, the company who manufacture the cleanser Mr Morton was using when he died." Nothing like a bit of economy with the truth. Let them think I was here to talk about the compensation if they wanted.

The woman pursed her lips. "You'd better go on up, then. It's going to cost your lot plenty, killing Joey like that." She gestured towards a door marked "Private."

I smiled my thanks and opened the door on to a flight of stairs. The door at the top had a Yale, but when I tapped gently and turned the handle, it opened. "Hello?" I called.

From a doorway on my left, I could hear a voice say, "Hang on," then the clatter of a phone being put down on a table. Gail Morton stuck her head through the doorway and said sharply, "Who are you? What are you doing up here?"

"The cleaners sent me up," I said. "My name's Kate Brannigan. I'm a private investigator working for Kerrchem."

She frowned and cast a worried glance back through the doorway. "You'd better come through, then." She moved back smartly into the room ahead of me and swiftly picked up the phone, swivelling so she could keep an eye on me. "I'll call you back," she said firmly. "There's some private detective here from the chemical company. I'll ring you after she's gone . . . No, of course not," she added sharply. Then, "OK then, after one." She replaced the phone and turned to face me, leaning against the table as if she were protecting the phone from hostile attack.

All my instincts told me that phone call was more than some routine condolence. Something was going on. Maybe it was nothing to do with anything, but my instincts have served me too well in the past to ignore them. I wanted to know just who she'd been talking to who needed to know a private eye was on the premises. "Sorry to interrupt," I said. "Hope it wasn't an important call."

"You'd better sit down," she said, ignoring the invitation I'd dangled in front of her.

The room was as much of a cliché as Gail Morton herself. Dralon three-piece suite, green onyx and gilt coffee table and side tables, complete with matching ashtrays, cigarette box and table lighter. Naff lithographs in pastel shades of women who looked like they'd escaped from the pages of those true-romance graphic novels. The room was dominated by a wide-screen TV, complete with satellite decoder. I chose the chair furthest away from Gail.

She moved away from the telephone table and sat down opposite me. She leaned forward to take a cigarette from the box on the table, her deep-cut blouse opening to reveal the tanned swell of her breasts. Philip Marlowe would have been entranced. Me, I felt faintly repelled. "So what have you come here for?" she asked. "Have they sent you to make me an offer?"

"I'm afraid not," I said. "Kerrchem hired me to try to find out who tampered with their product."

She gave a short bark of laughter. "Trying to crawl out from under, are they? Well, they're not going to succeed. My lawyer says by the time we're finished with your bosses, they'll be lucky to have a pot to piss in."

"I leave that sort of thing to the lawyers," I said mildly. "They're the only ones who can guarantee walking away rich after tragedies like this." I thought I'd better remind her of her role as grieving widow.

"You're not kidding," she said, dragging deep on her cigarette. In the unkind daylight coming through the window, I could see the incipient lines round her mouth as she kissed the filter tip. It wouldn't be long before her face matched her personality. "So what do you want to know?"

"I've got one or two questions you might be able to help me with. First off, can you remember who actually bought the KerrSter?"

"It could have been me or Joey," she said. "We used to do the cash-and-carry run turn and turn about. KerrSter was one of the things that was always on the list, and we usually had a spare drum in the cupboard."

"Who made the last trip?"

"That was Joey," she said positively. Given when the affected batch had gone out, that meant Joey had purchased the fatal drum.

"Where are your cleaning materials kept?" I asked.

"In a cupboard in the pub kitchen."

"Is it locked?"

She looked at me scornfully. "Of course it's not. There's always spills and stuff in a pub. The staff need to be able to clean them up as and when they happen, not leave them for the cleaners."

"So anybody who works in the pub would have access?"

"That's right," she said confidently. "That's what I told the police."

"What about private visitors, friends or business associates? Would they be able to get to the cupboard?"

"Why would they want to? Do your friends come round your office and start nosing about in the cleaner's cupboard?" she asked aggressively.

"But in theory they could?"

"It'd be a bit obvious. When people come to visit, they don't usually swan around the pub kitchen on their own. You must know some really funny people. Besides, how would they know Joey was going to open that particular container?"

Before I could ask my next question, a voice from the stairwell shouted, "Gail? There's a delivery down here you need to sign for."

Gail sighed and crushed out her cigarette. "I'll be back in a minute."

As soon as she left the room, I was on my feet. I wouldn't be getting a second chance to check out what had set my antennae twitching. I took my tape recorder out of my bag and pressed the "record" button, then I picked up the phone and put the machine's in-built mike next to the earpiece. Then I hit last number redial. The phone clicked swiftly through the numbers, then connected. A phone rang out. I let it ring a dozen times, then broke the connection and gently replaced the phone.

I heard steps on the stairs and threw myself back into my chair. When Gail entered the room, I was sitting demurely flicking through the pages of the *TV Times*. "Sorted?" I asked politely.

"I hate paperwork," she said. "But then, so did Joey, so we've got a little woman that comes in every week to keep the books straight."

"Did your husband have any enemies?" I asked. Eat your heart out, Miss Marple.

"There were plenty of people Joey would happily have seen dead, most of them football managers. But people tended to like him. That was his big trouble. He was desperate to be liked. He'd never stand up for himself and make the bosses treat him properly. He just rolled over," she said, years of bitterness spilling into her voice. "I told him, you've got to show them who's in charge, but would he listen? Would he hell as like. Same with the brewery. I'd been on at him for ages to talk to them about our contract, but he just fobbed me off. Well, they'll know a difference now it's me they've got to deal with," she added vigorously. Knowing the corporate claws of brewery chains, I thought Gail Morton was in for a nasty surprise.

"So, no enemies, no one who wanted him dead?"

"You're barking up the wrong tree," she told me. "You should be looking for somebody at that factory who has it in for their bosses. Joey just got unlucky."

"You benefit from his death," I commented.

Her eyes narrowed. "It's time you were on your way," she said. "I'm not sitting here listening to that crap in my own living room. Go on, get out of it."

I can take a hint.

When I walked into the office, Shelley had a look on her face I'd never seen before. After a couple of minutes of awkward conversation, I worked out what it was. The shifty eyes, the nervous mouth. She was feeling guilty about something. "OK," I said heavily, perching on the corner of her desk. "Give. What's eating you? Is it having to lie to the police about where I am?"

"I don't know what you mean," she said sniffily. "Anyway, I'm black. Isn't lying to the cops supposed to be congenital?"

"Something's bothering you, Shell."

"Nothing is bothering me. By the way, if you want your coupé back, it's on a meter round the corner. I wouldn't mind having my Rover back." She couldn't meet my eyes.

"Has he been here?" Try as I might, I couldn't keep my voice cool.

"No. He came round the house about eight o'clock this morning. I asked him to talk to you, but you're too good a teacher. That man of yours has really learned how to ignore. I was going to phone you, but he was gone by then, so it wouldn't have been a whole lot of use."

"Did he say where he was going?" There was a pain in my stomach which was nothing to do with what I'd had for breakfast.

"I asked him, but he said he wasn't sure what he was doing. He told me to tell you not to waste your time looking for him."

I looked away, blinking back tears. "Fine," I said unsteadily. "Though why he should think I can spare the time to chase him . . ."

Shelley reached out and gripped my hand. "He's hurting in his pride, Kate. It's going to take him a bit of time, that's all."

I cleared my throat. "Sure. I should give a shit." I walked through to my office. "If anybody wants me, I'm not here, OK?"

I closed the door and sat down with the tape recorder. I'd recorded the number dialling on high speed, and now I played it back on the lower speed setting so I could more easily count the clicks. Given the way my luck had been running lately, the call I'd interrupted had probably been made *to* Gail, and all I was going to end up with was the number of her dentist.

I wrote the numbers down on a sheet of paper. Unless Gail made a round trip of eighty miles every time she wanted her teeth fixed, it looked like I'd struck gold. The number I'd recorded from her telephone was a Liverpool number. On an impulse, I marched through to Bill's office, where the phone books live, and picked out a three-year-old Liverpool directory.

I looked up "Halloran." There it was. Desmond J. Halloran, an address in Childwall. The number didn't match.

"It ain't over till it's over," I said grimly, picking up the phone and calling Talking Pages. I asked for portrait photographers in Liverpool. The second number she gave me matched the number on the sheet of paper. DJH Portraits. I didn't think Ladbrokes would be offering me odds on those initials not standing for Desmond J. Halloran.

I shut myself back in my office and rang Paul Kingsley, a commercial photographer who occasionally does jobs for us when Bill and I are overstretched or we need pictures taking in conditions that neither of us feels competent to handle. Paul's always delighted to hear from us. I suspect he read too many Batman comics when he was a lad. I got him on his mobile. "I need your help," I told him.

"Great," he said enthusiastically. "What's the job?"

"I want to check out a photographer in Liverpool. I need to know how his business is doing. Is he making money? Is he on the skids? That kind of thing. Do you know anybody who could colour in the picture?"

"That's all you want?" He sounded disappointed. It was worrying. This is man whose assignments for us have included spending a Saturday night in an industrial rubbish bin, and standing for three days in the rain in the middle of a shrubbery. In his shoes, I'd have been delirious with joy at the news that his latest task for Mortensen and Brannigan involved nothing more hazardous to the health than picking up a phone.

"That's all I want," I confirmed. "Only I want it yesterday. DJH Portraits, that's the firm."

"Consider it done," he said.

My next call was to Alexis. "All right?" she greeted me. "Has dickhead turned up?" I told her about Shelley's encounter with Richard. "That doesn't sound like goodbye to me," she said. "You want my advice, give your insurance man a bell. Show

Richard you're not sitting around waiting for him to decide it's time to come home."

"Strangely enough, I'm seeing him for dinner," I told her.

"Nice one. Don't do anything I wouldn't do."

"That doesn't give me a lot of scope on a date with a fella, does it?"

"Exactly. Now, what was it you wanted?"

"You still got your contact in Telecom accounts?" I asked her.

"You bet. Like the song says, once you have found her, never let her go. What are you after?"

"I want the itemized bills for the last six months on three numbers," I said. "One Manchester, two Liverpool. How much is that going to rush me?"

"It's usually fifty quid a throw. I'll ask her if she'll give you the three for a hundred and twenty. You want to give me the numbers, I'll pass them on?"

I read the three numbers over to her. "Soon as poss," I said.

"If I catch her now, she'll fax them to you when she gets home tonight. That do you?"

"It'll have to."

"Is this something I should know about, KB? I mean, I'm the woman you were pumping last night about mysterious deaths in Manchester and Liverpool."

I chuckled. "If I said it was a completely unrelated matter, would you believe me?"

"Girl, if the Pope himself told me it was a completely unrelated matter, I wouldn't believe him. You've got no chance. You want to share this with me?"

"Do your own investigations," I told her.

"I'll catch up with you later. Have fun with the insurance man. I'll expect a full report tomorrow."

"Only paying clients get full reports," I laughed. I replaced the receiver and swung my feet up on to the desk. A vague shape was forming in my mind, but there were still too many questions that needed answering. Not least of them was the one Gail Morton herself had raised. If someone had been targeting Joey Morton specifically, how could they be sure he would be the person to open the fatal container?

I was still worrying at that point when Paul called back. "DJH Portraits," he said. "Desmond Halloran. One-man band. He used to work with another guy, doing the usual weddings, babies and pets. But he fancied himself as a bit of an artist, so he set up on his own, doing specialist portrait work. I'm told his stuff is really good, but the problem is that using the kind of processes he does is very labour intensive, as well as costing a fair bit on the chemicals. He was keeping his head above water to begin with, but the way the recession's been biting, nobody's got the cash to spare for fancy photographs that come in at five hundred quid a throw. My contact says he reckons he must be running at a loss these days. That what you wanted to hear?"

"Smack on the button," I said.

"This wouldn't have something to do with the fact that his wife has just popped her clogs, would it?" he asked eagerly, ever the boy detective.

"Now, Paul, you know I never divulge confidential client information."

"I know. Only, my mate, he says Desmond only kept afloat because his wife's business was a raging success and she subsidized him. He was wondering how Desmond's going to go on now."

Another piece of the jigsaw fell into place. "Thank you, Paul," I said. "Send me an invoice." It was a long shot, but if Desmond Halloran was having an affair with Gail Morton and they wanted to ditch their partners and run off together, they'd need something to live on. Quite a big something, if my impressions of Gail were accurate. But if Desmond divorced Mary, she'd doubtless hang on to the kids and to her business, leaving Desmond potless. And I suspected that Desmond potless was a lot less attractive to Gail than Desmond loaded.

Before I could do anything more, the door to my office opened and Della walked in. She looked at me, eyes reproachful, and gently shook her head. "Running out on Cliff Jackson I could understand," she said. "But running out on a promise you made to me? Kate, you checked your brains in with your bags at Milan and forgot to pick them up at the other end."

She didn't need to say any more. I could beat myself up. She was right. When I start letting my friends down, I know my life's starting to spin out of control. I got to my feet. "I'm sorry," I said inadequately. "You're right. You deserve better."

"Shall we go?"

I nodded. On the way out, Shelley said, "Sorry, Kate. I can lie to most people, but not to the rest of the team."

"No need to apologize," I said. "I'm the one in the wrong. You better phone Ruth and tell her to meet me at . . . where, Della?"

"Bootle Street," Della said.

"Oh, and Shelley? I think I might be a while. Better ring Michael Haroun at Fortissimus and tell him I need a rain check tonight."

I followed Della out to the waiting police car. I knew I was damn lucky not to be under arrest. I just didn't feel like I could risk walking under ladders.

# 24

It seemed to take longer to recount Richard and Kate's excellent adventure than it had taken to experience it. Asking the questions were Inspector Mellor from the Art Squad, who remembered me from our earlier encounter at Henry's, and Geoff Turnbull from the Drugs Squad, who thankfully owed me one on account of information received in a previous investigation that had provided him with a substantial feather in his cap. Della sat in on the interview, probably to make sure my brief didn't change my mind and persuade me to opt for the Trappist approach.

Even so, by the time I'd answered everyone's questions, it was past midnight. I'd come clean about all of my nefarious activities, on the advice of Ruth Hunter, my nonpareil criminal solicitor and, incidentally, one of the tightknit group of my female friends which Richard refers to as the Coven-ment—witches who run the world. "After all," she pointed out drily, "all your law-breaking took place outside their jurisdiction, and I rather think the Italian police are going to have enough to worry about without bothering you with such trivial charges as assault, kidnap, false imprisonment, burglary, data theft, concealing a body, and failing to report a murder."

Ruth, Della and I ended up eating steak in one of the city's half-dozen casinos. The great advantage with them is that they stay open late and the food's cheap. It's supposed to act as an incentive to make people gamble. I don't know how effective it is; most of the gamblers that night were Chinese, and none of them looked like a juicy steak was on their agenda. Not as long as the roulette wheels were still spinning. "Cliff Jackson's still going to want to talk to you," Della pointed out after we ordered.

"I know. His goons were sitting on my doorstep this morning."

Ruth groaned. "What now, Kate? Haven't you broken enough laws for one week?"

"That's not why Cliff Jackson's after me," I said stiffly. "It's just that I've been doing his job for him, and now I've tracked down his saboteurs, he probably wants to know who the real murderer is."

Della and Ruth both choked on their drinks. "Oh ye of little faith," I complained. "Anyway, I want to stay out of his way until I've got the whole thing done and dusted. If I leave the job half done, he'll only mess it up and arrest the wrong person. He's got form for it."

"Isn't it about time you went back to white-collar crime and left the police to deal with these dangerous criminal types?" Ruth demanded. "It's not that I think you're incapable of looking after yourself. It's just that you keep involving Richard, and he's really far too accident-prone to be exposed to these kinds of people."

"I don't want to discuss Richard," I said. "Anyway, Della, what have Mellor and Turnbull been doing for the last forty-eight hours with the info I handed them on a plate?"

"Luckily, Geoff's already had dealings with his opposite numbers in Europe about organized drug trafficking, so he was able to cut through a lot of the bureaucratic red tape. It turns out his Italian oppos have been taking a long hard look at Gruppo Leopardi and its offshoots, so the info you brought out of there has slotted in very nicely. You were right, by the way. They've been organizing art robberies all over Europe, not just in the UK, and using the art works as payment for drug shipments," Della said. "With the data you stole, it looks like they'll be able to set up a sting that will pull in some of the big boys, for a change."

"What about Nicholas Turner?" I asked.

Della fussed with a cigarette and her Zippo. "They found his body in the van, where you left it. A couple of the lads went over to Leeds this morning and spoke to his wife. She's denying all knowledge of anything shady, of course. She's going for the Oscar as the grieving wife of a legitimate art and antiques dealer. Grieving she may well be, but nobody believes for a minute she's as innocent as she wants us to think. Apart from anything else, there's evidence that she's accompanied him on several of his trips to the Villa San Pietro."

"He still didn't deserve to die," I said.

Ruth shrugged. "You take the money, you take the risks that go with it. How many lives have been destroyed by the drugs Turner was involved in supplying? Half the people I defend owe not a little of their trouble to the drug scene. I wouldn't lose any sleep over Turner, Kate."

I didn't.

Jackson's goons were on my doorstep again the following morning. I figured that by now he'd probably be staking out the office as well. I rang Shelley. "Have you got company of the piggy variety too?"

"Of course, sir. Did you want to talk to one of our operatives?"

That told me all I needed to know. "Is it Jackson himself or one of his gophers?"

"I'm afraid our principal isn't in the office at present."

I'll say this for Shelley, nothing fazes her. "There should have been an overnight fax for me," I said. "Can you stick it in an envelope and have it couriered round to Josh's office? I'll pick it up there."

"That's no problem, sir. I'll have Ms Brannigan call you when she comes back to the office. Goodbye now."

Whoever said blondes have more fun obviously didn't garner the experience wearing a wig. I went through the disguise-for-beginners rigmarole again and made my exit through Richard's bungalow, pausing long enough to do a quick inventory of his wardrobe. If he'd been back, he hadn't taken any significant amount of clothing with him. His laptop was gone, though, which meant he was planning to be away long enough to get some work done.

I arrived at Josh's office ten minutes after the fax, and settled down at an empty desk to plough through the phone numbers. It was a long, tedious process of crosschecking, made worse by the fact that Alexis's contact had come up with a more detailed breakdown of calls than the customer receives. The fax she'd sent listed every call from all three numbers, even the quickies that don't cost enough to make it on to the customer's account. But at the end of it, I'd established that there were calls virtually every day between Desmond Halloran's office number and the private number of the Cob and Pen. There were also a couple of long calls from the Hallorans' home number to the pub.

There was one other curious thing. A Warrington number cropped up on both bills. I checked the dates. Every Monday, a call a few minutes long was logged on one bill or another. It appeared most often on Desmond's office bill, but it was there half a dozen times on the Cob and Pen's account too. Of course, I had to ring it, didn't I?

"Warrington Motorway Motel, Janice speaking, how may I help you?" the singsong voice announced.

"I'm meeting someone at the motel today. Can you give me directions?"

"Certainly, madam. Where are you coming from?"

"Manchester."

"Right. If you come down the M62 and take junction nine, you go left as you come off the motorway and right at the first roundabout. We're the first turning on the left, just after the bridge."

"Thank you," I said. "You've been most helpful." If I had my way, Janice was going to be a lot more helpful before the day was out.

❧❦❧

There was nothing to mark out the Warrington Motorway Motel from the dozens of others that sprang up around the motorway network in the late Eighties. A two-storey, sprawling red-brick building with a low-pitched roof, a car park and a burger joint next door, it could have been anywhere between the Channel Tunnel and that point on the edge of the Scottish Highlands where the motorways run out. Rooms for around thirty quid a throw, TV but no phone, no restaurant, bar or lounge. Cheap and cheerless.

Late morning wasn't a busy time behind the reception desk. Janice—or someone who'd stolen her name badge—looked pleased at the sight of another human being. The reception area was so small that with two of us present, it felt intimate. On the way over, I'd toyed with various approaches. I'd decided I was too strung out to try for subtlety. Besides, I still had a wad of cash in my bag that had no official home.

I dropped one of my cards on the desk halfway through Janice's welcome speech. Her pert features registered surprise, followed by an air of suppressed excitement. "I've never met a private detective before," she confided, giving me the wide-eyed once-over. I hoped I wasn't too much of a disappointment.

I followed the card with a photograph of Gail I'd persuaded Alexis to lend me. "This woman's a regular here," I stated baldly. "She comes here once a week with the same bloke."

Janice's eyes widened. "I'm not supposed to release information about guests," she said wistfully.

I leaned on the desk and smiled. "Forgive me being so personal, Janice, but how much do they pay you?"

Startled, she blurted out the answer without thinking. "A hundred and seventy pounds a week."

I opened my bag and took out the five hundred I'd counted out on the way. I placed it on the desk and pushed it towards her. "Nearly three weeks' money. Tax free. No comebacks. I don't even want a receipt."

Her eyes widened. She stared at the cash, then at me, consternation clear in her face. "What for?"

"All I want to know is how often they come and how long they stay. I want to know when they're due here next. Then I want to book the room next door. Oh, and five minutes in their room before they arrive. There's no reason why anyone should know you've helped me." I nudged the money nearer to her.

"It's for a divorce, isn't it?" she said.

I winked. "I'm not supposed to release information either. Let's just say this pair shouldn't be doing what they've been doing."

Suddenly, her hand snaked out and the dosh disappeared faster than a paper-wrapped prawn off Richard's plate. She tapped Gail's photograph with a scarlet fingernail. "She's been coming here with this bloke for about a year now. They always book as Mr and Mrs Chester. It's usually a Wednesday. They arrive separately, usually about half past two. I don't know when they leave, because I go off at half past four."

I nodded, as if this was exactly what I'd expected to hear. "And when are they booked in next?"

"I think you've dropped lucky," she said, consulting her screen. "Yeah, that's right. They've got a room booked today." She looked up at me, smirking. "I bet you knew that, didn't you?"

Again, I winked. "Maybe you could let me into the room they'll be in, then book me in next door?"

Eagerly, she nodded. Funny how excited people get when they feel like they're part of the chase. "I'll give you their key," she said. "But bring it back quick as you can."

I picked up the key and headed for the lift. Room 103 was a couple of doors down the corridor from the lift. The whole floor was eerily silent. I let myself in, and gave the room a quick scan. I could have drawn it from memory, it was so similar to every motel room I'd ever camped out in. Because I hadn't been able to get into the office to pick up proper surveillance equipment, I'd had to rely on what I could pick up from the local electronics store. A small tape recorder with a voice-activated radio mike hadn't made much of a dent in my payoff from Turner. I took out my Swiss Army knife and unscrewed the insipid seascape from above the bed. I stuck the mike to the back of the picture with a piece of Elastoplast, then screwed it back on to the wall. There was a gap of about a quarter of an inch between the picture and the hessian wallpaper, but I didn't think Gail and Desmond were there for the décor.

I quickly checked the mike was working, then I was out of there. I returned the key to Janice and went over to the burger joint for supplies. I settled down in my room with a giant cheeseburger, fries, a large coffee and a bag of doughnuts. I stuck the earpiece of the tape recorder in my ear and waited. I couldn't believe myself. I felt like I was playing the starring role in the worst kind of clichéd private-eye drama; staking out the seedy motel for the couple indulging in illicit sex. All I needed was a snap-brimmed trilby and a bottle of bourbon to feel like a complete idiot.

While I was waiting, I rang Michael Haroun. "Sorry about last night," I said. "I was helping the police with their inquiries."

"They *arrested* you?"

"Behave. They only wanted a friendly chat. They were just a little insistent about having it right that minute."

"My God, you like to sail close to the wind, don't you?"

"My yachting friends tell me that's where you have to be if you want to travel fast," I said. What was it about this man that brought out the portentous asshole in me?

"So is this a social or professional call?" he asked.

"Purely social. I wanted to offer you dinner tomorrow as a penance for cancelling yesterday."

"You cook, as well as everything else?"

"I do, but that's not what I had in mind. How does the Market sound?"

"Fabulous. My favourite restaurant in town. What time?"

"I'll see you there about half past seven," I promised. To hell with Barclay.

The feeling of wellbeing that I got from talking to Michael didn't last long. There's nothing more boring than sitting around in a featureless motel room waiting for something to happen. Patience and I aren't normally on speaking terms, so I always get really edgy on jobs like this. It's not so bad doing a stakeout in the car; at least I can listen to the radio and watch the world go by. But here, there was nothing to do but stare at the walls.

The monotony broke around twenty past two. My earpiece told me that the door to the next room had closed. At once, I was on the alert, my free ear pressed to the wall. I heard the toilet flush, then, a few minutes later, the door closed again. There was a mumble of what sounded like greetings and endearments, irritatingly incomprehensible. At a guess, they were still in the passage by the bathroom, rather than in the room proper.

More mumblings, then gradually, I could make out what they were saying.

" . . . taking a risk," a man's voice said.

"You said what I told you to, didn't you?" Gail's voice. Unmistakably.

"Yeah, I told my mother I needed some time on my own, that I was going for a drive and would she look after the kids."

"And did she act like she thought you were behaving oddly?"

"No," the man admitted.

"Well, then," Gail said. There was the instantly recognizable sound of kissing, the groans of desire. "I needed to see you," Gail went on when she next surfaced. "I wanted you so bad, Dessy."

"Me too," he said. More of the kind of noises you get in Tom Cruise movies. I half expected to hear "Take My Breath Away" swelling in the background.

"We did it, you know," Gail said exultantly in the next break. "We're going to get away with this. Nobody suspects a thing."

"What about that private eye? You sure she doesn't know anything?"

"Positive. She was just on a fishing expedition, that was obvious. If she'd had anything solid to go on, she'd have let me know. Cocky bitch."

I wasn't the only one who was cocky. Only I had better reason to be. I checked that the tape was still running.

"Have you seen the news?" Gail asked.

"What news?" Desmond said, sounding nervous.

"About the chemical company," she said. "It was all over the *Evening Chronicle* and the local TV news."

"We haven't had the TV on much. We're supposed to be in mourning," Desmond said cynically. "What's been going on? Are they admitting liability?"

"Better than that," Gail said. "Apparently, somebody's been trying to blackmail Kerrchem. Product tampering, they said it was. The police have arrested a man and a woman. Hang on, I've got the paper in my bag." There was the sound of rustling, then silence.

Then Desmond let out a low whistle. "Fantastic!" he exclaimed. "The icing on the cake. Nobody's going to look twice at us now, are they?"

Famous last words, I thought to myself.

"Exactly. It's turned out even better than we planned. The police might think I had a motive for wanting rid of Joey, but they're not going to bother digging around in my life when they've got a perfect pair of scapegoats."

And even though his access to photographic chemicals meant Desmond Halloran could probably get his hands on cyanide without too much trouble, I reckoned the police weren't even going to think about suspecting him while they had Simon and Sandra behind bars. Besides, according to Alexis, the Hallorans were supposed to have an idyllic marriage. No one had an inkling that Desmond Halloran's Wednesday afternoons were spent in a motel room near Warrington.

The smooching noises had begun again. Then Gail said, "In a year or so, when we've got to know each other because of the court cases we'll be filing against Kerrchem, no one will be surprised when we decide to get married. After all, we'll have had so much in common."

Desmond giggled, an irritating, high-pitched whinny. Never mind his murderous instincts, that giggle alone should have put any reasonable woman off him for life. "Talk about coincidence," he cackled. "I bet those two blackmailers are sweating."

After that, things got a lot less interesting for me, though Gail and Desmond obviously thought different. There was a lot of kissing and groaning and embarrassing lines like, "Give it to me, big boy." Then they were grunting like a pair of Wimbledon champions. I pulled out the earpiece in disgust. It's not that I'm a prude, but it felt like this pair were shagging in an open grave. I sat patiently on the bed, watching the winking red light on the tape machine that told me it was recording. After an hour, I reckoned I'd got more than enough to nail the scumbags.

It was time to go and play at good citizens.

# 25

I dumped another oner on Janice's desk. "You've got an office through the back?" I asked.

She nodded, never taking her eyes off the money. "I'd like to use the phone there for a couple of minutes. I know you're not supposed to allow customers access to your phone, never mind your office, but if anyone kicks off, tell them I said it was an emergency." I winked again. Strange how I develop that tic whenever I'm sharing my wealth with the less fortunate.

Janice lifted the access flap at the side of the reception desk and I went through to the tiny office, closing the door behind me. I rang the familiar number of Greater Manchester Police and asked for the Stockport incident room. The detective who answered didn't seem very keen to put me through to Inspector Jackson. He told me firmly that anything I had to say to the boss could equally be said to him. Clearly a man desperate for Brownie points. "I know he wants to talk to me," I insisted. "He wants to talk to me so badly that he's had two of his lads sitting outside my house for the last two days."

"Hold on," he said grudgingly. "I'll see if he's free."

Jackson came on the line immediately. "At last," he said grimly. "Why have you been avoiding me, Miss Brannigan? I thought you were very hot on civic duty the last time we spoke."

"I'm sorry, Inspector, I've been a bit busy. And I knew you wouldn't be very keen to take me seriously since the last criminals I handed over to you weren't exactly what you were looking for."

He sighed. "Cut the smartarse remarks and get to the beef," he said. "When are you coming in to talk to me?"

"I rather thought you might want to come to me," I said sweetly. "I have something I'd like you to hear. I'll happily play it over the phone, though I don't know how well you'll be able to hear it."

"If you've been interfering with my case again . . ." he said heavily, letting some unspoken threat hang in the air. I wasn't scared; I've been threatened by experts.

"Just listen, please." I pressed "play" and held the speaker of the cassette player up to the mouthpiece of the phone. I'd rewound to the crucial exchange where Gail had conveniently outlined the murder plan. I let the tape run for a few minutes, then clicked it off. "The voices you just heard are Gail Morton and Desmond Halloran. I've only just made this recording. The pair of them are still in Room 103 at the Warrington Motorway Motel. If you hurry, you might just catch them at it."

As I replaced the receiver, I heard a splutter of rage from Jackson. Like the man said, I'm into performing my civic duty. I didn't want him to waste time cursing me out when he should be jumping in a motor and shooting over here, sirens blaring and lights flashing.

I thanked Janice politely for the use of her phone and handed back my room key. I went out to the car park and sat in my car. I don't know what I was planning to do if they'd left before the police got there, but I didn't have to make any decisions. A bare twenty minutes after I'd called, a pair of unmarked police cars screamed into the car park. I was impressed. They must have really hammered it.

Jackson jumped out and ran across to my car. He looked as if he wanted to hit me. "They still in there?" he demanded.

"Present and correct."

"Wait here," he commanded.

"My pleasure," I said.

Jackson went back to his officers and the six of them went into a huddle. After a moment, the only woman there peeled off from the main group and walked across to my car. She opened the passenger door and plonked herself in the seat next to me. "It's nice to be trusted," I commented drily.

She grinned. "After the way you've been giving him the runaround, just be grateful you're not cuffed to the back bumper of his motor," she said. "I'm Linda Shaw, by the way. DC Shaw."

"Kate Brannigan," I said.

"Oh, I know exactly who you are, Ms Brannigan. My guv'nor says you've got something for us?"

I watched Jackson lead his troops into the motel. I had a momentary pang of sympathy for Janice. I hoped the six hundred would be enough to make her feel reasonably cheerful about having been had over. Once they'd gone inside, I took the tape out of the recorder and handed it to Linda Shaw. "I take it this will come under the heading of anonymous tip-off when the case comes to court?"

"I'd imagine so. I don't think giving your agency good publicity is high on my guv'nor's Christmas list. Now, where else would you expect us to go looking for evidence that might strengthen our case?"

I liked Linda Shaw. She spoke my language. None of the bluster or intimidation of her boss had rubbed off on her. Like me, she'd developed her own style, complete with techniques that got quicker results than the heavy-handed approach without alienating everyone along the way. I made a mental note to mention her name to Della. Any woman trying to make it through the male-dominated hierarchy of the police needs all the help she can get. I stared straight ahead and said, "For it to get as far as murder, this affair must have been going on for a while. I'd have thought the hotel records would indicate how long. So they must have had some means of communication. If I had access to that sort of information, I'd take a long hard look at the phone bills at the Cob and Pen and at DJH Portraits."

Linda smiled and took out her notebook. As she scribbled a reminder to herself, she said, "You do realize you're going to have to come back with us and give a full statement this time? Not just about this, but about the Kerrchem sabotage?"

I sighed, resigned to my fate. "I spent yesterday evening in the nick helping the Art Squad and the Drugs Squad with *their* inquiries. Much more of this, and I'm going to be asking for overtime."

Linda chuckled. "You've got more chance of getting it out of your clients than out of our budget. Listen, would you prefer it if I took your statement?"

Another careerist. But this time, it suited me to go along. "Do you really think Jackson's going to give up the opportunity to make my life seriously uncomfortable?"

Linda nodded towards the door of the motel. A man I took to be Desmond Halloran was stumbling towards the car park, wearing nothing but a pair of jeans and a policeman on each arm. "I think Inspector Jackson's going to have his hands full with those two. Just thank your lucky stars that from here on in, you're a bit player."

Next came Gail Morton, more respectable in leggings, scoop-necked T-shirt and the kind of fashion leather jacket that makes you angry on behalf of the cow. Jackson held her firmly by one arm, with the other two officers bringing up the rear. The lovers were each thrust into a separate car, and Jackson came over to us.

"I'll see you back in Stockport," he said darkly to me, his eyes menacing behind the tinted lenses.

"I thought the police were supposed to be grateful for cooperation from members of the public," I said airily.

"We are," he snarled. "What we don't like is smartarses who think they know how to do our jobs."

He walked away before I could come up with a snappy rejoinder. Probably just as well. I didn't want to miss tomorrow night's date with Michael Haroun. I started the car and pulled in behind the two police motors. "If they smash the speed limit on the way back, I want immunity from speeders," I told Linda.

"You don't have to keep up with them," she pointed out. "I do know where we're going, even if you don't."

"Listen," I said. "Your boss is so paranoid about me that if I disappear from his rear-view mirror he's going to put out an all-points bulletin to stop and shoot me on sight for abducting a police officer."

"You're probably right. He's just brassed off because he was looking at the angle of possible collusion between the two bereaved spouses. Unfortunately, we're handicapped by having to operate inside the law, so we hadn't managed to make as much progress as you," Linda said ironically.

"Touché. I'll remember that when I'm making my statement."

"I would, if I were you. Certain of my colleagues would love to have something to charge you with."

I reached over and pulled my mobile out of my bag. "I'd better cover my back, then." Ruth was going to be thrilled. Much as she loved me, holding my hand twice in two days was stretching our friendship more than somewhat.

For the second night running, I was in a police station past midnight. Most of the time had been spent hanging around while Linda Shaw acted as liaison with Jackson, returning every now and again to ask me fresh questions, most of which I didn't have the answers to. No, I didn't know how they met. No, I didn't know exactly what chemicals Halloran had used. No, I didn't know where he bought his chemicals. Eventually, in exasperation, Ruth said, "Detective constable, do you believe in God?"

Linda frowned. "What's that got to do with it?"

"Do you believe that my client is God?"

Linda tipped her head back, stared at the ceiling and sighed. "No, Ms Hunter, I do not believe that your client is God." Waiting for the punch line.

"Then why do you expect her to be omniscient? We've been here for seven hours and my client has cooperated fully with you. Now we've reached the point where either you arrest her, or we're going home to bed. Which is it going to be, Ms Shaw?"

"Give me a minute," she said. She was back in just over five. "You can go now. But we may have some more questions for Ms Brannigan."

"And she may or may not answer them," Ruth said sweetly as we headed out the door.

When I got home, there was still no sign of Richard. I was too wound up to sleep, so I switched on the computer and played myself at snooker until my eyes were so tired I couldn't tell the reds from the black. I staggered off to bed then, only to dream of Gail Morton running naked across green fields pursued by a gigantic white cue ball.

The next morning, I had to deal with the depressing job I'd been avoiding ever since I'd got back from Italy. I drove out to Birchfield Place, noticing that the leaves were starting to fall. I hate the autumn. Not because it heralds winter or symbolizes the death of the year or anything like that. I just hate the way fallen leaves turn to slime on country roads and bring on four-wheel drift as soon as you corner at anything more than walking pace.

It was one of the days the house was open to the public, and I found Henry hiding from the masses in his little office in the private apartments. He didn't look particularly pleased to see me, which I put down to the pile of paperwork threatening to topple over and cover his desk. But the upper classes never let mere irritation interfere with their manners. "Hello, Kate," he said, pushing back his chair to stand up as I walked in. "Good to see you."

"And you, Henry." I sat down opposite him.

"Mr Haroun from the insurance company tells me you've been having a rather exotic time lately," he said. I thought I detected a slight note of reproach in his voice.

"Exotic. Now, there's a word," I said. "I'm sorry you heard it from him rather than directly from me, but I've been a bit hectic the last few days, and I thought the main priority was to make sure you could get reinsured at a decent premium as fast as possible."

"Oh, absolutely, you did quite the right thing. And you must let me have your bill for your trip to Europe. It sounds utterly dreadful, but the one positive thing to come out of it is that Mr Haroun has agreed to pay some of your bill as a quid pro quo for your putting a stop to these burglaries." All of a sudden, he'd gone motormouth on me.

I looked at him. "Don't you want to know about your Monet?" I asked.

He flushed. "Mr Haroun said you hadn't managed to recover it. I . . . I didn't want to remind you of your lack of success in that respect when you'd been so successful otherwise."

The smell of bullshit filled my nostrils. "What I didn't tell Mr Haroun is that the painting showed up in the paperwork," I said. "What it looked like to me was that the painting had been received by the drug runners, but hadn't yet been swapped for a consignment of drugs." I sat back and let Henry work that one out for himself. Right from the start, I'd been convinced he was holding out on me, and an idea of why was starting to form at the back of my mind.

"You mean it might still turn up?" he asked. Too nervously for my liking.

"It's possible," I said. "But there could be another explanation."

By now, he wasn't even trying to meet my eyes. "I'm sorry, I'm not following you." He looked up, caught my glance and looked away, his boyish smile self-deprecating. "I'm obviously not as well up in the ways of criminals as you, Kate."

"You want me to spell it out, Henry? You've been nervous about this investigation right from the start. I worked with you on the security for this place, and I think I got to know you well enough to realize you're not the sort of bloke who gets wound up about something like a burglary where no one's been hurt. So there had to be another reason. I only grasped it some time during the fourth hour of close questioning by the Art Squad. Henry, if what you had nicked off your wall is a Monet, I am Marie of Romania."

# 26

There was a long silence after I dropped my bombshell. Henry stared blankly at the papers in front of him, as if they'd inspire him to an answer. Eventually, I said quietly, "The rules of client confidentiality still apply. You'd be better off telling me what's going on. Then, if what they stole from you does turn up, we're ready with a story to cover your back."

He glanced up at me quickly, then looked away again. He was pink to the tips of his ears. "When my parents died, there wasn't a lot of money. I did my sums and realized that with a cash injection, I could make this place work. I was talking over my problem with an old friend who had had a similar dilemma himself. He told me what he'd done, and it seemed like a good idea, so I did the same thing." More silence.

"Which was . . . ?" I prompted him.

"After I'd had the Monet authenticated for insurance purposes, I took it to this chap my friend knew. He's an awfully good copier of paintings. No talent of his own, just this ability to reproduce other people's work. Anyway, once I had the copy, I sold the original privately to a Japanese collector, on the strict understanding it would never be publicly exhibited." Henry looked up again, his eyes pleading for understanding. "I didn't want to admit what I'd done, because the Monet is one of the main visitor attractions at the house. People come here to see the Monet because they're interested in his work, people who otherwise wouldn't cross the threshold. And no one ever noticed, you know. All those so-called experts never spotted the swap." He perked up as he pointed out his one-upmanship.

"And then when the thieves took the copy, you couldn't own up because that would mean admitting to the insurers that you'd been lying all along," I said, feeling depressed at the thought of the risks I'd taken over a fake.

"I've been feeling terrible about taking their money under false pretences," he admitted. "But what else can I do? If I tell the truth now, they'll never reinsure me, and I'll never get cover anywhere else. I've painted myself into a corner."

"You're not kidding," I said bitterly. "Not to mention putting my life at risk."

Henry sighed. "I know. I'm sorry about that. I simply didn't know how to tell you the truth. You've no idea what a weight off my mind it is to have told someone at last."

"Yeah, well, the Catholics wouldn't have stuck with confession all these years if it didn't have some therapeutic effect. The thing is, Henry, now I know for sure what I already suspected, I can't sit back and watch you defraud Fortissimus to the tune of seven figures. I've done some hooky things for clients over the years, but this is a few noughts too far," I said, the iron in my voice matching the anger inside me.

He met my stare at last, panic sparking in his blue eyes. "You said this came under client confidentiality," he accused. "You can't betray that confidence now!"

My first inclination was to say, "Watch me," and walk. But I'd got to like Henry. And I believed him when he said he was sorry about the shit I'd been through. Besides, it doesn't do in my business to get a name for selling your clients down the river. "Henry, this isn't about betrayal. You're making me party to a million-pound fraud," I said instead.

"But even if it does come out, there will be no suggestion that you knew about it. After all, if you'd known the painting was only a copy, you wouldn't have made such strenuous efforts to recover it," he argued persuasively.

"But I'd know that I knew," I said. "That's the bottom line for me."

Henry ran a hand through his gleaming hair. "So what did you come back here for this morning, Kate? To get the truth and then throw me to the wolves?"

His words stung. "No, Henry," I told him sternly. "I hoped you'd tell me the truth, that's true. But I don't want to shaft you. What I think we can do is stitch up a deal."

He frowned. "You want a cut, is that it?" Luckily for Henry, he sounded incredulous. If he'd seriously offered me a bribe, all bets would have been off.

"No, Henry," I said, exasperated. "What I mean is that I think I can do a deal with the insurance company."

"You're going to *tell* them I was trying to defraud them?"

"I'm going to tell them what an honest man you are, Henry. Trust me."

⊱⋅☆⋅⊰

An hour later, I was waiting to see Michael Haroun. I'd taken the time to get suited up in my best business outfit, a drop-dead gorgeous, lightweight woollen tailored jacket and trousers in moss green and grey. This was going to be such a difficult stunt to pull off that I was going to need all the help I could get. Call me manipulative, but this was one occasion where I was willing to exploit testosterone to the full.

I only had to hang on for ten minutes, even though the claims receptionist had warned me he was in a meeting that could take another half-hour. That's the power of hormones for you. Michael grinned delightedly at me, plonking himself down next to me on the sofa. "What a great surprise," he said. "I hope you've not come to call off our dinner date tonight?"

"No way. This is strictly a business meeting," I told him. I didn't let that stop me brushing my knee against his.

"Right. Well, what can I do for you, Ms Brannigan?" he said teasingly.

"This is all a bit embarrassing, really," I said.

He raised one eyebrow. Sexy, or what? "Better get it over with, then."

I pulled a wry face and tried to look innocent. "I've just come from our mutual client, Henry Naismith. He's finally got round to clearing out some boxes of papers that were lurking in a dark corner of the cellar at Birchfield Place. And he found something rather disturbing." I paused for effect.

"Not the Monet, I hope," Michael joked.

"Not the Monet. What he did find was a bill of sale, and a note accompanying it in his father's writing." I took a deep breath. "Michael, the Monet was a fake. Henry's father had it copied a couple of years before he died. He secretly sold the original to a private collector on the understanding it would never be displayed publicly, and the fake's been hanging on the wall ever since."

I'd never believed the cliché about people's jaws dropping till then. But there was no other way to describe what had happened to Michael's face. "A fake?" he finally echoed.

"That's about the size of it."

"It can't be," he protested. "We had an expert go over all those paintings when we first insured Birchfield for Naismith. He authenticated all of them."

I shrugged. "Experts can be wrong. Maybe he was misled by the paperwork. I'm told the Monet had an immaculate provenance."

"I don't believe this," he exploded. "We used the leading expert. Shit!" He turned away for a moment. Then, slowly, he swung round to face me. "Unless we're really talking about your client, not his father."

He was smart. I like that in a man, except when I'm up against him. I opened my eyes wide, aiming for the injured innocent look. "What is this, Michael? I come here telling you your company's just saved itself a million quid payout and you're giving me a bad time? For Christ's sake, look at the bottom line here!"

His eyes narrowed. "You're telling me he's dropping the claim?"

"As far as the painting is concerned, of course he is. Now he knows the painting was a fake, he sent me to tell you the painting was a fake. If he was as dishonest as you're trying to make out, he could just have kept his mouth shut and pocketed the readies. Come to that, would he be paying to send me schlepping halfway across Europe in a head-to-head with the Mafia over something he knew was a copy? All Henry wants to do is set the record straight and sort out the reinsurance on what's left of his art collection."

By now, Michael was scowling. "And how do we know the rest of the collection aren't fakes too?"

"They're not. Henry is willing to let you do any tests you want to on the other paintings. Experts, X-rays, whatever. He'll stand by the results. Michael, you owe us a bit of leeway here," I continued, building up a head of righteous anger. "If it hadn't been for the investigation Henry instigated, this bunch of robbers would still be emptying your clients' stately homes more regularly than the phases of the moon. Thanks to Henry, that problem has gone away. And now his honesty is saving you a sizeable hole in your balance sheet. Can't you just be grateful for that?"

I watched his eyes as he calculated his way through what I'd just told him. After a few moments, the clouds cleared and he smiled. "I have to hand it to you, Kate," he said. "You are one smart operator. We have a deal. We don't pursue your client for fraud, and we reinsure, subject to more than the usual checks. In exchange for which, your client withdraws his claim in respect of his stolen Monet. Get him to put that in writing, will you?"

I held out my hand. "Deal."

Michael shook my hand, holding on to it rather longer than was necessary. "I do realize I've been listening to *Jackanory*, but this is an outcome I can live with," he said, needing to end the negotiation in the driving seat.

I let him. I'd got what I wanted. I stood up. "See you tonight."

"Half past seven, the Market Restaurant. I'll be there."

By the time I'd walked back to the office, my brain felt like a bombsite. For once, Shelley took pity on me, leaving me alone to work my way through the pile of paperwork that had accumulated while I'd been roaming the mean streets. After my recent adventures, I was longing to get back to the relative peace of a tasty bit of computer fraud or even some routine process serving.

Alexis rang just before lunch, demanding to know what part I'd played in the dramatic arrest of Gail Morton and Desmond Halloran. Her own researches had come up with how the couple had met. Apparently, Halloran had been doing a portrait of one of Gail's friends and she'd gone along for the session to keep her mate company. It had seemingly been lust at first sight. There was a warning, if I'd needed one, about the consequences of letting physical attraction cloud one's judgement.

In exchange for that nugget, I gave Alexis the lowdown as deep background, and promised her the full story on the drugs-for-art scam just as soon as the various police forces had coordinated their efforts and done their sweep-up of the villains.

When I came off the phone, Shelley wandered into my office with a memo. "New client," she said. "He's got a chain of record shops in the Northwest and his stock seems to be shrinking rather more than it should be. I've set up a meeting for you in the main lounge of the Charterhouse at half past three. OK?"

"Fine," I sighed. "Make that the last business of the day, would you? I need some quality time with my bathroom."

"No problem," Shelley said. Nothing ever is to her. Sometimes, I hate her.

I walked through the impressive doors of the Charterhouse Hotel at twenty-five past three. The huge red bullshit Gothic building, complete with looming tower, is one of Manchester's landmarks. It used to be the headquarters of Refuge Assurance and occupies a vast block on the corner of Oxford Road and Whitworth Street, bordered on a third side by the brown and sluggish River Medlock. Inside, the decorative glories of Victorian tiling and wood panelling have been left miraculously intact, a monument to a time when labour and materials were cheap enough to make every public building a cathedral to commerce.

I checked at the reception desk, but no one had been asking for me, so I settled down in a chair where I could comfortably see both entrances and where anyone coming in would be bound to see me.

At 3.32, Richard walked in. I breathed in sharply, while my stomach contracted in a cramp. At first, he didn't see me, since he was heading single-mindedly for the reception desk. I had a moment or two to study him. He looked satisfyingly hollow-cheeked, the shadows under his eyes visible even at ten yards. I reminded myself sternly that he probably hadn't been pining, merely enjoying too many late nights on the razz with the rockers. He was wearing Levis and a baggy Joe Bloggs T-shirt under the leather jacket I'd bought him in Florence. As I watched him talk to the receptionist, I felt a pain in my chest.

I saw the receptionist shake her head. He looked around then, and saw me for the first time. I tried to keep my face frozen as our eyes locked. He took an uncertain step in my direction, then stopped.

I stood up and moved a couple of steps away from my chair. It was a Mexican standoff. Shackled by pride and stubbornness, we remained firm, neither willing to be the one to back down. Before the deadlock could set in stone, a familiar voice from behind my shoulder boomed out, "This isn't *High Noon*, you know. You're supposed to use your gobs."

I swung round to see Alexis emerge from behind a pillar. "You bastard," I said.

"I didn't set this up just to watch the pair of you imitating Easter Island statues," she complained, walking over to stand midway between us. "Now, one step at a time, approach."

By this time, both Richard and I were clearly fighting not to smile. In sync, we moved towards each other. God knows what the receptionists were making of the scene. When only Alexis stood between us, she stepped back and said, "I'm out of here. Get it sorted, will you? The pair of you are doing everybody's heads in."

I suppose she left then. I wasn't paying attention. I was too busy staring at Richard and remembering all the reasons I felt bound me to this man. Thinking too how right he'd been to resent people's perception of him as a wimp, when actually he's the strongest man I know. He's strong enough to step back and let me get on with my own life, strong enough never to make demands he knows I can't meet, strong enough to understand that our relationship gives both of us what we need without all the crap neither of us wants.

Somebody had to speak first, and I reckoned it might as well be me. "I missed you," I said.

"Me too. I'm sorry," he added, his voice cracking.

"Me too." I reached out a hand across the space between us. He linked his fingers with mine. "We need to talk," I said.

Then he smiled, that cute smile that cut me off at the knees the first time I encountered him in a sweaty nightclub, minutes before he reversed straight into my car. "Later," he said. "Let's book a room."

Richard was pouring the last of the vodka from the mini-bar into a glass for me when I noticed the time. I hoped Michael Haroun wouldn't still be waiting in the restaurant two hours after we'd arranged to meet. Deep down, I knew I didn't really care if he was. Sure, picking up some business from Fortissimus would have been nice. But being grown-up means recognizing that some prices are way too high to pay.